"I do not care to be kept waiting."

"Do you not?" In two long strides, he was much closer than she appreciated. "Well, I strive never to keep a lady waiting—especially so eager a chit." He seized her by the shoulders, bent, and kissed her, long and hard.

Sophia sometimes allowed her fingertips to be lightly kissed, but aside from her immediate family, no man had ever been permitted to kiss her on the lips. For an instant she was so stunned she didn't move. His hands gripped her shoulders like iron bands. He smelled of rain and wet earth and shaving soap, with no trace of pomade or perfume.

"Allow me, my lady," he said with new and chill politeness, "to introduce myself. *I* am Camille Damon!"

Also by Patricia Veryan:

LOVE'S DUET

Patricia Veryan

FAWCETT CREST • NEW YORK

To my Mother

A Fawcett Crest Book
Published by Ballantine Books
Copyright © 1979 by Patricia Veryan

All rights reserved under International and Pan-American Copyright Conventions. Published in the United States by Ballantine Books, a division of Random House, Inc., New York, and simultaneously in Canada by Random House of Canada Limited, Toronto.

ISBN 0-449-21607-1

This edition published by arrangement with The Walker Publishing Company, Inc.

Manufactured in the United States of America

First Fawcett Coventry Edition: June 1980
First Ballantine Books Edition: July 1988

Chapter 1

"The toss of a coin!" Deirdre Breckenridge's lovely face, lit by the sunshine of this bright morning, was a study in dismay. She leaned forward from the squabs of her luxurious barouche to peer into the twinkling violet eyes of her companion. "You jest, surely? Do you love him or not?"

Lady Sophia Drayton's ringlets, the colour of ripe wheat in moonlight, bounced against her ivory-muslin morning dress. "I am...not sure," she shrugged.

"Then you do not!" Deirdre gave a small but vehement nod. "And must not even consider him!" She leaned back, surveying the pleasant Kentish countryside they travelled as though the matter were quite settled.

Lady Sophia gave a little ripple of laughter. "Deirdre, we are not all as single-minded as you. Most ladies meet and like—perhaps love a little—many gentlemen before they decide. And too many of us, alas, marry with no thought of love, though we may be so fortunate as to have several from whom to choose."

5

"Several!" Deirdre scoffed. "Hartwell's offer *must* constitute your...well, you have received more than twenty offers by my count?"

"Thirty-one, were I to include my Italian beaux..."

"Oh, my! And is there none you favour above the others?"

A furrow appeared between the smooth brows, and the beautiful head tilted as Sophia said musingly, "I suppose...Hartwell is the leading contender."

"You *suppose*? Lud! Sir Amory Hartwell is young, handsome, and wealthy. One of the finest prizes on the matrimonial market! And you—*suppose*?"

"You forget, love. I am a widow and past all such dreams as finding my heart's desire." A roguish dimple hovered beside my lady's sweetly shaped mouth as her friend uttered a sound that—in any but one of London's leading toasts—must have been designated a snort.

"You were a seventeen-year-old sacrifice! Married off in your first season to a man old enough to be your Grandpapa in an effort to retrieve your family fortunes! Oh, never bother to deny it, Sophia! I was truly fond of Sir Edgar, but"—she giggled—"I often think of how furious your Papa must have been to discover his wealthy friend was totally under the hatches and that he himself was obliged to pay Drayton's funeral expenses!"

Sophia gave a sigh at this reminder of her charming but improvident father. "You," she scolded mildly, "are, and ever were, a saucy scamp! Papa sought to provide for me, God rest his dear soul. But,"—she scanned her friend's face anxiously—"Edgar died...happy...do you not think?"

"Very happy," agreed the Breckenridge, adding wickedly, "and of anticipation!"

"Deirdre!" Sophia threw a hand to her scarlet cheek but, meeting those mirthful dark eyes, could not hold back a giggle. "I vow I shall never cease to feel guilty that the poor old fellow died at his own wedding reception!"

"His *third* wedding reception! And it was very naughty of him to offer for a beautiful young girl at his age. Especially when he was pockets to let! At all events, your cousin Clay told me they found Edgar sitting in the garden as if asleep and with a rapturous smile on his face. What a blessed way to go!" She chuckled, then, sobering, asked, "Do you contemplate another *mariage de convenance*, Sophia? I beg you will

6

not. You know that if things go badly, you and Stephen are more than welcome to come—"

"Of course, I do, you goose!" Sophia squeezed her hand affectionately. "And as for marriage—why, I may decide against it altogether."

"*Against*...it?" Deirdre gasped. "But whatever shall you do?"

Lady Sophia folded her hands in her lap and tilted up her chin. "Look after Whitthurst, of course." And, quick to sense her friend's indignation, she added, "He needs me."

"He needed you when he was so terribly ill," frowned Deirdre. "And you were beside him. What he needs now is a wife, not a sister!"

"Perhaps, but he vows he will never marry. And he goes out so seldom, Deirdre. Poor boy, he is so very subdued."

"Scarce to be wondered at." Deirdre shook her head sadly, then asked cautiously, "Sophia, does he feel...I mean, is he...?"

"He is maimed, love. And proud. But it's more than the loss of his arm, I fear. He seems to have...lost heart." Deirdre said nothing, but her dark gaze was filled with compassion, wherefore Sophia brightened at once. "Listen to me grumbling like an old lady! Whitthurst will make a full recovery—in time. It is, after all, only four months since Waterloo, and—Oh! My goodness!"

They had passed through some rather drooping ornamental iron gates and now traversed a small park. Ahead was Singlebirch, a gracious old sprawling, half-timbered house with a look of welcome and comfort, albeit the woodwork needed fresh paint, and the shrubs were overgrown. It was not the shabby appearance of her ancestral home that alarmed Sophia, however, but the lady who stood upon the terrace, watching their approach in an attitude of anxiety. As soon as the barouche pulled up at the foot of the steps, she was out of the vehicle and running to the faithful housekeeper. "What is it, Hettie? Is the Viscount worse?"

"He's gone, milady! Oh, my sweet soul...he's gone!"

The kindly face blurred before Sophia's eyes. Then Deirdre's arm was about her as she said calmly, "Speak plainly, Hettie! Is Lord Whitthurst from home?"

"Yes, yes!" The plump little woman wrung at her apron. "Your cousin come, milady. Sir Harry. And when he left, the

7

Viscount was all of a state and went tearing off in his curricle."

"The curricle! Heavens! But where does he go?"

"To see his wicked uncle! The one wot lives in Dorset and come and shouted at him so drefful whiles you was in Italy!"

"Good God!" gasped Deirdre, tightening her arm about her friend's swaying form. "Whitthurst will be all right, love. Never worry so!"

Sophia scarcely heard her. "Hettie," she managed in a thread of a voice, "you never mean—you *cannot* mean... My brother did not go to—*Cancrizans Priory?*"

The housekeeper nodded vehemently. "To see that horrid Markwiss!"

"All the way to Dorset?" marvelled Deirdre. "Whitt must be vastly improved."

"He may stop at my cousin Clay's home in Surrey." Sophia was very white. "I must leave at once!"

"But—surely there's no cause for such a taking? Whitthurst has his man and his groom, does he not, Hettie? There—you see. You could—"

"No, no! You do not understand!" Sophia wrung her hands but, pulling herself together, said with a twitching attempt at a smile, "Forgive me, Deirdre. You go on. If I can, I shall join you in Town to help you choose your bride clothes. Hettie! Call Meg and Miss Jarrett at once and tell them to pack for several days. They must both accompany me. I will tell James to prepare the carriage. *Hurry!*"

Leading the way down the back steps of the pleasant house, the elderly butler said, "The Major went out to sit quietly for—" He paused, shook his head, and turned away. Her ladyship was already hurrying across the grass to where Clay dozed on his favourite bench under the old laburnum tree.

So it was that Marcus Clay, who had known little of sleep these past weeks, awoke from a troubled slumber to find his most beautiful cousin descending upon him with a flutter of petticoats, agitated little hands, and a breathless spate of enquiries. He sprang up, but even as he bent to kiss her smooth cheek, she asked, "Is Stephen here? Have you seen him today? It looks like rain now. Do you not smell it in the

8

air? He is not *well* enough, Marcus, to be careering about all over the countryside, with only—"

Clay threw an arm about her and, half laughing, said, "Hush, Chicky! You chatter like a magpie! Do you seriously mean that Whitthurst is out driving?"

"Yes, yes! And I am half out of my wits worrying lest he exhaust himself!"

"You worry too much about him, Sophia. Come." He drew her down on to the bench beside him, noting as he did so that the skies had darkened and the air was becoming more chill. "We've had so little time together since you returned from Italy. You shall simply have to spare me a moment or two, dear girl, and tell me—calmly—where Whitt has gone. And why."

Sophia would not be calmed. "To see his uncle. And I do not know why. Harry Redmond stopped at Singlebirch whilst I was out, and Stephen went rushing off, and—oh, Marcus! I *must* catch him before he reaches Cancrizans, else he will—"

"*Cancrizans*?" he interpolated. "The Priory? But—it's in Dorsetshire! Surely Whitt would never be so corkbrained as to start out with weather blowing up, and him just this side of having turned up his toes—" He broke off at the flicker of pain in Sophia's great eyes and added a repentant, "Clumsy clunch that I am! Sorry, coz. This whole mess must be a most ghastly coil for you to come home to. Had you no idea he meant to join up?"

"None!" She clung to his hand and said tremulously, "For he promised Mama he would not. Surely you realize I would never have left her else?"

"Of course not," he soothed. "How could you have known? Not like old Whitt to break his given word. Though ... he *was* mad to get into it, Chicky."

"Mad, indeed," she said with a touch of bitterness. "Heaven knows, with the service record of our family, we might have been spared the sacrifice of one more life to this dreadful, unending war!"

He pointed out gently that the war *had* ended. "And Whitthurst did not lose his life, praise be!"

"No," she sighed. "Only his right arm. Four and twenty—and ruined."

"You know that's not true," he scolded, pulling her to her

9

feet. "Whitt's too fine a fellow to be written off so easily." They started towards the house together, and he asked thoughtfully, "Who travels with you?"

"My maids and James."

"What?" Shocked, he drew her to a halt. "Two frippery abigails and an elderly groom? By God, that will not do, Sophia!"

"It shall have to do!" Her little chin set in the manner he knew so well. "I fought hard for Stephen's life, and I do not intend to lose him now because he rushes out in the rain and takes an inflammation of the lungs!"

"But you cannot go to see Damon alone! Ain't...decent!"

"I have no choice...unless—" She bit her lip and was silent.

Clay swung open the side door to the library, his eyes troubled. So the headstrong Sophia was determined to journey to Cancrizans Priory. How strange a coincidence that she must visit the Marquis, the very man who might be able to help him. He knew Damon very slightly, and it was doubtful that Sophia knew him at all. Certainly, she could not be allowed to go all that way without a proper escort. To accompany her would be no hardship, for he always found her delightful, and if the undertaking of so pleasant a journey would also further his own hopes, he must be a paperskull to hesitate. He made up his mind. "Esther is in good hands. I will ride with you, Chicky."

Sophia leaned back in the comfortable wing chair in Clay's study and sipped gratefully at her tea. Thank heaven Marcus had agreed to accompany her. She was very fond of him, and his presence would offer her both company and protection. If they were unable to overtake Stephen before he reached the Priory, she would not have to face Damon alone. And with a fighting man like Clay beside her, even if the Marquis had learned of her revenge, he would not dare harm—

"Pssst!"

Smithers' honest round eyes peered at her around the French doors to the verandah. She hurried to close the hall door and beckoned the groom inside.

"'Scuse Oi, marm, but ye said as how Oi was to tell ye if Major seemed downhearted loike." He tiptoed clumsily across the room. "Just afore ye come"—he bowed his face into his

10

hands imitatively—"like that'n were 'ee. Major don't never get squashed by bad times. But squashed 'ee were! Never seed un' like that—even at the storm o' Badajoz!"

Concealing her anxiety, my lady asked, "Do you know why? I saw little Douglas when I arrived and thought he looked less frail. Mrs. Clay seems to be recovering nicely from her lying-in—and the baby is doing splendidly."

"Oi couldn't say, milady." He frowned, scratching his head. "Less'n it were summat as Mr. Gordon says s'marnin'."

"Major Clay's solicitor was here? Oh, dear! Whatever can be amiss?"

The young man racked his rather obtuse brain and admitted, "All Oi heered 'un say was about the new gate. That's all they seemed to talk on. Blessed if Oi can see why the Major should be so squashed account o' a new gate!"

Sophia thanked him, pressed a coin into his hand, and when he had gone, returned to her chair to puzzle at it. Stephen said Marcus was under the hatches, and, with Esther for a wife, that was understandable. But surely the Duke of Vaille would help with financial problems. Clay would not come into his inheritance for more than a year, but as executor of Benjamin Clay's estate, Vaille could release sufficient funds to help the Major over this heavy ground. Of course, the Duke had been against Clay's marriage, but to deny him his due would be Turkish treatment, indeed.

Clay had fallen in love with the beautiful but feather-headed Esther five years earlier. His affection had been returned, and Esther had happily married the dashing young cavalry officer, only to be devastated by his frequent and perilous absences. Left alone save for his brief and infrequent leaves, she had become increasingly miserable and, during her second pregnancy, had pleaded to be allowed to join him. Clay had been sorely tempted since in that summer of 1815 so many of the *haut ton* had gathered in Brussels. His wife's health was poor, however, and her doctors had advised Clay against it. He had kept their warnings from her, saying only that with Bonaparte on the loose again, it was too dangerous and, at least until the child was born, she must remain in England. At once, the sick girl had deduced she was not only unwanted but unloved. Bored and heartbroken, she had indulged a taste for gaming, and to such a degree that when Clay returned from Waterloo in a blaze of glory, it was to find his finances

11

a shambles, his remorseful wife near death from grief and guilt, and his creditors pressing in from every side.

In view of the fact that Clay was heir to a considerable fortune, Sophia had assumed that most of his creditors would be willing to wait. There were, however, some terrible tales of the relentlessness of moneylenders.... Frowning into the fire, she reflected that the shatter-brained Esther, with the best intentions in the world, seemed unable to do anything right. Clay, adoring her, would say nothing to her discredit, however she served him. But it stood to reason that if Gordon had come all the way from Town, it had not been to discuss the acquisition of a new gate. She stiffened. A new...gate? Dear God! Had they, in fact, been speaking of the dread *Newgate*? Was the valiant Marcus now facing incarceration in Debtors Prison? Frightened, she nibbled at one knuckle. Clay had readily agreed to accompany her. Why? Damon! Of course! The Marquis was the only son of the Duke of Vaille! Clay hoped to persuade Damon to intercede for him, to attempt to sway his father to a more kindly attitude! Vaille must have refused Clay's appeals. In which case, the Duke of Vaille had a heart no less cold and inhuman than that of his murderous son!

"Don't like this weather!" Clay turned on the rocking seat of the chaise as the beauty shrank closer, ducking her head against his sleeve. A glaring lightning flash sliced the lowering afternoon skies, and thunder racketed in pursuit of it. "If the bridge looks in the least unsafe," he resumed, patting her wrist absently, "it's back to 'The Wooden Leg' for you, ma'am."

"No, but Marcus," she pleaded, sitting straighter and clasping her gloved hands, "the landlord did not say the bridge was definitely *un*safe."

"Said his eldest crossed first thing this morning, and it looked about to flop again. Why in the deuce Damon don't build a decent bridge, I cannot fathom."

"No, dear," she said meekly. "Will you not please see if they follow?"

Muttering beneath his breath, he lowered the window, leaned out quickly, withdrew his head, struggled with the window again, and sat down, glaring sodden and speechlessly at the Lady Sophia.

12

She gave a musical little laugh and, taking a tiny piece of lace-edged cambric from her reticule, wiped at his face, pushed back his wet brown curls, then leaned to kiss his cheek. "My poor coz! James follows, I gather?"

He nodded. "Why you need your maid *and* dresser when you merely hope to capture Whit and bear him back to Kent is beyond me."

The truth was that she needed their support, but she said nobly, "If Steve is ill, we may have to rest at 'The Wooden Leg' before we start back."

"In heaven's name why? I hear Cancrizans is enormous. Damon could certainly find room for us. Though I hope to God we can get in and out fast." Sophia looked taken aback, and Clay said apologetically, "I want for manners, do I not? If Douglas made such a crude remark, I'd likely spank him! But—well, I'm sure you must have heard of the place, Chick. And of Damon...?"

She had, indeed, and wondered for the hundredth time why Stephen must put her into such a dreadful position. But she looked away and said lightly, "You must remember I have never seen Cancrizans. Nor met my uncle. He may—"

"*Your* uncle!" He gave a shout of laughter. "What fustian!"

"The Marquis of Damon's sister," she said demurely, "was Stephen's Mama."

"Yes, but a daughter of the Duke's first wife—not at all blood related to Damon. And *you* were born to *your* father's second wife."

"Stephen and I share everything," she smiled. "Marcus, is Damon truly a cranky old recluse with a face like a washboard? Deirdre says he is appalling."

She was obliged to wait for a reply as Clay blew his nose, groaned that he must be catching a cold, and asked breathlessly if she had not met Vaille.

"The Duke? No, but I hear he is a formidable old gentleman, though he cuts a fine figure..." Her voice trailed off, her smoothly arched brows drew together, and she mused, "Which must be remarkable considering..."

"Considering he is senile?"

"I find that unkind in you, dear," she reproved mildly. "Shall he be at the Priory, do you think? Or is it true that he and Damon do not deal very well?"

"I've heard the same." Clay sighed and stared out at the deluge.

13

Sophia watched him narrowly. "I simply cannot understand why your Papa stipulated you must be eight and twenty before you could inherit. Surely he loved you."

"He did. But fancied I'd squander the fortune on Esther. Or fall in with some choice group like Cobra. Or—"

"Never even *think* such a dreadful thing!" Sophia's eyes were wide with revulsion. "As if someone as clean and honourable as you could sink to the level of those depraved monsters! Now tell me—do you mean to ask Damon's help?"

Astonished, Clay said, "How shrewd you are!"

"Shrewd enough to realize the Duke must have refused you. What did he say?"

Vaille had said a good deal, beginning with the observation that Clay had wed, against his advice, a lovely henwit, and ending with a suave, "You were certainly aware of her want of good sense, and I knew you'd retain sufficient of your wits to guard against her excesses. My confidence in you was not, I trust, misplaced?" With a wry smile, Clay answered, "He was not—sympathetic."

"The beast! Does he know you face Newgate?"

Too bedevilled to wonder how Sophia was aware of that hideous fact, Clay shuddered and shook his head. "I did not know of it at the time."

"Then perhaps you should approach him again, dear."

Gordon had said the same, and Clay realised they were both right, but in the face of Vaille's attack upon his repentant Esther, he'd drawn back from confessing the extent of her recklessness. To have to face those icy eyes again, to have to admit that she had brought the threat of Newgate upon him, reduced his courage, so firm in battle, to quivering shreds.

Sophia read a great deal in his expression and flared, "How *dare* he humiliate you! He is doubtless shamed by your military record since his own son can only suffer by comparison! Cavorting about Europe with his fancy Frenchwoman—at his age! The man should have been wed long since and his sons out of Eton already!"

Both amused and touched by her vehemence, Clay grinned. "My sweet champion! But in all honesty, Chick, Damon's—ah—liaison with the beautiful Mademoiselle Gabrielle was ended some time back."

"I am not surprised," she sniffed. "Even a lightskirted

14

Parisienne could have only contempt for a man who shirked his duty."

Clay frowned a little. "Patriotism takes many forms, Sophia."

"It does, indeed. And, in our noble uncle, it took a very cunning form. He served his country vicariously, if you will." She uttered a brittle laugh and said, "My Lord Damon purchased Stephen's colours. Were you aware?"

"No, by gad! Jolly decent of him, since your Papa could...not..." Sophia was regarding him in horrified disbelief. He regrouped. "What d'you mean—vicariously? You never hold it against him that Whitt—"

"Near died and is cruelly maimed?" Her small fists clenched, and she said with unfamiliar bitterness, "Lud—why ever should I do such a thing? Because Damon cursed and bullied Stephen into doing his fighting for him while *he* stayed safely at home? Good gracious—no!"

After a small, tense silence, Clay asked softly, "Do you intend to tax him with it? If so, I'd best not ask his help."

"Oh—I'd not thought of that! If *only* I could help you." Her worried eyes brightened suddenly. Her early marriage had left her with only a title, and...

"My emerald! That's the answer! Marcus, you could—"

"I most certainly could not!" he said, his eyes flashing indignation. "What the deuce d'you take me for? I vow you're becoming positively totty headed!"

"And you too prideful for your own good! Wherefore, I collect I'm obliged to be all sweetness and light at the Priory—and shall be, never fear. Until I am able to spirit Stephen safely away from my infamous uncle. Or until you have secured his promise of help." Her heart constricted violently. If the Marquis of Damon already knew of her vengeance, Clay could expect short shrift!

Misunderstanding her expression, the Major said uneasily, "Gad—I'd not intended to stay longer than one night."

Nor had she! The thought of even dining there made her toes curl with fear. But she must not let Clay know that and therefore laughed. "Gracious! You sound bereft of all hope. You love to fence. You and Damon could—"

"He don't fence."

"But—he must! Has he not fought several duels?"

15

"Was challenged each time. Chose pistols. He's a dead shot, I hear, but hates swordplay."

"Well, then, you could ride. He's said to have a splendid stable."

"He don't ride. Loathes horses."

"*Loathes...horses?*" Shattered by such infamy, she gasped, "Lud! Then what *does* he do for diversion? Spar? Or is he too dainty for that, either?"

"Don't fence," Clay mourned. "Don't ride; don't spar."

"Good...God! My poor uncle must have led a solitary life aside from his French baggage. Surely the Bucks and Corinthians shun him?"

"Matter of fact," said Clay thoughtfully, "he was well liked in Town before he debunked. Ran with Saxon and Bolster and that crowd. Our cousin Redmond thinks the world of him, I gather."

"Harry? How odd. They must be years apart. And Harry's a dear."

"Wouldn't describe him in just that fashion," he grinned. "But I'll agree Redmond don't seem the type."

"For what?"

"Your uncle's diversion—as you called it." Sophia waited, intrigued, and Clay said with a chuckle, "Only thing he does that I know of, m'dear, is play the harpsichord."

Chapter 2

Her bags beside her, Sophia stood on the far bank, pulling her cloak tighter and watching Clay anxiously. The swollen river roared thunderously in her ears, and she tried not to notice the rubble its broadened girth had claimed from the banks to propel along the boil of the water. The bridge *looked* safe enough, but hovered scant feet above the turbulence. Clay had refused to order the chaise across. He had walked over with her, carrying her most necessary possessions. At least the rain had lessened, now becoming a steady light fall so that she was not drenched as she waited through Clay's brief conference with his groom. Smithers swung down from the chaise with obvious reluctance and crossed to the carriage to climb up beside James. *Clay* was going to drive the chaise across! She realized with a pang of fear that he'd judged it too hazardous to require his groom to attempt it.

The greys were balking, frightened by the cacophonous uproar. Sophia held her breath as Clay guided them expertly onto the timbers. It was little short of idiotic, she thought angrily, that the Marquis chose to live in such a godforsaken spot with this one rickety bridge providing the only means of access.

And then her heart jumped into her throat. The bridge moved! She heard a scream from the carriage. The greys began to plunge, and Clay sent the whip snaking over their heads. "Dear God!" she whispered. "What have I done?"

A great mass of debris rushed on the crest of the littered waters to slam deafeningly against the pilings. Smithers jumped down from the carriage, ran over the swaying bridge and clung to the back of the chaise as it shot forward. The horses had barely reached the far side than an uprooted tree hurtled into the weakened structure. The greys screamed with fright. For an instant the chaise seemed to hang over empty space as the bridge disintegrated with an ear-splitting roar. Then the wheels bounced onto the bank. The horses strove, eyes rolling in panic. Clay, his face white, flailed the whip, and with a wild plunge, they were clear.

Sophia swayed, weak with terror, and then was crushed close in her cousin's arms. She clung to him, half sobbing, "Oh, Marcus!" He kissed her, said a cheerful, "Silly chit!" just as Stephen would have done, and bustled her into the chaise while Smithers shouted to James to await them at "The Wooden Leg."

From the top of the rise, Sophia viewed the Priory with a sinking heart. The rutted apology for a drive swept around a small pool, beyond which lay the great sprawling building, stark and unwelcoming in the gloomy afternoon. The central structure was flanked on each side by long wings extending back to create a wide "U" shape. The windows were narrow, deeply inset, and few. The front door crouched under a heavy Gothic arch, and only faint gleams of light showed from those lurking windows. There were some fine old trees, but the lawns were a collection of weedy grasses bearing little resemblance to the velvet turf surrounding her own Kentish home.

Dismayed, she felt inclined to run back to the chaise. It was little short of miraculous that they had not overturned when the wheel, badly sprung when the chaise had bounced onto the river bank, had split. Tired of watching the men

18

struggle to repair the damage, she had set out in search of the Priory, which, with his usual optimism, Marcus had assured her was "just around the next bend." Instead, she had tramped at least a mile. She was cold, and her feet hurt from the long walk in shoes not designed for such endeavours. But she was here at last! She climbed the steps and approached that forbidding door.

No baying of dogs, no grooms, no welcoming footman or butler greeted her. The Priory seemed to leer malevolently, defying her to persist in her invasion. The wind howled, sending her hood flying. She pulled it back up and, finding no bell, pounded on the heavy door defiantly. Silence. She pounded again and gave it a few angry kicks for good measure. It creaked open. Alarmed, she jumped back, then ventured to peer inside. She saw a vast hall panelled in dark wood that added to the depressing dimness. It was sparsely furnished with only one huge old table, which held a branch of flickering candles and was flanked by several ancient and decrepit chairs. The massive hearth on the right end wall yawned black and empty. A broad flight of steps opposite the front door divided at a wide landing into two separate staircases leading to either side of a railed balcony on the upper floor.

Sophia walked reluctantly into the unprepossessing interior, murmured an ironic "Charming!" and called, "Is somebody here?" No whisper of life answered her. 'Lud!' she thought. 'What an awful place! Just what I expected of him!'

Two corridors led back into the wings of the house. The one to the right was dark, but to the left, light gleamed faintly. She traversed the hall and walked nervously along the corridor, passing several closed doors on either side. It was chill and damp and smelled of paint, but the last door was slightly open, sending a beam of light across the flagged floor. Again, her knock won no response, and she stepped in. Something white flew at her with a loud hissing. She gave a shriek of terror and shrank back. A large goose advanced, with neck outstretched in evident hostility. "N-nice...birdie," she quavered. The creature eyed her with beady displeasure. Sophia reached blindly for an object of defence and, grasping something from a side table, glanced down at her prize. It was a sculpted bust, the name across the man's chest identifying 'Wolfgang Amadeus Mozart'. She smiled faintly, but her smile faded as the broad wings of her antagonist began

19

to rise and the neck to stretch once more. She replaced the bust hurriedly, but when she took a tentative step forward, the goose hissed like a veritable dragon. Sophia thought of Marcus and Smithers labouring in the rain. Vexed, she shook her cloak at the bird and cried, "Oh, go away, do!" The goose squawked, made an ungainly dash for the rear of the room, and squeezed through a French door that was not quite closed.

The victor looked around in some surprise. She stood in a large and gracious room. A fire blazed in a lovely Adam fireplace. The walls, with Gothic panels picked out in gold, were a soft cream. Heavy brocaded draperies of cream and beige were closed over all the windows. The furnishings were tasteful, and at the far end of the room, stood a magnificent old harpsichord, the top littered with music. She walked toward it curiously, then, glancing to the door through which the goose had vanished, caught a glimpse of someone outside.

She hurried on to a broad, rain-swept terrace below which lawns stretched out. At once the wind blew the door wide, whipping the music from the harpsichord into a paper cyclone that whirled out to surround her. A servant, inadequately clad in breeches and a leather apron over an open-throated shirt, had been labouring to retrieve similar sheets apparently kidnapped by an earlier gust. He looked up from the foot of the steps, saw the new disaster, and roared an exasperated, "Oh hell and damnation!" It was not an endearing greeting, and the startled Sophia collected herself and favoured him with her most daunting frown.

He was undaunted. "Close the door, you ninnyhammer!" he shouted.

It had been several years since anyone had addressed her in that fashion.

"How...*dare* you!" she said with regal displeasure.

Unintimidated, he started towards her, bellowing, "Close the door, woman! Are you daft?"

He was slim but tall and with broad shoulders. Sophia backed away and, intending to escape this insolent brute by returning to the house, was thwarted as the door blew shut. Her attempts to open it were fruitless: it was either locked or jammed. The servant was again gathering up the sheets of music that the disobliging wind blew in all directions. The goose, she saw, lurked beside him, scurrying around, keeping the man ever between itself and her, peering at her uneasily from beyond him each time he halted. She looked around for

20

some other door into the house. She *must* try and find someone rational who could send help to Marcus.

"Don't stand about!" the servant shouted. "Get down here
and help!"

She wondered if he always addressed his master's guests
in such a fashion and decided he was either mad or drunk
as a walrus.

"*Will* you get down here—or must I drag you?"

Given pause by that irate snarl, she looked at him again.
He was reaching for an errant sheet of music, but she
glimpsed black, wet hair and darkly scowling eyebrows. She
had best placate the lunatic. She walked reluctantly to the
steps. He thrust a sheaf of wet papers at her. "Since you
cannot take 'no' for an answer, make yourself useful, girl!
Put these under your cloak."

Sophia stared. The unbelievable impudence of the fellow!

He waved his salvaged collection at her impatiently, then
burst into a torrent of French, so rapid that she caught only
the beginning, which conveyed the information that she was
totally wits to let, and the ending, which was a pithy "*ce n'est
que le premier pas qui coûte!*"

She regarded him with the hauteur that had shattered
many a too persistent admirer. "Were it up to me, sir, *my*
first step in this house would be to discharge *you!*"

"God!" he groaned. He came slowly up the steps. Sophia
looked down into a lean, finely chiselled face, possessed of a
straight nose, firm chin, and the most unusual eyes she had
ever seen, wide and deepset, and of a clear, light turquoise
colour. She had heard someone speak of such eyes and now
remembered silly little Brenda Smythe-Carrington mooning
over her latest "true love," "Cam" somebody or other, whom
she had described as "the handsomest man in London."
Whoever Brenda's Cam may be, thought Sophia, slightly
dazed, he would surely be put in the shade by this man! She
stood motionless, her own features shadowed by her hood,
watching the rain drip off the end of that slim nose and course
down the aquiline features.

"Put these under your cloak!" he repeated with tight-
lipped emphasis.

Finding her voice, she said, "I most assuredly shall not!
They are muddy."

"Of course, they're muddy! Largely because you left the

21

blasted door open! I'll buy you a new dress, girl! Do as you're told!"

"No!"

For an instant, he stood still, then stepped even closer. Those incredible eyes were hard and cold, his beautifully shaped mouth curving to a terrifying smile. Speaking very softly, he said, "Put...these...under..."

She grabbed the sheets and thrust them under her cloak.

He turned away, muttering a sardonic, *"Voilá! Coup de maître!"*

As soon as he reached the lawn, Sophia made a mad dash across the terrace, passed a wide central court between the two wings of the house and, at the far side, found to her inexpressible relief a door that admitted her to the dark hall.

She ran a little way, slowed, and stopped. It was very dark in here, and the quiet held an odd brooding. Darkness had always terrified her, and she knew suddenly that someone, something, watched her. Her heart fluttering, she began to back away. Something touched her elbow, and she almost fainted from shock.

"I am persuaded, ma'am," said that same deep drawl, "that I have been most rude to a poor soul not in possession of her full faculties. You have been misinformed as to our needs. I shall provide transportation for your return to the village if you will be so good as to come this way."

She felt weak with relief and, ignoring his sarcasm, followed his tall figure back onto the cold, wet terrace. Long before they reached the door to the lighted room, however, she was fumingly rehearsing the speech she intended to make to her uncle about this obnoxious secretary or music master, or whatever he was.

He tried the door handle, muttered, "Confound it!" and gave the door a hard kick while roaring, "Horatio!"

Sophia took an uneasy step back into the rain. The goose honked behind her, tore past triumphantly as she jumped aside, and took refuge behind a graceful Hope chair. The man stood aside, said a cool, "Your Majesty," and swept her a mocking bow. Outraged, she marched in, tossed the dirty papers on to a sofa of brocaded cream satin, and crossed to the fireplace, well aware of the cry of rage that had burst from her companion. Her depredations were incomplete, however. Her hand left a blur of mud along the pristine mantle

22

even as a tiny but very muddy shoe gratifyingly sullied the hitherto immaculate brass rail before the fire.

"You, madam, are a full-fledged disaster!" came that irate voice behind her. "We've no need for a maid who ignores requests and in one minute desecrates an entire room! That I can assure you."

It was apparent there had been a misunderstanding, but how dared this arrogant upstart use that tone with her? She put back her hood and gave a shake of her lovely head. The gleaming ringlets did not bounce softly on to her shoulders, as expected. The gleaming ringlets were, in fact, one wet straggle. Raising an exploratory hand, she realised too late that it was muddy and began to form an unhappy estimate of her appearance. Ignoring the Creature, who had dropped to one knee before the sofa and was scanning his sheets of music with anxious intensity, she sought in her reticule for her small mirror. It revealed her appearance to be even more shocking than she'd anticipated. She went swiftly to work and, when her repairs were completed, turned again to her busily occupied companion.

His wet hair still sent occasional trickles of water down his face. His skin was bronzed by the sun—not at all the thing! The white shirt clung wetly to broad shoulders that tapered to a very trim waist, and his muddied grey breeches revealed slim hips and long legs.

Disposing herself beside the fireplace, Sophia waited for him to get his first real look at her. The wait became interminable. With growing indignation, she realized that he had completely forgotten her. "If there is a butler in this asylum," she said haughtily, "be so good as to summon him."

"You'll find him in the kitchen."

She tensed with rage. A china figurine—the charming but inexpensive replica of a boy and a dog—was closest. She took it up and dropped it into the hearth.

The servant's head shot around. His eyes widened predictably as he saw the fragmented china.

"I gave you an order," she nodded. "I do not care to be kept waiting."

"Do you not?" In two long strides, he was much closer than she appreciated. "Well, I strive never to keep a lady waiting—especially so eager a chit." He seized her by the shoulders, bent, and kissed her, long and hard.

23

The Drayton sometimes allowed her fingertips to be lightly kissed, but aside from her immediate family, no man had ever been permitted to kiss her on the lips. For an instant, she was so stunned she didn't move. His hands gripped her shoulders like iron bands. He smelled of rain and wet earth and shaving soap, with no trace of pomade or perfume. Her eyes shot open. 'Good God! What am I doing?' She groped back, found the fireplace tongs, and swung them upward. A crystal vase toppled from the mantle and joined the ex-figurine.

"Hey!" Long fingers closed about her wrist, and he laughed down at her as he took possession of the tongs. She was pale, her great violet eyes flashing with rage. Awe crept into his expression, to be replaced by shock as her open palm cracked across his cheek so hard that a lock of hair was bounced down his brow.

"Filthy...lecherous...brute!" Sophia wiped her mouth fiercely. "My brother will kill you for that!"

"While I await death," he said, an infuriating quirk tugging at the side of his mouth, "I'll have you taken home." He crossed to pull on the bellrope and, turning back, touched his glowing cheek thoughtfully and stared at her stomach.

Sophia glanced down. Her cloak had fallen open. Her new brown travelling gown was very muddied, and she gave a distressed wail.

"I told you I would buy you another dress," he said with an uneasy surveillance of that modish gown.

"So you did. That will be one hundred and thirty-five guineas, if you please!"

"One...hundred,—" he gasped, with a simultaneous shiver of cold.

"Lud, sir," she mocked, "I'd no thought to make you shake in your shoes."

"And I've no thought to be made a monkey by some pert lass who—"

"Energy wasted," she intervened loftily, "since t'was accomplished before ever I came upon the scene!"

He glared; then mirth began to twinkle in his eyes. "What a madam fire and destruction! Who in the deuce are you?"

"I am come," she said, her nose well elevated, "to find my brother."

"Well, he's likely at 'The Wooden Leg' and well foxed by now."

24

"My brother's habits," she said quellingly, "are scarcely your concern. However, you may be of service. My cousin and his groom need help to repair our chaise. The wheel came off soon after that ridiculous bridge collapsed—"

"Devil it did! Well, the blasted thing can stay down for all I care!"

"You will scarce be consulted," Sophia said with disdain. "However, your master must be told of it, and I shall also advise him of your impertinence and your language, both insupportable." She tossed her cloak onto the sofa.

Undaunted, his eyes travelled appreciatively down her sleek but well-rounded little figure. So appreciatively that her teeth grated together.

"My...master?" he repeated with obvious amusement.

"My uncle," she nodded. "The Marquis of Damon."

His jaw dropped. The laughter died from his eyes, and he all but gaped at her. "Your...*uncle?*" It was a near croak.

Triumphant, she smiled and said loftily, "You sense retribution, I perceive. You may announce that the Lady Sophia Drayton is here and desires to make his acquaintance. If the old gentleman is not already abed."

His jaw snapped shut. "Allow me, my lady," he said with new and chill politeness, "to introduce myself. *I* am Camille Damon!"

Chapter 3

"I do not see," Lady Sophia complained, "why this could not have waited."

Mrs. Hatters poured more hot water around the girl in the hip bath. "Milord says you be chilled and must be bathed," she said in a dry, expressionless voice. "He says. I does. That's it."

"But all my things are in the chaise."

"Robe on the bed. It's clean. It'll do for now." She started away, and when my lady requested that a maid be sent up, shrugged. "Ain't got none."

Momentarily bereft of speech, Sophia stared, her mouth falling open slightly. Almost she thought to see a smile creep into those cold eyes before the door slammed, but her indignant "Come back!" went unanswered. It was, she thought, applying soap to sponge furiously, the outside of enough! Why Stephen should have so deceived her was incomprehensible. And that Clay should have allowed her to continue to believe that wretched viper of a Marquis to be her—Steve's—uncle was downright perfidy! The man was not a day over thirty, if that. He was every bit as evil as she'd imagined, that was quite clear—a lecher, as well as a craven! Her hands slowed. Brenda had been right, though. The Marquis of Damon was assuredly her "Cam"—and the most handsome man she'd ever seen. She scowled at her own stupidity. It just went to prove the old adage that looks were only skin deep, for Damon was still the monster who'd bullied her brother into the hussars and sent him off to be near killed while he huddled snugly in his wretched Priory!

She smiled grimly, recalling how furious he had been when he'd realised she was not simply a traveller seeking aid who would then resume her journey, nor a local girl applying for a position as a domestic, but that he would be required to provide accommodations for several unwelcome guests. When the butler, Mr. Thompson, had appeared, Sophia had thought him well suited to his environment. He was a stocky, middle-aged man of untidy appearance, and he was quite foxed. The Marquis had fixed him with a searing glare and apprised him of the fact that the front door had been left unlocked. Thompson had cringed before his master's wrath and departed, white-faced, to send grooms to aid Clay and require the housekeeper to show Lady Drayton a bedchamber.

Mrs. Hatters, coming on the heels of the Priory, the atrocious Marquis, and the butler, was quite as expected. A thin, dark little woman, she was possessed of piercing pale-blue eyes that held a sour look. Her manner had been little short of rude as she'd led the way upstairs, grumbling under her breath. She'd taken Sophia to her own pleasant and commodious room at the rear of the north wing, muttering, "Have to put your bath in here. Can't get another room warm on one minute's notice!"

Despite these depressing experiences, the bath was restoring, and Sophia had dried herself, donned the threadbare robe the housekeeper had left for her, and was curled up in the comfortable armchair before the grate when Mrs. Hatters returned, carrying her bandbox and valise.

"Oh!" cried Sophia, jumping up eagerly. "Major Clay is here?"

Mrs. Hatters gave a brief nod and set down the luggage.

"Is he all right? Have they repaired the chaise? Is there any word of Lord Whitthurst?"

27

"One yes. Two no's."

Sophia's chin and her brows lifted simultaneously. What a cold, unfriendly person. And how utterly insolent. He deserved her! "What do you mean—there are no maids? There certainly must be servants to run a big house like this."

"Me. His lordship's valet, Thompson. Ariel, he's the cook and looby if you was to ask me. Four grooms. Two gardeners. Two daily maids come in from the village." She stared meaningfully. "Won't stay. Scared of the place."

Sophia returned that stare to such effect that the woman flushed and her eyes dropped. "Do you mean," asked her ladyship, "that Mr. Thompson is Lord Damon's valet *and* butler?"

"Yes, my—" The woman bit her lip for all the world as though the address she'd begun had escaped against her will. "Yes," she finished gruffly. "When you're ready, ring the bell, and I'll show you to your room. Oh, and Thompson's a mite deaf. Cannon at Ciudad Rodrigo. He can hear if he watches your mouth."

Astonished by this volubility, Sophia recovered in time to request that she be shown to her room at once. This precipitated a battle of wills. The housekeeper seemed determined to present rooms that were totally unsuitable, and Sophia, suspecting the existence of more comfortable accommodations, stubbornly refused such quarters. Her fourth turndown, being on the grounds there was no connecting door, appeared to baffle the woman, and when Sophia pointed out that she desired her maids to be close to her, Mrs. Hatters actually paled and gulped, "They in the chaise...with the other lot?"

"If you mean with Major Clay...no. They are at 'The Wooden Leg' in Pudding Park and will come tomorrow as soon as the bridge is repaired."

Despite Mrs. Hatters' scornful pronouncement that it would be "weeks afore they gets that done," Sophia remained adamant and enquired whether all the rooms on the south side of the corridor were occupied. She refused to admit, even to herself, that the north wing had frightened her to death and said she had rather look out on to the countryside than into the central court. Mrs. Hatters was reluctant. Her ladyship would not like "them rooms." Her ladyship would be better served across the hall. Sophia was obdurate, and a few minutes later, watching the door close behind the scowling woman, she danced a jig of triumph. Mrs. Hatters had flung

28

open the last door on the left of the long hall to reveal a large bedchamber charmingly decorated in a soft orchid and white and having a beautiful four poster bed, a mahogany press, chest of drawers and escritoire, and a fine marble fireplace flanked by a comfortable sofa and armchair. The connecting door led to another spacious and pleasant bedchamber, the whole being far more than she had hoped for. Oddly, she had thought to see a gleam of amusement in Mrs. Hatters' cold eyes, but it had instantly vanished if it had existed at all. An obviously reluctant offer had been extended for milady to return to Mrs. Hatters' room "'til I can find that dratted fireboy and send him up here." Sophia's pride forbade she accept. It was positively frigid in the big room, but once between the blankets and she would soon be warm. She made a dive for the bed and pulled back the coverlet. The bed wasn't made up! "Oh, fustian!" she exclaimed, and pulling the bell-rope so that she might send for her clothes, curled up in the coverlet.

Ten minutes later, her teeth chattering, she eased the door open and peeped into the hall. No sign of life. By now, Mrs. Hatters was doubtless busied downstairs. She tiptoed along the hall, drawing the robe closer. The sash came untied and fell to the floor. Clutching the robe about her, she bent to pick it up. A slim, tanned hand was before her. She knew by the length of the fingers whose hand it was and could have sunk. She fairly leapt upright with disastrous results and, her cheeks flaming, dragged the parting robe savagely together. Too savagely. It ripped all down one side. In an agony of mortification, she shrank against the wall and raised her scarlet face to encounter those mocking eyes alight with laughter. The Marquis had seen a great deal more of her than any other man had ever witnessed, but he managed somehow to maintain a grave countenance. He bound the sash swiftly about his eyes, turned and groped his way along the hall, singing softly in a fine deep baritone, "Believe me if all those endearing young charms, which I gaze on so fondly today..."

She hoped with all her heart that he would fall down the stairs.

Edward, the Earl of Ridgley, ran a hand through his light, crisp hair, beamed down at Clay, and said, "Couldn't be more pleased, Marcus! Tell the truth, it gets confounded lonely at times. Though Damon's the best of company, of course," he added with a quick glance to the library door. "Still, do you plan on staying a bit? Perhaps you and I could go a round or two or get in some riding."

Clay was warm at last and enjoying the chair closest to the fire. He acknowledged his old friend's pleasure with a lift of his wine glass. "Delighted. A great piece of luck for me, your being here, Ted." He, too, glanced at the door through which the Marquis had departed a few minutes earlier. "You're related to Damon in some way, ain't you?"

"Vaille's my cousin." Ridgley's eyes hardened. "Fond of old Cam, y'know. Good boy."

"I heard," said Clay, "that he used to give some jolly fine parties. But that he—er—don't like company these days. I hope he ain't greatly put out."

The Earl frowned into his wine glass and chose his words with care. "This old place belonged to his mother. Beautiful creature..." His eyes became blank for a moment. "She was French, y'know. But she'd a grandfather who was English, and his family owned Cancrizans for two hundred years. Damon's hoping to completely restore it. Take him a lifetime probably. But he loves the old pile."

"I suppose between this and his hotel, he's kept busy all the time."

"So you'd heard about that. It's to be a sort of spa, actually. About five miles north on t'other side of Swallow Lake. Lovely spot. He plans for boating, fishing, riding. He's installing a series of canals—Venetian style."

"Gad! Must be costing a fortune, between both projects!"

"He has other investors in on the spa. Sunk a great deal of his own—" The Earl checked and asked with a change of tone, "How does your lovely Esther go on?"

Clay imparted that his wife, Douglas, and the new babe were well, added that he hoped Vaille was the same, and stared, astounded.

He'd known Ridgley since he was a boy. The Earl had been several years younger than Benjamin Clay, but they'd seen service together in India and become close friends. Clay had always liked the genial man and had never seen him angry. Now he found himself looking into eyes from which all warmth had vanished. As swiftly as it had come, however, that grim expression was gone. "I have not," said Ridgley mildly, "the remotest idea of how Vaille fares."

Clay was silent. If this same relationship prevailed between the Duke and Damon, his goose was cooked. He'd no sooner had the thought than the head of a large goose lifted like a serpent above the arm of his chair and voiced a loud honk into his startled face. He looked disbelievingly at his glass.

Ridgley gave a crack of laughter. "You're all right, Clay! It's Horatio. Camille uses the dratted bird as a watchdog because—"

"Because," said the Marquis, returning at that moment carrying a full decanter of wine, which he set on the reference table, "he doesn't tear up my gardens nor bite the grooms. And he gives me lots of warning"—he turned to Clay and finished with blunt rudeness—"in case of—er—unwanted company."

Clay flushed darkly and sprang up, yearning to stalk out of this place and knowing he dare not. "I sincerely apologize for intruding upon you," he began.

"Not at all," Damon put in with a smoothly disarming smile. "I am delighted to have...overnight...guests." The emphasis on the qualification was slight but unmistakable, and he added, "Do sit down, Clay. I'm not your Colonel, you know."

"Most definitely not," smiled Sophia, walking gracefully into the room. Her blue gown, its swooping neckline demurely edged with white lace, fell in a slim line from beneath the snug bodice, the soft fabric revealing to advantage the full curves of her beautiful body. A single sapphire gleamed against her fair skin, and matching drops hung from her ears. A blue band, decorated with tiny seed pearls, held back her shining hair, and her hand-painted fan showed little blue flowers against the ivory. She had dressed with care, knew that she looked extremely well, and was pleased by the awe in the faces of the nice-looking blond gentleman and her cousin.

Lord Damon watched her expressionlessly. He wore a rich, dark maroon-velvet jacket that fit his wide shoulders to perfection. The lace at his throat and the falls beneath the cuffs of his sleeves were like snow. A large diamond winked from his cravat. Sophia noted that he wore pantaloons instead of knee breeches, but since he lived in such squalid conditions in the country, it was not to be wondered at. It escaped her memory that Whitthurst would likely have told her she had maggots in her attic had she suggested knee breeches in a country house. She was forced to admit that Damon looked startlingly handsome and thought it a great pity that he was

31

such a thorough cad. She realized suddenly that they were staring at one another and that a silence had fallen. Breaking it, Clay came to take her hand and tell her that the Marquis and his men had been so kind as to convey the chaise to the Priory and hopefully it would be repaired by the morrow.

Clay introduced the Earl, who bowed over Sophia's hand with courtly charm and escorted her to the chair beside the fire.

Offering her a glass of ratafia, the Marquis asked, "Have you any idea what your brother wishes to discuss with me, ma'am?"

Despite the mildly bored air, his eyes seemed very penetrating, and Sophia lowered her lashes. "I know only that he is much too ill for such a journey, my lord. Save for that knowledge, I would never have prevailed upon my cousin to attempt the bridge and thus force ourselves upon your—er—hospitality."

She failed to disconcert him. "*Au contraire*," he protested with his quirkish grin. "It has been no imposition, but most—revealing, my dear lady."

She knew she was blushing and, remembering with savage rage his barely contained mirth on the balcony, said sweetly, "I am sure Whitthurst is close by and will come as soon as possible."

"Then by no means must he be delayed. I shall instruct my foreman to cease work on the spa tomorrow in order to rebuild the bridge."

Perversely, Sophia thought, 'Why, the wretch cannot wait to be rid of us!'

Horatio burst from behind Clay's chair and started to rush around the room with much honking and flapping of wings. A taut look crossed Damon's face. The butler came into the room and, staring at him, announced in obvious consternation, "Lady Fanny Branden and Miss Charlotte Hilby, my lord."

"Good...God!" Damon half whispered, and locked glances with Ridgley.

Sophia was surprised to note that the Earl, who impressed her as being a warm and kindly gentleman, looked almost as dismayed as his kinsman. For herself, she could have screamed with laughter. It appeared that one antisocial, would-be hermit was about to be inundated with company!

A tall, husky woman stamped into the room. She wore an ill-fitting riding habit, the train of which she held draped across one arm, revealing a startling expanse of high-buttoned boots. An enormous white feather soared up from a dejected-looking hat of the same brown as her habit. She was undoubtedly on the far side of forty, but her mousy brown hair, escaping in all directions from beneath that wilting hat, was unmarked by silver. Her eyes were dark and scanned the room in a brief sweep as she advanced on the Marquis. "There you are, nephew," she barked redundantly, arms outstretched. "I bring you a surprise."

Sophia had the distinct impression that the Marquis winced as he was caught in that crushing hug, and his "Feather!" was more a gasp than a greeting. He planted a dutiful kiss upon her upturned cheek, however, and thanked her for having braved such a storm.

"Where'd you spring from?" enquired Ridgley, submitting to her embrace uneasily. "Thought we was cut off!"

"Phinny Bodwin's," she roared. "Decided to pay you a quick call but, with the state of the roads now, may have to camp here a few days!" She fetched the Earl a slap on the back that deposited most of the contents of his glass onto the sleeve of his jacket, then marched to the door. "Charlotte! Where in the devil are you, girl?"

Sophia, meeting Clay's mirthful glance, fought back a giggle and saw Damon slant an amused look at her. The Earl, smoothing wine from his sleeve, muttered, "Same old Feather..."

Another woman entered. She was tall and willowy and younger than her companion by a good decade or more. Coppery curls, coiffed in the newest short style, framed features of classic perfection, enhanced by long green eyes. She moved in a smooth glide, her cloak swinging apart to reveal an apricot-hued gown that emphasized the colour of her hair.

Damon took her hands and bowed over them, pressing each to his lips. "Welcome, my dear lady." His smile had become very tender, and the affection in his eyes made him seem, or so thought Sophia, almost human. The beauty's white hand caressed his cheek in a revealing gesture before she proceeded to the Earl, who planted a kiss on her brow and muttered it was "stupid he ain't yet wed you!"

Damon presented Sophia and Clay to the large woman, who was his aunt, Lady Fanny Branden. Lady Branden cut him off with the pronouncement that her friends called her "Feather." "We already know of you, Major." She extended her hand to Clay. "Your gallant exploits against Old Boney

33

had all England by the heartstrings! You must tell us of Waterloo. Can't get you lads to speak of it."

"I rather imagine Clay is tired of speaking of it, dear Aunt." Damon's voice held boredom. "Meanwhile, Lady Sophia has not met Miss Hilby."

It was all Sophia could do to hide her disgust. How logical that he should so summarily turn away any discussion of the fighting he himself had so carefully evaded. She schooled herself to respond suitably as she was presented to the beauty, but her forced smile encountered a thoughtful green stare, and she sensed that her resentment had been discerned.

Thompson came in to take Miss Hilby's cloak, but Feather refused to be divested of her hat, pointing out rather illogically that she was still chilled through from that beastly drive. "Should have ridden!" she observed. "Get the old blood going, eh?" She turned to Damon. "You found the gumption to straddle one of your fine cattle yet? Suppose not! Likely never will at your age! Lud, what a waste, with legs like those!" She slapped a large hand on her frozen nephew's thigh. "Splendid! Ain't he got splendid legs, Ridgley?"

"And a red face." The Earl grinned.

Damon's face was more white than red, but he managed a tight smile and murmured, "Dear Feather, won't you sit here by the fire?"

"No," she stated unequivocally. "Shut your eyes!"

Amused, he obeyed, but she peered at him with suspicion. "Don't trust you! No man should have great long lashes like that! Cover your eyes, sir! And do not dare to peep!" Laughing, he followed orders. Lady Branden held one finger to her lips, tiptoed heavily to the door, and beckoned.

The girl who now entered was small, dark, and vivacious. She was not beautiful, for her upper lip was too short, her nose too *retroussé*, and her bone structure lacking the fineness associated with true beauty; yet she appeared beautiful, perhaps because she radiated warmth and affection. She paused briefly, her soft brown eyes peering around the room in a myopic stare. She had discarded her cloak and wore a gown of brilliant orange silk that displayed to advantage an astonishing figure, bountiful of bosom, round of hip, and tiny at the waist. The Earl blew her a silent kiss. Lady Feather clasped her hands and beamed in the manner of a magician who has pulled a very fat rabbit from the hat. Her face alight with love and mischief, the girl began to run toward the

34

Marquis, only to stumble over excessively high heels.

At her small shriek, Damon's head shot up. He cried a delighted "Genevieve!" and jumped forward in time to catch her.

"Ah, Camille!" she exclaimed, hugging him tightly as he swung her around, her feet high above the floor. Lapsing into French, she went on. "At last, I have found you! And how well you look, dearest of all cousins! But why in the name of the good God must you hide and rusticate in such dreary desolation? This hideous ghost ridden mortuary, when you had London at your feet! Name of a name! The most beautiful man in all England, buried! Lost to—"

Since all of this impassioned speech was liberally interspersed with kisses, the Marquis had evinced no inclination to disrupt it, but now he laughed and said also in French, "Speak English, my little cabbage. We have company."

He set her down, and upon the Earl's complaining that he did not rate a kiss, she went to pull him down and plant a generous buss upon each cheek. "Are you, *mon pauvre*, sacrificed upon the altar of my foolish cousin's...seclusion?"

"If this is seclusion, m'dear"—Ridgley beamed—"I'll spend the rest of my days here!"

"You most assuredly will do no such thing," Damon said coldly.

A scowl replaced Ridgley's grin, and he met the Marquis' level gaze resentfully.

"Damon, you've become a clod!" snorted Lady Branden.

"Total," Ridgley confirmed.

"Will no one introduce me to this lady?" asked the French girl hastily, "whose beauty is of such perfection."

"And who blushes so admirably," murmured the Marquis, peering at Sophia through his quizzing glass.

Flustered and longing to scratch him as all eyes turned to her, she stammered, "W-Why, I am...overwhelmed by such a pretty compliment. Though perfect beauty, or perfection of any kind, must surely be inhuman."

"Not in the House of Branden," grunted Ridgley, still having a resentful set to his jaw. "One would not dare be otherwise!"

The quizzing glass, which had been allowed to swing idly from the Marquis's hand, jerked slightly. Miss Hilby directed a reproachful look at the Earl and reminded Damon that his introductions remained incomplete.

For a second, his eyes challenged those of his kinsman,

35

and Ridgley flushed and looked away. Then, with perfect composure, Damon presented Sophia and Clay to his cousin, Mademoiselle Genevieve de la Montaigne. Clay bowed politely. Sophia held out her hand, and Genevieve took it, frowning a little. "The name I do not know...and yet we have meet—*oui*?"

Sophia said that she did not think they had met and was astonished when the French girl suddenly wrapped her in a hug.

"Is of the *peu d'importance*! I have know in this one minute you shall be a special friend! Some of the times I have this feeling—here." Her hand fluttered to her shapely bosom, a movement followed with interest by the eyes of the three gentlemen. "Come." She drew Sophia toward the fire. "Here we sit and have the happy cose."

"Which I shall join." Feather marched to seat herself to Sophia's left on the comfortable leather sofa. "Knew your Papa. Fine seat. And a grand fighting man. Served with my husband in Holland." Her hard eyes softened briefly; then, with a little shrug, she went on in her bluff manner. "Sorry to hear about your brother. But you can at least be proud of your men."

Instinctively, Sophia glanced at Damon. A cynical smile twisted his mouth, but he said nothing. "It seems, my lord," she smiled, "that if my house is blessed with courage, yours is blessed by its charming ladies."

Genevieve hugged her, and Feather gave a barking laugh. Damon watched her with a thoughtful expression, and she realized he had read an innuendo into the words that she had honestly not intended but that was, she felt, well justified.

He turned to Miss Hilby and said a meaningful "It is indeed."

"Oh," said Sophia artlessly. "Are you also of the House of Branden, ma'am?"

Miss Hilby, her fond gaze steady on the Marquis, said, "Not yet, my lady."

Chapter 4

Lady Branden, Mademoiselle de la Montaigne, and Miss Hilby had retired to their rooms to refresh themselves after their journey. The Earl and Clay were engrossed in a military discussion regarding the shrewd tactics employed by the French at Quatre Bras, and Sophia looked at Damon with an ingenuously hopeful smile. The westering sun chose that moment to flood the room with belated brilliance, and, having stared rather blankly at her, bathed in that warm glow, he mumbled an offer to show her around the Priory, adding deprecatingly, "Though it is a dusty old place, and I doubt you'd be in the least interested, ma'am." She dashed his hopes by saying she would find it delightful, and, Clay raising no objection to the idea, Damon sighed and bowed her wearily into the hall.

Despite his apparent ennui, he was nothing if not thorough. He conducted her through a succession of chill and gloomy rooms, some holding furniture protected by Holland

37

covers so dusty they looked as if the doors had not been opened for several years. He gratified her expressed curiosity politely, drawing many objets d'art to her attention and discoursing with surprising knowledge on the various pieces. He then related the gruesome history of the house, which had originally been a famous keep, the catacombs all that now remained of the ancient structure. Knowing her host was thoroughly bored, with outward gravity and inward glee, Sophia asked countless questions and generally conducted herself very much in the fashion of a bright student on tour with her tutor. But, gradually, as they went, her coy duplicity began to be replaced by a real interest, and, sensing this, his condescension became less pronounced and his comments more informal.

Last to be viewed was the portrait gallery on the third floor. It was dusty and festooned with cobwebs. Yet, in the beautifully arched sweep of the roof, the low, recessed windows, the graceful pillars and random-planked floors, there remained an echo of a simple elegance that drew from her a little cry of mingled regret and admiration. She swung around to find him watching her intently. "Oh! But how lovely it...could..." She faltered into silence. The Marquis said nothing, but in his steady gaze she thought to detect a shadow of sadness, and she stood motionless, her head uptilted. Perhaps it was the crimson glow of sunset or the peaceful quiet. Perhaps the very age of the house created a mellowing aura. Whatever the cause, they were both swept into a strangely isolated span through which violet eyes held to eyes of turquoise. Scarcely breathing, Sophia experienced a haunting sense of irrevocability—as if a clock not previously wound had suddenly begun to measure the seconds and hours of a tapestry woven of time.

Something scampered across her foot, shattering that fragile illusion. She gave a shriek as the mouse fled into a hole in the wainscoting. Instinctively, her hand went out, and at once Damon's vital clasp tightened around her fingers. Shrinking against him, shivering, she glanced up, saw laughter in his eyes, and felt her cheeks grow hot. Only then did it dawn on her that they were most improperly alone in this remote part of the Priory. She pulled away and, because he made no attempt to restrain her, at once felt flustered and missish. It was foolish to think of Damon as her uncle, yet

38

she could well imagine Stephen's impatience with her unease.

"This, ma'am," said Damon in his languid drawl, "is the home of many of my illustrious ancestors."

Somehow his very tone reassured her. She looked pointedly after the mouse and murmured, "So I see."

He gave a muffled snort, then, as if unable to recover his aplomb, burst into a peal of laughter. When mirth overcame him, he seemed a totally different person, warm and devastatingly attractive. It was evident that he possessed a lively sense of humour, and it was equally apparent that he was determined to stifle it. Even now, although amusement still sparkled in his eyes, he swung hurriedly away and sauntered to the nearest painting. She followed, wondering why his irrational temperament should cause her to feel so troubled.

She learned much of the House of Branden in the next half hour. Damon had a droll wit, and she found herself chuckling at his anecdotes, her own humour complementing his so naturally that the moments flew past. And then they stopped before the last portrait, and he was silent.

Sophia stared upward, fascinated by the face above her. The man was startlingly handsome, the face thin, with high, finely etched cheekbones and a sensitive arched nose. The thick light-brown hair was split by a white streak at each temple, giving him an oddly winged look. The mouth above the firm, cleft chin was neither as generous nor as perfectly shaped as Damon's, and the fine blue eyes held a trace of sorrow, wherefore, womanlike, she felt drawn to him and breathed, "Is this?"

"My father. Philip—Duke of Vaille."

So this was the doddering old fellow whom the wicked Clay had allowed her to believe "senile"! "What a splendid gentleman," she acknowledged, and then, with a naïvete quite foreign to her, added, "You are not at all like him." She could have sunk the instant she realised what she had said. Mortified, she started to apologise, but he overrode her words, regarding her with the lift of an eyebrow and saying a glacial "You are not the first to remark it, my lady. Alas, one does not always inherit the—ah—'splendid' characteristics of one's sire. But I assure you he *is* my father."

Blushing to the roots of her hair, she frowned, "What a dreadful thing to say."

39

"Not at all. He has many splendid characteristics."

"Odious!" she snarled, her small fists clenching with wrath. "Why must you insist upon misunderstanding everything I say?"

"Your remark was perfectly understandable. Especially since your own brother, if I recall correctly, is *his* noble Papa—in every way."

She was very conscious of the widespread and unhappily justified opinion that her father had been a hopeless wastrel. Sure that Damon's sneering words held such a hidden barb, she countered, "Thank you. Stephen will be here soon to refresh your recollections of him."

"Oh, gad!" With an affected little laugh, he raised his quizzing glass to survey her flushed face. "Is *that* why Whitthurst rushes here?"

"Of course not," she snapped. "He has urgent business with you."

"Indeed? Then how sad that he will be unable to complete his journey. Unless he takes the western loop." An arrested look came into his eyes. "That must be the answer. We shall escort you to 'The Gold Crown' to meet him. The Toll road will certainly be open by tomorrow, and—"

"Stephen's groom, my lord, is most devoted, as is his man. Neither would allow him to attempt the western loop in such inclement weather. He will wait at 'The Wooden Leg' until it is safe to cross the bridge. And, by your leave, I shall await him here." The pucker between those black brows was deepening, and in a sudden guilty recollection of Clay's predicament, she said meekly, "Am I an annoyance? I do assure you that just as soon as my brother arrives, we will no longer burden you with our presence."

For a moment, he was quiet, then murmured a bored "How fortunate..."

Sophia tensed, rage flaring anew at this insufferable rudeness.

"...that I was able to show you some of Cancrizans before your...imminent departure," he added smoothly, and with a graceful wave of his quizzing glass, ushered her to the stairs.

Sophia had assumed the tour finished, but when they reached the Great Hall, he took up a branch of candles and started toward the north wing. "You will certainly wish to

see our famous catacombs, ma'am?" He smiled unpleasantly.
"Not afraid of the dark, are you?"

She had, in fact, been thinking how horribly black and
eerie that corridor seemed, but the mockery in his voice so
irritated her that she tossed up her chin and followed.

How many times Whitthurst had teased her because of
her fears of darkness. She would overcome her weakness!
And he would be so proud. Only...it was so *very* dark, and,
again, there was that horrible feeling that something crouched
in wait. The air began to smell musty and stale, and the
occasional creak of a board beneath their feet set her heart
beating faster. She hastened her steps so that she was very
close behind Damon.

They came to the last door in that interminable corridor,
and she was appalled to discover that it opened onto a winding stair, the stone steps worn away by age and possessed of
an icy coldness that penetrated the soles of her dainty slippers. The wretched Marquis was all outward consideration,
holding the candles aloft and requiring that she hold his hand
as well as the iron railing. If he was aware of the chill of that
little hand and how it trembled in his own, he gave no sign,
merely commenting in a casual fashion that they were coming now to the oldest part of the Priory. The lowest level, he
said, dated to the thirteenth century and had been the dungeons and torture chambers of the keep wherein many helpless victims had met a horrid death. He waxed so eloquent
on the subject, detailing the horrendous punishments meted
out for such vile crimes as the theft of an apple or some
tardily completed task, that Sophia's dread of the place
mounted. His voice seemed to become positively sepulchral
as they reached the foot of the steps. Walls and floor were
dank and chill, sloping ever downward. To either side were
even older doors than on the preceding level, with tiny barred
slits for windows, through which she could imagine some
agonized victim stretching imploring hands while begging
in vain for mercy.

He pushed open one of those frowning doors and, stooping,
entered. She made herself follow despite the onset of a smoth-
ering need to escape. This blackness seemed a velvet curtain
hung directly before her eyes. The candles dipped lower, and
she realised that Damon was starting down the last flight
of steps that wound into stygian gloom. She did not move.

41

Her palms were wet now, her breathing rapid and uneven. Damon glanced back and held out one hand, but she shook her head mutely.

"Whatever is it?" His cynical sneer enraged her. "You do not believe in ghosts, surely?"

Her rage fled. "G-Ghosts...?"

"Nonsense tales spread by peasants and witless bumpkins. They say that one of the monks, long ago when this place was a Priory, loved a village maid. He smuggled her down here one night, but—like you—she panicked and tried to get away..." He paused, and Sophia, paling, took a step closer to him and whispered, "And then...?"

He said nothing, staring down with sombre eyes. The silence grew more intense, throbbing in her ears until it seemed to Sophia that she heard the faintest of footsteps coming softly up the stairs. She felt goosebumps break out on her flesh and all but jumped when Damon resumed in a hushed tone. "They struggled here—just where we stand..." (She stepped back hurriedly.) "She pushed him, but as he fell, he seized her, and they both went over the rail..." He held the candles lower, and, impelled by some morbid curiosity, she took two hesitant steps and saw dimly, far below, the broken iron railings of the winding staircase, sticking up like so many spears. Had their bodies broken the rail, she wondered? Had that poor girl been impaled and—

"Down through the centuries," breathed Damon, his lips at her ear, "the monk has appeared often—on these very stairs. And sometimes the girl's screams can be heard...all the way to—"

A voice echoed distantly through the stillness: a woman's faint yet piercing cry. Sophia gave a sob of horror. A weakness spread through her, and she felt her knees buckle...

Her face was against his cravat; his arm was about her, and she was in the corridor. "Good gad, ma'am," he said scoffingly, "I'd not thought you the type to become vaporish over such nonsense!"

She took a deep breath, tore herself free, and stood straight despite her wobbly knees, her eyes holding, she hoped, all the disgust she felt.

His expression changed subtly, and when he spoke again, his voice was very gentle. "I am truly sorry. I had not meant to frighten you so."

She knew that he'd had just such a thought, that his every intent had been to so terrify her that she would leave his

42

mouldering old ruin by shanks' mare, if necessary. She was not accustomed to subterfuge. If only she could say what she really thought! But to do so would be to destroy her cousin's one hope. And, therefore, she managed a cool "Of course you did not, my lord. How could you possibly intend such a thing? No gentleman worthy of the name would be so loathesome."

For an instant, he gazed at her in silence. And then, again, that cry disturbed the awful quiet, and my lady's pride crumbled into dread; her face grew deathly pale, and she fairly jumped for the safety of his arm.

He chuckled. "It is only Mrs. Hatters, calling us to dinner, ma'am." He gestured politely for her to precede him and, with the candles held high so that she might see, followed her to the stairs.

Sophia was led in to dinner by the Earl. She made a determined effort to appear lighthearted but was still unnerved and full of forebodings that Clay, knowing her so well, would detect her emotional state. Her cousin was a gentleman in the fullest sense of the word. He would merely have to suspect that the Marquis had behaved toward her in so despicable a fashion and they would leave the Priory at once if, in fact, the two men did not come to cuffs. Anticipating his concern over her distress, she prepared to allay it by revealing her increasing anxiety about Whitthurst. Her fears proved unwarranted; Clay, escorting the vivacious Genevieve, was so delighted by that young lady he scarcely noticed his cousin's arrival. Sophia at once experienced a perverse resentment of his neglect. Fortunately, Ridgley was an excellent dinner partner and soon had her chattering merrily, her dismals forgotten.

Despite his extreme shortage of servants, the Marquis possessed a most excellent chef, who had, however indignantly, contrived on short notice to provide a superb meal. Sophia ate very little of the asparagus soup, poached fish, roast game hens, and a magnificent mutton pasty. She only began to feel renewed when Thompson carried in the desserts. He was assisted by Nancy Hooper, Miss Hilby's abigail, a ruddy cheeked, comely girl, pressed into service in this emergency. The Earl's attention having been momentarily claimed by Genevieve, Sophia could not but admire the charm of her surroundings. The dining room was large and might easily

43

have appeared barnlike. The walls had been remodelled into a design of slightly recessed arched panels. The main colour throughout was a soft blue, while the areas within the arches were papered in a shadowy floral design of blue, lavender, and green, an effect she found pleasing. Fearing to appear unmannerly, she glanced up to catch Damon turning amused eyes from her.

Lady Branden, allowing Thompson to place a dish of cherries blancmange before her, said, "I was sure you'd be at Amanda's come-out Ball, Damon. Everyone was asking why you are become such a recluse. Lucinda was most put out and well justified in view of your close friendship with Bolster."

The Marquis was spared the necessity of a reply, as Genevieve cried dramatically, "And I was into the blackest despair cast! My rascal of a cousin have abandon the entire human race. Why you do this so strange thing, Camille?"

"Because, my pretty creature, I have business here."

"You never mean the spa?" Lady Feather's howl vibrated the glasses. "You do not go on with it, Camille? Good God! You must be mad! A commercial venture? And against his wishes? Vaille is raving, I'll wager!"

"Quite possibly, ma'am. But *I'd* have wagered no one could reach my Priory tonight—instead of which I am surrounded by...charming guests."

His Aunt leaned forward and waved her spoon at him. "Not so charming as to be turned aside from unwanted subjects. Take care you do not provoke him too far. Philip will stand for just so many queer starts and then pull the rug from under you. What on earth possessed you to build an hotel out here? God knows there are enough of 'em in Town—or Bath, or Brighton!"

"True." His polite smile was unwavering, but he was irritated that such a discussion had been forced upon him in front of strangers. "But my hotel stands upon the shore of a jewel of a lake, and—"

"Lake!" she snorted. "If it has a lake, why should you be so daft as to surround it with canals? Or has some cloth head filled my ears with stuff?"

Sophia was so diverted as to meet Damon's glance and surprise an echoing gleam in his eyes before she hastily lowered her lashes. "The land was very cut up about the site," he explained. "It was Whitthurst's thought to install the ca-

44

nals, Venetian fashion. We shall have gondolas on summer evenings and wandering musicians. It should be very effective, I think."

"And romantic," sighed Genevieve. "Ah, but I can scarce wait to see it."

"Egad!" frowned Lady Branden, more practically inclined. "Must be costing a bowl of lettuce! It had *better* be a success! Though I doubt it."

"Never say so," he laughed. "Some of my stockholders are here tonight. You'll put them into high fidgets with your gloom!"

Lady Branden looked around in surprise. "They are? Which of you poor innocents has been gulled by my slick nephew?"

Damon uttered a groan and cast his eyes at the ceiling.

"Me, for one," the Earl chuckled. "And Charlotte and Lady Sophia's brother."

"True," said Damon. "Without Whitthurst's contribution my spa could never have been built. He deeded us much of the land about the hotel itself, and all the lake frontage."

His words seemed to blast in Sophia's ears. She kept her eyes downcast, her heart thumping so violently it was all she could do not to betray herself. How smug he sounded, doubtless gloating over how he had, as Lady Branden said, "gulled" his trusting nephew! Well, the treacherous Marquis was in for a rude shock. He did *not* have "Whitthurst's contribution"! The fact was that Stephen owned only a half interest in the lands Damon believed to have been deeded to his precious spa. Poor Steve, having no head for business, had apparently forgotten that his sister's signature must be obtained before the lands could be disposed of. When she'd first returned from Rome, Sophia had been too desperately occupied with striving to keep him alive to bother with the mountain of papers awaiting his attention. When at last she had settled down to that dreary duty she had discovered most of them to be unpaid bills, and had been astonished to come across the Deed, already signed by Stephen in readiness for a transfer of ownership. Accompanying it had been a letter from Sir Horace Drake, pointing out that Lord Whitthurst was *half*-owner, and asking that he require his sister to sign the deed also, in order that Title might be transferred to the Marquis of Damon's Spa of the Swallows, now under construction in Dorsetshire. Incredulous, Sophia had skimmed through the

45

long and involved letter, deducing that for some inexplicable reason, Stephen had been persuaded to give a great deal of property to the man who exerted such a great influence over him—and that without the acquisition of that property Damon's ambitious plans would be ruined. Seething with resentment, hurt by her brother's suffering, dreading lest at any moment she lose him, and crushed by the burden of their financial disaster, she had signed the Deed. Instead of returning it to Sir Horace Drake however, she had sent for the faithful Amory Hartwell, entrusted the Deed into his hands, and begged him to act as her agent and borrow as much cash as possible against their acreage. Her only stipulation had been that under no circumstances was it to be built upon. Delighted to be set a task by the lady he hoped to win, Hartwell had departed vowing he would persist until he obtained such terms as must delight his goddess.

Through it all, she had never dreamed that today she would be a guest in the house of the very man against whom she plotted. Nor that his relations would be so kind to her. She told herself defiantly that her revenge had been well justified. She had suffered a twinge of anxiety just now when Ridgley said her brother was a stockholder, not merely a victim of Damon's smooth-tongued chicanery. But from the moment of her arrival, the erratic behaviour of the Marquis had branded him a Creature; and one whose unscrupulous cunning would eventually have duped her gentle and trusting brother out of every last sou, stockholder or not! Despite these reflections, she was shaken, and recovered her composure only when the servants left the room, and Feather changed the subject, making a pointed remark about Genevieve's reputation.

"I have not the smallest notion of what you speak," said that young lady, albeit shooting a guilty glance at her cousin.

"Well, I have, *mon petit chou*," said Damon sternly. "You left a trail of broken hearts all across Europe!" Ignoring Genevieve's prompt but rather wistful denial, he asked, "Has she been at it again, Feather?"

"I doubt there's a whole male heart left in Devonshire," affirmed Lady Branden, "Including that of your old friend, Hartwell."

Sophia caught her breath, and her hand tightened convulsively on her spoon. Hartwell? Amory had never mentioned that he knew the Marquis.

Damon was leaning forward eagerly. "I was not aware he is in Devon."

"I doubt he is," said Miss Hilby, her tone chill, "if he has learned of our departure."

"Gad!" The Marquis settled back in his chair, smiling reminiscently. "Haven't seen Amory since..." He checked abruptly.

"Since that nasty business in Town," the Earl finished. "Very close shave, that. Did you hear—" He stopped with a gasp and glared at Damon indignantly.

"Hear what?" demanded Lady Branden.

Damon's face was a suave mask. "You were speaking of Hartwell, dear lady."

She continued to regard him suspiciously. "What's all this about nasty—"

The Marquis glanced to Miss Hilby. "Oh, Feather," she intervened, "let's not speak of that sordid business. It was horrid, and Lady Sophia looks tired."

Startled, Sophia protested, "No, but really, I am not."

"'Course the child's tired." Lady Branden slammed down her serviette. "After the day she's had and worried about her brother! Ladies, shall we leave?"

The ladies stood, the gentlemen pulling back their chairs and promising to join them very shortly. Clay ushered them to the door, and Thompson began to remove the covers. The Earl leaned closer to Damon and grumbled softly, "That hurt, if you must know, Cam. Caught me right on the blasted shin bone!"

"Apologise. But we don't want Feather nosing about, do we, Ted?"

Ridgley paled. "Gad! You're right, of course. She'd be here forever!"

As the last notes of "Eine Kleine Nachtmusick" died away, there was a moment of quiet in the music room. Sophia was deeply moved, as music had the power to move her. The Marquis of Damon played magnificently. She joined the enthusiastic applause, the men rose to their feet, and Genevieve ran to embrace her cousin.

Feather, seated beside Sophia, fumbled for her handkerchief and dragged it fiercely across her eyes. "Wretch!" she

47

growled. "He plays so divinely, and weeping women always make me want to cast up my accounts!"

Struggling against a laugh, Sophia said, "Then he should never play."

"God forbid! I look forward for weeks to the time I can hear him—and weep. Silly great creature that I am!"

"Let's have something else!" cried Ridgley eagerly.

"It grows late, and you've all had tiring journeys." Damon shot a mischievous glance at Sophia and added "And other—wearing experiences."

Sophia contrived to maintain a look of complete unawareness.

"Besides,"—Miss Hilby nodded—"you must be up early, Camille, in case his grace arrives."

Damon gasped, and the Earl stared at the beauty as though her copper curls had become writhing adders.

"Your...your pardon, Charlotte?" Damon stammered.

"You expect your Papa, do you not? In London, the Duke told me distinctly he would visit you within the month. I rather gathered it would be this week."

Sophia and Clay exchanged tense glances.

Damon took a deep breath and said, "I hope not—since the bridge is out."

"But your working men will have it newly made by to-morrow, you say—no?" asked Genevieve.

"Perhaps, my lord," murmured Sophia innocently, "your Papa could stay with us at 'The Gold Crown'?"

"What?" Feather exploded. "You're never throwing us out, Damon?"

"Not tonight, of course, dear ma'am." His face betrayed only affection. "But longer, I am persuaded, would be unendurable for you. The workmen are here from dawn to dusk, you see, for we are renovating one room at a time. And—"

"And are no sooner opening the door to us than you wish us gone—is that it?" The eyes of the formidable Feather were angry, yet also held hurt.

Damon spread his beautifully expressive hands in a gesture of helplessness.

"Of course, it is not, Feather." Miss Hilby clasped one of those outstretched hands. "Stop scolding him so! He'll not banish us from his gloomy—and now isolated—old dungeon. Will you, Camille?"

A long look passed between the two. It was a romance

48

beyond doubting, thought Sophia. But surely the lady was too old for him. 'Five and thirty if she's a day.' Still, she was certainly lovely enough to follow in the wake of his beautiful French mistress, and— They were all smiling at her. "Oh! Your pardon!" she gasped. "I was woolgathering. How terribly rude of me!"

"Not at all, m'dear," said Feather kindly. "I was only telling my fiendish nephew he cannot heave us all out of his ruins since it would be improper for you to be without a chaperone while you await your brother's arrival."

"But, dearest of Aunts," said Damon, "Whitthurst is an invalid, and the Priory's swarming with noisy workmen all day! Not salubrious, you see."

"Then stop 'em!" rasped Feather. "The Priory's been mouldering for centuries. Won't collapse if it has to wait a few days to get its face lifted."

"Whitt must be improving," Ridgley put in absently, "if he can survive riding all this way through a howling storm. Surprising. Felt certain he was going to turn up his toes, but—" He stopped as Feather dug an elbow into his ribs.

"Clumsy oaf!" she scolded. "Sophia's worried to death for the boy."

"He is not a boy," Damon corrected sharply, "but a courageous fighting man who was well aware of the risks when he undertook to serve his country."

Sophia was shocked by such blatant hypocrisy. Mistaking the reason for her pallor, Ridgley patted her hand. "Sorry, m'dear. Ain't the soul of tact, am I? But Cam's right, y'know. Whitthurst acquitted himself very well."

"He did, indeed!" Unable to restrain herself, she said ringingly, "And I am excessively proud of him. And of those other gallant gentlemen willing to sacrifice everything for the sake of—those of us who stayed at home." Fully aware that Miss Hilby had frowned at these words and that the Marquis was very still, she swept on. "Where would England be, I wonder, without such selfless dedication?" And seeing Clay's stunned expression, she could have cut out her tongue.

The Marquis raised his glass in salute and with his cynical grin murmured, "Where, indeed?"

Chapter 5

Despite the fact that she was bone weary, sleep was long in coming to Sophia that night. As soon as she turned down the wick on the oil lamp, she was wide awake and lay there, her feet cuddling the hot brick, her brain whirling. It had been so odd to undress and prepare for bed without Meg and Miss Jarrett to aid her. They were more like family than maids, and she missed them as much for their companionship as for their services. They had been with her since she left the schoolroom, had both accompanied her to Italy, and been pillars of support through the nightmarish fiasco of her home-coming.

Her first intimation that anything was amiss had been a letter from Mama saying that she had accepted an invitation to accompany friends to India. She had long wished to visit her favourite brother who was stationed in Darjeeling, and she hoped, she said, that her health might benefit by the avoidance of an English winter. It had sounded logical, yet the decision seemed to have been reached in such haste, and there was little mention of Whitthurst. Trying not to worry, Sophia had at once written to her brother, but receiving no answer had despatched an urgent enquiry to her Uncle George in Hampshire. His reply had been long in coming and couched in such vague terms that her anxiety had increased and she had sailed for England on June 22, only four days after the Battle of Waterloo.

Her housekeeper, Hettie Adams, had run out to meet her on the terrace of her loved Singlebirch. Sophia had been kissed, wept over, drawn inside, and there told the shattering news that the Viscount had joined a crack hussar regiment three months earlier. Her Mama had refused to impart this information for fear she would feel duty bound to terminate her happy stay in Italy and come home. Still struggling to absorb these facts, she had been ill prepared for the shock of learning that the Viscount had fought in the great battle and even now lay severely wounded in his room. She would never know how she had concealed her heartbreak when she first saw the dashing half-brother she had grown up worshipping. The loss of his right arm at the elbow had been a bitter blow to the athletic young man, but he'd borne it bravely and, had greeted her with a loving, though weak, smile and a show of spirit that had inspired her to fight tears away and attempt to emulate his own courage.

In the days that followed, he had seemed to improve. A week later, however, an infection had set in, necessitating a more severe amputation. It had been a ghastly experience, both physically and mentally. Whitthurst, already weakened, had lost heart, and Sophia had been faced with a full-scale battle for his life. She had waged it well, and now he was much improved. He was certainly not hardy enough, however, to go jauntering about all over the countryside in inclement weather. That he had even essayed the journey was surprising. His long and painful illness had taken much of his spirit. He always had a cheery word for her, but too often she would find him staring into space with a sad emptiness in his eyes. His boundless energy was gone, and he seemed to lack all desire to return, however gradually, into the society he had once so loved.

Sophia thought wistfully of their earlier years. Such happy years...Mama, joyful and proud of the children she adored;

51

Papa, always good natured; Stephen, brimming with vitality, constantly involved in some madcap scheme and as constantly in hot water. During his Oxford years, she had railed at him for his wildness, but he'd continued on his merry way, ever the Corinthian. When his studies were over, they had ridden together, hunted together, partied together. Steve had been amused by her devastating effect upon his friends, proud of her popularity, but horrified by her brief, early marriage. And then dear Papa had died very suddenly, and Stephen had become the head of the family. The Peninsula campaign had been raging in full fury, and, longing to go, he had promised his grieving stepmother he would not do so. A year later, Signor Bertolini had made Sophia his dazzling offer to join his family in Italy for further studies. It had been Stephen who, knowing how desperately she wanted to go, had ridden roughshod over her doubts and practically carried her onto the packet. She could see him still, standing on the dock, waving. Tall and strong and handsome. Her eyes blurred with painful tears. He would never wave that arm again.

The Marquis, his powerful hands about her throat, was forcing her back over the steps in the catacombs, toward those hideous broken railings below... A series of crashing discords woke her. Starting bolt upright, her heart pounding frenziedly, she stared at the faint glow surrounding the curtains. That was not Damon playing! Whatever else, the Marquis was a musician par excellence. She winced before another onslaught, turned up the wick of the lamp, and looked to the ormolu clock on the mantle. Half past two o'clock! It occurred to her suddenly that Horatio must be stamping about on the keyboard. But with a house full of company, why did no one attempt to stop the wretched bird? Pulling the pillow over her head, she lay there, seething with rage. She began to contemplate various ways of dealing with the feathered musician. They progressed in violence until, as time ticked past, there was nothing for it but to slaughter the monster!

She gave a sigh of relief as the bizarre concert ceased, but just as she was dropping into an exhausted slumber, another crashing chord sent her heart leaping into her throat. It was the outside of enough!

Two minutes later, burning with fury despite the frigid atmosphere, she marched along the hall, candle in one hand, poker in the other, her dressing gown buttoned up tightly, a cap neatly arranged over her hair. All was still.... And suddenly she knew why. The music room was directly below her! And her bedchamber undoubtedly shared the same chimney! That Machiavellian housekeeper had known her master allowed his sadistic pet to dance on the harpsichord in the small hours of the morning! Disregarding the fact that it had been her own insistence that had resulted in her occupation of the bedchamber, Sophia hastened on, the trumpets of war soundlessly blaring her advance, murder in her heart.

Throwing open the door to the music room, she swept in, poker held high, prepared to separate one goose from his musical aspirations.

The Marquis sat at the harpsichord. He wore no jacket and frowned (understandably!) as his long fingers moved firmly and unfortunately over the keys. Sophia halted, stupefied by the fact that even he could be so inconsiderate as to perpetrate such an uproar at this hour. His fist pounded down with a crash. He ran his fingers through his already rumpled hair in a gesture of furious impatience and grated, "Blast and damn the stupid thing!"

Horatio, snoozing on the rug before the fire, woke with a start, caught sight of Sophia's warlike pose, gave a screeching honk, trundled to the far corner of the room, and disappeared behind the drapes.

With lightning reaction, the Marquis sprang to his feet and spun around, a grim scowl on his face. To Sophia's horror, a long-barrelled and wicked-looking pistol had apparently leapt into his hand and was aimed unwaveringly at her heart.

For an instant, they stared at one another. Then the pistol was whisked from sight. "Ah..." he smiled. "Charades...!"

Recovering her wits somewhat but still trembling, she lowered the poker.

"Let me think..." He picked up his jacket and shrugged into it. "It could not be Boadicea, for you have no helmet, unless...that so charming cap?"

"W-why"—she breathed faintly, ignoring his nonsense,— "did you p-point that ugly...thing at me?"

He stepped towards her but stopped as she backed away. "We have had some thievery, ma'am. 'Pon my word, but your energy astounds me! I'd have thought that after such a tiring day you would be sound asleep."

"So would I," she said, her heart settling back into place once more. "When I heard the...noise, I thought Horatio was jumping about on the keys. I see now that I was mistaken."

53

He contemplated the upward tilt of her little nose and said gravely, "Most mistaken, my lady. He has been known to waddle, has made a few attempts at flying, and occasionally, I believe, might be said to rush. But I honestly cannot say I have ever seen him—jump."

That disconcerting dance of mirth was in his eyes. But she was not going to be taken in again. "I regret the error," she said coldly.

"Ah, but are you quite sure, ma'am?"

"Your pardon?"

He took another step towards her. "I have"—out went his hands in a charmingly Gallic gesture—"a sort of—er—*je ne sais quoi...*"

Sophia was obliged to remind herself sternly that this was the same vicious man who had so cruelly teased her in the catacombs. But she could not resist asking, "About me, uncle?"

"*Mais non*—niece. About Horatio."

She affected disinterest, and he went on. "Perhaps it is that, had it not been for my presence, my faithful friend might have joined his feathery ancestors this night. And with no picture gallery to assure his immortality!"

"Good God!" she gasped. "I never meant to kill—er—well, that is to say, I would *not* have! It was just that awful uproar!"

"Alas. My music does not please you."

"Nor you, evidently. To judge by your profanity."

Immediately, he was all seriousness. "Your pardon, Lady Sophia. I trust you will believe I'd not heard you come in."

"Of course. You could not *possibly* have done so." She gave a weary sigh and, lowering her lashes, said nobly, "I shall leave you to your...practising, my lord, and *try* to get some sleep." Looking up with saintly martyrdom, she discovered not repentance but a near grin on his face and was hard put to it not to abandon her tragic pose and favour him with one of her famous set downs.

"That I should disturb your slumbers, dear lady, cuts me to the heart," he mourned, entering her drama by resting one hand gracefully upon his chest. "However, since this house is built like a fortress, I cannot quite understand how my miserable stumblings should disturb you, had you been tucked beneath the covers of your—most fortunate bed."

His twinkling eyes travelled her dressing gown. She pulled the neck closer, an unnecessary movement since she

54

was far more fully clad than she had been at dinner. "Sounds," she snapped, forgetting her meekness, "travel up the chimney!"

Abruptly, all traces of humour vanished from his face. "Mrs. Hatters put you in my mother's room? Now truly this is unforgivable! Of course, you were awakened! My profound apologies, ma'am. I shall be silent as the grave." He bowed, but with anger lurking in his eyes.

"You are all consideration," she murmured. "I bid you goodnight, sir. And pray convey my apologies to Horatio."

With this Parthian shot, she turned away, feeling very much the conquering heroine. A loud "Honk" tarnished her glory. Flushed, she glanced back. Horatio's head protruded from beneath the drapes, the folds wrapped like a great cloak around his long neck. The Marquis stood, hands on hips, watching her, his teeth a white flash in his dark face. He strode to the door and swung it open, and she fled, her cheeks scarlet.

At the stairs, she paused. How angry he had looked when he'd discovered that Mrs. Hatters had given her the Duchess's room. His temper certainly matched those eyebrows, and it had not been Mrs. Hatters' fault. She retraced her steps. On the threshold of the music room, she stopped. The Marquis was seated at the harpsichord, leaning forward, his tousled head bowed onto arms that were crossed upon the edge of the lid. He looked a man totally defeated. Confused and unable to cope with such puzzling behaviour, she hurried away.

Sophia's second awakening was scarcely more propitious than her first. Her bed appeared to lift into the air, shake, and bounce back to the floor again. She gave a gasp, sat up, and then quailed as another crash shook the room. A sudden flood of sunlight blinded her, and she threw up one hand to shade her eyes.

"Good morning, m'lady," said a soft, husky voice.

Charlotte Hilby's maid, wearing a cap over her soft brown curls and with a welcoming smile lighting her blue eyes, placed a tray across Sophia's knees and imparted that it was past eleven o'clock and the workmen "hard at it." The tray held toast and jam, a soft boiled egg, a pot of tea, and, beside the monogrammed serviette, a crystal vase containing a red rose. She took up the rose and admired its rich fragrance.

55

"Lord Damon picked it special for 'ee," Nancy volunteered.

Instantly remarking that it was full of ants, Sophia requested the bloom be removed. Nancy peered curiously at the antless rose, and while pouring her tea, Sophia said a hurried "How very kind in Miss Hilby to allow you to help me. Did Lady Branden and Mademoiselle de la Montaigne bring their maids, also?"

"No, m'lady. We was only thinking to stay one night, and Lord Bodwin said he could be sure they'd go back if their abigails was at the Hall." She frowned a little. "So here be I, and not a body to talk to save for Mrs. Hatters and Ariel. And he..." She sighed and, searching through the press, asked, "Will you be wanting your habit, m'lady? They others has gone riding."

Sophia declined the chance for a ride and chose a morning dress that Nancy hurried away to iron. To the accompaniment of much pounding and hammering, Sophia finished her breakfast, then got out of bed and crossed to the windows. The wide lawns, bathed in bright sunshine, sloped down to an enticing fringe of flower gardens, among which a fountain played. Behind was a long line of birches, and beyond those the countryside spread in low tree-rich hills, girded by the sparkle of the river. Under her windows were the terrace and steps from which she had watched the Marquis struggle to retrieve his music in yesterday's storm. A drive path ran along the foot of the terrace, dividing at each side of the house to continue to the front and also winding away on both sides of the back lawn until it was concealed by the slope of the hill to the left and vanished among some trees to the right.

"Why," she murmured in surprise, "it's lovely!"

From behind her, the returning Nancy agreed and, upon learning that her ladyship had not visited the Priory before, confessed with a meaningful giggle that she and Miss Hilby had been here "lots o' times."

With a sudden and uncharacteristic streak of Puritanism, Sophia decided that Nancy was given to making lewd remarks. However, the girl was also pleasant, willing, and deft, and in no time Sophia was dressed and her hair arranged into clustered curls beside her small ears. Her lilac gingham was a pretty thing, if a little out of the present style, the low-cut bodice having a set-in bib, a white froth of lace that tapered to a snug waist below which the full skirt swept out

56

over several petticoats. She wore no jewellery save for a large amethyst ring that had been a gift from her brother. She touched it tenderly, wondering how he was faring on this beautiful autumn morning.

In the Great Hall a polite but decidedly unfriendly Thompson informed her that the master had not gone riding. His advice as to where "the master" was was lost in a burst of shouting and hammering that emanated from a room at the head of the south wing. Sophia gave him one of her most bewitching smiles and made her way to the rear terrace.

It was a heavenly morning, the sunlight warm, the air like wine. She felt refreshed and lighthearted as she wandered down the steps and across the lawns toward the flower beds. She turned back then to survey the house. From this vantage point it appeared even larger than she had supposed and much less gloomy. The lawns rose humplike behind each wing of the house in two long mounds that stretched out beyond the slope of the hill like crumbling arms, digging deep into the ground.

"Those," said a familiar deep voice at her elbow, "are the upper levels of the catacombs."

The Marquis wore dark-brown corduroy breeches and an open-throated white shirt, the collar folding back over a leather hunting jacket. He carried a gun over his left arm but had no game bag, nor was he accompanied by either loader or dog, which she thought peculiar.

He scanned her appreciatively and observed that she appeared to have enjoyed a good night's sleep despite its interruptions. She assured him that she had scarcely slept a wink, but the twinkle in his eyes so flustered her that she added hurriedly, "Is it not rather unusual to name a home after a crab?"

"Perhaps. But it was built in reverse, you see. The kitchens and servants' halls are at the front. The main rooms of the house, to the rear."

He turned as he spoke to survey the rambling building. Pride came into his face, and she realized he loved the Priory. With an effort she tore her gaze from him and turned, also, to the house. "Surely it was built to embrace the view," she mused. "Whoever designed it catered to beauty rather than custom. And very wisely. It is much prettier to the west."

He was silent, but she sensed that he was pleased. His eyes were on her again, and her heart began to beat faster.

57

With nervousness, of course. "The rooms you have remodelled are perfectly lovely," she remarked. "Do you really intend to restore the entire building?"

"Money thrown away?" he asked, with a faintly sardonic smile.

She thought of the fortune her father had squandered and of Esther Clay's foolishness that now caused her husband to be shadowed by the fear of shame and imprisonment, and a frown touched her brow.

"Alas," he sighed. "Again, you do not approve."

Irritated, she flashed, "I can think of no reason why you should seek my humble opinion, my lord."

"No more can I," he shrugged carelessly.

She gave an outraged gasp, then saw that his eyes twinkled at her through those long thick lashes and that a grin hovered about the corners of his mouth. He looked at her fully, his smile widening. "However," he went on, "in view of my advancing years and our relationship, humour your poor old uncle, I beg."

Why must he be so changeable? One moment cold and insulting, and in the next, displaying such devastating charm? He had maggots in his attic, that was the reason! He belonged in Bedlam! She determined to toss her head and walk regally away and was considerably surprised to hear herself saying, "I think it would be tragic to let it decay further. Already the library is delightful, the music room very fine, and the main dining room a joy."

Delighted, he asked with boyish eagerness, "Which is your favourite?"

She was tempted to answer "the Great Hall," which had not been restored and which she thought hideous. But for Clay's sake, she considered and said at last, "My bedroom. It especially has been decorated with love, I think."

His face became closed. "Thank you," he said, the words rather clipped. "My father had it remodelled many years ago. For my mother. I have kept it maintained, but it was his plan, not mine."

Disconcerted, she asked if she might see the stables. He brightened and, telling her it was a rather unusual arrangement, led her across the lawn, skirting the jutting bulk of the basements and continuing around to the north wing.

It was indeed unusual. The slope fell sharply away on this side, exposing part of the catacombs that had been converted into stables. A yard had been built around the area, with shrubs and young trees planted to conceal it from the front approach. The stalls looked clean and neat, and many fine horses were here.

Damon halted when they were still some distance away. Clay, dressed for riding, was talking animatedly with one of the grooms, and Sophia's heart lifted. She watched him with both affection and admiration, noting which, the man beside her scowled.

Beaming, Clay came toward them. Sophia slipped her hands into his, and he kissed her cheek and wished her a good morning. "Egad, Damon," he said, his eyes aglow with enthusiasm, "You've some dashed fine hunters here. That bay stallion's splendid!"

"Viking? Then by all means ride him," said the Marquis, looking bored.

"D'you mean it? I thought perhaps he was your personal— er, I mean..." Clay floundered, his excitement having betrayed him into forgetting the incredible fact that this man, with those legs, never rode.

Sophia had also been brought up in a household where horses were both a necessity and a passion and found Damon's attitude so incomprehensible that her pose slipped. She eyed him as though he were an oddity, and, very well aware of this, a faint flush stained his cheeks. "Do you never ride at all, my lord?" she asked.

"I find," he replied with a curl of the lip, "that horses— smell."

"Good God!" gasped Clay.

Damon's eyes were solid ice. "Unfortunately, if one spends a great deal of time around such cattle, one tends also to— smell."

The insult was calculated. It was more than enough to provoke any gentleman to an instant challenge. Clay's jaw set, and he had to bite his tongue to check a furious rejoinder. Sophia, however, was quite unable to restrain herself. "How fortunate, my lord," she said in a brittle tone, "that you have such a love for music, which, however poorly played, does not have an—*apparent*—odour." Her chin came up as she voiced those fateful words. Her eyes flashed fire. And, once more, she was seized by horrified remorse, while, at her side, Clay felt his heart sink, and he thought a miserable 'That's that!'

The Marquis, his face enigmatic, bowed perfunctorily,

swung away, and walked with his lazy stride past the stables. They watched in miserable silence as he disappeared beyond the line of trees; then Sophia moaned, "Oh, Marcus—I'm so sorry! My wretched temper!"

He smiled wryly, squeezed her fingers reassuringly, and said, "Don't blame you a bit, love," and, by mutual accord, they started back to the house.

Distantly, a shout of laughter rang out. Sophia spun around. Two grooms were coming through the trees, their faces alight with mirth. She turned back, not looking at Clay. How ridiculous that she had thought for a minute it had been Damon who laughed. And how even more ridiculous that she had hoped it was so.

"The thing is, you see," said Clay, shifting uneasily in the comfortable leather chair in Damon's pleasant and well stocked library, "I'm in rather a devilish fix. Quite"—he bit his lip and, forcing pride away, gulped—"under the hatches, to tell the truth."

The Marquis, watching him thoughtfully through the cloud of smoke that curled up from his favourite pipe, said, "And my revered parent is—ah, reluctant to accommodate you?"

"Well, he ain't without justification," said Clay honestly. "I'd a considerable fortune but—it all...sort of frittered away."

"The tables?" Damon asked dryly.

Clay flushed, and his gaze lowered. "Yes. Matter of fact."

"How very unwise." There was scorn in the deep voice. Clay gripped his fists very tightly on the arms of his chair and fought to control his rage. Damon all but sneered. "Are you asking me for a loan, Major?"

"No!" He choked back the 'blast you!' "Only your—help."

"I see." Quite aware of what this interview must be costing the other man, Damon leaned back his head, watching the smoke drift upward. "How long shall you have to wait for your inheritance if Vaille proves...ah...intractable?"

"A little over a year."

"Not so very long, surely?"

The sardonic tone, the slight lift of those heavy brows, sent Clay's nails digging into his palms. "I would not be here...begging," he said hoarsely, "except—two of my cred-

60

itors won't wait. They've started proceedings for Newgate."

Damon gave a gasp, and his eyes narrowed, and Clay, hope rekindling, waited.

"You were at Vitoria and Waterloo, so I understand?" Damon frowned. "And now they want to clap you up? Pretty shabby. Does my father know of it?"

"The last time I spoke with him, I wasn't quite that badly pressed for blunt. But—well, he was so...that is, I thought, if you—being his son—" Clay bit his lip. "I *won't* go to the cents-per-centers!" Damon waited with raised eyebrows and a faintly supercilious smile. Clay lunged out of his chair and strode to stand with his back to the fireplace. His nerves shredding at this total humiliation, he almost choked over the plea. "If you'd...put in a good word for me...I'd be most devilish—obliged."

Damon met those strained brown eyes in thoughtful silence, put down his pipe, and inspected a fingernail. Clay's hands were shaking when at last the Marquis stood, stretched lazily, and sauntered to the reference table. Taking up some papers, he murmured, "Regrettably, I fear I am quite unable to be of assistance to you, sir."

Clay wrenched around and placed one wet palm on the mantle, staring down into the hearth, knowing this desperate hope was gone. Surely, Damon had not refused him carelessly? Could it be that he was well aware his father had no intention of intervening? With his inexorable and judicial disdain, had Vaille decided a lesson was both deserved and desirable? Clay bit his lip, accepting the bitter fact that he must now throw himself upon the Duke's mercy. Esther's money lender was incurably ill and had no intention of leaving this vale of tears without balancing his accounts to the last farthing. The mantua maker was retiring to Spain and wanted her money at once, believing, apparently, that with him incarcerated, Esther would be driven to raising the cash. If Vaille was immovable, Newgate was inevitable. Newgate! God! That would kill Esther!

His head came up. He squared his shoulders, turned, and said brightly, "Quite understand. Sorry I bothered you at all," and started for the door, his smile set, his face taut and drained of colour.

"No bother," said Damon mildly. "Think nothing of it."

Clay, ignoring him, thought savagely, 'I won't, damn you!' and closed the door quietly behind him.

61

Chapter 6

The smokehouse was situated among some trees a short distance from the north side of the Priory and down a little rolling bank. Sophia was sure she had seen someone enter those trees just a few moments ago. She had only glimpsed the disappearing shadow, but if it was the "Heartless Viper," she intended to confront him.

She smiled faintly, pleased by this appellation. One way or another they had all been caught in his toils: Mama, herself, her adored brother, and now Marcus, whose gallant attempt to conceal his despair after Damon's refusal to help had wrung her heart. She was not quite sure whether vipers were constrictors, or if they merely bared their fangs, but since Damon did both, she decided to keep his new title. Of one thing she *was* sure, her words at the stables earlier had resulted in his cruel refusal to aid poor Marcus. If begging his forgiveness would help, she would try it, and with no qualms of conscience, since he had so much to answer for.

Something struck her calf with painful force. Her shocked yelp was accompanied by a loud hissing, and Horatio rushed past, wings low spread, honking his triumph. Muttering angrily, Sophia inspected the damage and was again startled by a man's shout, followed by a storm of profanity. Uneasy but curious, she crept into the trees, only to halt, staring her astonishment.

A giant of a man was doubled over just ahead. Upright, he must have been taller than six feet. His white hair curled in a muddled fashion all over his head, while an equally curly beard grew in lush but contained profusion about his chin. His white apron and the linen sack in one huge hand proclaimed him to be the cook, and remembering that Mrs. Hatters had said he was looby, Sophia ventured no closer. He was making odd grunting sounds, and his left arm swung back from time to time, accompanied by breathless cursing. He looked like a berserk gorilla, and, thoroughly frightened, she began to edge away. At once, he stopped moving and bellowed, "Who be there?"

Her breath fluttering, she prepared to run.

"Please," he called beseechingly, "if there do be some'un there, will'ee help me?"

She regarded him uncertainly. He had made no move to attack her, nor did he appear to be foaming at the mouth, which she'd heard was a sure sign of madness in dogs or men—women apparently being spared such unseemly manifestations of dementia. She called a timid identification of herself and asked what was wrong.

"It's that little bas—er, it's that naughty little goose o' his lordship's," he gasped. "Run 'twixt me legs and made me put me back out good and proper, milady. Ever since I picked up the cannon at Rodrigo, it ain't been the same."

"Good gracious," she cried, hurrying forward at once, "I am scarce surprised." She stepped around his bulk anxiously. "What can I do, Mr. Ariel?"

"Deal me a good 'un, ma'am. 'Bout midway 'tween me breadbasket and me shoulder blades, if'ee please. Hard like."

Sophia clenched her fist and, as requested, dealt him a good 'un.

"Yes," said Ariel encouragingly, "right there, milady. Now don't'ee never worrit, ma'am. Haul off and whack me."

"I did!" she cried with righteous indignation.

63

"You did!" he echoed. "With what?"

She clenched her fist and shoved it out for his inspection.

"Oh Lor'..." he groaned. "Well, try again, milady. Put both on 'em together and whack away."

She clenched her hands tightly, swung her arms down with all her might, and jumped back with a small scream, folding her hands under each arm.

"Ain't no use," sighed Ariel. "You'll just break them little hands o'yourn."

"Here," said a soft voice, "I'll help'ee, Mr. Ariel."

Nancy, armed with a sturdy branch, stepped past and swung the branch high.

"No!" cried an alarmed Sophia.

But the branch whipped down and broke with a crack across that broad back.

Ariel gave a sigh of relief, stood erect, then bent forward a little. "I do truly thank'ee, Miss Nancy," he said with an odd upward tilt of his head.

"And it do pain ye, I see," she observed kindly. "Let me help'ee. Come now, lean on me. 'Tis bed for ye, Mr. Ariel. My father has the very same kind of back. Why, I remember once..."

Sophia smiled as they walked away, the cook's massive arm resting carefully across the girl's shoulders, his eyes glued to her face with rapt fascination. It was quite apparent that anyone else had ceased to exist. She gathered up the sack the cook had dropped and followed them back to the house.

The Priory seemed very quiet and still. Sophia wandered rather disconsolately into the music room and found it as empty as the library had been.

"The workmen is eating their lunches, m'lady." Nancy's bright face beamed from the doorway. "Big Luke asked me to thank'ee for trying to help him. Doan't ye worrit about him; he's had trouble with his back since he come home from the wars."

"And you are expert at repairing it, I collect," Sophia teased. "Have you known him long?"

"Long enough, ma'am." The blushing but firm assertion augured ill for Ariel's continued bachelorhood.

"Aha." Sophia smiled. "I thought I sensed a fondness."

"No, ma'am. I love him. And will wed him—when he do ask me proper and civil like. Three times he do have spoken, but..." She took up the hem of her dainty apron and began to roll it between her fingers. Then, a dimple flashing beside her mouth, said shyly, "But—not quite the way I want, y'see."

"Minx!" laughed Sophia. "So you keep him dangling and sighing for you."

"What's worth having is worth waiting for, m'lady." Nancy smiled. "And Lord Damon be in the garden."

Sophia drew herself up, anger bringing a frown to her face. "I fail to perceive your meaning," she said austerely. "Explain, if you please."

"Oh, ma'am," Nancy whimpered, pale with agitation, "I doan't mean nothing. I only means as how ye'd been looking for my lord earlier! I only thought..." She wrung at her apron, her eyes filling with tears, and fled.

Staring after her, Sophia was almost equally affected. Why had she become so angry? The pretty creature had meant no harm, and she had frightened her. Probably, she thought with a scowl, the gracious Miss Hilby never said a harsh word to her. Probably, the gracious Miss Hilby never said a harsh word to anyone but drifted through life like an elegant swan, bestowing an aura of serenity on all about her. The Lady Sophia Drayton, on the other hand, rushed tempestuously from pillar to post, always blowing hot or cold but never lukewarm. The last word pleased her and was undoubtedly how Stephen would view Miss Hilby. It was obviously, however, not how my Lord Damon viewed her. Their hands had touched often at dinner the previous evening. Later, during the brisk conversation that had ensued when the gentlemen joined them in the music room, the golden beauty and Damon had several times murmured low-voiced asides to one another. When the Marquis had handed Miss Hilby her candle at the foot of the stairs, he'd bent his dark head to attend her remark, and her hand, placed familiarly on the lapel of his jacket, had patted him with a fondness also reflected very clearly in those limpid green eyes.

Sophia scowled at the painting that hung over the music room mantle, a small landscape, inadequate for such a large expanse of wall. She suddenly became aware of a workman watching her through the open door, a puzzled expression on his face. Flushing hotly, she all but ran into the garden and crossed the lawns toward the flower beds. Damon was well hidden. And then she heard voices from the clustering young trees between the rose garden and the cutting beds. An angry man was barking in a belligerent tone. "...and wot I want is a answer! Quick like. I ain't got all day, me good John or Tom or Wilbert! Speak up!"

After a brief silence, Damon's voice, mildly curious, asking, "Wilbert...?"

"Knowed a fella name of Wilbert. Hod carrier he was. Fell off'n the scaffold an' broke his neck. Wot's wrong with that?"

"A great deal, I would think," the Marquis pointed out, "if you happened to be Wilbert."

"Ar—but I ain't. And you, me poor chap, seem to have a deal o' trouble understanding wot I means. And wot I mean is—wot's wrong with Wilbert?"

"Why—he's dead, I imagine."

"Shows how wrong a cove can be, don't it? 'Specially a cove wot talks so fancy and don't understand nothing! Wilbert ain't dead. He goes around sorta sideways is all. But you, being so high and mighty, don't like the likes o' Joshua Jenks a'calling of you 'Wilbert'. Right?"

"It merely seemed an odd companion to John or Tom. However," Damon conceded equably, "if you are happy with it, Mr. Jenks..."

"I *ain't* happy with it, my cove! Wot I *am* is thinking on fixing up yer nostril tubes for yer! Considering it very serious I is, as you might say. All I done was to ask a honest question, and all I get is jaw! Well? Wotcha waiting on?"

Thoroughly irked, Sophia stepped closer. The Marquis, wearing a leather apron over his shirt and breeches, was cutting flowers. Cutting flowers! How much good it would do this indolent young aristocrat to settle his noble seat into a saddle and essay some sporting endeavour for once!

"I was not," Damon explained, inspecting a brilliant red rose critically, "'waiting on'-anything."

Mr. Jenks carried a sheaf of papers beneath his arm. He was tall and burly with a red, bloated countenance. His jacket and worsted breeches were too tight and his neckcloth greasy and ghastly. "Oh, you're a'waiting on something all right, me young bucko," he opined, mopping at his brow with a dark-blue kerchief. "An' I'm the very one to hand out just wot it is! So if you like, I'll fix up yer nostril tubes!"

Damon sighed, straightened, and turned to face him. It was odd. The irate Jenks was taller and heavier, yet somehow, when that dark head came up, it was the Marquis who appeared to look down upon his companion. "In what way, sir," he enquired patiently, "does it appear to you that my nostrils require assistance?"

"They're all stuck up," replied Jenks ferociously. "Need to be brung down a sight if you was to ask me!" And he waved a large and knotted fist under Damon's chin.

"The fact is," the Marquis pointed out, removing that fist with his own slim hand, "your opinion in the matter has not been solicited."

Mr. Jenks looked down in some bewilderment at the white marks those long fingers had left upon his wrist but blustered on. "Cor, wot a mouth! Did you ever," he enquired of the nearest cloud, "hear the like of it? Anyone'd take this here tuppeny-halfpenny gardener fer the high mucky muck his own self!" The cloud proving uncommunicative, he advanced another step and, thrusting his face under that straight but offending nose, snarled, "I'll say it one more time, blast yer eyes and toenails... Where's that old goat, Thompson?"

"And I shall tell you," the Marquis replied with quiet but firm emphasis, "as I did before, that I am not acquainted with an 'old goat'."

They faced one another thus for a few seconds. What the man read in Damon's steady gaze, Sophia could not tell, but he retreated hurriedly. Several of the roses the Marquis had already cut lay in a wicker basket at the edge of the flower-bed. A crafty light came into Jenks' small eyes. He edged closer, and his boot lifted.

Damon said a mild "Do not."

The tilt of his chin was suddenly ominous, and Jenks, who had already noted the width of those shoulders, backed away, snarling. "You'd best not be here when I come back, Mr. Top Lofty!"

The Marquis regarded him without noticeable terror. Jenks stamped toward the house, expounding at length on the sauce and lack of respect of today's young folks when all a body done was to ask of a simple, civil question, wot only needed a simple, civil answer.

Damon shook his head and turned to encounter a blaze of disgust in Sophia's eyes. A brief look of consternation was hidden as he bent to scan his flowers again and murmur, "An unexpected pleasure, ma'am."

"Why do you say what you do not mean?" she demanded.

"You, my lady, have been saying what you do not mean from the moment you came."

His calm but shrewd perception so flustered her that she had no rejoinder and therefore resumed the attack. "Why did you let that beast talk to you like that?"

The Marquis, selecting another rose, answered, "I fancy he was capable of little better."

"Had you told him who you are, he'd not have dared address you so."

"True," he admitted, turning the rose admiringly. "I should instead have been fawned upon and toad eaten." He shot a wry smile at her. "Infinitely worse."

Undaunted by this inescapable logic, she said fiercely, "Stephen—before he was crippled—would have shaken him like a rat and tossed him out the window!" Seeing his hand jerk a little when she said the word "crippled" caused her to become slightly muddled at the end. But declining to take advantage of the obvious fact that there were no windows readily available, he answered, "*Sans doute*, madam," after a pause. "And did you come seeking me to discuss my lamentable lack of courage?"

Meeting those wideset eyes, she had not the slightest notion what it was she had come to discuss. "The...bridge," she said, recovering but rather breathless. "I hope it is finished?"

She felt her cheeks redden at this bald rudeness, but his reply was just as lacking in grace. "I do so wish it was, ma'am, but you may be assured I have every available man rushing it to completion."

"Then you and—poor Ridgley—will soon be free once again to enjoy this—unique solitude. Until"—she glanced at him sideways—"your spa is completed. That will destroy your privacy to some extent, I suppose?"

"Scarcely, ma'am. It is five miles distant."

"And you could, of course," she murmured, touching a marigold with one dainty finger, "have a fence erected around the Priory."

"It might be less expensive. But my wall shall serve, I am sure."

"Wall? A *wall*? All around?"

"Gad, no! Just enclosing the house and grounds. The first ten acres should be sufficient. Do we build it to seven feet." Sniffing a white rose, he regarded her gravely across the petals. "Do you not agree?"

She recovered her poise with an effort. "Oh, I do. And you could have it topped with rusty nails. Just as a little—extra precaution."

He laughed. "What a monster you think me!"

She wished his laughter wasn't quite so infectious and that his incredible eyes didn't hold such a merry light. "I was only funning," she smiled.

"Of course, you were! Nails, indeed! No, no, dear lady. I am sure the broken glass will be quite adequate."

Chapter 7

The Marquis did not join his guests for a delightful luncheon served on the terrace. Afterwards, they scattered to their respective rooms. The workmen's undiminished uproar made a nap impossible, so Sophia settled down to write a letter to her housekeeper and, upon finishing it, went in search of the Marquis so that he might frank it for her. He'd implied the Toll Road might be passable; surely they could not be completely cut off here. There must be *some* way to have letters delivered to a post office.

A tremendous hammering came from a room at the head of the corridor, but the music room was quiet, the drapes drawn across all the windows. She had been sure she would find Damon there, but disappointed, she was about to look elsewhere when her attention was caught by a yellowing sheet of parchment on the music rack. The notes had an odd squared structure, and there were no time values or any symbols of instruction. There was no title; no composer's name, and the melody, if any, was weirdly inharmonious. It

dawned on her that this was the piece with which the Marquis
had wrestled so devastatingly during the night, though why
he should bother with the silly thing was beyond her. Curious, she peered at the faded notes. It was too dim to see
clearly, and she walked to the rear wall and drew back the
curtains, admitting a flood of light to the room.

"Close them, if you please," came a growl from behind her.
So he *was* in here and in one of his black humours by the
sound of it. She turned and said sweetly, "Why, uncle, I'd not
realised you were taking a nap. I do beg your pardon."

The Marquis, sprawling in a chair before the fire, deigned
to stand and fix her with a chill stare. He then stalked over
to slam the drapes shut, while remarking, "If you have come
to enquire about the bridge again, it appears—" A deafening
crash, followed by a tattoo of hammers interrupted him.
When comparative peace was restored, he continued, glaring
at her through the gloom. "It appears that the supports were
not as badly damaged as was first thought. My men already
have a framework erected. The bridge should be safe for foot
traffic in the morning."

Curiously depressed, she asked if he would be so obliging
as to frank her letter, and he was finishing that small task
while noting the utter absurdity of despatching a letter that
would probably not reach Kent until after she herself had
returned when Horatio rushed into the room, honking his
warning. At once Damon's eyes flashed to the door, his mouth
becoming set and grim. Sophia was disgusted. It was, she
thought, downright reprehensible that he should so dread
company. Her criticism was swept away by shock as she
heard a familiar voice outside.

"Never mind, Thompson. I'll announce myself to the old
curmudgeon!"

Chestnut curls wind tossed, grey eyes bright even in that
dim room, Sir Amory Hartwell strode in, checked, gaped,
then cried a joyous "Sophia! Egad, what wonderful luck to
find you here!" He bowed over her outstretched hands, and
pressed each to his lips. Turning reluctantly from her, he
crossed to Damon. "Why the surly look, *bon ami*? And what
the devil are you doing alone in the dark with my lady?"

Damon's eyes widened and directed a searching glance at
Sophia as he took his friend by the shoulders, smiled in return, and answered, "Welcome, *mon cher*! How good to see
you again!"

71

"And you, Cam. But what are you doing down here when—" He paused enquiringly as Damon's gaze shifted.

Mrs. Hatters trembled in the doorway, her face twitching with nervousness.

"Millicent?" said the Marquis. "Whatever is the matter?"

"Oh...my lord!" she faltered, wringing her hands. "It's Ariel. His back again—very bad! Mr. Thompson says he'll be confined to his bed for days!"

An odd expression flickered across Damon's face. Watching him, Sophia sensed that he was pleased! This gave him the excuse to be rid of them all. Before he could respond, however, the solid figure of the valet lurched into the doorway. Mrs. Hatters took one look at his vacuous grin, moaned, and fled.

Damon's eyes narrowed. "Jack," he said menacingly, "by thunder! Have you been at my brandy ag—"

Thompson raised one hand in a lofty gesture, placed the other against the wall to steady himself, and announced throatily, "Your Dukeship! His Lord, the Vaille of grace!"

Sophia gave a gasp. Hartwell snorted with mirth. Thompson bowed low and lower yet until he lay comfortably outstretched across the threshold.

Damon groaned a soft "Oh, my God!"

A clear, mellow voice protested, "You do me far too great an honour, Camille. It is only—your father."

The man who entered the room seemed to fill it with his magnificent presence. Tall, poised, elegantly clad, he stepped across Thompson's recumbent form without the slightest evidence of disapproval. To Sophia's delight, he then paused, bent to straighten the butler's neckcloth, and again proceeded to his son.

Damon shook the slender white hand held out to him, then stepped back, murmuring, "You are most welcome, sir."

The Duke neither moved nor spoke. His hand still extended, he stood there, his head tossed back a little, the fine brows lifting, a faint smile still playing about his mouth. He was an inch or two above his son's six feet but seemed at that moment at least a head taller.

Damon flushed and bowed to touch the thin fingers to his lips.

"How pleasant," said Vaille languorously, "that you have not forgotten your manners completely. Might I prevail upon you to draw the curtains?" He raised a jewelled quizzing glass to peer down at Thompson with new interest. "Unless you

72

are conducting a seance, perhaps?"

Sophia strove unsuccessfully to choke back a gurgle of laughter and marvelled that she had ever imagined this dynamic individual to be aged and infirm. Damon shot a glance of desperate entreaty to Hartwell and crossed to pull back the curtains. Sir Amory, moving quickly past Sophia, bent to slip an arm under Thompson's shoulders, then half dragged him to his feet and out of the room.

Vaille ignored the muddled protests emanating from the retreating butler and addressed Sophia admiringly. "I can readily see, dear lady, why my son would seek to keep you hidden."

The Marquis stepped forward to perform the introductions, but his father stopped him with an airy wave. "Lady Drayton, is it not? You bear a remarkable resemblance to your gallant brother, ma'am."

His eyes, very blue and keen, flickered over her in a shrewd appraisal. Briefly, she knew how a bird must feel when trapped by a cat. That gaze seemed to penetrate to her guilty conscience, and she bowed her head to hide scarlet cheeks as she made her curtsey. The Duke kissed her hand and vowed that the descriptions of her beauty were inadequate, adding, "Do you not agree, Camille?"

"Yes," said Damon curtly as his friend returned and threw him a reassuring wink. "Your grace has met Sir Amory Hartwell, I believe?"

Vaille raised his quizzing glass, the better to scan Hartwell from head to toe in a critical fashion seemingly lost upon the light-hearted young man who bowed before him. "Servant, sir," Sir Amory beamed.

"Thank you," said Vaille without warmth, and, strolling to the mantle, looked thoughtfully at the small painting above it.

Following his gaze, Damon made haste to offer refreshments, but the Duke, without shifting his attention, murmured that he had taken lunch at "The Wooden Leg" and then frowned slightly as a cacophony of hammering split the quiet.

Damon could barely contain his incredulity until the noise lessened. "You walked across the ... scaffolding?"

"Of necessity," Vaille replied absently, "since I have not yet mastered the art of flight. And why so surprised? I am not yet totally decrepit." He managed to tear his eyes from their preoccupation with the painting and, glancing at Sophia, sighed hopefully. "At least, I trust I do not appear so."

"I venture to believe, your grace," she said, a dimple dancing in her cheek, "that anyone foolish enough to think so would commit a most serious blunder."

At once, that wistful mouth curved to a smile, and his eyes lit in a way she found delightful. "Thank you, my dear. I perceive that my son has indeed become a connoisseur."

Hartwell, who had been previously amused by the exchange, now looked rather annoyed, then smiled, "By George, sir! I hope I'll have your energy when I've reached your age! Did you trot all the way from the bridge?"

"I never—*trot!*" the Duke imparted as from a great height. "I rode."

"A—horse, sir?" asked the mystified Damon.

Vaille replaced the poker, which had been left out of the holder. "A wheelbarrow."

Both young men gasped at this, and Sophia gave a trill of laughter that brought new admiration into the piercing blue eyes that were turned upon her.

"Most obliging fellow. A little—ah, reluctant at first. Said he had some business with a gardener's nostrils, of all things!" He saw the laughing glance that passed between his son and Lady Drayton and nodded. "A most ridiculous excuse, I agree. Added to which, the fellow had the gall to order a workman to give the 'old loose screw' a hand. Oh, don't faint, my boy! He was somewhat justified since I had to make a rather hasty leap for the bank. The wind was coming up, you see. However, I persuaded him to provide the necessary propulsion himself."

His smile was very bland, but, knowing his father, the Marquis chuckled despite himself. Vaille, shared his mirth for a moment, then asked, "What *is* that?" and gestured toward the painting.

Damon sobered. "A painting, your grace," he said with wooden impudence.

"It is?" The Duke raised his glass and peered curiously at the article in question. "A conversation piece, beyond doubting. We are, I take it, to guess what it depicts?"

Damon's jaw tightened. Hartwell grinned broadly, and Sophia sensed that a small truce had just ended. The Duke's eyes twinkled merrily at her, however. "We must let your beautiful guest play first. What is it, dear lady?"

"I believe you quiz me, your grace," she smiled. "It is a landscape."

74

"Landscape?" Enlightened, Vaille peered upward, again employing his glass. "By gad! I do believe you are right! And here I'd thought it a still life!"

Hartwell laughed aloud, and Sophia looked curiously from father to son, wondering what it was all about.

Damon, his face totally closed, said with formal politeness, "I shall have it taken down while you are here, sir. Since it offends you."

"No, no, Camille. I'd not dream of putting you to such inconvenience."

"Not at all, your grace. I'll certainly not miss it. For one night."

Hartwell's mirth faded, and his jaw dropped. Stifling a gasp, Sophia surprised a swiftly concealed but so stricken expression on the Duke's face that she was conscious of a near overpowering impulse to run and comfort him.

"If you insist, dear boy," Vaille murmured. "I realise it is the fashion these days to move paintings about, but I must admit I thought the portrait of your mother looked especially well there."

"It is being cleaned, sir."

"I realise I am seldom here," Vaille said slowly. "It must be five months since last I saw it. Yet I do not recall that it appeared soiled."

"We had trouble with the chimney," Damon explained, his eyes fixed upon the ruby in his father's cravat. "Smoke, you know. Quite damaging. In truth, I am positively beset by disasters."

"Yes," agreed Vaille. "I stepped over one when I arrived."

Unmoved by the smile that touched his father's eyes, Damon said a bored "A comparatively minor problem, your grace."

"Oh? Not so major as the demands upon your... hospitality, perhaps."

"I am desolated"—Damon gave one of his eloquent gestures—"but I fear my hospitality can best be evidenced by conveying my guests to the nearest hostelry."

"Is this," Vaille probed gently, "a French custom?"

Damon's eyes flickered, but his tone was as cool as ever. "My chef is abed with a sprained back, sir. The bridge collapse prevents the maids from coming, and even were Thompson not—ah—indisposed, the poor fellow could not possibly attend to all our wants in addition to his other duties."

"How terrible for you," Vaille murmured. "My man—you

will recall Orpington—follows this afternoon. But that would be little consolation, I collect?"

"Alas," sighed Damon, "Thompson cannot cook, your grace. But my family and friends will not be inconvenienced. I am advised Rowan's Bridge has been repaired. 'The Gold Crown' on the Toll Road is a splendid posting house, and you shall be much more comfortable there than in my poor old . . . haunted . . . ruin."

That there was some hidden meaning in the last words was obvious, and Vaille all but winced. That any gentleman could so wound his father was beyond Sophia's comprehension. Controlling her disgust with an effort, she said timidly, "Your grace, might I beg a word?"

The Duke started as if he had forgotten that others were present and begged her pardon for having subjected her to this foolish discussion.

"It is only," she offered, "that since you have come all this way . . . Well, I scarce dare enter my own kitchen, my chef is so militant about his territory. But I love to cook. It would give me great pleasure to repay Lord Damon . . . in this small fashion." And she smiled upon the Marquis with much sweetness.

Briefly, Damon's expression reflected stark fury, then became unreadable. Hartwell's face was a mask of astonishment. The Duke, a gleam of unholy joy in his eyes, exclaimed, "A lady of quality in the kitchen? How shocking, ma'am!"

During luncheon, Lady Branden had invited Sophia to join her later in a game of two-handed patience. Driven by curiosity, Sophia now availed herself of the offer and, during a bewildering course of instruction, watched her hostess place a red eight upon a black nine and remark that she would delay greeting the Duke until he might have "cooled down," "for I vow his rages terrify me!"

Sophia abandoned all pretence at understanding the rules of this erratic game. She placed a black queen below a red queen and, deciding that they looked nice together, asked, "Does the Marquis resemble his Mama?"

"Have you never seen Ninon?" Feather looked up, her eyes sharp. "Oh—I forget the portrait is gone from the music room. Does Vaille know of it yet? And didn't like it, I'll wager! Yes—Damon resembles her. More's the pity! She was much too beautiful for this world, just as he is too blasted hand-

76

some!" She sighed, stared at her cards, then said, "You know the story, of course?"

Sophia admitted her ignorance, and Feather brightened. "Then I shall enjoy myself with a cosy gossip! Pour me another cup of tea if you will, and I shall regale you with the details, though 'tis not a pleasant story." She waited while Sophia obligingly refilled her cup, then, stirring at it dreamily, began. "When Vaille was younger, he was a wild young Buck, a veritable terror around the ladies, but such a charm..." She sighed, saddened by memory. "Even today, no woman with eyes in her head can fail to see it in him. Suffice to say that he ran off with the leading Toast, a widow ten years his senior, who already had a child, a pretty little twelve-year-old girl. Come to think on it, that same little girl grew up to become your brother's Mama—but that's another story. Anyway, Vaille was a reckless young firebrand. He was travelling in France when his carriage chanced upon a band of rabble attacking the coach of a noblewoman and her daughter. Philip immediately flew to the rescue. He and his coachman and valet succeeded in driving off the murderous crew, though it was a hard-won struggle. Vaille himself was wounded, and the Comtesse de la Montaigne insisted he be taken to her chateau. Ninon was little more than a child, but you can guess the effect it had on her. She never forgot him, and four years later, when his first wife died, she married him." She paused, her eyes sombre.

After a moment, Sophia prompted curiously, "Were they happy, ma'am?"

"Feather!" the big woman scowled, and when her companion smiled and nodded, she resumed. "Ideally so. Ninon worshipped him and was so lovely—angelic is the only word could begin to describe her. Only..." Her hands clenched as though she were deeply distressed. "I'll not go into the nightmare that followed. Enough that when Camille was nine years old they quarrelled bitterly. Ninon ran away—with the boy. Poor Vaille's world had fallen apart, and he could not tell what prompted it all. He thought Ninon had taken a pet and, his own hackles roused, took himself to Dover and his yacht. Ninon was racing to Town in a fast chaise. The groom said later that she kept urging him to greater speeds despite a heavy storm. She was afraid, I suppose, that Vaille would follow...poor child..."

Aghast, Sophia murmured, "There was an accident?"

"The chaise overturned. A wheel came off, I believe. Ninon—rest her soul—was mortally hurt. Poor Camille. His beloved Mama lay dying, and his father had vanished. We could not inspire in him the will to live, although he was not badly injured. Just before Ninon died, she made us send for her Mama. The Terror had chased the Montaignes from France by then, and they were living in Brussels. The Comtesse came at once. She was a lovely woman, almost as beautiful as her daughter had been and with the same pretty way of speech. She was the saving of Camille. He crept back to life again, but he lost all memory of that entire week and has never regained it."

"Did you send for the Duke?"

"We tried." Feather gave a helpless shrug. "We could not trace him. It was, in fact, four months before he returned to England. By that time...well, what could we do? The Comtesse was devoted to her husband, and they were preparing to remove to their chateau near Ghent and make it their permanent home. She had to return. Camille's life still hung in the balance. He loved her and had lost the mother he worshipped. The Comtesse took him with her. And he stayed. For seventeen years!"

"Good gracious! Whatever did the Duke say? Did he make no attempt to get his son back?"

"He did, indeed!" Feather shuddered. "But the Comtesse prevailed. Damon stayed in Belgium, and France, when it was safe. And only came home two years ago."

Sophia thought, 'And even now, after all his father's heartbreak, cannot find it in him to be kind...' "Poor Vaille," she said softly.

"Poor, indeed, for he lost all in life that mattered."

"And he seems so kind. So reaching out for warmth and affection."

"And so curst obliged to correct the world." Feather chuckled. "To straighten every errant branch and leaf—uncurl each shrivelled petal. I vow he'd right the earth on its axis if 'twas within his power!"

Remembering how the Duke had restored Thompson's cravat, how fastidiously he had replaced the poker, Sophia smiled. "Not such a dreadful trait, surely, does one view the whole man. We all have failings, God knows."

"Yes," sighed Feather. "I wish Camille could see that..."

78

Chapter 8

Sophia awoke with a start and, glancing to the clock, saw that it was a little past the hour of four. The hammering had ceased, which would account for her having been able to sleep. She was thinking that the Duke was probably responsible for the peace and quiet when she heard his voice drifting from the fireplace. It would be wicked to listen. There was, surely, nothing more contemptible than an eavesdropper. She swung her feet off the bed and tiptoed to the mantle.

"I am surprised," he was saying, "that Géant tolerates Horatio."

A pause, and Damon replied without expression, "Géant died."

"How sad for you. What dreadful luck you have with dogs."

"*Che serà serà...*" Damon yawned. "Horatio suits. And it was some months ago, nor of such import that you should let it influence your decision, sir."

"You are so shrewd," mused Vaille. "But you always were a bright lad. You did fare well in school, didn't you?"

"I did not go to school, sir." Damon sounded bored. "*Grandpère* preferred a tutor."

"Of course. How absent-minded I am become. For myself now, four years at Magdalen—yet I was not a good scholar. I could never make a lecturer, I fear."

"And yet," murmured the Marquis resignedly, "are about to essay the task."

Vaille laughed. "Merely as a preamble to my—decision. It seems incredible that we have never before been—ah—able...to discuss the matter of your Mama's death. It has been nineteen years, Camille. Shall you never forgive me?"

It came so suddenly and Vaille's tone grew so wistful that Sophia was taken by surprise. She fancied the voice of the Marquis to be a little unsteady when he answered, "I thought we enjoyed a satisfactory relationship, sir."

"Satisfactory?" breathed Vaille. There was an edge of steel to the words now. "Did you, by God! I have seen you less than a dozen times these past nineteen years! In truth, I scarcely know you! Since you returned to England, I have been granted the pleasure of your company on a few brief occasions I could count on one hand, and otherwise consistently avoided, though I've offered you every inducement to share my various houses—even if you have no desire to share my company! You were educated in France—one must not expect too much, I realise! You are skilled in literature and the arts, play the harpsichord and pianoforte tolerably well, certainly employ a fine tailor. And—oh, forgive me—do I overlook something?"

Sophia flinched a little and was surprised. Her initial estimate of the Duke had been one of power. Diverted by sympathy, she'd come to think him soft. But there was nothing meek about the tone he now employed! Damon had made no response, and she could picture his eloquent shrug.

After an instant, Vaille resumed. "Ah, yes. I *knew* there was something more. You are a fine shot." His tone hardened. "Which you prove with distressing frequency."

"One fatality only, your grace."

"Perhaps, did you choose more manly pursuits, your behaviour might prove less unsettling. To men, at all events."

"My tastes," drawled the Marquis, "do not run to fisticuffs, sir. Nor to racing madly about the countryside clinging to the back of a brainless animal while looking and smelling like some crude aborigine!"

80

"Beast!" breathed Sophia between clenched teeth. "Foul...viper!"

"And *my* tastes," the Duke flashed, "do not run to a grown man who fritters away his time tickling the keys of a harpsichord like some dainty miss and skulking sullenly in a...a maudlin mausoleum!"

Sophia raised a soundless cheer, licked her finger, and scored a triumphant mark upon the marble of the fireplace.

Damon sighed. "Then how extreme fortuitous that, pleasing you so little, I contrive to remain where you must not be constantly reminded of my—er—inadequacies. To the furtherance of which, I shall remove my offensive presence."

Sophia, her breath snatched away by this supreme insolence, heard the movement of a chair and all but fell into the fire in her eagerness to catch the Duke's reply. When it came, the words were quietly uttered, but that soft voice made her tremble. "I do not recall having granted you my permission to leave." A breathless hush. Vaille's words whipped across it. "Sit down!"

"I am aware," the Duke went on, still in that tone midway between an arctic winter and the thrust of a rapier, "that you hold me to blame for the death of your mother. I have given you time because I know that her death wounded you deeply. Nineteen years is, I think, time enough! During those years, you have distinguished yourself neither as a scholar nor a sportsman. I dared to hope you might remember that you are predominantly an Englishman and feel some obligation to fight for your country. You evidently did not experience such a commitment." Another pause, and he enquired with chill politeness, "Do I detect a protest?"

"Not at all, your grace," Damon sighed.

"For shame!" whispered Sophia contemptuously.

"Instead," Vaille resumed, "you contrived to keep your own precious skin intact while gallant gentlemen by the thousands, including many of your personal friends, were sacrificing their lives. I was downright shocked to learn that you have made not the slightest attempt to visit poor young Whitthurst, despite—" He stopped speaking, and Sophia jumped when he thundered, "What in the devil d'you think you're about?"

"It's one of Horatio's feathers, sir," Damon chuckled. "See here—caught in my sleeve, begad! Why, that little rascal, I vow he—"

81

"I do not," rasped Vaille, "give one good God damn about your feathered playmate! You will attend me when I address you, my lord!"

The Marquis muttered a plaintive excuse that he had, indeed, been attending. Sophia, her heart palpitating, prayed she might never be present when the Duke was this provoked.

"I watched you pouring money into this...ruin..." —Vaille sounded slightly strangled—"and said nothing, deeming it infinitely preferable than that you squander your fortune on the tables at White's or Watier's or one of the hells I know you to frequent! I observed your prowess with your bits of muslin and waited patiently in the hope you might become more—anglicized. However! I hear you are become involved in that which I *will not* condone! That you were, in fact, closely acquainted with Sir John Stover and that wretched Bartholomew Mullins!"

It seemed to Sophia that she detected a gasp. She frowned, trying to think where she'd heard those names before.

"Of one thing I am quite sure," said Vaille grimly. "No son of your mother's could possibly sink so low as to join that—unspeakable sect!"

Cobra! Mullins and Stover had been exposed as having been members! But—the son of the Duke of Vaille? That *could not* be! Horrified, Sophia drew a step away from the fireplace, staring at the flames as though the devil himself capered amongst them.

Vaille rasped, "Is Craig-Bell also numbered among your friends, my lord?"

"I—I know him...sir..." stammered Damon in a shaken voice.

"And admire him?"

"I dislike him—intensely."

"Thank God you've that much discrimination! In my opinion the entire membership of that stinking club should have been shot out of hand! Which would be too decent a death for most of 'em. When I think of all the grief they brought about with their vicious pranks and blackmail, their lust and savagery and treason! And all in the name of 'fun'! Gad! It makes me want to vomit! One can only thank God they are disbanded at last and—hopefully—destroyed!"

"Then...you have no further cause for concern on—"

"To the contrary! Since you choose to associate with Cobra

82

members, the time has come for me to intervene in your checkered career!"

Apparently regaining his composure, Damon now sounded amused. "So I am to leave Cancrizans and return to London. I must marry and breed many Brandens with some dull and dutiful wife... *n'est-ce pas, mon père?*"

"The prospect amuses you. I, however, am *not* amused by such an address. You are a peer of this realm, Damon. Not a French *émigré*. Try to remember that fact!"

Sophia shrank. The vitriol in Vaille's tone was too much for her. She knew that her behaviour had been unpardonable and tardily put her hands over her ears as she retreated toward the bed and stepped into her slippers. How ghastly for the Duke that his son had chosen such foul company. And how repelling Damon's insolence to the father who had known so little of happiness.

She tidied her hair and hurried downstairs to the kitchen.

"Good God!" boomed Feather, having swung open the kitchen door. "Sophia! I couldn't credit it when Mrs. Hatters said you was in here! What on earth are you doing?"

"Grating cheese," said Sophia, mourning a broken fingernail. "Somebody has to cook dinner." She apprised Feather of Mr. Ariel's lamentable condition, and noted, "Mrs. Hatters is too nervous to attempt a meal for so large a group."

Bestowing a feeling look on her new friend, Feather sighed, "Poor Camille. A house full of company and a lack of suitable food—horrors! How kind of you, dear child, to help the boy. And what skill you must possess! Did you learn to cook in Italy?"

"Er... no..." Sophia admitted, attending diligently to her grating.

Feather nodded and began to stamp about, swinging open doors and drawers until she discovered several immaculate aprons, one of which she proceeded to fasten about her bulky person. "All my days I've longed for such a golden opportunity," she said blithely. "Oh, I'm not timid, Sophia. But my chef would have my liver in a trice did I dare venture into his domain! And—oh, how I have yearned to dabble in eggs and flour! Oh, for the joy of serving a man a dish beyond

83

words delectable and knowing 'twas I and I alone who created it!"

Sophia gave a little laugh and was at once crushed in a fierce embrace.

"I should have known in the first instant I saw you that you were a jewel of the first water!" Feather exclaimed. "Now tell me—am I not the very essence of a chef?"

She wore a rose-coloured gown of the finest silk, and the bodice, swooping low, was edged with small pink feathers, while in her already crumbling coiffure reposed two larger such adornments. With the apron wrapped about her middle, she resembled no chef Sophia had ever laid eyes upon. However, agreeing with this willing accomplice, she enquired what deliciousness Feather planned to concoct.

"Here is Ariel's menu for tonight—he always prepares 'em in advance..." Feather drew a paper from a drawer and peered at it. "Vichyssoise...skewered scallops...roast chickens stuffed with chestnuts...veal pasties...spinach flambé...creamed green peas and pearl onions...potato balls...trifle...lemon puffs..." She stopped as a small whimper emanated from her companion and asked innocently, "Do you intend to make all that, love?"

"I...only," Sophia croaked, "know how to make cheese soufflé! And I only made that once!"

Feather gave a shattering roar of laughter. "I knew it! Else I'd never have dared join you! I can make trifle. I think."

"For why," called Genevieve from the open door, "do you gather here?" Her eyes became very round. "Ah...How *delicieux*! I may play, too—yes?"

"Oh, gad!" Feather chortled. "This will be a meal to drive that wretched nephew of mine straight back to Town!"

84

Chapter 9

It required the combined efforts of Sophia and Mademoiselle de la Montaigne to convince Feather she must lie down upon her bed. She sang heartrendingly all the way upstairs and once staggered backward in a plunge that near sent them all toppling. Genevieve giggled irrepressibly throughout, but Sophia was in a fever of dread lest Vaille or the Marquis catch a glimpse of their thoroughly inebriated kinswoman.

She had not dreamed that a simple disagreement over whether one added rum, sherry, or cognac to a trifle would result in this shocking *débâcle*. Obviously, Feather's decision to sample a little of each on a finger of sponge cake had not resolved her dilemma, necessitating a second or even a third round of sampling. She heaved a sigh of relief when they were safely inside the room. Feather tossed herself with complete abandon on to her bed, breaking two of the plumes in her hair and lying on her back, arms tossed wide, still singing disjointedly.

"You, *ma cherè*, shall run down the stairs now," said Genevieve between spurts of laughter, "and tuck the white sauce for your soufflé into the pantry. My *poulets* shall not be done for several of the hours. Your soufflé—you must delay." She tugged at Feather's apron and giggled. "Am I not the clever poetess?"

Obediently, Sophia returned to the wreckage of the kitchen and placed her bowl of grated cheese and the white sauce on the pantry shelf beside Feather's custard. She reflected sorrowfully that there was little to choose between their efforts; both sauce and custard were inclined to be brown and lumpy. She had burned the sauce when she'd been paralyzed by the shock of seeing Lady Branden suddenly sit down in the middle of the floor and start to sing 'Les Marseillaise'. Genevieve, who had insisted upon standing rigidly at attention during this rendition, had eventually, if hysterically, consoled her by observing that "the *fromage* shall cover the multitude of sins."

That multitude seemed magnified when Sophia shudderingly surveyed the once-neat kitchen. She was hot and weary and, deciding she had fought the good fight and was entitled to a respite, went into the cool glory of sunset to pick some flowers. She lingered in the garden for quite some time and had a full basket of fragrant blooms when she stepped up to the scullery door. It swung open before she touched the latch. Damon's tall figure loomed before her, and her heart began to hammer. He reached for the basket, and she allowed him to take it, then slipped past. He said nothing, but the frown in his eyes added to her trepidation.

He set the basket beside the rear sink and sneered, "Had I suspected such a fount of energy, I'd have hired you when you first applied, ma'am."

Sophia smiled coolly. She had scored a major victory in offering to cook dinner, thus preventing him from ousting his unwelcome guests. That he was thoroughly enraged was evidenced by the tight set to his lips. Considering his preoccupation with such mild pursuits as music and architecture, it was odd that there was an aura of power about the man. Yet even with her new knowledge that he was linked to Cobra members, she was not afraid of him. She picked up the small shears and snipped off a broken leaf. "I try always to help where there is need, sir," she said piously.

86

"Good gad! An inveterate do-gooder! The plague of the world!"

Sophia maintained her saintly pose with difficulty and, cutting a daisy much too short, pointed out that his own servants could not be expected to find the time for such trivial matters.

"You surprise me, ma'am. I've always thought flowers charming. Still, you're probably right. Shall we discard them?"

He reached for a handy bucket. Longing to ply her shears on his reptilian throat, she placed herself between the Viper and his intended victims and wondered aloud if Mrs. Hatters had gone to lie down. "For the poor soul must be quite exhausted." She cast a look of reproach at his expressionless features. "In truth, I never have seen so large a house with so small a staff. You are indeed fortunate, my lord, that these hard times enable you to—er—retain such tireless servants."

Damon blinked at this excellent counter-attack. "They are adequate for my needs—usually," he allowed. "And Mrs. Hatters has most certainly *not* gone to lie down. She knows I do not permit laziness in my menials."

"*Laziness!*" Sophia spun furiously to brandish a rose at him but caught a glimpse of a twinkle that so confused her she had to pause an instant before she was sufficiently recovered to warn, "Take care, my lord, that the poor lady does not collapse from pure exhaustion. As did Mr. Thompson."

She'd not intended to add that last sentence, but his smothered chuckle recalled the scene so vividly that she all but laughed aloud.

Damon opened a cupboard stocked from floor to ceiling with vases, urns, bowls, and figurines. "Should Millicent fall ill, it is a comfort to know how"—he cast an ironic eye upon the littered kitchen—"how—er—efficiently you can step into the breach. I cannot but admire your stamina, but then you are from Kent, and country-bred girls are always the strapping ones, are they not?"

Sophia's pretty mouth was quite literally hanging open by reason of this revolting testimonial. He reached to a high shelf, thus concealing his mirth, and went on. "I rather suspect Mrs. Hatters has merely gone down into the catacombs to feed the fireboy."

"Oh, my heavens!" Sophia gasped, her own abuses forgotten in the face of this new infamy. "Do you force a child to labour in that hideous place...at this hour?"

"Indeed not, ma'am. We feed him when his work is done. He has to rise early so as to set the fires and stoke up the stove for Ariel. And there is wood to be chopped for the day. But once he is finished with the windows, he has only to scrub the kitchen, steps, and terraces, haul the refuse for my gardeners, and clean out the stables. He is usually returned to his cell by eight of the clock at night." Her beautiful eyes were almost as round as her mouth, and struggling to maintain his composure, he handed her a huge silver urn.

Sophia took it numbly and essayed a faltering "C-Cell?"

"Why, they run away, you see," he sighed. "Or was used to. Ungrateful brats! But now I've had the chains installed, I've not lost a fireboy since the last one got stuck in the chimneys somewhere..." This last touch proved his undoing, and he failed hopelessly to keep the quiver from the side of his wide mouth. Sophia, becoming aware of it, fought to remain angry, but, despite herself, laughter leaped in her heart and danced into her eyes. She thrust the urn back at him and, endeavouring to sound stern, decreed that it was much too large and that the amber crystal vase would serve.

The amber crystal vase was barely visible at the back of the top shelf. Damon glanced with some resentment at the lady and surprised a dimple that made the task well worthwhile. He went to work, removing vases, bowls, and bric-a-brac; thinking the way clear at last, he barely caught a valuable porcelain patch box after it bounced off his head. He was a little out of breath when he handed her the desired object, and beholding the sparkling look on her face, his breathing was stopped altogether.

For a still moment, they gazed at one another. Their hands both supporting the vase, were very close together. It seemed to Sophia that she was caught in an amber haze, drifting helplessly toward Damon's incredibly tender mouth.

She tore her eyes away and, scarcely knowing what she said, stammered, "You have been teasing me, sir—and—I deserved it for appearing to criticize. I am quite aware we impose upon you and you do not care for company." And never dreaming how close she was to being seized and crushed and kissed, she felt the tension between them still and, panicky, chattered on. "My own home, of course, is open to our friends at every season of the year, and always shall

88

be." She realised at once that she made Singlebirch sound more like Blenheim and with sinking heart waited for him to ridicule such a fatuous remark, but he only said gravely, "I trust that holds true also for—elderly relations, ma'am?"

"Y-yes..." She took up a rose and staring at it, mumbled, "of course."

"Then I shall not need to bring my man, since you doubtless keep several 'gentleman at chambers'?"

She did not see the smile that accompanied these words and thinking herself thoroughly (and deservedly) set down, retorted sharply, "No, we do not. But neither do we keep a skeleton staff and make of *them* skeletons."

His eyes flashed to her in a narrowed appraisal. "My people, ma'am," he frowned, "are quite at liberty to leave my service if they are unhappy."

"Were you a servant, my lord, could *you* be happy in a house such as this?"

His chin lifted at once. "It is the House of Branden." Pride was in his face and the hauteur in his voice abrasive. Or was it that in her heart she knew she was behaving badly? Spurred by vexation and angered by the whisper of conscience, her reply snapped before she could stop the words, "The House of Branden at one time boasted many great warriors—or so I was taught in the nursery."

Damon tensed. A dark flush swept his features, but he made no slightest attempt to evade her eyes until he murmured with a slight bow, "Thank you."

Sophia turned away. That had been unforgivable, especially since she was a guest in his home. She could imagine Stephen's anger. She could apologize, but knowing she was too close to tears to speak, bent her energies upon arranging the flowers, ignoring the Marquis as he rather savagely replaced the items he had taken from the cupboard. Gradually, her rioting emotions quieted, and when her task was completed she was relatively calm again.

Damon carried the vase into the Great Hall for her and she asked that he place it on the large table before the fire. At once he protested that no one would see the flowers in the dark room.

"It could be a charming room," she observed impulsively, "were you to install large windows." And, remembering Clay, she said, "Oh! Your pardon!"

"Not at all." He set the vase in the spot she indicated and

89

asked eagerly, "Like those in Lucian St. Clair's Beechmead Hall?"

"Yes," she responded with enthusiasm. "*Exactly* what I had thought."

"What of the floors? Marble?"

"Oh, no! That would ruin it!"

"I agree. Pegged oak would be better, wouldn't you say?"

"Much. And the panelling is too dark, also. You could— Oh! Your grace!"

Vaille, looking extremely handsome in a blue jacket that emphasized the blue of his eyes, came gracefully toward them. Sophia sensed an immediate withdrawal in the Marquis as his father exclaimed, "What a pleasant splash of colour in this gruesome hall. And so beautifully arranged. Your work, my dear?"

She admitted such was the case, and he complimented her upon her skill and, leaning closer to straighten an errant bloom, singled out a bright pink rose. "What a delightful shade. Such a pity it is faulted. The bud's contour is poor, don't you think?"

Damon removed the rose at once and tossed it into the fire. If Vaille was startled by this cavalier behaviour, he hid it well, smiling warmly at Sophia as he strolled toward the south wing.

As usual, indignation robbed her of diplomacy, and she crossed to where the Marquis leaned with one hand upon the mantle, frowning down at the scorching petals of the rose. "Why did you do that?" she demanded in a low tone. "The bloom was lovely, and I don't think he meant to be critical."

"Do you not?" Damon glanced cynically toward the Duke's retreating figure. "It was imperfect. And my father finds imperfection in anything quite offen—"

In full cry, Horatio trundled into the hall, wings spread, passing Vaille who stepped back, lifting his quizzing glass and gazing after the bird incredulously. Damon scowled at Thompson, who hurried downstairs, anguished remorse written on his weathered countenance. Vaille returned to Sophia's side, still watching Horatio, who was making his second full-throated lap around the room. "Good gad!" quoth the Duke.

Damon groaned, "Oh, no!"

"Poor chap," commiserated Vaille, with a grin and a wink to Sophia.

Thompson hurried to open the door, revealing a dignified, elegant gentleman possessed of thickly waving grey hair, piercing grey eyes, and a languid manner, who sauntered across the terrace with a flourish of his cane.

"Lord Phineas Bodwin," announced Thompson.

"How very charming," the Duke smiled.

"Hell!" grated Damon under his breath, and, stepping forward, hand outstretched, said, "Phinny! How kind in you to come and see us..."

Clay's eager search for the Marquis appeared destined for failure. There was no sign of him in the Great Hall. The music room was occupied by the Duke and Lord Bodwin, who sat politely conversing. The library was empty. He was proceeding to the kitchen when he noticed Horatio huddled against a closed door on the left of the north corridor. Clay entered cautiously and was greeted by so fluent a stream of invective that he closed the door hurriedly behind him

He was in what appeared to be a combined study and work room since it held a fine old walnut desk in addition to bookcases, leather chairs, and an ample table. At the far end, another long table was piled with architects' drawings and plans. The flickering light of a branch of candles revealed Damon standing before the fire, a half-full wine glass sagging in one hand. Even as Clay watched, he launched into a renewed spate of cursing, this time in French, and topped it off with a growled "After all these years!" He despatched the remainder of the wine, flung the glass savagely into the fire, and pounded his fist on the mantle.

Impressed, Clay laughed and applauded. Damon spun around, revealing a scowl that might well have daunted a lesser man. "What the hell do you want?"

"By George, but you swear like a cavalryman, if I say so myself!"

The harsh glare relaxed very slightly. "Long association with the breed. St. Clair and Vaughan and others of their ilk. Uncouth devils."

"Yes," said Clay. "Which should have told me something. Now don't fly into the boughs again. I came to thank you. I trust you won't find it necessary to shoot me for my pains."

"Don't count on it," said Damon, but meeting only a

91

friendly grin in response, the remaining anger faded from his eyes.

"Your noble sire," Clay said levelly, "has just—as they say—saved my bacon. And he tells me that it is thanks to your impassioned plea that I am spared the gruesome spectre of Newgate."

"He never did! Well I assure you I'm quite incapable of—er—impassioned pleas...in behalf of myself, let alone some fribbly Major of hussars!" Clay's chuckle was accompanied by a look that caused the Marquis to shrug and say hurriedly, "Do not refine overmuch on it, Clay. My Papa probably took a closer look and decided you were not all that worthless. I had very little to do with it."

"Lie like a cavalryman, as well," Clay smiled. "And there's not a damned bit of good your glaring at me like that. I'm sorry, old boy, but—" He moved closer and put out his hand. "You cannot possibly know what these past few months have been like." Damon's long fingers closed firmly around his own. "This will be"—Clay blinked, and gulped hoarsely—"probably...the first night I'll get any sleep since—" He checked, gasping.

"Oh!" Damon released his hand hurriedly. "Sorry, old boy."

Clay stared in astonishment at his bloodless fingers, looked up into the amused eyes of the Marquis, and muttered an awed "Gad...!"

"I really do apologize," said Damon. "It's all the music, you see. Tends to improve the grip." His whimsical grin brought a deepening of Clay's instinctive liking. "And, I had to stop you somehow. Couldn't have you falling on my neck. Too dashed hard on the cravat!"

"I cannot think where our Nancy have go," said Genevieve, busily fastening the many tiny buttons down the back of Sophia's gown. "I have think she is with Charlotte, and Charlotte have think she is with me. Her family have the farm near at hand, so I heard, but that is a very naughty cabbage if she have leave without the ask for permission!" She peered at Sophia in the mirror. "How lovely you are, my new friend! If only I might wear such a gown! But me—alas! Always I go so far out and so far in! Such a gown on me would look"—she laughed roguishly—"not so polite, *n'est-ce pas?*"

Amused by the girl's description of her rich little figure, Sophia had to admit it was true to an extent. The pale-green silken sheath that clung to her own body with soft and revealing sleekness would seem improper if worn by the more voluptuous Genevieve. She lifted her arms for the overskirt. The darker green net allowed the sheath to be seen, but tantalizingly, sometimes revealing very little, sometimes allowing her slender shape to be quite visible. With a jade pendant about her throat and carven jade drops dangling from her ears, her beauty was inescapable.

Genevieve, adjusting the back of the overskirt, was speaking of Lord Bodwin's unexpected arrival. "He have come to fetch us back to his big mansion. Poor Phinny is lonely, you know. He say the roads are *affreux*—er—how you say?"

"Horrid," Sophia translated. "Then how did he reach here?"

They started toward the hall together, and Genevieve answered, "He have the estate *magnifique* just this side of the Toll Road, so he can journey by the new road my Camille have build for some of the ways. And whatever happen to be the weather, when Phinny want something—" She shrugged expressively. "But you will know him better than I, perhaps...?"

"I know only that he is one of the richest men in England. But—wasn't there something not too long ago? Some sadness in his life?"

"Ah, yes—his nephew. Did you not know Irvin? Such a wild creature, that one. He and Damon were fine friends and once come to see me in Copenhagen. They take me out—oh! What a night was that! My cousin was jolly then, Sophia." She grimaced fiercely. "Not like now he is! They have behave very naughty." She paused as they came to the top of the stairs and, catching Sophia's arm, said, "We go into a club, and you know what they do, those bad boys? They have all the wineglasses put on a shelf, and Irvin, he say Damon must give him the—how you say? Arm-hat—something like these?"

Sophia knit her brows, then, starting down the stairs, laughed, "Oh, you mean handicap."

"*Bon!*" Laughing merrily at her own mistake, Genevieve linked her arm through Sophia's. "How clever you are to unwound my so bad language. So this 'handicap,' as you say it, was that Irvin will shoot all the glasses through their fat tummies, while my Damon he must shoot all the stems, and whoever reach the end of the line first have to pay nothing for the evening. To make it, as they say, 'not so easy,' they blow out all the lights but one candle! And then—oh, *horrifique!* The noise! Worse than my Damon's working peoples! But everyone they laugh, and make the big wagers, so I do this, also!"

"Lud! They must have wrecked the place! Who won?"

"Damon, of course! And I win five hundred francs! Irvin, he shoot nicely. But my Damon—no one shoot like him!" She paused, and her eyes, staring down at the empty Great Hall, had lost all merriment. "Poor dear Irvin. He have the most silly accident a few months since. He clean his pistol, and it go off!" She shivered. "So young and so dead. No war, no illness, no duel. Just—pouff! He is gone, and his poor uncle left to mourn him."

"How dreadful! But Lord Bodwin does not look to be in black gloves?"

"No—this is not Irvin's way. He say people who grieve for their men lost in the wars weep for themselves—not their loved ones, who go on to better living. Phinny honour that *credo* and will have no wailing at his Hall." She sighed and added slowly, "Sometimes, I think our Phinny is—"

"Genevieve! Thank heaven!" Lady Branden stood on the balcony behind them, her wrapper clutched about her, a broken feather dangling beside her left ear, one hand held to her brow. "Oh, how I need my maids! That horrid Phinny Bodwin is squirming, if my thoughts reach him! For God's sake, come and put your drunken Aunt back together, love—else Damon, the wretch, will never cease to quiz me!"

Genevieve flew to aid the stricken lady. Watching her slip a comforting arm about the large waist, Sophia thought how delightful they were, each in her own fashion, and could not be sorry she had come.

Continuing down the stairs, she sniffed. The aroma wafting from the kitchen proclaimed that Genevieve's chickens were almost done. She must look to her soufflé.

Order had been restored; the kitchen looked as immaculate as ever, and the smells were truly delicious. She was a little taken aback to find the Marquis standing beside the sink in deep converse with Mr. Thompson. Mrs. Hatters, busily peeling potatoes, hummed to herself, and none of the three noticed Sophia enter.

"...the portrait of my mother," said Damon, "so I told him

94

it had been sent to be cleaned. Now you must not forget, Jack, it—" He stopped as the valet's gaze alerted him.

Sophia, watching closely as he swung toward her, saw admiration come into his face and as quickly vanish. Then he strolled to inspect her through his detestable quizzing glass and drawled, "I protest, ma'am, you'll have us poor gentlemen quite unable to notice the food you've so cleverly prepared."

She was no less impressed and thought his artfully tumbled dark hair became him admirably, while the jacket of bottle-green superfine fit his shoulders to perfection and emphasized the depth of those vivid eyes. But she also suspected his praise to be a hollow mockery and therefore shrugged, "Any such omission after our inspired labours, my lord, would rate instant death!"

He smiled. "One can only hope that the *results* of your inspired labours do not have a similar effect."

"Oh! What a wretched thing to say!"

"I am a wretched man, my lady, who puts his guests to work."

She assured him loftily that there was no least need for him to feel beholden. It had been, she said, a most rewarding experience. "For when I set up my own household, I shall have a better understanding of the problems to be encountered in a kitchen."

Mrs. Hatters, having spent over an hour cleaning up the wreckage, cast her eyes to heaven at this.

"And do you," asked Damon thoughtfully, "anticipate setting up your own household in the near future, ma'am?"

Sophia lowered her eyes. This kind of flirting was so familiar. "I am well past my come-out, sir. It is time I was looking to my future."

"Cheer up, ma'am," he said kindly. "I think you carry your years very well."

Her meekly bowed head flung upward, wrath flaming in her eyes. The Viper was surveying her critically through his glass. "On the other hand," he mused, "does one chance to be a silly goose..."

Mrs. Hatters dropped her potato.

"You," spluttered Sophia, "are—are—intolerable!"

"I suspect you are right," he sighed. "Only—he does not think so."

"He?"

95

"Horatio," he said innocently. "Why—whom did you think I meant?"

A muffled snort came from the direction of the sink. Sophia blushed to the roots of her hair.

"Horatio," Damon went on, his eyes dancing, "has voiced the only criticism of which I am aware. Do you not agree, Millie?"

Mrs. Hatters, however, had recalled an urgent errand and was whisking into the hall.

"Alas," Damon said, "she apparently does not. But do not despair, dear ma'am. Such a cook as yourself shall not remain for long on the—er—shelf."

"You . . . offer me hope . . . to cling to," she grated. And resisting the urge to bare her teeth at him, she crossed to where the saucepans were hung. She had intended to take one down and deftly slip her white sauce into it, shattering him with her competence. Unfortunately, they were all hung so high.

"May I be of assistance, Lady Sophia?"

His voice was close to her ear. And why, oh why, must her foolish heart start to pound and her breath to hasten? She concentrated on Stephen's dear thin face and was able to say coolly, "The medium-sized pan, if you please."

She did not turn to face him, wherefore he was able to continue to view the pale glittering gold of her hair and to breathe the soft fragrance of lily of the valley that clung to her. One curl flirted brazenly on the snow of her shoulder. His finger touched that cool silk . . .

Sophia swung around, frowning, and found my lord inspecting an offending cuticle. "*That* one," she repeated emphatically, "if you please."

"That one" was very high. Damon reached for it unsuccessfully.

Sophia pointed out with more than a hint of scorn in her voice, "There is a stool beside you, my lord."

There was. He eyed it without enthusiasm.

She gave a tiny snort of impatience, and in a movement so fast he caught only the flash of a beautifully turned ankle, she was standing above him, slim and lovely, reaching up to grasp the elusive pan. Enraged out of all proportion to the incident, she stepped back too swiftly, misjudged the confines of the sophisticated silken gown, and, with a little shriek, toppled.

Strong arms caught and held her and crushed her close

96

and captive. Her breathing seemed to stop. His eyes were filled with an intense yearning. His lips, slightly parted, hovered above her own. Sophia waited, a new and frightening emotion gripping her: the sure knowledge that not only was she about to be kissed but that she wanted nothing more in the world.

Damon set her down and, with his twisted, mocking smile, said, "Egad, ma'am! Such athletics! I vow you are most amusing..."

Excusing himself on the ground that he must join his guests in the music room, he begged she would soon grant them the pleasure of her company and sauntered to the door, the quizzing glass swinging from one tanned hand.

Throughout this little performance, Sophia stood as if frozen, holding "that one" against her bosom and staring after the Marquis with dazed disbelief. Again, he had made her look a total idiot! She had lain in his arms like some trollop, with no sign of a struggle, no indignant outcry, no slightest attempt to slap his cruel face! She was losing her mind—as well as her moral values!

Swinging up the pan, she gave a choking cry of rage and brought it down with all her strength on the inoffensive potato Mrs. Hatters had just peeled, thoroughly smashing it and wishing with every fibre of her being that it was a certain smug, sneering face.

Chapter 10

It had been a long time since Cancrizans Priory had welcomed so glittering an assembly as now gathered in the spacious music room. The fire leaped in the fireplace: candles awoke an answering glow on silks and laces: Thompson moved quietly about proffering nuts, mints, and wine, aided by Smithers, who had been pressed into service and was flushed and uncomfortable in his footman's attire. The guests chattered and laughed softly, to all outward appearances thoroughly enjoying themselves.

Sophia was early captured by an admiring Lord Bodwin. Genevieve came in late, but her vivacious little trill of laughter was soon charming all about her. Miss Hilby, a vision in cream lace and wearing an emerald choker and long drop earrings that accentuated those deep green eyes, hovered close to the Duke, who treated her with kindly paternalism. No doubt, thought Sophia, setting her traps for the father's approval since her designs on the son were perfectly obvious.

Feather came in, vast and impressive in silver, with white and silver feathers nodding in her hair. She greeted the Duke with deep affection and Lord Bodwin with sympathetic concern. She was pale and responded to Genevieve's anxious questions by saying she'd turned the wrong way and, finding herself wandering along the unoccupied north wing, had become convinced she was not alone and had "fairly flown" back the way she had come. She cast an aggrieved glance at Damon and all but collided with Hartwell, who entered at that moment. He caught the lady in his arms and laughingly guided her to a chair, into which she sank gratefully, placing the fingers of one hand only briefly against her temple.

Damon, watching his aunt with a deep frown, warned that the north wing was very old and probably unsafe. Sophia, remembering that miserable tour, shot him an outraged look that he ignored as he asked sternly that they all keep away from the area, "For it would grieve me were any of my guests to be hurt."

"Egad, Camille," smiled Bodwin, "you contrive to lead an exciting life, even here in the country."

Vaille asked with apparently casual interest, "You refer to my son's unfortunate propensity for duelling, I take it, Phinny?"

The Marquis was bending to murmur something into Miss Hilby's ear. He raised his head and directed a steady look at Lord Phineas, who muttered a thoughtful "Er—of course, Duke."

"Oh," said Hartwell brightly, "I thought you meant the assassination, sir."

Damon's face reflected total exasperation, and Vaille, with unhurried calm, probed gently. "Assassination...?"

"Why, yes," nodded Hartwell, apparently unaware of the daggerlike glare he was receiving from his host. "It was on Sackville Street. About—three months back. Cam and Redmond and me were coming home from the Westhavens' rout and ran into that Count fella...what'shisname? Rondell!"

The Duke stiffened, his gaze flashing to his son, who had lost interest and stared drowsily at the fire. "Rondell? You were with him when he was shot?"

"Standing right next to him, sir!" Hartwell answered excitedly. "Gad, if old Cam hadn't chanced to step back, he might have caught the ball instead! Put the fear of God into me, I don't mind telling you! Beastly close!"

"If ever a man deserved to be annihilated," said Bodwin, "it was Rondell!"

"Annihilated?" asked Ridgley, hurrying into the room at that moment. "What are you—" He broke off with a gasp. Vaille had stiffened at the sound of his voice and jumped to his feet, turning to the door. The eyes of these cousins met like engaging swords and held through a long moment that twanged with tension.

Sophia became aware of several things simultaneously: that Ridgley's pleasant features had become pale and very grim; that the Duke was equally pale, his blue eyes holding a deadly glare; that Damon, looking from one to the other, received from each a flashing glance filled with anger; that Genevieve, Feather, and Miss Hilby were all aware of the reasons behind this behaviour since they watched with obvious anxiety.

"I forgot to mention, your grace," said Damon quietly, "that Ted has been visiting me these past few weeks."

"So you...did." The Duke's aquiline features were still drawn. He smiled a smile that held the warmth of the northeast wind and, with eyes every bit as chill, raised his quizzing glass, surveyed his cousin with haughty deliberation, and murmured, "You are looking quite well, Edward."

Ridgley drew a quivering breath. His hands were clenched at his sides, and his jaw moved slightly as though his teeth had been clamped together. "I am, fortunately, in excellent health, Philip."

His failure to enquire after the Duke's health was painfully obvious, and Feather's voice, unusually fretful, sliced the silence. "If we are done with the medical reports...Tell us Damon—have you yet found your treasure?"

Sophia became aware that Lord Bodwin had drawn her hand through his arm and was patting it kindly. She gave him a grateful smile but withdrew her hand.

Damon said with a rueful shrug, "Unfortunately, no."

Genevieve, who had been obviously frightened by the taut emotions of the past few minutes, now enquired, "Camille? What is this treasure?"

"If you've lost some, I'll be glad to help you," Clay grinned. "Nice stuff."

Sophia stared at him in astonishment. Why he should be
100

so cordial to this beast who had refused the help he might so easily have extended was beyond her.

Hartwell was saying he had already offered to help Damon find his treasure. "Half a dozen times, in fact. Old Cam's not about to open these grounds to a full-scale treasure hunt. Not that I blame him. In one day, this place could be torn to shreds by a greedy rabble."

"Do you really think so?" Vaille brightened. "How intriguing!"

Ignoring his father's remark, the Marquis explained that a hoard of gold and jewels, gathered by Jacobite sympathizers to finance the uprising of 1745, was believed to have been hidden somewhere in the priory. "Unhappily," he said "the gentleman who concealed it did his work too well. Legend has it that he was captured as he sat in this very room and executed before he was able to reveal the location to his friends. It is said he told his gaoler that he left a message any educated man could read."

"And in all these years," Sophia asked interestedly, "has no trace of it been found?"

"Evidently not," said Vaille. "To discover its location would be quite a windfall for you—eh, Damon?"

The Marquis, meeting his father's dry smile, answered gravely, "It would, indeed, sir."

Bodwin claimed Sophia's full attention at this point, telling her with pride of his nearby home, which he insisted she was to visit very soon. The wine flowed liberally, the guests grew more relaxed, the conversation easier; and still Bodwin rambled on. "...And the fountains, dear lady, I had copied from two I had admired. Not so sophisticated as mine, but a good starting point." He glanced up as the Earl wandered over to join them. "You've seen my fountains and the pool, Ridgley?"

"Very impressive," the Earl nodded. "Copied Mullins', didn't you?"

"Mullins?" Feather frowned. "Wasn't he a Cobra member? Dreadful!"

Bodwin frowned as though he resented his maze being linked to such an ugly matter but admitted it was the same man, and added rather testily that he thought the entire Cobra business had been greatly sensationalized by gossip and the newspapers.

"To the contrary," said the Duke, a flare in his eyes, "I

doubt the general public will ever know the full horror of that hideous organization. But we must not discuss such vulgarities while the ladies are with us."

"Lud, Philip"—Feather shrugged, removing a hand hurriedly from her aching brow—"I've no doubt but that all of us here know of Cobra, though I confess I could scarce credit such a cult flourished in our gentle little island."

"They were of the aristocracy, were they not?" Genevieve asked curiously. "Bored young gentlemen who devise the odd and nasty ways to divert themselves. It is true that no one knew who they are—not even they themselves?"

"It is very true," Vaille answered. "They were known to one another only by code names. For instance, if a member was called Lizard, the likeness of the creature was embroidered on his mask. And because the Runners were always seeking them, to avoid the chance of an imposter infiltrating their group, each man had his symbol tattooed upon his upper arm. Only the leader and his lieutenants were aware of the true identities of all the members."

"But," puzzled Miss Hilby, "why so much secrecy? If they were so ashamed of the terrible things they did—why continue?"

"The secrecy, dear lady," said Hartwell, "was for fear of blackmail among themselves. Their 'amusements' ran the gamut from malicious vandalism to murder to espionage. Rather potent material."

"And they *had* to continue," Ridgley put in, scowling at his glass. "Couldn't get out."

"True," Hartwell agreed. "I knew a good chap who became caught in their web. He went to dinner with a friend, got thoroughly foxed, and—" He checked at Vaille's warning frown. "Well, at all events, next morning, he discovered that sometime during the night he'd joined Cobra and participated in some very illegal pursuits. After that, he was forced to continue under the threat of exposure, which would have ruined him and shamed his family. He was with the Foreign Office, you see. The poor fellow got in deeper and deeper. Shot himself eventually. You knew him, Cam. Poor Flanders."

Vaille started. "Good God!" he cried, much shocked. He turned to his son. "Hilary was a member of Cobra? That defies belief!"

102

Damon shrugged with bored indifference. "I heard something of the sort."

"Why you all use the past tenses?" demanded Genevieve, very intrigued. "They are caught at last? I hear your Running people cannot discover them."

"Our Runners," snorted Vaille, pulling his irked gaze from the Marquis, "could not find the ends of their own noses on a clear day in Hyde Park! And this is not a proper subject, as I said before. Let us change it, if you please."

"*Oui*—of course, dear Uncle Philip," she said, adding roguishly, "in just a tiny moment. It is the exciting tale! What happen to Cobra?"

They all laughed, including Vaille, who then exclaimed fondly, "You're a minx, Mademoiselle! Very well, then, since you yearn for the macabre . . . Have you ever met Lord Sumner Craig-Bell?"

Genevieve's eyes widened, and she gave an instinctive shudder.

"I see you have," the Duke nodded dryly. "One of the richest men in England and the leader of Cobra. He has a grotesque country seat called Green Willow Castle in Essex. It was the perfect location for their headquarters and might shield them today had it not accidentally caught fire."

"There is some question," demurred Bodwin, "whether that fire *was* accidental."

"Then if 'twas not, whoever set it deserves the highest commendation this nation can bestow because that fire destroyed Cobra."

"They were all . . . burned to cinders?" asked Genevieve, her eyes very wide.

"No, no, m'dear." The Earl laughed. "But the men who came to help fight the fire found enough evidence to call in the Runners, and that was that!"

"Ah . . ." breathed Genevieve. "Then the members are now unmasked!"

"Unfortunately not." Vaille scowled.

"Might not have been so dashed unfortunate," Ridgley apparently addressed the fireplace. "Lots of those poor fellows were entrapped and comparatively innocent."

"I fail to see how any 'innocent' man could have become involved with so hideous a group," said Sophia.

Damon murmured an amused "Judge not . . ."

103

"Agree with the lady," Bodwin put in heartily. "They were a scurrilous crew. The Runners searched Green Willow from dungeons to flagpole, so I heard, but all old Sumner's dossiers, lists, and records were in ashes."

"Were none of the villains captured?" asked the persistent Genevieve.

"Three, so I heard," Ridgley nodded. "They were brought to trial, but they only knew the identities of a few members, and the men they did name had vanished by the time they were sought. Craig-Bell was fortunate to escape with a whole skin."

"He is," said Miss Hilby, a little pucker between her eyes, "not a man I should care to upset."

"Upset! Now there's a prime understatement," observed Ridgley with a laugh. "His home burned; all his records destroyed; his hold on his victims broken; his lucrative blackmail and espionage operations wiped out!" He slapped his thigh and exulted. "Gad! But I'd love to have seen that blaze!"

"Your eloquence," murmured the Marquis, with a twitch of his thin nostrils, "moves me so that I can almost smell it."

For an instant, Sophia stared at him blankly, her thoughts still on Cobra. Then she gave a small cry and rushed to the door, closely followed by Genevieve and urged on by the exhortations of the would-be diners.

In the corridor, a more pronounced smell of burning greeted them. A crash was followed by a distant scream. Sophia and Genevieve halted, and somebody rushed past. Sophia realized it was Damon, and fear lanced through her.

"Stay there!" he commanded in a tone that brooked no argument.

He disappeared into the Great Hall. She heard him swing open the kitchen door, and casting obedience to the winds, she hurried forward. A great shout of laughter rang out, that same glad peal that had followed her sarcastic quip about the aroma of his music. So it *had* been Damon who'd laughed...

As she entered the kitchen, chaos greeted her eyes. Damon leaned against the wall, sobbing with mirth. The roasting pan into which Genevieve had crammed her four chickens was on the kitchen table. The rope with which they had tied on the lid hung smouldering from it, but the contents had largely disappeared. Mr. Thompson and Mrs. Hatters stood in the pantry doorway, staring at the carnage in stunned

104

disbelief. Chickens and rice were spread liberally about the room; legs slid slowly down cupboard doors; rice stippled the walls; one wing hung from the chandelier, while another had settled across the back of the petrified kitchen cat. Even as Sophia stared dazedly, a drumstick abandoned the ceiling and fell into the pan of gravy.

From the doorway, Genevieve whispered an awed "Mon...Dieu" and Feather, staggering up, squawked, "Oh... my God!"

The cat, evidently deciding enough was, in this case, too good of a feast, abandoned her wing and shot with a yowl into the pantry.

Thompson and Mrs. Hatters stepped gingerly into the kitchen.

"Are you...quite sure," moaned Damon, "that neither of you was...burned?"

"The rope caught on fire, m'lord," croaked the valet. "I hauled that pan out. It weighed a blooming ton! And it was all sorta...shivery. So I grabbed Millie, and we run into...the pantry." He put a hand behind him and added an uneasy "Oh Lor'!"

"Oh!" cried Mrs. Hatters. "You're all over rice, Jack!"

Thompson glanced in turn at the back of the lady. "You, too, Millie! Good gawd! Now what'll we do, sir?"

Damon merely lapsed into renewed peals of mirth, his feeble gestures of no help whatsoever.

"What on earth," gasped Sophia, "happened?"

"Why, they—exploded," said Mrs. Hatters, looking at the three amateur cooks with a valiant but not altogether successful attempt at sympathy.

"Exploded? But for heaven's sake! How?"

Damon, wiping away tears, sighed. "Look at all...the blasted rice! If all *that* was in the poor brutes...it's a wonder they didn't blow...the roof off!" He leaned back, a hand over his eyes, shoulders heaving.

Flashing him an outraged glance, Genevieve wailed, "My poor little ones!" Grasping a clean bowl, she began to rush around retrieving the remains.

Tearfully, the Marquis asked, "What are you doing...*mon petit chou?*"

"Do not little cabbage me—*sauvage!*" she cried fiercely. "How may you stand there and laugh at this so *tragique* thing? Have you no heart?"

He sobered a little and, standing away from the wall, said, "Millie, you'd best go and change. You, too, Thompson. We'll get started here."

Sophia realized suddenly that she was staring, bewitched by the rather shattering effect of his mirth. "Oh, heavens! My *soufflé!*" She grabbed two pot holders, rushed to the oven, slipped on the riced floor, and would have fallen had not Damon caught her and, urging her to strive to be less boisterous, swung open the oven door.

The *soufflé* was a masterpiece. High and golden brown and crusty. Sophia gazed at it, awed by her own skill.

"Oh, my ... !" sighed Feather, scraping rice from the clock.

"Aha!" breathed Damon admiringly.

"Get a spoon!" Genevieve snarled. "And help with my rice!"

"Help?" he echoed. "It's past help! What you need, m'dear, is a shovel! How in the name of— How did you get it all in? And keep it there?"

"I spoon it," she said defiantly. "Your foolish Ariel hide the chestnuts I am supposed to use in their tummies, so I have to use the rice. And he also hide his pans. I can find only this one to fit with properly, but however we may tuck in *les poulet*, they are still too much for the pan, and I fear they will pop out, so I take the rope, and Sophia have help me to tying the lid on."

"We tied it very securely, my lord," Sophia confirmed, her own eyes abrim with laughter.

"Gad." He chuckled. "I still cannot see how ..." A glimmer of comprehension touched his eyes. "You did—*cook* the rice?"

"Cook it? Why should you ask so stupid of a thing? Can you not see it have cook? Really, Camille! The rice cook inside the bird, inside the pan!"

"Yes," wheezed the Marquis. "It most assuredly ... did. And when the rope caught fire—made good its escape!"

"Here," hissed Genevieve, thrusting a spoon into his hand. "Begin! *Vite!*"

"Look, my pretty, why don't we just scoop up the beastly stuff, and—"

"*Beastly ... stuff!*" she cried furiously. "Do you imagine for one of the moments, my Most Honourable the Marquis of Damon, that all of the work most hard I have do all days is onto the rubbish pile going?"

He stared speechlessly as she pounced on a chicken breast

hiding modestly behind a Toby mug on the shelf. "You're...never going to offer—my guests...?" and he waved feebly at the scattered remains.

"It will rightly serve you," she snapped, "if your guests expire! Here!" She thrust a piece of meat between his jaws. "Try it!"

He obeyed and gave as his opinion that it really was not half bad. "A little hairy, but—"

Genevieve brandished a wing threateningly. Damon stepped back. "Now be serious! You cannot—"

Feather interpolated, "She is perfectly right. What the eye don't see, the heart don't grieve for. By the time we get it cleaned up a little..." She peeled a rose petal from a piece of breast and shook her head. "By the time we get it cleaned up a little, they'll never know the difference."

Chapter 11

It was, as they all agreed later, a most remarkable meal. The conversation proceeded at a brisk pace, eventually turning to the Regent's famed Brighton Pavilion, which the Duke referred to dryly as George's House of Horrors. Bodwin, the group's authority on art and architecture, immediately embraced this delightful characterization and exploded into peals of laughter.

Sophia, outwardly joining in the amusement, was inwardly taut with anxiety as the dishes were carried in. She was inexpressibly relieved to note that her soufflé was holding up very well. Deluged with compliments on its majestic appearance, she blushed with pleasure. Genevieve and Feather had worked wonders with the salvaged chicken. It looked quite inviting when served on a bed of rice and well sprinkled with chopped parsley. Vaille declared the dish incomparable, and Sophia, nobly emulating his example, managed not to wince as she bit down on a piece of candle wax.

Damon, who had turned his attention first to the soufflé, kept his head downbent for a minute, then slanted a brief and decidedly hilarious look at Sophia and complimented her on her culinary art.

Apprehension seized her. She tasted a morsel of her creation. It was light, fluffy, and extreme weird! It was, in fact, positively sweet! Numbed with horror, she realized what must have happened and, casting a frantic glance to Genevieve, found that lady frozen into immobility, her big eyes having an expression of such total guilt that she knew her fears confirmed. Genevieve had volunteered to complete Feather's trifle by adding the cooled custard to the top. She had mistaken the bowls. The soufflé contained not white sauce but Feather's custard!

Feather, looking up with a puzzled expression, said, "Sophia, your soufflé has the most—"

"The most delightful flavour," interposed the Duke smoothly, turning twinkling eyes upon the devastated chef.

"It has, indeed," agreed Lord Bodwin. "I confess it is quite new to me—Italian, I suspect, eh? Whatever does it contain, my dear lady?"

"Oh," said Sophia faintly, well aware of Damon's smothered chuckle, "it is an old family secret, my lord."

"Good God!" gasped Ridgley, removing a rose petal from his rice. "You French will stop at nothing to achieve an exotic flavour!"

"Nothing!" Damon put in.

Feather burst into a paroxysm of coughing. Damon blinked rapidly into his water goblet. The Duke murmured a polite appreciation of the "inspired efforts of our magnificent ladies." Genevieve grinned irrepressibly at all and sundry.

Sophia thought "Oh, heavens! What about the trifle?"

"No cards for me," the Earl decreed, shaking his curly head. "Afraid that delightful meal has made me sleepy. If we're to toddle over to Phinny's in time for luncheon tomorrow, I'd best not start into a long game at this hour."

The ladies exchanged surreptitious and amused glances. Despite its initially unusual flavor, the trifle had been the success of the meal. Lord Ridgley had partaken of three servings and been so well pleased he had begun to sing softly to himself as the gentlemen were left to their port. Bodwin had declared it by far the jolliest evening he had enjoyed in years and once again implored Sophia to join the group that would journey to Bodwin Hall next day. She was eager to see the famous mansion and had declined with reluctance, but Damon had said the bridge would be completed by the morrow. Whitthurst would certainly come, and she intended to be here to care for him as soon as he arrived. The Earl had accepted his invitation, however, and it was apparent that only his loyalty to his cousin kept Clay from going along.

Damon turned to the Duke. "Do you care to play, sir?"

"Thank you—no," said Vaille. "However, if *you* would be so kind."

Amazed, the Marquis asked, "Play? The harpsichord...?"

"I hoped," explained the Duke, "we might persuade Lady Sophia to sing."

Gratified by the astonishment on Damon's face, Sophia assented. Damon escorted her to the harpsichord and, seating himself, glanced up, hands poised, one brow questioningly raised.

She leaned to him and murmured, "Do you know...'Believe Me If All Those Endearing Young Charms'?"

He grinned, breathed a soft "Touché!" and started into the introduction.

Feather, who had suffered through many an ear-splitting musicale, resigned herself and settled back with a small sigh. Sophia began to sing. With the first notes, Damon tensed, and his eyes reflected awed incredulity. She had an exquisite voice; a rich mezzo soprano, magnificently trained, and she sang the poignant words with such warmth and feeling that Feather was in tears before the first verse ended...Sophia looked down at Damon and could not look away...

> For it is not while beauty and youth are thine own
> And thy cheeks unprofaned by a tear
> That the fervour and faith of a soul can be known
> To which time will but make thee more dear.
> No, the heart that has truly loved never forgets
> But as truly loves on to the close;
> As the sunflower turns on her god when he sets
> The same look which she turned when he rose.

The last notes died tenderly away. There was no movement, no rush of applause, the guests by their rapt silence bestowing the highest tribute any performer can receive. Having woven this magic, Damon and Sophia were each trapped by it. Time ceased to exist, and they gazed upon one another through a breathless suspension of all else.

Lord Bodwin, applauding frenziedly, leapt to his feet, crying an enthused "Bravo! Bravo!"

And the spell was broken. Damon started and looked away. Sophia gasped and straightened, feeling not a little frightened as the guests crowded around her, overwhelmed by admiration.

Vaille caught her hand, pressed a kiss upon it, and exclaimed, "My dear child! That was—truly—perfection!"

Blushing, Sophia said, "Thank you, your grace, but without Lord Damon I—"

"The entire evening has been pure delight," Bodwin avowed. "Lady Sophia, may we beg another song? Will you so honour us?"

"Oh, please do," gulped Feather, wiping fiercely at her eyes.

"I would be delighted"—smiled Sophia—"if my accompanist will..." She stopped, her smile fading. The bench was empty. My Lord Damon had gone.

The courtyard was chill now, as a cool night wind swayed the weeds that sprang between the mouldering old bricks and whispered in shrill whines among the chimneys. The Marquis, seated on the rim of the time-ravaged fountain, drew on his old pipe, which was shaped like a lion's head, and stared down the hill with eyes that saw neither the cloud-wracked sky, the tossing trees, nor the pipe's glow. Nor the dark shape that crept upon him.

The man sprang forward. In a lightning movement, Damon was on his feet, crouched a little, his eyes narrowed and deadly. Ridgley said severely, "Much too slow, Cam!"

"If you've made me break my pipe, damn you, *you'll* be slowed!"

Ridgley picked up the treasured article and handed it over. "All of a piece, I think. And how dare you talk to an aged relation with such flagrant lack of respect?"

Damon answered in French and so explicitly that Ridgley

gasped a shocked "Have a care! The women might hear you!"

They started to wander together along the terrace and down the steps.

"Your retreat," said the Earl dryly as they followed the curve of the drive, "has not endeared you to your sire. They were all clamouring for The Drayton to sing again." Receiving no answer, he murmured cynically, "Didn't mean you to fall into flat despair, dear boy..."

Still, Damon said nothing. Watching him covertly, Ridgley was favoured by the wind, which, tearing apart the tenuous clasp of shifting clouds, allowed the moon to illumine the stern face beside him. He frowned worriedly and observed, "You're tired, Cam."

Damon drew back his shoulders at once but then abandoned the subterfuge and muttered, "If they don't all leave soon, I—I think I'll run mad!"

His unease mounting, Ridgley placed a hand on the younger man's arm. "You say so damned little. How do you feel these days?"

The Marquis pulled away. "Exasperated beyond belief!"

The Earl vouchsafed only a grunt at this, and when he next spoke, the very quietness of his words conveyed the depth of his resentment. "You could at least have warned me Vaille had arrived."

"I'd sink lower than that to reconcile you. Nineteen years is too long to carry hatred. Especially between first cousins who were once closer than brothers."

"Or—father and son..."

The pipe glowed very brightly, and Damon stopped walking. "That's not true."

"It's an odd kind of love that keeps you apart."

"You should be well informed. You're such an odd kind of lover!"

They glared upon one another. Then Damon, remorseful, said, "I'm sorry Ted. That was a stinking thing to say. Forgive me."

The Earl cuffed him lightly on the arm and, as they resumed their stroll, sighed, "I'm a fool to say it, the man disgusts me. But—in spite of everything, he loves you, Cam."

"Ah," said Damon softly, "but you see he does not know—everything. Yet. Still, he's cutting me off. Financially, at least. Without even the proverbial shilling." He gave a faint and bitter laugh.

"Good God!" Ridgley halted once more. "You never mean it? Does he realise the position that will place you in?"

"God forbid! It would send him into whoops!"

"But—what shall you do? Shall you be able to complete your spa? Perhaps that'll save your neck."

"More like to break it! I'm already in debt to the tune of twenty-five thousand and will need three times that to finish."

"Well, of all the cork-brained cod's heads!" cried the exasperated Ridgley. "Why did you not come to me? I could have gone to my bankers and—"

"And done what? Arranged another loan? You've already sunk ten thousand into the Spa, and had I known how short of blunt you are, I'd never have allowed you to invest at all!" Cutting off his kinsman's attempt to speak, Damon raised a peremptory hand and said, "No, Ted! As soon as I can get a groom across the bridge, I'll send word to Town and have Gillam call a meeting of the investors. They shall have to dig a little deeper—or let some new money in."

They had come to a wrought-iron bench beyond the looming bulk of the north wing's catacombs and sat down, each man busied with his own thoughts, smelling the stable smells, hearing the occasional shifting of an animal in a stall, all mingled with the myriad voices of the night and the stirrings of the wind.

"Damme!" Ridgley exploded in sudden irritation. "What a cold-blooded devil he is! Did he offer you no alternative?"

"Of a certainty," Damon acknowledged wearily. "I'm to marry within three months, give up Cancrizans, and remove to Town."

"Ah... And would you consider his demands?"

Damon favoured him with a glance of withering scorn.

"But—if you've swallowed a spider?" Ridgley blinked.

"Not quite. I still have Mother's jewels."

"What? You wouldn't, by God!"

"May have no alternative, old chap. The jewels would buy me a respectable life—were I to live quietly. I'd have to give up Cancrizans, of course. And the Spa. But—I suppose I could live in Town. My house on Green Street is not encumbered."

"You'd be doocid welcome to move into either of my places. You know that, I hope."

"I do, and thank you." Damon gave a wry grin. "You may host me sooner than you expect."

113

After a minute, Ridgley growled, "He has learned this much. Did it ever occur to you what he'll do when he learns the whole?"

Damon flinched a little. "It has occurred to me."

"Christ! Better by far to have been with the Guards in that blasted chateau at Hougoument! I don't know which of us he'll slaughter first! If you'd a spark of decency, Cam, you'd tell the man before he hears it from someone else."

Damon slanted a cynical look at him. "Is that what you would do?" he sneered. "How noble!"

"Noble, hell! Of course, I'd tell him! Whatever else, he's my own flesh and blood! D'ye think I am a hunk of ice—like you?"

"No, sir," said Damon politely. "I think you're a god-damned liar!"

The Earl smiled at the moon and responded without rancour. "Foul-mouthed young whelp."

Bodwin Hall lay to the northwest of the Priory, and the sound of Lord Phineas's carriage rumbling down the rear driveway awakened Sophia from her reverie. She was startled to find that it was after two o'clock, and she stood, resolution chasing the dreams from her eyes. She had sat here for over an hour, and there was nothing to be gained by mooning over a man who was the antithesis of everything she honoured! She must find Amory instead and discover whether he had completed the assignment with which she had charged him. During this entire day, she'd not had one instant alone with him. It was doubtful that he had yet retired, and hoping to intercept him on the stairs, she took up a candle and crept into the hall. There was no one in sight, but light still gleamed from downstairs. She hurried to the balcony. The very man she sought was hastening across the Great Hall towards the north wing. She called to him, but fearing to wake the other ladies, her cry was soft and went unheard. She hurried downstairs, crossed the hall, and turned into the north wing, following the rapidly disappearing glow ahead.

There was no sign of Amory when she came to the first winding steps leading downward, and her nervousness mounted as she recalled the tragic story Damon had told her. It was all nonsense, of course, a figment of his wicked imagination. There was no reason to fear darkness. Beginning to tremble, she crept down those clammy steps. Whatever was Hartwell about down here? His close friendship with the Marquis would imply he was no stranger to the Priory— perhaps he had come down to get something...

At the foot of the stairs, the corridor loomed ahead, her light piercing only a short way into the gloom. The heavy, rounded doors began to appear, one after another, like so many eyes, lurking in their recesses to watch her as she passed. Very mindful of Damon's monk, however she strove to dismiss him, she called a quavering "Amory?" that lay flat against the blackness.

She came at last to a wider place in the narrow passage and a half-open door and, holding her candle high, peered inside. No sign of Hartwell, but many things were stored here: a broken wicker chair from the garden, a pile of rusting iron gates, abandoned tools; and, in one corner, sedately alone, a portrait was propped. The lady must have been extraordinarily beautiful. She had glistening dark hair, pale skin, and exquisite, darkly lashed eyes, wide set and of a rich and familiar turquoise colour. The rest of her features were indeterminate. The portrait had been slashed so many times that the canvas sagged; only the hair and eyes remained intact. Her identity, however, was beyond doubting, and Sophia's fear of this gloomy place was eclipsed by a new terror. She stood unmoving, her candle held aloft, her eyes riveted to that savage destruction. Almost she could hear the Duke asking, "Where is the portrait of your Mother?" And Damon's cool "It is being cleaned, sir..." Why would he lie? And, even more horrifying, why would he bring that painting of his so beauteous Mother down into this dank dungeon and slash it to shreds?

She heard footsteps and saw the glow of an approaching candle in the hall. Amory! At last! She ran through the doorway. The welcoming cry on her lips died to a sobbing gasp. The slim figure was too tall; instead of the rich gleam of Hartwell's auburn curls, the hair was black and thick and slightly waving, with the rumpled look that she knew came from his running his hand through it while he puzzled at his music.

Damon stopped, lifting the branch of candles he held and scowling at her. "What the devil?" He looked so forbidding; with that savaged portrait fresh in her mind, she instinctively took a step back. He lifted the candles higher and, in a voice like the crack of a whip, commanded, "Come here!" Instead, she moved back. He must know that she had seen what he'd done to the portrait. Perhaps he—

She gave a little cry of terror as he pounced on her. "Let me go!" she gasped, struggling desperately. "Filthy beast! You shall not—"

There was an ear-splitting creak. Dust billowed about them. Choked and half blinded, she was whirled around in arms of steel and deafened by a thundering crash. The floor shook, and debris flew through the air. She was paralyzed by the fear that the entire roof was folding in upon them as the darkness became absolute. She knew somehow that Damon's head was bent over her; coughing and spluttering, she clung to him desperately.

"It's...all...right," he wheezed, stumbling through the blackness. "Don't be...afraid."

"What happened?"

"One of the beams collapsed. Are you all right?"

He loosened his arms, but she shrank against him in a frenzy of terror. "Yes, but don't leave me!"

"Of course not." His voice became steadier and was very tender as he asked, "Sophia—are you quite sure you're not hurt?"

"Just...so frightened. I've never known such awful darkness!" She heard a scrabbling sound. Perhaps that collapsed ceiling had opened the way for rats—in a building this old. She threw her arms about his neck, burying her face against his chest.

And then his hands clamped on her shoulders, and she was being pushed away. Light was beginning to glow through the dust-laden air, and, looking up, she saw his face covered with grime, the tousled locks heavy with dust, the light eyes blazing. Shaking her, he demanded fiercely, "What in God's name were you doing down here? I told you to keep away! Are you daft, woman?"

Speechless with shock, she gazed up at him. Were these bruising hands the same hands that had held her so safely against him? Was this harsh snarl the tender voice that just a moment ago had asked if she was hurt?

Other voices rang out, followed by the sounds of running feet. Damon shoved her roughly towards the oncoming light. "Little fool!" he gritted. "Go with them! And since it has to

116

be spelled out for you—as soon as may be, I'll thank you to leave my house."

She gave a gasp at this unthinkable behaviour, yet did not move, watching as he turned and went back into the drifting clouds of dust, peering up at the shattered remains of the ceiling.

A familiar voice called a worried "Damon...?"

"Marcus!" With a sob of relief, Sophia ran to her cousin's arms.

"Good God!" he exclaimed, and then shouted, "He's here, sir. And Sophia as well!"

The Earl came running up, his face strained with anxiety. "Are you all right, ma'am?"

"I am...now," she faltered, suddenly weak in the knees. Clay held her protectively. Ridgley eyed her with frowning concern, then went to Damon and demanded angrily, "Why in the deuce did you bring her down here at this hour?"

Damon threw him a disgusted look and, ignoring the question, said curtly, "The beam gave way, and—By Jupiter! Amory!"

Candle in hand, Hartwell clambered over the debris. He was covered with dust, and blood streaked his forehead. The Earl hurried to help him over the rubble, and he at once rushed weavingly to Sophia. "What are you doing down here? My God! Were you under that confounded crumbling ceiling?"

"Your poor head," she cried, her fears forgotten in her concern for him.

"I would suggest," said the Marquis sardonically, "that this is neither the time nor the place for *l'amour*. The rest of this ceiling looks quite ready to come down on us."

Sophia tossed him a disgusted look, but they lost no time in retreating. Upstairs, Vaille met them in the corridor and assisted Hartwell to one of the wide settles before the still-smouldering fire in the Great Hall. Miss Hilby fled in search of water and bandages, and Sophia, refusing stubbornly to go to her room, sat beside Hartwell. Vaille examined the young man's scraped forehead. "It doesn't look too bad. Can you tell us what happened?"

"And why?" asked Damon glacially.

He received outraged glares from both his father and Sophia as Hartwell muttered a rueful "Don't really know, Cam. Thought I saw someone trotting down the corridor, so I followed. When I got all the way to the catacombs, I heard

117

someone behind me and turned back." He held his head and sighed weakly, "Whole...blasted roof came down."

Miss Hilby returned with a bowl of water and strips of white linen, and Sophia began to bathe Hartwell's lacerations.

"And you, ma'am," Vaille probed, "why were you down in that ghastly place?"

"I wanted to talk with Sir Amory," Sophia mumbled, colouring as she realized how foolish and improper that sounded.

"Had I known you were behind me," sighed Hartwell, "I should have rushed back."

"And had either of you been so courteous as to heed my warnings," Damon put in with a curl of the lip, "there would have been no need for any of this nonsense."

Chapter 12

Sophia rose early the next morning. It seemed imperative somehow that she look her best, and to this end she donned a frock of jaconet muslin sprigged with tiny orange garlands, and of a colour almost the shade of her hair. Her gleaming curls she piled high and tied about them a riband of orange velvet. Her toilette required a good deal of time, and when she went downstairs at last, it seemed to have been laboured over in vain, for there was no one to be seen. She had hoped to find Marcus, or Sir Amory. She needed to talk to someone, for she was still quite shaken from the horrible events of the previous evening. Troubled and restless, she wandered into the library and stood staring blindly at the empty hearth, the old heavy bricks... Again, the nightmare of that disintegrating ceiling swept over her. She forced memory away and, walking briskly to the bookshelves, scanned the volumes. She seemed to have halted before a section devoted almost entirely to the history of music. Much as she loved the subject, she was not in the mood, and was about to look elsewhere when she spotted a copy of Lord Byron's "The Corsair." Pleased, she reached up for it, but it was quite tightly wedged in, and when she removed it several other volumes toppled. She gave a little squeal as one landed on her head. Exasperated, she bent to gather up the fallen books. Her head had suffered quite a rap. She thought of how much more it would hurt if she had been nearer that massive beam last evening. Damon had saved her. There could be no doubt that if he had not acted swiftly she would have been seriously injured. She was most assuredly in his debt now! Yet what a hopeless enigma he was—saving her one moment, snarling at her the next! Heaven help the woman who loved him, for she'd not know from one second to the next how his temper might—

The murmur of voices reached her ears. She had dropped to one knee and was in a quite inelegant position, still not having retrieved the fallen volumes. She gathered them up, stood, and gave a gasp as in her haste she stepped upon the hem of her frock and the high waistline ripped disastrously. The voices were closer. Vaille and Miss Hilby. Catching sight of herself in the glass of a framed print, she uttered a moan of dismay. Her carefully arranged coiffure had been torn loose by the falling book; no longer neatly upswept, the entire left side flopped in total disarray. She tossed the books onto the reference table. She'd not the least intention of allowing Miss Hilby to see her looking such a fright, and so made a dive for one of the deep window bays. She knelt on the cushions, slid the curtains closed as quickly and quietly as possible, and crouched back, waiting for them to pass.

They did not pass. She could have wept when she heard the door close. She had no least desire to eavesdrop upon another private conversation, and reached for the curtain, determined to reveal her presence.

Already however, the Duke was speaking, and in a gentle tone she'd not heard before. "...my poor girl, of course I do not wish you to be unhappy. I am assured you honestly imagine yourself in love, but—"

Frowning a little, Sophia drew back her hand.

"Imagine!" Miss Hilby sounded between tears and anger. "You *know* my heart is given. And my love *is* returned. You cannot convince me otherwise!"

There was a small pause, then Vaille said carefully, "I am

sure many men have loved you, Charlotte. You are an exceeding beautiful woman. I merely seek, once again, to warn you that there will be no offer of marriage."

"Camille does not agree," she retaliated with quavering defiance. "He says that soon or late we shall be wed!"

"Does he, by God! Then I should take a horsewhip to that young scoundrel! My dear child, you must surely realize he has deceived you!"

Sophia gave a shocked gasp as Miss Hilby sobbed, "No, no! He has *not*! Oh, Philip, when he speaks to you, *promise* me that you will at least listen to what he has to say."

"That will not be necessary, for I am convinced he has no intention of coming to me on such an errand. Waste no more years, my dear. Nor throw your life away on one who is—quite ineligible."

"Oh..." Charlotte wailed. "How c-can you say such... cruel...things?"

For a moment the Duke made no response. Then, with slow reluctance, he said, "One must sometimes be cruel...in order to be kind. Despite what my son may have told you, ma'am, you do but delude yourself. I may not know him well, but I suspect Camille was merely—"

There was a wild outburst of sobbing, the sound of running feet, and a door slammed. Sophia, kneeling motionless, heard the creak of a chair and a deep, groaning sigh.

It was a sigh she echoed as she stared blindly at the closed curtains. How despicable that the Marquis should so injure those who loved him. It was hard to know which of them she most pitied: poor trusting Miss Hilby, or the much tried Duke of Vaille. It must have been exceeding difficult for so well bred a gentleman to utter such a deplorable indictment of his son...yet had Miss Hilby one ounce of sense, she would have listened, for he had spoken honestly. It was folly for her to continue to delude herself. Damon *might* be fond of her. She *was* very beautiful, but he would not marry a woman older than himself. Besides, if he *truly* loved her, he would certainly...never have— Sophia bit her lip, appalled to find herself entertaining such unkind thoughts. It was nothing to her if Miss Hilby chose to throw her silly self at Camille's head, just because— She gave a gasp, mentally pinched herself for her wickedness, and hearing the door open, peeped through the curtains. Vaille was leaving. His head was bowed, but as she watched, he straightened his shoulders and

121

stepped into the hall, his carriage as proud as ever. Her heart aching for him, Sophia waited a few minutes, then slipped from her hiding place.

"Marcus!" Sophia withdrew her hand from her cousin's arm, spun to face him, and cried furiously, "You really are insupportable! You should have told me at once so that I could have thanked Damon instead of—" She frowned and stopped.

He took up her hand and, again pulling it through his arm, led her across the lawns on this bright morning and soothed, "It was jolly decent of him to speak to the Duke, and I'm sorry I neglected to tell you of it, but—no great harm done. You seem to—er, be going along well together. Cannot say I blame you. He's a handsome devil, and they say in Town all the hopeful mama's are hot on his trail. I hear he's become most adept at dodging 'em, and so charmingly that the ladies sigh and languish just the same."

"Sigh...and languish," murmured Sophia through set teeth. "Do they now?"

"So they say. There are some odd whispers about him, but—I must confess, I'm devilish drawn to the fellow even though he ain't a sportsman and don't—"

"Ride or fence or spar—or do anything a gentleman should do," she intervened scornfully.

"Such as," Clay said stiffly, "saving your life?"

Sophia caught her breath. If Marcus knew how Damon had shaken her in the catacombs and the insulting things he'd said, her cousin's obviously spiralling opinion of their reluctant host would undergo a drastic change. Her brow furrowed. Too drastic! Clay was the soul of honour. He would confront Damon, and they would very possibly come to a challenge. God forbid! Despite his splendid military record, Clay was no great marksman and no match for a crack shot like Damon! She looked away, therefore, and merely said, in what she hoped was a calm tone, "I am not unmindful of my obligation and intend to express my thanks at once."

Clay's brow cleared and he patted her hand approvingly. He was a happy man this morning: not only was his financial situation resolved so that the crushing spectre of Newgate no longer haunted him, but he was about to join the party preparing to depart for Bodwin Hall. Despite his reluctance to leave her at the Priory, Sophia, knowing how much he wanted to see the showplace, had argued that although she was most anxious to greet Stephen upon his arrival, her brother had business with Damon that he would wish to conclude before leaving for Kent. This, she had pointed out, would give Clay ample time to look around the hall and return to escort them on the journey home.

When they reached the stables, Feather, Genevieve, and Ridgley were getting mounted. Vaille, poised and elegant as ever, was admiring a splendid grey stallion that a groom attempted to restrain from devouring Genevieve's fine chestnut gelding. Clay called eagerly to the other riders that he would be "going all the way" with them, a statement that was received with jubilation.

Damon stood at some distance from the stables, engaged in earnest conversation with his head groom. He glanced over as the glad cries rang out and called sharply, "Hold him, Trask! He's too full of fight! Saddle up the bay stallion for the Major."

Trask started away, but the Duke was intrigued by the big horse and went over to take the reins. The grey quieted and stood docilely as Sophia and Clay walked to Vaille's side. "You look as radiant as ever, my lady," he smiled. "Sorry about this fire-eater, Clay. I suspect you are disappointed."

"Not at all, sir. Especially since your son has given me leave to ride the bay. He's perfect."

"Pretty fair," Vaille qualified. "Inclined to throw out his right knee."

Mindful of her intent, Sophia slipped away and approached the Marquis. He did not see her coming, having rudely turned his back upon them all, and when she realized he and Mr. Quinn were discussing the absent Nancy, she paused, eager to learn of the girl's whereabouts.

"...not like the lass at all, m'lord," Quinn was saying. "She sent word by one of the locals as how she will take an accommodation coach to London so soon as her Dad do be better off. Reckon she knows how soft her mistress do be." He shook his head. "More'n one of my men would do—I can tell'ee! Still—" He broke off, glancing enquiringly to Sophia.

The Marquis swung around. "Good morning, ma'am. Dare we hope you shall leave us without any further uproars?"

His eyes were sneering, his mouth curving to an unpleasant leer. Sophia felt her face become hot and was rendered

123

speechless with shock that he should so address her in front of a groom.

Quinn, also taken aback, stammered, "My lady—er—have you seen our Viking? He do be mortal fine..."

She wrenched her mind from its preoccupation with casting the Marquis to the lions and followed the man without another word. The bay truly was magnificent, and she joined the others in her admiration of the animal. Vaille passed the reins of the grey stallion to Trask as soon as Clay took possession of the bay. Sophia managed somehow to concentrate on the remarks the Duke addressed to her and to respond with some degree of sanity. From the corner of her eye, she saw Damon saunter toward the house; a few moments later, the riding party left, Clay calling to her that he would be back by three. They headed along the driveway, and Damon paused on the steps, turning to wave as they drew level with him.

It was a brilliant morning, the sky blue, a few white clouds standing about, a gentle, if rather sultry, breeze blowing. Although she was still raging inwardly, Sophia could not but admire the beauty of the scene. The vivid green of turf and trees; the vibrant colours of the flower gardens; the sparkling plumes of the fountain; the fine, high-spirited animals; Genevieve looking poised and lovely; the Earl, still red in the face from having tossed Feather up into her saddle, but both he and Clay such splendid examples of British manhood.

And then, suddenly, Genevieve turned her gelding, calling something to Damon. Trask, who had been standing smiling rather vacuously at the handsome group, had let the reins slacken. The grey stallion, fired by a new sight of the hated gelding, thundered straight for his enemy. Genevieve was taken by surprise as the chestnut reared in fright. Thrown, she fell with a shriek. The stallion plunged to the attack, eyes rolling, ears laid back, teeth bared. The chestnut bucked frenziedly, rear hooves slicing the air only inches above the prostrate girl. The Earl and Clay swung their mounts simultaneously, but the animals panicked and collided.

Without a second's hesitation, Vaille left Sophia and raced toward Genevieve, but Damon was closest. He started forward. The stallion reared, hooves flailing, screaming his defiance. Damon froze. He shrank back and quailed, one arm flung across his terrified face.

Vaille, running, shoved his son aside and, with unflinch-

124

ing valour, reached up to grasp the reins, somehow avoid those flashing hooves, and with strong hands and firm words pull the raging beast down.

Sophia, also running, tossed a disgusted look at Damon. She was briefly aware that his face was haggard and streaked with perspiration; then she was past and rushing to help Genevieve.

Cancrizans Priory seemed a very quiet place now. As she left the stables, Sophia experienced an odd feeling that a chapter had closed in her life that was of more importance than any preceding it. She wandered toward the sprawl of the house, thinking of Genevieve. The plucky girl had seemed more concerned for Damon than for herself. After assuring Vaille she was unhurt and perfectly able to undertake the ride, she had run to the steps where her cousin waited silently and clasped him in her arms. Speaking in a low rush of French, she had pulled down his dark head and kissed him resoundingly on each cheek. He had muttered something, and she'd laughed and shaken him chidingly, but whatever it was she'd said had failed to bring an answering smile. When they had ridden away at last, the Duke had come to thank Sophia for helping. His eyes had swept through Damon as though he were not there, and the Marquis had sauntered back into the house, his faintly ironic grin reflecting no trace of the shame he should have felt.

Sophia had accompanied the Duke to the stables where he had decided to give the grey stallion an exercise before himself departing. Her initial consternation had been soon dispelled. Vaille was a superb rider and handled the fiery animal with ease. He had ridden off at a full gallop, the grey soaring over a low hedge, Vaille leaning forward in the saddle, his hair flying, looking a man much younger than his years.

Irritated by her continuing inability to talk with Hartwell, Sophia determined to seek him out as soon as she had thanked Damon for coming to her rescue in the catacombs. Whatever the Marquis' motives may have been, his actions had most assuredly saved her. Certainly, he had made no attempt to protect himself but had used his own body to shield her. Her brow wrinkled as she sought to equate this behaviour with the fact that when faced with an incipient tragedy

125

involving his beloved cousin, he had acted the craven. Little wonder Vaille had stalked past him with such cutting contempt. She could well imagine what Papa would have said had Stephen behaved in such a fashion when a lady was in peril.

Pondering thus, she crossed the terrace and entered the house. It was cool inside after the rather muggy warmth of the gardens. She could hear the harpsichord and was intrigued by the poignant sweetness of the unknown melody. Horatio was not with his master, and Sophia entered the music room without announcement. She had only listened for a few seconds, however, before the Marquis tensed and jumped to his feet, turning to face her. As she drew nearer, something in his eyes shrank, and she was seized by the knowledge that he *was* ashamed and in this moment completely vulnerable.

She felt strangely disoriented and, forgetting what she had come to say, was silent as she moved to the harpsichord. A sheet of half-completed music was on the rack, and she looked at it curiously, wondering if this was the melody she had just heard. His hand fairly shot out and covered it with another page. Sophia drew back in embarrassment, and Damon removed all the music from the rack, his manner clearly implying that she intruded.

Obviously, he had regained his self-control. He met her startled gaze with one of ice and said, "You wished something, ma'am?"

'I wish your haughty nose may drop off,' she thought furiously but managed to keep her eyes as cold as his and say formally, "I have come to thank you for helping my cousin and for—rescuing me in the catacombs last night."

"Had I followed my natural inclinations, ma'am, you'd have been spanked instead of 'rescued'."

He looked quite capable of performing such a deed, and it was with difficulty that Sophia maintained her aplomb. "Whatever your natural inclinations, my lord, you contrived to rise above them. For that, at least, I am grateful."

Damon granted her an ironic bow and turned back to his horrid harpsichord.

"Excuse me, your ladyship..."

Sophia wrenched her glare from the Viper. Mrs. Hatters stood in the doorway, addressing her, but with an anxious gaze fixed upon her employer. "Miss Hilby sends her com-

126

pliments, ma'am, and might she have a word with you at your convenience?"

Wearing a dark-blue riding habit, Miss Hilby was as lovely as ever, but there was a haunted look behind her smile. "I know that Philip would be relieved to see you safely home," she said as they sat together in the pleasant bay of her bedroom window. "Can I not prevail upon you to accompany us?"

Sophia thanked her but reiterated her conviction that Stephen was on his way and that she must be here when he arrived. Miss Hilby nodded, moved to her dressing table, and placing a small blue velvet hat on her curls, expressed the conviction that, without Nancy's deft attentions, her hair looked a fright. "I am a little worried, Sophia. I would have allowed her to see her father at once, of course. Still"—she adjusted the large pale-blue feather so that it curled down beside her face—"it is not at all like her to leave without telling me. She is a very good...girl..." The words trailed off, her wistful gaze fixed upon a wall plaque on which was carved the coat of arms of the House of Branden.

Her heart touched, Sophia crossed to put a hand on her shoulder. "My dear, do not grieve so."

Those liquid green eyes flew to meet her own. A wave of scarlet warmed Sophia's cheeks, and she stammered, "I—I overheard you talking with the Duke this morning." Miss Hilby gave a gasp, and Sophia admitted wretchedly, "I was in the library. I tried to reach a book on an upper shelf and it fell on my head and knocked my hair all askew...and then I trod on the hem of my gown and the waist tore. I was so terribly embarrassed...and I heard you coming. And you are always so—so elegant. It was deplorable. But I had to hide my tattered self...and..." She gave a little gesture of helplessness.

"Of course." Recovering, Miss Hilby patted Sophia's hand kindly. "I quite understand. We have all had such horrid moments, have we not? And how very unfeminine it would be not to shrink from them! Now don't look so grieved, my dear, for, indeed, everybody knows my secret."

"I did not know. I might have suspected, perhaps. But a woman can usually sense heartbreak in another woman, do you not think?"

She had spoken sympathetically but had not expected her

127

companion to suddenly bow her head into her hands and burst into tears. Sophia offered her handkerchief, sat beside her, and patted the bowed shoulder through the storm. And in a very little while, Miss Hilby blew her classic but rather pink nose, wiped her eyes daintily, and sniffed, "Forgive me, I beg of you. I . . . I do not usually give way like this. But—oh, I love him so! And have waited such . . . such a very long time. But it is useless. I must accept that he will not offer for me. And I'll . . . oh, I'll never find a husband . . . now!"

"What nonsense! I vow, Charlotte, if you so much as showed your face at Almack's, the men would be flocking—"

"Oh!" wailed Miss Hilby damply. "That horrid marriage mart—at my age?"

"Tush and a fiddlestick! *Your* age, indeed!"

"Thank you for the kindness. But it's true—my salad days are long past. I should have accepted another offer years since. Damon insists he . . . loves me. But—oh, Sophia—it's our ages, you see. He—he feels there is too large a gap."

'He would!' thought Sophia, striving rather unsuccessfully to feel indignant and succeeding only in wanting to burst into tears. "Was there never anyone else?"

"Not that I cared a fig for. I had so many beaux when I first met him. It was at Almack's, in fact . . ." Haunted by memory, she looked extremely lovely despite her tear-stained face. "I shall never forget it as long as I live. He came straight across the room to me—and I thought him the handsomest, the most elegant gentleman I had ever beheld. He looked at me with those splendid eyes of his, and—I was lost, Sophia. And so I refused all others. And although I knew how he felt, because he has never lied to me, I waited. I have begged him." She gave a forlorn little shrug and, looking at the younger woman with shamed eyes, admitted, "That's how desperate I am, you see. But he won't hear of it. And so, I just wait . . . and hope . . . and pray." She bowed her head again, and Sophia stood and walked to the windows.

The Marquis was in the courtyard below them, hands on hips, talking with two grooms. He looked every inch the aristocrat, and, noting the proud tilt of the head, the carriage of the shoulders, the respect with which the men attended his every word, her heart ached. A hand slipped through her arm, and Charlotte stood beside her, a humble smile on her face. They hugged one another, and struggling for composure, Sophia forced a smile. "No matter what you say, you could

128

have any one of dozens of men with just a snap of your fingers. But if you feel it must be him—or no one, why it's better to have known such a love than to endure a *mariage de convenance* with someone else. Or so I should think." And she sighed, knowing drearily that very few marriages these days had anything whatsoever to do with love.

The maid said her name was Patience, that she came from the village daily—when there was a bridge to cross—and that the Marquis begged the pleasure of her company in the library, adding with an envious sigh, "At your convenience, my lady."

Sophia thanked her and hurried past the rosy-cheeked lass, her heart leaping with hope. If Patience could have come across, surely it would be safe for Stephen...

Damon was standing before the library windows, scowling down at a paper in his hand. When she entered, he folded it hurriedly and thrust it into his pocket. "A message from the landlord of 'The Wooden Leg.' Whitthurst came—and has gone. You would do well to accept—"

"Gone?" she interposed, aghast. "What do you mean— *gone*?"

"What the deuce should I mean? Your brother arrived at the inn not an hour after you had left. When he learned the bridge was down, he at once returned to Kent—quite the worse for wear, I am informed. I've no doubt he needs you at—"

"Is that what the note says?" she demanded angrily, and when he gave an exasperated gesture and nodded, she asked if she might read it.

"Gladly, ma'am. However, there is also a personal message for me. And our innkeeper is, I fear, a crude individual at best." His eyes were bland and empty. "Since my father has already offered to—"

"To be taken many miles out of his way? And before you tell me that he will be glad to change his plans for my sake, I have no doubt of it." Her lip curled. "Surely, sir, you can restrain your impatience. Directly my cousin returns, we shall leave you to your precious solitude."

Two hours later, however, she was beginning to repent her decision. Clay was still among the missing, and Vaille and Miss Hilby had departed better than an hour since. Now, beginning to be really worried, Sophia went downstairs.

In the music room, the maid Patience stood beside the harpsichord, her fingers touching the keys gently. She looked up, her eyes dreaming, and, seeing Sophia, started and gave a small scream. "Oh, ma'am! Oh, my stays! I am that *sorry*! I clean forgot, and it do be almost a hour, too! Sir Amory, ma'am. He do be waiting for'ee down by the fountain!"

"Twelve thousand...pounds?" Sophia's voice squeaked a little. "But—the agreement I signed said *two* thousand!"

Hartwell sprang up from the wrought iron bench in the rose garden, bowed theatrically, and handed her a bank draft. "I bullied the old curmudgeon into coming up a trifle! And—was ever a man so fortunate as to complete his lady's errand and win so glowing a look in return?"

He watched her adoringly, his handsome face reflecting his love. And she was desolate. Why, oh, why had she begged him to handle the transaction for her? Why had she decided to borrow against the land? She'd had no right—not without consulting Stephen...no right at all! At the time, it had seemed—

"...is wrong?" Hartwell was asking anxiously.

She gathered her wits. "I just do not understand. They *do* realize I am just *borrowing* against the land? It...it was not a *sale*, Amory?"

"My dear, when I brought you the preliminary agreement you said— You *did* ask Whitthurst, or your man of business to look it over, as I urged you to do?"

"Yes—well, I did, of course," she lied. Amory had arrived at Singlebirch one rainy afternoon, soaked to the skin, and with a preliminary agreement form requiring her signature. "May not be able to get the old chap to sign it, even now," he said cheerfully. "But you and Stephen look it over m'dear and see what you think. If it appeals to you, sign on the bottom line and I'll rush it back to him with the Deed. Must go and change now—have to be back in Devonshire first thing in the morning. Strike while the iron is hot, y'know! Don't want Prendergast to change his mind!"

After he'd left she had begun to struggle through the voluminous pages of crabbed writing, much in Latin, with endless clauses and long words. She'd deciphered the fact that Prendergast Associates were willing to loan the sum of two

130

thousand pounds against the properties, the amount to be repaid in full within twelve months. She had also noted that they were willing to halt any building currently under way upon said properties, and to prohibit any additional construction prior to the termination of the agreement. But this was as much as she had been able to establish before Amory returned, eager to be upon his way once more. She had longed to be able to turn to one of her uncles, or the family solicitor for advice, but it had been more than she'd dare do. Even if they agreed not to discuss the matter with Stephen—which seemed unlikely—they were sure to mention it to their wives. The word would have swept the family like a forest fire, returning inevitably to her ailing brother's ears.

Amory had assured her that "old Prendergast" was true blue and sound to the backbone. "Never one to hand you over to the cents-per-centers," whatever that meant. He looked weary, but denied it with cheerful vehemence. He had worked so hard in her behalf and been so delighted to think he had helped her in this emergency. Grateful, she had signed, and he'd left promising to return with the bank draft as soon as possible.

Now, watching her narrowly, he exclaimed, "Oh, Lord! I pray I've not caused you to be worried? I'm the last one to understand all that legal flummery. If anything goes amiss, Whitt's liable to think I've been up to some skullduggery!"

"Indeed, he will not! You have been a true friend, Amory. As if we could ever entertain such wicked doubts!"

He took her hand and pressed it to his lips. "Had you only allowed me to be of greater assistance than merely arranging a fribbly loan for you . . . it would have made me the—the very happiest fellow in all England."

"You are too good." She gave his hand a slight squeeze before removing her fingers from his clasp. "But it would not be at all proper, you know."

"Then let me make it proper! Dash it all, Sophia, I shan't let one turndown stop me! I love you! My lovely lady, won't you allow me to start planning the biggest ball, the grandest wedding, the most delightful honeymoon money can buy?"

She looked into his eager face and felt a deep liking. She looked into those wide grey eyes and knew herself the veriest fool among fools, for here was total devotion. And she did not love him. Her glib advice to Charlotte came back to haunt her. 'Better to have known such a love than to endure a

131

mariage de convenance...' "Dear Amory..." she said haltingly, "I—I am most...deeply honoured and truly thank—"

He gave a muffled sound of despair, leapt to his feet, and turning from her, began to stride down the slope.

"Amory!" She ran after him. "Wait! Please wait!"

The grass was still slippery from the rains and the soles of her slippers somewhat worn. She slipped, tumbled, and gave a small cry as she sprawled with a revealing display of petticoats and ankles. Hartwell turned with a shocked gasp and, running back to her, slipped also and went to his knees. Heedless of his immaculate breeches, he crawled up to ask breathlessly, "Sophia—are you all right?"

Laughing, she said, "A trifle muddy, but—" Horatio shot through the trees and flew at her with a hiss and a flap of wings. Amory pulled her close, waving his arm menacingly. She shrank against him, and the goose trundled on past.

Damon, bursting from the trees, cried, "Is something wrong? I—" He halted abruptly, looking utterly taken aback. Then a fierce glare travelled from Sophia's bare ankles to the arms that Hartwell clasped about her. Two spots of colour appeared high on his cheekbones. "I do apologize," he said acidly. "Pray forgive the interruption of such a...pleasant pastime." The contemptuous curl of the lip, the lift of those dark brows, relegated Sophia to the status of Haymarket ware.

"The devil!" Amory spluttered indignantly. "I vow you're becoming positively caper-witted, Damon! You go beyond the line—the lady fell, merely!"

But noting how his arms gathered the stunned Sophia a little closer, the Marquis bowed and was gone, sauntering gracefully back through the trees, Horatio squawking grumpily after him.

Chapter 13

When Sophia entered the house, the harpsichord was crashing in a furious boil of music. She recognized Bach's tempestuous "Toccata and Fugue" as she flung the door wide. The room was, as usual, almost dark.

"Excuse me," she snarled. Her plea went unnoticed. She stepped closer. Damon's head was bent, his supple fingers flying over the keys. "Your pardon, my lord," she enunciated, loud and clear. His head went back, the thick hair tossing. One slim hand shot up, poised, and then he was leaning forward, the notes rippling out again.

"Viper!" she hissed. Bach enveloped her and was her only response. Marching forward, she threw the drapes open.

A crashing chord terminated Mr. Bach's music. Damon stood, scowled at her, then went to the mantle and began to ram tobacco into his pipe. "I do apologize, my lady, for bursting in so rudely upon your little... tête-à-tête." And, again, there was the insinuating, offensive smirk.

From earliest childhood, the Lady Sophia Drayton had been schooled in the arts of grace and graciousness, but never had her reputation been so impugned. Her many beaux variously worshipped, admired, or desired her. To be blatantly insulted was something so foreign to her experience she could scarce comprehend it. And thus it was that, facing him, she was all but panting with rage. And very lovely.

"If it is any of your business, my ignoble lord," she half sobbed, "I had fallen. Sir Amory was merely—"

He gave a tiny shrug, a gracefully deprecating wave of the hand. "I beg you will not fatigue yourself with explanations. I, in fact, owe you my felicitations." His eyes glared suddenly. "Since Hartwell is the man of your choice. At least, one must assume so, in view of your—er—torrid embraces."

She stamped closer and thrust her small chin at him, her eyes blazing with wrath. "Oooh!" she choked. "How I wish I were a man!"

Damon's eyelids assumed a bored droop. "That, dear lady, is a desire you can scarce expect me to share."

"I expect nothing from you, sir! *Nothing!*"

"Alas," he sneered. "I am become unnecessary, I perceive. While Hartwell is so—ah—accommodating."

Sophia flushed scarlet, her fists clenching. "How monstrous you are!"

"True," shrugged the Marquis. "Wherefore, being monstrously unnecessary, I am sure you wish to be gone, for you surely cannot care to be—"

"To be spied upon!"

"But, of course. No one would. Under *those*—circumstances."

It was incredible how much scorn he could convey with just that cynical lift of one eyebrow.

Her teeth bared, Sophia grated an impotent "How—*dare* you!"

"You, ma'am, were the one who dared. I must confess I thought it not quite the thing. *En plein jour*, as it were. But I am, I collect, rather old-fashioned."

She paled. For an instant, she stood quivering and silent. Then her hand slapped hard across his cheek.

It was the second time she had struck him. A lock of his hair was bounced down his brow by the impact, but he made no movement of either anger or retaliation, merely regarding her levelly.

"By what right," she bit out, almost incoherent, "do *you* censure *me*?"

She was quite visibly shaking with rage. Looking down at her, the glare faded from Damon's eyes. He made no response for a moment, then gave a slight bow. "Not censure, ma'am. Merely observe. But you are ...... apologize. I have neither the right nor the desire to bandy words with you."

"Of course not," she sputtered. "That is not your way, is it? Having insulted me, you think ...... away—like the coward you are!"

His eyes fell. "Yes. If you ...... ma'am," and he started away.

"Well, I shall not!" She ...... front him. "You have ...... your nasty ...... you will have the decency to hear me out!"

...... halted at once. "I ......"

...... Valour? ...... aware ...... and have k...... ...... death ...... How fortunate ...... did not ...... came a guest ......

Damon stood rigidly si...... ...... and begemmed snuff box, def...... ...... pinch with infuriating languor, and in...... "...... not aware," he said, dusting his cravat with a lac...... "that I mentioned such a word ...."

He had spilled more snu...... ...... hand shook so. The movements of the h...... ...... cast a small cloud, and Sophia, her mouth ...... for ...... blasting attack, paused, gasped, and gave so violent a sneeze that a comb was shaken from her hair. Damon, his eyes at once abrim with laughter, scooped it up and offered it.

Sophia snatched at it angrily but dropped it as she sneezed once more. His faint chuckle added to her fury as she thought up a scathing indictment, waved her arms preparatory to devastating him with her acid words, only to explode into another sneeze. "Beast!" she choked inadequately.

He grinned and held out his handkerchief.

She took it, turned as she felt another paroxysm building, and ran a few quick steps toward the harpsichord. The sneeze was magnificent. It rocked her to her slippers; gasping, she reached out blindly for support. Her hand struck the rack, sending music flying helter-skelter. Damon hurried over and began to retrieve the pages, and Sophia, recovering some-

135

what, bent to collect the sheets that were close to her. Something inside her became very still. The topmost sheet was the melody she'd heard him playing just before Vaille had left, the music he had snatched away so hurriedly. It was still unfinished, but these notes had been penned by the sure hand of a skilled musician—quite different to the clumsy efforts on the old parchment. At the top, a bold, firm scrawl provided the title "Sophia."

Stunned, her eyes flashed to Damon. He was on one knee, searching anxiously through the pages he had gathered. He looked up at her, saw the music in her hand, and froze. For a very brief instant, his face reflected shocked guilt. She saw the white teeth catch at his lower lip. Then he took a breath, stood, met her amazed stare, and said an aloof "My Great Aunt..."

He was lying, she was sure of it. All other considerations became of no importance; her boiling fury was totally forgotten. "Oh?" she murmured, and hummed the melody. "You must be very fond of her. This is beautiful."

He thanked her with bored indifference but from the corner of his eye saw her suspicious regard and said hastily, "You were quite right. I am devoted to her. Though she's a pitiful old thing."

Sophia expressed the hope that the lady was not ill.

"No. Fat." The words were gravely uttered, but again laughter gleamed in his eyes as her chin swung up in that betrayingly defensive fashion.

"Fat!" It had occurred to my lady of late that her hips might be just a shade too rounded. "Very fat?"

"Enormous," he said, warming to his creation. "And tall—well over six feet."

She gasped. "Six feet! Has she a husband?"

"Twice widowed," he mourned. "And she has a—" He looked into her lovely and faintly aghast violet eyes and said irrepressibly, "A squint, poor thing."

"A squint? And twice widowed! She would seem overburdened with afflictions."

"True. And with lovers."

"L-lovers...?"

"Well, only one at the moment," he qualified gravely. "Terribly jealous. But—very devoted."

Sophia, her own eyes beginning to sparkle with mirth, echoed, "Only one?"

"At the moment. Fine chap. A bit short for her, unfortunately. Stands about four feet, ten."

"They must," she observed, her voice a trifle unsteady, "present a rather odd appearance."

"*Mais oui.* But then he has such an air about him."

"He does?"

He nodded. "Most decidedly. Cannot escape it." His lips quivered. "He's a cockle and mussel merchant, you see."

Choking, she said, "Cockle...and mussel."

"Alive, alive-oh," he grinned.

"How fascinating," she said with a ripple of laughter. "No wonder you were so inspired as to write that lovely song for her."

"Well," he admitted, "she loves me. And, after all, when someone...loves you..." Mesmerized by her laughing face, he faltered into silence.

And, again, that shimmering magic encompassed them. Sophia scarce dared to breathe. His eyes seemed to pierce her soul...

A log rolled in the grate. Damon's shoulders jerked. He looked away at once and, with a hand that trembled, picked up the old sheet of music and began to battle it.

Thoroughly unnerved, Sophia moved to the fireplace, her breathing rapid now, her heart beating wildly. How could he have summoned a store of humour at such a moment? And why must she forget so soon the indignities he seemed to delight in heaping upon her? Another moment and she'd probably have been clutched in his arms again—a willing captive! The man was a mesmerist—and she, a stupid, henwitted widgeon. She picked up something, thinking, 'Fool! Fool! Fool!' and realized suddenly that she was staring at the small china figurine she had smashed on that first afternoon. It had been glued back together, only a small chip of the dog's tail having been lost. The repairs had undoubtedly entailed much time and patience, and it followed that the piece must have some deep sentimental value. Dismayed, she swung around.

The Marquis was watching her. "It was a gift from my mother," he said.

"Oh! And I broke it deliberately! My horrid temper! I am so sorry..." Her distressed words trailed away as she stared down at the figurine.

"Are you sure?"

She looked up, saw his half smile, and carefully replaced the piece upon the mantle. "I cannot quite understand," she said, moving to the side of the harpsichord, "why you would strive so hard to repair it when the portrait in the catacombs has not been—"

She stopped. His eyes held a frightening glare. The hand, draped lazily over the music rack, clenched convulsively. He began to play the discordant notes once more, his fingers hard upon the keys. She knew she had trodden in some forbidden area and drew back to leave.

"And what do you think of this melody, my lady?"

"I doubt it will ever become popular," she replied with considerable understatement. "The notes appear to have been arranged without rhyme or reason. Much as a child might toss a pile of alphabet blocks onto the floor and hope to find them arranged into words. Whoever composed it might better have bent his energies to some more rewarding hobby."

"Yes," he mused, and added whimsically, "Like plumbing or bricklaying."

She smiled, "But perhaps—"

"Sophia!"

Her heart jumped into her throat. She spun around. Viscount Whitthurst leaned in the doorway, his buckskins muddied, his jacket rumpled, his thin face pale and drawn with exhaustion. "What in God's name...are you doing...here?"

"Stephen!" She started toward him.

Whitthurst took one stumbling step, swayed, and crumpled to the floor.

Unaware that an anguished cry had escaped her, Sophia was beside him on the instant and, kneeling, began to gather his head into her arms. A firm hand on her shoulder stayed her.

"Do not, ma'am. He'll be better off if you let him lie flat."

She glared up at him through a sparkle of tears, her eyes blazing with disgust. "You lied! He had not been at 'The Wooden Leg' at all! *You lied!*"

"True," he admitted and, as he strode to tug urgently on the bellrope, added with a sigh, "I wanted to be rid of you. It didn't work—unfortunately."

Sophia leaned back in the chair beside the bed and put a hand across her eyes. The drapes were drawn and the room dim, but she felt drained and exhausted and was still trembling from the reaction of her confrontation with the Marquis and the shock of her brother's collapse.

The Viscount stirred in the big bed, mumbling something incoherently. She stood at once and bent over him, touching the thick dark hair with a fond hand and murmuring comfortingly, and he quieted at once. She watched him, grieving because he was still so thin and his face marked by suffering—old beyond his years. Dear Stephen—so typical of the gallant young men Britain had lost by the thousands in these endless years of warfare. He did not move again, and she returned to the chair and leaned her head back wearily.

She was calm now, her emotions under control, but she felt hurt and betrayed. "I wanted to be rid of you..." The brutal words rang in her ears. Believing her departure imminent, he had indulged her with that humourous interlude. Probably, the music had indeed been written for another Sophia—one of his many lightskirts. He had lied to her about Stephen, neither knowing nor caring how desperately the injured man would need help and rest, caring only that his priceless privacy be restored to him.

She gave an impatient shrug. All that mattered now was Steve. Damon was—as she had said—beneath contempt. Yet try as she would, she could not force him from her mind. However determined she was to concentrate on her brother, within a very few moments she would find her thoughts on some event in these crowded few days: mostly upon the laughter, grief, or anger contained in one pair of darkly lashed eyes, and his final treachery which made her glad, in a heartsick fashion, that her revenge would be complete and so devastating...

The door swung open silently. She glanced up, then jumped to her feet and, with a strangled sob, flung herself into her cousin's arms.

Clay wrapped her in an affectionate hug and, looking anxiously over her shoulder to the bed and the young man who lay in it, was alarmed both by the deathly pallor of the Viscount's face and by Sophia's weeping. Stroking her hair, he pressed a kiss upon it and groaned remorsefully, "Cam told me what happened—in truth the poor fellow seems little less distraught than you, my dear coz. I truly am sorry!" He drew her into her own room, sat beside her on the sofa, and comforted her until, her fighting spirit asserting itself, she accepted his handkerchief and, having blown her nose and dried her tears, essayed a tremulous smile. "What a...feather head! I might have woken Stephen with my nonsense!"

The Viscount, however, did not wake all that day or night. Next morning, Sophia, who had snatched what sleep she might in the chair beside his bed, awoke to find him tossing feverishly. She was immeasurably relieved when Damon imported a plump and motherly midwife from the village to help care for him. The poor young gentleman, Mrs. Gaffney advised, was merely exhausted, on top of which he'd taken a chill. He would be all the better for a long rest and, provided her instructions were followed, would doubtless be fully recovered in no time.

Sophia was willing enough to follow whatever orders the kindly woman issued. She hovered close at hand, however, refusing to be chased away, and Clay spent much time with her, entertaining her with tales of Phineas Bodwin's magnificent showplace of a home. "He's determined you shall see it," he informed her during one of these conversations. "If Steve improves as Mrs. G. says, you could go back with Ridgley. He'll be coming here day after tomorrow for Cam's meeting." The questioning arch of her brows elicited the information that the Marquis expected a number of gentlemen on Thursday afternoon to discuss "some kind of urgent development with his spa." Sophia's knees turned to water. For an instant, she was so dizzied she almost tumbled from her chair. It took her every effort not to betray her terror, and she was relieved to be able to look away, feigning shyness when Clay asked, "By the by, how fared your eager Lothario?"

She mumbled that she was not ready to make a decision. Seemingly amused by this, Clay grinned. "Turned him down again, eh? I heard he went roaring off. Well, old Whitt won't shed any tears when he hears that news. Begad! If it ain't starting to rain again!"

By noon the rain had become a downpour. Mrs. Gaffney ordered Sophia to bed after lunch, and assured the invalid was in excellent hands, she obeyed and slept for several hours. When she awoke, she found the midwife had been urgently summoned to the village. Mrs. Tibbett's firstborn was arriving early. "But milady is not to worry! Poor Lord Whitthurst is sleeping peaceful and will likely be much better in the morning."

Sophia stayed beside her brother for a while. He was snoring gently, his skin cool, the flushed look of fever gone from his face. She tied one of her scarves to the bellrope and secured it beside the bed where he might easily reach it. Then she tidied her hair and wandered downstairs. The Marquis and Clay had driven off in a closed chaise to inspect the ravages this new storm had wreaked upon the spa. The house was quiet—not even Horatio in evidence—and she went into the library and curled up in the big leather chair. She was still drowsy from loss of sleep and was beginning to nod when she noticed an odd shadow cast upon the wall by a twist of paper that, having fallen short of the fire, had become caught between two logs in the basket. Retrieving it, she was about to toss it into the blaze when she saw part of an excellent sketch. She spread the crumpled sheet. There were no words. At the top was a scorpion, quite a sinister creature, though very well drawn. Below it was a bare-headed, elegantly dressed man of middle age. Next came the sketch of another man, thickset and powerful looking, with a dog on either side of him, one a bloodhound and the other a setter. And lastly, the figure of a woman, young and of the quality beyond doubting, magnificently gowned, but her face not completed. And, beside her, a question mark. Gazing at the drawings curiously, Sophia jumped, her heart all but stopping as a slim hand reached over her shoulder to take the paper.

"Gad, ma'am," Damon rasped, "what a busy person you are, to be sure!"

He might as well have said "busybody." His eyes, hard and angry, reduced her to total embarrassment. She knew she was reddening and mumbled apologies, not helped by the sneer on his face. She was vastly relieved when Clay hurried into the room, asked eagerly about Whitthurst, and imparted the information that it was raining cats and dogs and the canals at the Spa were half filled already. His chattering lent her the time to compose herself, and as soon as was decently possible, she left them explaining that she must spend the evening at Stephen's bedside.

"I shall come up directly after dinner," said Clay kindly, "and keep you company."

"Good God, Chicky!" Clay tossed his cards onto the table and, shoving back his chair, eyed her with pained resentment. "That's the second time you've played through!"

"Oh, dear!" Sophia laid down her own cards and admitted ruefully that she never had been very good at piquet. "I am sorry, Marcus." Her eyes turned to the dim room in which Whitthurst still slept peacefully. The eiderdown had slipped again, and she hurried to pull it gently over his maimed shoulder. Returning, she found Clay sprawled in an armchair. When she had seated herself, he asked smilingly, "What is it you've been trying to bring yourself to tell me?"

She gave a little laugh, her pulse quickening. "You know me too well!" It was the opportunity she'd waited for. Gathering her courage, she asked carefully, "Marcus—what does Vaille intend? Shall he pay off all your creditors and—"

He straightened at once. "Nothing for you to worry about, m'dear. Can't tell you what a weight it is off my mind not to have to contemplate being shackled up and hauled away to Newgate!"

"Of course, poor dear, I can well imagine! But, Marcus— shall you have to practise very strict economies? Esther will worry herself ill again if she realises how badly strapped you are."

She would realise, of course, thought Clay. However he tried to account for it, when he disposed of the Town house and let the servants go, she would be bound to worry. Still— it was better than Debtors Prison, praise God! "I am well satisfied, Sophia. You just look after your harum-scarum idiot in there, and do not worry your pretty head with my problems."

She rose and, looking down at him gravely, took the bank draft from her pocket and handed it to him.

"Oh, Lord!" gasped Clay. "*You* asked Vaille, too?"

"No, dear. I took out a loan on some property."

"I see." With a doubtful frown, he passed it back to her. "Whitt know?"

She pushed the draft back into his hand. "You can repay us when you come into your inheritance, coz. So there's—"

"*I can what?*" he growled, his eyes kindling.

Five minutes later Sophia sat with her handkerchief pressed to her lips and sniffed realistically while observing him with a shrewd and tearless gaze. Clay stared down at the draft. Twelve thousand pounds! What a magnificent difference that could make! He found Sophia watching him and flushed painfully. Before he could utter any more protestations, she leaned forward. "Marcus, I wish you will be kind. I can endure no more grief, and you don't want me having the vapours all over the floor?" A faint smile lit his eyes, and she pressed her advantage at once. "You can pay us lots and lots of interest if it will please you. You really have not the right to refuse, you know. The baby and Douglas depend on you, as well as dear Esther! And, in Christian charity, Marcus—I've enough to keep me awake at night without fretting about your little family!"

He stood, seized her hands, pulled her to her feet, and embraced her with such fervour that she gasped for mercy. "You are the very dearest girl," he proclaimed. "But—what of you and Stephen?"

She assured him they would be perfectly comfortable, for she still had the emerald, she thought, if things became really grim. "If nothing else, this visit has paved the way to several invitations. Stephen and I are asked to visit Vaille House, to say nothing of spending a week or so with Miss Hilby. And I have an open invitation to Feather's Viewpark, besides—"

Mrs. Hatters came into the room with an agitated expression on her narrow features. Sophia's thought that she had heard Horatio in action was confirmed.

"It's your valet, sir. Rid all through the rain he done. Something very urgent, he says, Major."

Clay cast a scared glance at Sophia, excused himself, and strode out. Begging Mrs. Hatters to remain, Sophia waited. Clay returned in a few minutes, looking pale, and she went to him with considerable apprehension. "Not—Esther?"

"No. It's Douglas. That idiotic Nanny let him play in the rain, although he had a cold. You know how frail the little fellow is! Sophia—I'm most devilish sorry, but I must go at once!"

"Oh, Marcus! Do they know what it is?"

"No. But it don't sound too good," he said distractedly. "What a beast of a coil! You alone here! Ain't proper at all! Shall I send word for Feather to return?"

"I wish you will not. She doesn't like this place above half. Besides, Stephen is looking much better. Tomorrow, if Lord Phineas sends the big coach for us, as you said he would, we shall doubtless be able to join him."

"He'll be in transports," Clay nodded. "And Damon's gone out on business, thank God! He won't be back tonight and,— Oh, excuse me, Mrs. Hatters! I only meant...cousin
143

...unchaperoned, y'know."

"Yes, Major," said the housekeeper, nodding at his flushed face. "Which is why his lordship went to Pudding Park."

Sophia shot a startled glance at her, then urged her cousin to leave at once. "And do not worry. Mrs. Hatters will bear me very proper company."

When Clay had gone, and Mrs. Hatters was preparing a room for herself across the hall, Sophia went over to the windows. The sky was black as pitch, rain lashing the glass. She thought she heard a shout and swung the lattice wide. The wind blew out the candles at once; in the sudden darkness, she saw a glow approaching around the corner of the house. She thought at first it must be Clay but doubted he'd yet had sufficient time to be outside. Puzzled, she watched. A man's dark shape hove into view. A man wearing a long, many-caped coat that blew in the wind. He was tall, and even in the bulky coat, she could see that he was slender and walked with a pronounced limp. He turned away, raising the lantern and, as Clay's voice was raised in a shout to his groom somewhere, drew back swiftly, as if afraid to be seen. Sophia gave a gasp of terror. The lantern was extinguished, but just before it died, she saw a steely blue glint in the man's other hand. The long, deadly barrel of a pistol!

Chapter 14

Sophia's mind seemed so beset with troubles she was sure she would get very little sleep that night, but she slept deeply, her slumbers undisturbed by dreams, and awoke shortly after eight o'clock, feeling refreshed and able to cope with whatever might befall her. She had left the connecting door open so as to hear Stephen in case he called and, glancing that way, was surprised to find it shut tight. Perhaps Mrs. Gaffney had returned. She pulled on her dressing gown and hurried to the door. It was locked! How could anyone have been so stupid? She rattled the handle, but the sound was lost as the Marquis thundered, "You will damned well do no such thing!"

Sophia's mouth fell open a little. The monster had come home very early and was losing no time in berating Stephen—even when he was so very ill! With her fist upraised to pound on the door, she paused as Whitthurst's voice rang out, equally angry. "I shall, by God! What the devil d'you take me for? A damned dog in the manger? You gave me your word, Cam! Of all the cork-brained starts!"

Delighted to hear her brother in such a fine fettle, Sophia gave a contemptuous snort. The word of the Marquis of Damon was likely as worthless as the rest of his treacherous person. Stephen should have known him better than to rely on any promise he made!

"Keep your blasted voice down," snarled Damon. "D'you want her to hear?"

"She might as well! She'll hear the whole curst thing as soon as she wakens at all events!"

"The hell she will! I want you out of here, Whitt! And I want that shrewish termagant of a sister of yours out! God knows my life has been hell on earth since she arrived!"

Sophia's eyes glazed. 'Shrewish! Termagant? Hell on earth?' Well, Stephen would wipe the floor with him now—arm or no arm! Waiting smugly for the sound of a blow or, better yet, a shot, she gasped as her brother gave a smothered shout of laughter. "Ran into that fiery temper of hers, did you? Gad, but I'd love to have seen it!"

"You would! So far—nephew—she's put my staff into a state of shock by taking over my kitchen. I've had exploding chickens, cheese soufflé with custard— Stop laughing, blast you! To say nothing of a trifle topped with white sauce and so damned laced with cognac—yes, *cognac*! that Ridgley was in his cups before the meal was done!" Here, despite herself, memory and the sound of Stephen's hilarity conspired to bring a smile to Sophia. "On top of all that," the Marquis continued aggrievedly, "your confounded sister informed me in no uncertain terms that I'm the blackest villain since Lucifer and slapped me so damned hard I've two loose teeth, I vow!"

Sophia tensed. Stephen would challenge him for that! Instead, Whitthurst sounded reduced to a state of near imbecility. It was quite a few seconds before he was sufficiently recovered to gasp out something comparatively mild, to which Damon replied, "Never! Take her out of here, Whitt. In truth, I count the minutes!"

Counted the minutes, did he? Well, wait until he had his confounded investors meeting! She'd give him some minutes to count!

The conversation became calmer and harder to follow. With her ear pressed to the door, she heard Stephen say something about a "filthy damned mess" and Damon respond hotly that he didn't need to be taken to task by a maggot-

146

witted young loose screw! Stephen, his temper obviously warming, started to retaliate, only to burst into a siege of coughing. Fear seized Sophia, and she pounded on the door; receiving no instant response, she kicked at it angrily, succeeding only in stubbing her toe. She was bent over, clutching at her foot when the door opened and the Marquis enquired, "Morning exercises, ma'am?"

She cast him a glance that should have scorched those raised eyebrows and swept past to her brother, who looked pale but gave her a loving smile. "Dearest," she said, bending to kiss him. "Thank heaven you're better. I am so sorry you had to be"—and here she glared at Damon—"so upset!"

"What the deuce," demanded Whitthurst, "are you doing here?"

"I followed you, of course," she replied, more than a little put out by this attitude after all she had endured for his sake. "And might," she added, "ask you the very same thing. Really, Steve, of all the foolishness, to go rushing off like that! You know you are not strong enough to undertake so long and arduous a journey."

Damon strolled to the window and gazed out in silence. The Viscount slanted an uncomfortable look at those broad shoulders and muttered, "I'm sorry if you were put about, Chicky, I had no—" He stopped, seeing the shocked roundness of his sister's eyes. "Oh," he said unhappily. "Egad!"

Damon, turning from the window, quizzing glass raised, scanned the furiously embarrassed Sophia with amused eyes, then excused himself and left them. The door had scarcely closed, and Sophia's mouth was just opening to chastise her brother for his use of that childish nickname, when the Marquis stuck his head back in again. He levelled a meaningful glare at Whitthurst. "Have a care, nephew! You will regret it if you cross me in this—I warn you!"

"That villain!" cried Sophia as the door closed. "How *dare* he threaten you?" Her brother offered nothing more substantial than a frown, and, a thought striking her, she asked a dismayed "Stephen—you're not—?"

"Afraid of him?" he finished with a faint smile. "No. But— I never missed my arm so badly! By God! I'd give all I have to have it back!"

"Of course, you would, love," she said sadly.

Still glaring at the door, Whitthurst went on as if she'd not spoken, "So I could knock that top lofty devil down!"

Mrs. Gaffney returned, pronounced the Viscount much improved, and gave her sanction for the journey to Bodwin Hall, so long as they did not depart until afternoon, and Lord Whitthurst rest after the drive. Sophia was urged to go downstairs, have a decent breakfast, and then get some sunshine. "For in truth, my lady, you look positively hagged!" To the accompaniment of a hoot of laughter from Whitthurst, she took this kind advice and made her way downstairs.

She found the Marquis alone in the breakfast room. He was slumped back in his chair, coffee cup in one hand, the newspaper folded beside his plate. It was a small fold, and she thought it should take him only a few seconds to digest the information it contained, but he was either a very slow reader or not reading at all because he made no movement, continuing to stare downward, head bowed.

Sophia had donned her prettiest morning dress. Of white India muslin, it had a low-cut bodice laced with violet ribands over a pale-lilac placket. Puff sleeves were also laced from the shoulder, and a straight skirt fell softly from beneath the high bustline. Damon looked up as she entered, and she received a momentary impression of unutterable weariness before he sprang to his feet, ushering her to a chair.

"I have come—" she began as she sat down.

"Obviously," he said dryly. "Shall Whitthurst be joining us, ma'am?"

At once irritated, she was thrown off stride and blinked up into his cold eyes. "Of course not! Mrs. Gaffney says he must rest this morning."

"A thousand pardons." He waited as she rejected the eggs, cold beef, or haddock Thompson came in to offer and, when the butler had poured her coffee and left the room, said, "I imagine you are anxious to make your announcement."

Guilt caused Sophia to buckle her toast and spread jam on her thumb. "A-announcement?" she gasped, whitening.

He shrugged. "Your engagement to Hartwell."

At first inexpressibly relieved and then just as annoyed, she stabbed butter onto her second piece of toast and said a frigid "I am betrothed to no man, my lord."

"Really?" He had the gall to look astonished. "But—surely he's a good catch for you, ma'am? Very flush in the pockets, I understand." His thick lashes dropped after this insult, but the infuriated Sophia knew somehow that he was still watching her and realized suddenly that the provocation was deliberate. Shocked by that knowledge, she then felt a new power and, smiling sadly, admitted, "True. But I am, you see, a very foolish fool. I mean to wait until I meet the man I can...love." The last word was very hard to speak. Especially looking straight at him.

In an offhand fashion, he enquired, "And what if your—love—has no funds?"

Before, she would have lusted to scratch him for that. Now she merely said meekly, "Why, then I must needs learn to sew and mend and clean. And"—she darted a glance at him and finished with a dimple—"and cook."

Damon stooped hurriedly to retrieve the serviette he contrived to drop. When he straightened, he said a wooden "What a dismal prospect."

"Less dismal than being so vastly rich it is necessary to employ armed guards."

The hand that had been reaching toward a muffin checked briefly. The eyes that were turned upon her were totally blank. "Ma'am?"

"You have no need to dissemble. I saw one of your men last evening. I must allow I was startled until Mrs. Hatters explained that you have been bothered by thieves and vandals. Horrid. And you have quite spoiled your muffin, sir."

Damon's gaze lowered to the wreckage of the muffin. "Dry. I cannot recommend them, ma'am. Unlike some of my *objets d'art*, which are quite fabulous."

"Which is why you discourage visitors? Alas—I must have been a great trial. But you shall not have to strain your manners beyond this afternoon. Lord Bodwin is sending his carriage for us."

"So I understand. I trust it will not inconvenience you to wait until after the investors meeting. It should be over in time for Whitt to—"

"Whitthurst is much too ill to attend your silly meeting!" Sophia flashed, her poise vanishing. "I should not really allow him to journey to the Hall."

"Spoken like a true martyr," he said with his twisted smile. "No wonder poor Whitt found it necessary to escape to Cancrizans."

"Escape? Oh! *Oh!* You most—most *odious*—"

149

"Viper?" He leaned forward. "Whitthurst is a fine fellow, and I know you love him. But he's blue-devilled just now, and if you continue your overprotective coddling, he may never regain his spirits."

Infuriated, she hissed savagely, "He near died—if you care!"

"I do. And it was admirable that you pulled him back to life—"

"And unspeakable that *you* almost pushed him to his death!"

He met her flashing eyes, then drew back and began to toy with the salt cellar. "For some men, perhaps. But you should not lose sight of the fact that I am...beneath contempt."

His lazy grin mocked her, but she noted the shadows under his eyes and, remembering her earlier impression of weariness, said in a gentler voice, "If I love my brother so deeply, it is because he is kind and honourable and thoroughly decent. I admire him for those qualities. And for his gallantry."

She had spoken with unconscious pride and now blushed as he sneered, "'And will seek those same traits in a husband, no doubt?"

"I would not settle for less!"

His eyes fell. He was undoubtedly aware of his shortcomings, and Sophia could not help but be sorry for him. "I suppose every gentleman has some doting lady in his life who tends to smother him with affection," she said. "Even you, uncle."

"*Assurement!*" he said cynically. "My mistress. For which she was extreme well paid."

"Of course he wants us out of here," said the Viscount, talking softly so as not to start himself coughing again. "He cannot have the workmen pounding away while I'm lying here like a curst, grizzling girl."

"Grizzled might be a better term," smiled Sophia.

He felt his chin. "Lord! Regular gooseberry bush! You might ask Thompson if he could spare the time to shave me. I cannot seem to manage it myself yet. But I'm improving, only took off half my ear lobe last time!"

She concealed the pang that went through her and said,

"Dearest, I know you don't like me to mention it, but—does it still hurt very much?"

"No," he said brusquely. Then, relenting, sighed, "The worst thing, Chicky, is the dreadful time some people have trying not to notice. Don't know what to do with their eyes. Drives me wild!"

"Oh, and I thought—when St. Clair asked you how you were getting along with one wing to fly with it was dreadful of him. I suppose—it wasn't?"

"Well—he was *there*, you see. Any of the old sportsmen who went through it understand. It's the men who didn't go...and the women. Gad!"

"I see," she said in a very small voice.

"Oh, I didn't mean you, little Chick. You've been not half bad..." His fond grin negated the begrudging nature of the praise. "But the girls I've met the few times I've gone out try so wildly not to stare. They struggle frenziedly to make conversation..." His fist clenched. "But they can't wait to get away from me, they're so nervous and embarrassed. That's what I've become, you see—an embarrassment...One poor girl almost fainted, I think, because she was honest enough to say she was 'up in arms' about something!"

He stared at the ceiling, his face very strained, and Sophia, remembering how many times she had cautioned friends against "noticing" his injury, could have wept. Damon had said she was overprotective. But Whitthurst had been so horribly close to death... "Stephen," her voice trembled, "I'm sure they don't mean to be unkind. They're just so afraid of hurting you..."

"I know." He took a breath and smiled brightly. "Don't pay no attention to me. This is my 'be sorry for Stephen hour'. It's...it's only..." He stared at her little slipper and ground out, "If just once—just *once* a girl would look at me and say, 'Oh—you lost an arm, I see!' By God, I think I'd marry her on the spot!"

She gave a shaken little laugh in which he joined, and some of the strain went out of his face.

"You're much too young to be thinking of marriage," she chided.

"I'm only four years younger than the old Nunks—or Hartwell. And I hear *he's* been dangling after you again. Get another offer from the fellow?"

151

"Yes, as a matter of fact." He hadn't sounded pleased—as Clay had implied. Curious, she asked, "Would it displease you if I accepted Sir Amory? Don't you like him?"

He hesitated, then said reluctantly, "No."

"Why? He's one of the most popular young bachelors in Town. And a real catch—as your gracious uncle has already informed me."

Stephen looked at her sharply, then grinned. "He would! Cam thinks Hartwell's a bang-up sportsman. Blind spot. They grew up together, y'know. Hartwell was from a very impoverished house."

"He was? But I thought he was extreme wealthy?"

"Is now. Inherited it—some distant relation in America, I believe, who had the kindness to pass to his reward a few years ago. When they were children, Hartwell practically lived here. And they spent a lot of time together in Europe. But—I don't think Cam really sees him these days."

"And you do?" Her brother was frowningly silent, and she said, "Stephen, I wish you would tell me. If you *really* disapprove..."

"Don't be such a peagoose," he grinned. "Your life is your own, Sophia. You must marry the man of your heart."

"Then—you'd give your consent?"

He stared at her, at the end posts of his bed, at the rich rug on the floor. "No! Be damned if I would!"

She burst into laughter. "But—you just said..."

"I know I did. Hadn't really thought it would come to that, I collect. I don't really know why I don't like the fella." He scowled, thinking about it, then said sapiently, "Perhaps it's because he never says anything he fears might displease anyone. Everything is so carefully calculated—almost as if he plays a part. And—he's got such perfect white teeth!" He glanced at her in some embarrassment. "You think I'm corkbrained, I don't doubt. Not much to take exception to, is it?"

"Not really. Cam—er, the Marquis, is much better looking, yet you don't seem to object to him."

"You never asked me about the Viper." She gave a start at the use of her nickname for their host, and he chuckled. "Must admit I'd not realized you were considering keeping it in the family."

"Of course, I am not!" she bridled. "As if he'd ask me! He knows I purely despise him!"

152

Whitthurst, who loved his sister slavishly and seldom scolded her, now looked upon her with cold eyes and said sternly, "I sincerely hope you are not serious because until now I have not suspected you of being totally henwitted!"

The air was crisp and fresh after the rain, and as Sophia guided the black Arabian mare through the copse of beeches, the sun burst from diminishing clouds to edge each leaf with diamonds and enrich the green of ferns and grasses. The mare was a spirited creature, her hooves prancing so rapidly they seemed scarcely to rest upon the earth before they were picked up again. It was a pleasure to exercise her, as Damon had requested, despite the fact that at first Sophia had suspected this was merely a ruse to separate her "overprotective" self from her brother. She had assented reluctantly but now could only be delighted of the chance to ride through such a bright morning after so many hours spent in the sickroom.

She had come a long way and was circling back toward the Priory when the mare gave a snort of fright and began to dance in so frantic a fashion that Sophia was almost un-horsed. Leaning forward to quiet the animal, she checked in alarm. The turf sloped downward to her right, ending against a small belt of silver birch trees. Before those trees, two men wearing breeches and shirts with sleeves rolled back circled each other warily. The one, a young giant with hair like snow in the sunlight; the other, slim and tall, with dark hair. And seeing these things, Sophia was out of the saddle in a second. She lifted her skirts and ran wildly down the hill with no thought for ladylike propriety or revenge or anything but the bright crimson that streaked the side of Damon's mouth and the terrible crouching advance of the mighty Ariel.

They closed even as she approached, Ariel's right arm flashing upward in a blur of movement. Damon swayed aside, leapt in to strike, and moved back awkwardly, his blow seem-ing to have made little impression, if any.

"Stop! Stop!" Sophia shouted. "Are you both gone mad?"

Damon, shooting a quick, desperate glance at her, called, "Stay back, Sophia! He *is* mad—poor fellow. Stay back!"

"Aye!" Ariel confirmed, that deep voice a husky sob. "Mad I do be all right, milady. And ye'd best be gone—less'n ye want to watch me kill this...this filthy vermin, what calls itself a man!"

With the last word, that mighty fist shot out. Damon ducked, lightning swift, and, eluding Ariel's guard, rammed home two savage blows to the midriff that staggered the big man. With a leap of the heart, Sophia thought, 'Well done!' but Damon was obviously already hurt and no match for Ariel, even had he been heavier by three stone.

"Luke," Damon cried. "I swear you're wrong! Luke—don't be a fool!"

If only, thought Sophia, she had not so cleverly eluded the grooms Damon had sent to escort her! What chance had she to stop this, all alone? She took up a rock and wondered if she could bring herself to smash at Ariel's great head with it. Damon, casting a quick look in her direction, called, "No!"

For one split second, Ariel's attention shifted. And, without hesitation, Damon jumped in. His right fist shot straight and true for the bearded chin, and even as that deadly arm swung up to block him, his left smashed again into the big man's midriff. Ariel gave a grunt. Incredibly, he staggered, went to his knees, and, pitching forward, caught himself on one hand.

Sophia ran closer and swung her rock high. And, again, Damon shouted a furious "No!"

She halted, and the chance was gone. Ariel was dragging himself to his hands and knees, and she backed away while Damon, standing ready, watched him.

Slowly, the abused head was raised, and a glitter of tears was in the cook's eyes. "Why did ye do this awful thing?" he groaned. "Ye that I loved like me own brother. Ye that took me up when everyone else wiped their feet on me...I'd have died for 'ee...don't ye know that?"

And even then he was leaping forward with surprising speed for so large a man and striking out. Damon dodged aside, but this time the left fist followed too swiftly, and his attempt to block that battering ram was only partly successful. The impact was stunning. He hurtled back and, falling heavily, managed to retain sufficient consciousness to roll aside as Ariel ran and jumped. Small branches snapped, and twigs and leaves flew as those great boots landed. Sophia gave a sobbing whimper and shrank, her hands flying to her mouth. Damon, rolling desperately, was somehow avoiding

154

those stamping boots. God help him if one landed! And then he was up once more, gasping for breath, clinging to a tree as he dragged himself on to unsteady feet, his face white and sweat streaked, his right arm tight against his side where that last blow had caught him.

"Luke," he wheezed. "For . . . God's sake, man . . . Don't—do this!"

Ariel, holding his own middle, groaned, "Ye knocked me right down, Damon! Right off my feet! Ye as was the last one I'd'a thought could stand up to me! How can'ee be so much of a man and so evil? Why did ye have to hurt her? Ye knows . . . how I do so love her."

"Luke, I swear! Luke—don't!"

But the grief-stricken Ariel was jumping forward. The movements of the Marquis were ever more faltering. He staggered under a welter of blows and fell yet again, but as the giant rushed him, he snatched up a branch and thrust it between those ready boots so effectively that Ariel also crashed down.

Filled with a terror such as she'd never before known, Sophia found a large branch. No matter what Camille said, this time she would wield it even if she should kill him, though that horrible prospect made her grow cold with dread. But as she reached out, she saw a note on the ground, and, her eyes caught by one word, she snatched it up and read, "Luke, my dere. Dont ye come looking for me bekos I have run far away where you wont never find me. O Luke—Lord Damon is just what they sed. Hees a devil. I dident no what they ment. I tride to get away for your dere sake as well as my own. But he was too strong for me. And so I must hide and you must find someone cleen and decent. And forget your poor, shamed Nancy."

The paper fluttered from Sophia's hands. She looked up slowly and saw that they were both on their feet again, Damon weaving drunkenly as he backed away. Even as she watched, Ariel charged forward. Damon struck at him desperately, but Ariel only shook his head, gave a harsh broken laugh, and unleashed that terrible fist. Damon was smashed back, went down hard, and lay unmoving. Ariel stepped closer, his jaw set, his eyes shining with inflexible purpose.

Sophia woke up and ran between him and that sprawled figure. The white bushy brows drew down. The narrowed

155

eyes glared, and her heart seemed as if it must burst, so great was her fear. "Luke," she begged. "Luke—don't! They'll hang you!"

"It'll be worth it. Stand away, milady!"

He looked quite crazed, but she held out her shaking hands beseechingly. "Luke—he's not worth it. He's just...filth."

"Yes," he said on a near sob. "That's just what he do be. And so I'll kill him, milady...and no more poor, innocent, gentle girls...will have to know that terrible fear...and disgrace."

He gripped her arm, and, stepping closer, she said, "Ah—no! Do not! She'll need you. Luke—you must be free to take care of her."

He took her up at the waist and lifted her aside.

Damon struggled onto one elbow. There was a puffy discolouration along the side of his face, and blood had dripped from his mouth to stain his shirt. But Ariel had struck mostly for the body. Feeling as if he'd been galloped over by a coach and four, he said thickly, "I...blacked your...eye, Luke."

Ariel touched that swelling. "And you caught me a good one in the breadbasket," he said chokingly, tears spilling down his cheeks. "No one never really hurt me before, Damon. Not in a fist fight. Whatever else you...are—you're a man." His fists clenched. "A dead man!"

Frantic, Sophia screamed, "Who'll look after Nancy? Who'll care about her? She'll hide from her family, Luke. Nobody will help her—if you hang!"

He halted. A puzzled look crossed his face and he turned to her slowly, as if he could not understand why she was there.

Sobbing, she ran forward and caught at his sleeve. "Oh, Luke—don't you see? He's nothing! If you kill him, you make him something worth dying for! She's worth *living* for, Luke. Isn't she?" And shaking his arm passionately, she pleaded, "Isn't she, Luke? Isn't Nancy worth living for?"

The light of reason dawned at last. "Aye...she do be that, milady."

"Then come away." She pulled at him eagerly. "You must find her. And help her. She needs you."

"Aye..." Some of the glare was leaving his eyes. "She do need me. My sweet little Nancy needs me now, don't she, milady?"

She nodded, blinking rapidly. He brightened, took two great purposeful strides, then swung back. "He can't hurt'ee now, ma'am," he said with a toss of his head toward the silent Marquis. "But will'ee come with me?"

"No, Luke. You go."

"If ye ever needs me, milady..."

"Thank you. If I ever need you, I shall call."

He peered at her, then hurried away.

Sophia turned wearily. Damon had dragged himself to where he could lean against a tree and half lay there, one arm pressed to his side, watching her.

She thought of Nancy and the love that had been so teasingly concealed from the humble giant who worshipped her. She thought of the gentlemen she had known all her life and their relentless code of honour that decreed a man, whether bachelor or benedict, may have his bits o' muslin but that no gentleman worthy of the name would force his attentions upon an unwilling girl. Nancy had been unwilling—of that she was very sure. Wherefore, her lips curled with disgust as she pulled the inadequate wisp of fine cambric from her pocket and walked toward the Marquis.

Dropping to her knees beside him, she asked, "Are you very much hurt?"

"No," he replied in a strained, breathless voice. "Thank you."

She wiped gently at the side of his mouth and said with detached calm, "I suppose you will say you didn't do it."

"Do you?" he countered gravely.

His left shirtsleeve was ripped and spotted with blood. She reached to it and began to pull the torn linen farther apart. "I suppose you and—your kind would say it doesn't matter. That she was just a country girl. Just a serv—" She gave a little cry, her hands flying back as though burned.

His forearm was badly grazed, but the thing that appalled her was infinitely more hideous. A tattoo that stood out clear and sharp upon his upper arm. The outline of a scorpion.

She stood, crept back a pace, and stared at him with total revulsion, her mind barely able to comprehend what should have been obvious for so long.

Camille, Marquis of Damon—heir to that proud perfectionist, the Duke of Vaille—*had* been a member of Cobra!

157

Chapter 15

"It just don't seem right," said the Viscount peevishly, lying back in his corner of the sumptuous travelling coach and fixing his sister with an aggrieved eye. "Ain't like old Cam to vanish like that, knowing we was leaving! I'll tax him with it next time I see him, you may be sure!"

"Yes, dear," said Sophia dully.

"Besides, you would think he'd have at least come back to the Priory and..."

She lost the thread of his words, her thoughts drifting. Damon *had* come back. She had sent Mr. Quinn after him the instant she reached the Priory. Whitthurst had been dozing and she and Patience busily packing when she'd heard wheels on the rear driveway and run swiftly to the window. The phaeton had pulled up below. Damon's dark head had been against Trask's shoulder and the man's arm about him, holding him steady. Quinn had jumped down and run around to help. She'd watched as the Marquis had roused sufficiently

158

to stumble out of the vehicle and come into the house, the men supporting him on each side. His head had been erect then, but he had seemed to favour his right leg, and she'd wondered if one of Ariel's boots had caused the damage.

"...go back!" cried the Viscount wrathfully. "By God, Sophia! You've been bamming me! You think I don't know a whisker when I hear one? Cam didn't cancel that meeting! You was afraid I'd get tired!" He read a confirmation in the horrified dismay in her face and leaned forward to call the coachman.

"I wish you will not! Please, Stephen! There will be no meeting—there couldn't be. He is in no condition to..." She stopped as Whitthurst's face paled, and he searched her eyes with such an expression of terror that she was startled.

"What do you mean? Is Cam—? My God!" He caught her wrist in a grip of steel, his green eyes reflecting a grimness she seldom witnessed, and demanded, "Tell me at once! Is Cam hurt?"

"Stephen!" She touched the fingers, so tightly clamped around her wrist. He let her go at once but still waited tensely.

Bewildered, she said, "He had a little...dispute with Ariel. But—"

He gaped at her. "Ariel? Cam—and *Ariel*? But the man worships him! You don't mean they really went at it? Bare knuckles?"

"Just a little, dear," she said, her conscience protesting that massive understatement.

Awed, he muttered, "And Cam's still alive?"

She nodded and, with what she hoped was a reassuring smile, said, "And when last heard from was shouting for a bottle of cognac."

"By Jupiter!" He was quiet for a moment, then frowned. "Why? D'ye know?"

"Something about a girl..."

"Oh." He drew a deep breath, seemingly much relieved. "Is that all?"

Under normal circumstances, such a remark would have caused Sophia to embark upon an impassioned denunciation of men and their intolerable conceits. Now she felt only a vague irritation and, sitting back, resumed her blind contemplation of the landscape. There was absolutely no reason

159

why she should feel so shattered. No reason at all. The tattoo had merely been the final proof of his infamy, had she needed any. Her initial assessment of his character—or lack of it—had—

She looked up as Whitthurst took her hand and asked gently, "Won't you share it with me, dear?"

She forced away her silliness and said with real indignation, "I confess I'm in a taking! Damon had the unmitigated gall to send my maids back to Singlebirch! Did you know it? I wondered why they had not come to me, but it seems his noble lordship sent a groom to 'The Wooden Leg' the instant the bridge was repaired, and told them to go home! Scarcely to be credited, is it?"

"More astonishing to me is the fact you didn't miss 'em until today," he observed dryly.

"I had...other things to think of," she stammered. "You came and..."

"And found you and Cam behaving quite civilized to each other. And since have the impression you're at daggers drawn, though I've not been given the straight of it."

"What would you imagine to be the—'straight of it'?" she demanded tartly. "A lover's quarrel?"

Unabashed, he grinned. She felt her cheeks burn. Her lashes drooped. And because sudden and unaccountable tears scalded her eyes, she said bitterly, "What a very peculiar standard of values you possess—that you object to someone as clean and decent as Amory Hartwell, yet would willingly bestow your only sister upon a member of Cobra!"

Whitthurst gave a choked gasp, and the colour drained from his thin face. Sophia could have cut out her tongue. Steve loved Damon and had no conception of how unworthy was his idol. This was not the time to have destroyed his illusions. She clasped his hand and, finding it cold as ice, said contritely, "My dear! I am so sorry. I am—a little upset, but—"

"What do you know of Cobra?" he demanded in a shaken voice.

"Nothing love," she lied, trying to soothe him. "Now do not—"

"What," he repeated, that appalled look on his face still, "what do you know of Cobra? *Answer* me, Sophia!"

Frightened by his horrified intensity, she said, "That they were the dregs of mankind. The lowest, most wretched beasts

160

who ever walked this dear land of ours. That they met in secret—and committed hideous crimes against the innocent, the helpless, for sport! That they should all have been hanged but could not even be found until they were destroyed by a fire. And some were caught and punished, though none would inform and, shamefully, most got away scot-free." She frowned and added slowly, "I once heard Papa say that if ever he had one of them before him and a pistol in his hand, he'd shoot without an instant's hesitation. And consider he'd done the world a service."

There was silence between them. Lost in her desolate thoughts, Sophia looked up at length and found Whitthurst's eyes upon her, eyes so dulled with grief that she was filled with sympathy.

"What makes you think," he asked, low-voiced, "that Cam was one of that miserable crew? The truth now, Chicky."

"Many things. I suspected at once, I suppose, that he was—" She bit her lip. Damon had already threatened her brother—it would not do to precipitate a real quarrel between them—a Cobra member would have no least qualms about striking at a maimed man. "I went to try and help him after...after he fought with Ariel. His sleeve was torn. I—saw the tattoo."

He closed his eyes as though his last hope had flown. "Of what?"

"A scorpion." She shuddered at the memory.

Whitthurst groaned. "What did you say?"

"Nothing. But he knew I had seen. I was too shocked to say anything."

"Didn't *he* say anything? No kind of explanation, or—?"

"No." She winced a little, recalling how she had left him lying there, unable to bring herself to touch him again. "He just watched me go...and...and, when I once glanced back, he seemed to...to be smiling."

"Oh...hell!" swore Lord Whitthurst.

At the top of the rise, Lord Ridgley leaned forward, craning his neck for a first view of the visitors' carriage. He had ridden part of the way to meet them and, catching sight of the vehicle, waved his beaver and made a great halloo until they stopped and, after he'd told one of the outriders to bring in his mare, joined his friends in the carriage. Sophia was

161

irked by his arrival, fearing he might mention the meeting and thus send Stephen into the boughs once more. In an effort to prevent such a contretemps, she chattered brightly about the luxurious vehicle that was conveying them so smoothly over the uneven surface of the road. As she exclaimed at some length over the white and gold exterior, the rich wood panels embellished with gold leaf adorning the interior, the powder blue and white velvet of the seat cushions and squabs, the hand-embroidered pulls of blue, white and gold, and the incredible ermine rugs, Sophia became aware that her brother viewed her aghast while Ridgley's brown eyes were alight with mirth. Unable to restrain herself she burst into laughter. "Oh...you dreadful men! You have no appreciation of beauty!"

"Spelled o-s-t-e-n-s-h—Gad! How *do* you spell it?" grinned Stephen.

"Ain't sure whether you mean—'stench' or 'ostentation'," quipped Ridgley. "Either one might suit!" Stephen having indicated the latter noun, Ridgley's sunny nature responded to the challenge, and they were soon all three embroiled in a spelling wrangle so that the miles passed very quickly.

Presently the Earl exclaimed, "Ah! Look, Sophia—you can see the Hall."

She looked, and gasped. Whitthurst said an awed, "By George!"

"Incredible," said Ridgley cheerfully, "ain't it?"

It was, thought Sophia, quite incredible.

Behind elaborately planted flower gardens in which every bloom was pink or white, Bodwin Hall towered to an impressive five storeys. The period was distinctly French, with lofty pitched roofs fringed by dormer windows and well supplied with tall, narrow chimneys. To the sides and back of the grey house, a high wall enclosed a private garden with many trees and shrubs and the two famous fountains, one on each side of an oblong pool. The stables were located behind the rear garden, while to the north, the spires of a tiny chapel peeped above the wall. And the whole was set in a small lush valley, rich with trees.

As the carriage swept down the drive and round the gardens, a mellow horn was sounded by the guard on the box, and at once the front doors swung open and an individual who was clearly the butler stepped out onto the wide terrace, followed by two splendid footmen.

The carriage came to a smooth halt. The grooms jumped down; the door was swung open, and the steps lowered. Trying not to look as awed as she felt, Sophia was handed down and greeted by the butler's respectful bow. Lord Bodwin hurried from the house to kiss her hand. "My dear Lady Drayton, what a *very* great pleasure!"

Ridgley introduced Whitthurst. Bodwin, his eyes very keen, was delighted to welcome the brother of so lovely a lady. The Viscount, his own eyes missing little of this elegant gentleman, took an immediate and intense dislike to him and therefore bowed with rare formality.

Once inside, Sophia was unable to conceal her amazement. The enormous central hall swept from front to back of the house. The floor was of white marble inset with rounds of sparkling green stone scattered haphazardly across the white expanse. To the right, a beautiful staircase spiralled upward, the delicate tracery of the iron railing, which was painted the same soft green as the round discs in the floor, rising through all the upper storeys to the roof. In the deep well hung a gigantic chandelier, the sunlight waking a thousand miniature rainbows from countless prisms. On each side of the front doors, windows soared to the ceiling and were so closely set in this central area that the wall was predominantly of glass. The far end of the room repeated the pattern, thereby preventing the huge area from becoming dark and forbidding. Looking up, Sophia discovered the ceiling to be magnificently carven, the center rising to a lovely dome intricately gilded and inset with superb oil paintings.

"My...heavens!" she gasped. "It is a palace!" And realizing the ghastly inadequacy of her present wardrobe, she could have sunk.

"It is, is it not?" beamed Lord Phineas, pleased by her perspicacity. "Though a palace lacking a Queen, I fear." His eyes dwelt upon her with a hunger that brought Whitthurst's brows sharply together. "I knew, my dear boy," Bodwin went on, taking the Viscount's arm as though he sensed his reaction, "that your beauteous sister would appreciate my home. Especially after that dismal Priory, eh, ma'am? Perhaps it was not kind in me to invite you here directly. But then, every man for himself! To the victor, eh, Captain? Being a—er—former military man, you can certainly appreciate that!" He led them toward the stairs, Whitthurst flashing a fulminating glance at Sophia as their host prattled on hap-

163

pily. "How pleased I am that you were able to come. When Damon sent me word, I could not wait until Ridgley left but sent the carriage especially for you both. And now I have the honour of entertaining the reigning toast *and* a hero of Waterloo!" The Viscount flushed, glanced back at Ridgley, and was treated to a low bow and a broad grin as that worthy sought entertainment elsewhere. "You shall have to tell me all about it, my lord," said Bodwin. "Never have had a first-hand report, and it must have been such a magnificent spectacle! Though they're saying now Wellington bungled, as usual, and it was more a defeat than a victory!"

Sophia cast an appalled look at her brother's suddenly pale features. Their well-meaning host could scarcely have managed so many wounding remarks had he tried.

Whitthurst stiffened, opened his mouth for a scathing comment, but was drowned in the tide as Bodwin rambled on, eventually apologizing for having chattered like a magpie and saying as they reached the top of the first flight, "You must rest, for I can see you are far from well, poor fellow. And you will both be wanting to view your rooms. There'll be no noise to disturb you *here*, of that I can assure you! Later, I shall insist upon showing off my home. I am vastly proud of it, for it's one of the finest in all England, I do believe. But you must stop me if I become verbose upon the subject!"

Whitthurst summoned a smile that Sophia was afraid might cause his rigid countenance to crack and, becoming very aristocratic—a demeanour that would have warned his friends—politely lied that he was not in the *least* tired and would enjoy to see the house now. Dismayed, she could do nothing but join in these sentiments, and Bodwin joyfully conducted them on a "brief" tour.

An hour later, they had still not seen all of the mansion, and Sophia had exhausted her supply of superlatives. Bodwin, however, was as full of words as enthusiasm. He had lectured on many paintings, carvings, and objets d'art contained in a bewildering succession of drawing rooms, lounges, and salons. They had been conducted through an overpowering music room containing an ornately carven and gilded harpsichord, a harp, and numerous smaller instruments. They had viewed at least four dining rooms beside the breakfast room; a study; a huge library; weapons room; game room; gymnasium, and a long gallery containing his lordship's col-

164

lection of the more precious works of art, together with a splendid array of antique jewelery. Shy-eyed, impeccably neat maids were everywhere, and there seemed to be an inordinate number of footmen standing about: tall, well-built men, splendid in livery of a dusty green satin that matched the stair railings.

Already, Sophia was slightly weary of such a surfeit of ostentation, and Whitthurst had become very pale, the dark shadows beneath his eyes bespeaking his fatigue. Bodwin, his attention equally divided between Sophia and his home, noted her anxiety and at once summoned the nearest hovering footman and desired him to show the Viscount to his room. Sophia managed to follow without too obviously betraying her concern. Entering the magnificent bedchamber, she was less impressed by it than she was relieved to find Stephen attended by an elderly and apparently kindly gentleman at chambers who was, Bodwin assured her, to devote himself solely to Lord Whitthurst. A footman was summoned and instructed to assist Mr. Byrnes "should he need—ah—help with his lordship." This last kindly remark brought a painful flush to the Viscount's handsome features, and it was with considerable relief that Sophia watched Lord Bodwin beam his way from the room.

She stayed for only a few moments and, aware that her brother was seething with rage, adjured him to have a good nap, after which she was sure he would feel better. He cast her a darkling glance; she smiled lovingly and withdrew.

The housekeeper waited in the hall. She was impressively gowned and properly welcoming, yet lacking that spark called warmth.

Having been silently conducted to the enormous bedchamber allotted to her, Sophia was again taken aback. In the center, a raised platform supported an incredible bed. The four posts were of carven ivory, and it must have required months of painstaking labour to complete the motifs worked in filigree from top to bottom and the bird that perched atop each post, wings widespread, its beak holding the edge of a delicate canopy of white silk edged with pale-pink tassels. The ruffles and curtains around the bed were also white silk, and the eiderdown was pink and white in a dainty floral pattern. The decor was pink, shading to reds, with white accents. In the lower area, three armchairs were charmingly grouped before the windows; there was a graceful escritoire,

165

a dressing table and bench, several chests of drawers, and two presses. The windows were many and wide, opening onto the eastern side of the house, allowing a pleasant view of the tranquil countryside.

Two maids curtseyed as Sophia walked into the room. They were shy country girls: one, plump and giggly, was named Constance, and the other, very tall and lantern-jawed, was Louise. The housekeeper took her leave, having sternly admonished them that she'd best not hear anything to their discredit. Sophia assured the alarmed girls that she was delighted to have the benefit of their services, and they brightened gratefully. She also told them, however, that they would have few clothes to care for since most of her belongings had been returned to Kent, and she had only the few garments in the valise and bandbox she had brought with her from the Priory.

The maids exchanged surprised glances, then Connie threw open one of the presses. Sophia was dumbfounded. The rack was crowded with her own clothes, just as Hettie Adams might have packed them for an extended journey. She spread the garments and discovered a ball gown she'd never seen before. It was of dusty blue silk tinged with lilac. Rather décolletté, the heartshaped neckline was edged around with tiny hand-embroidered flowers of a paler blue, centred by small sapphires that winked and sparkled even in the dim press. The gown might have been created especially for her, so perfect were both colour and style. Touching it admiringly, she felt paper rustle and found a note pinned inside. She frowned, recognizing that firm scrawl. "My regrets, niece, that I was unable to find a suitable travelling gown to replace the one you spread with mud." (*She* spread!) "I trust this poor substitute will prove satisfactory. Damon. P.S. You'd best try it on—it is probably a size too small." She choked back an indignant exclamation. Too small, indeed! The man simply did not know how to be gracious! And the gown would go unworn, of course! Lovely as it was. She sighed. It must have cost a fortune.

"Your other things is all unpacked, ma'am," said Constance, opening two of the drawers in a chest.

Sophia saw with delight that her toilet articles and under garments were, indeed, neatly disposed. So many of the small yet necessary items she had missed these past few days. "How very kind of Lord Bodwin!" she exclaimed.

Louise said, "The Marquis of Damon had your portmanteau brought from Kent, ma'am. His grooms drove all night to get here in time. This here"—she moved to open the connecting door—"is your parlour, milady."

Sophia followed, arguing fiercely with herself. She had no need to feel overset with guilt! The wretched Viper had merely returned articles he himself had most arrogantly snatched away from her.

The parlour was smaller than the bedchamber but no less splendid, though rather too full of ornaments for her taste. Among these, her attention was held by the rather insipid watercolour of a farmyard. She smiled at it sadly and could all but hear the Duke's well-modulated voice exclaiming, "I thought it was a still life." Again, staring wistfully at the painting, she sighed.

Thompson opened the front door and stood for a moment, speechless with astonishment. Impatient, Sophia stepped inside. Horatio was about to set forth on a second vociferous gallop round the Great Hall but, catching sight of her, checked so abruptly that he skidded and, having recovered himself, hissed his disapproval and made a mad dash for the kitchen.

"Lord Ridgley just come a bit ago—" stammered the butler. "He didn't say you was coming, ma'am. I dunno what—"

"He did not know," said Sophia coolly. "I have a message from Lord Whitthurst for the investors, though I told him the meeting had been postponed..." She searched his troubled eyes and, receiving no nod, asked, "It has—has it not?"

A distant roar of masculine voices raised in song, accompanied by the vibrant tones of the harpsichord, answered that question.

"Perhaps," said Thompson uneasily, "if your ladyship would wait in the—"

"That is perfectly all right." Sophia bestowed her bonnet and cloak upon the startled man. "I shall announce myself."

"But—it's a gentlemen's business meeting! You can't— you don't—"

"I can. And I do." She smiled and walked down the hall, her knees rubbery, her heart pounding like a hammer.

She had told Ridgley only that her brother was too exhausted to return for the meeting and had waved a goodbye

167

to him, betraying no hint she intended to follow. Lord Bodwin had agreed reluctantly to her sudden departure. Unable to abandon his other guests, he had insisted she travel with a guard, two grooms and two outriders, in addition to the coachman, and she'd promised to return just as quickly as her message was conveyed to the Marquis. Now, reaching the music room, she paused and took a deep breath. How she was to brazen it through she dared not think, but *she* had done the damage, and if—as she feared—Damon had learned of her vengeance, she must be the one to face him; he must not be allowed to upset Stephen! She touched the small but heavy weight in her reticule for reassurance, then pushed the door a little wider.

Damon was seated at the harpsichord. He wore no jacket; his neckcloth was loosened and his shirt unbuttoned, allowing a glimpse of black hairs on his exposed chest. Ignoring this vulgarity, her eyes flashed to his face. Despite the cut mouth, his pipe was clamped between his teeth. The left side of his face seemed one large bruise, and a piece of tape was affixed to his right temple. He must, of course, have had a few hours rest before his guests arrived, yet it was remarkable, she thought, that he was able to play resoundingly, betraying no sign of discomfort, as the investors sang lustily.

Ridgley leaned against the mantle; two gentlemen, arms linked, stood beside him, tankards waving in time with the music. Another young man with tow hair and a pleasant, ruddy-complected face, lay on top of the harpsichord, his cheek propped on one hand, a goblet in the other. A fifth gentleman sprawled on the sofa was almost invisible, with only his Hessians sticking out the far end; and sprawled in one of the armchairs was a bald, heavyset man, eyes closed, smiling dreamily and crooning something that appeared to have nothing to do with either the words or music of their song.

"Second verse!" roared Damon. "Oh, the noble Duke of York, he had—"

At this point, the man atop the harpsichord caught sight of Sophia. His reaction was ludicrous. His jaw fell; his eyes goggled; he almost dropped his tankard and swung himself off the harpsichord so hurriedly that he fell and disappeared beneath it. Damon, observing this performance with amusement, followed his gaze, stopped playing, barely caught his

168

pipe as it tumbled from between his teeth, and, starting up, winced, caught at his side, and sat down again.

Bereft of their music, the singers, one by one, faded into silence. The last to cease his enthusiastic braying was the man on the sofa. Perceiving belatedly the frozen consternation of his brethren, he raised an untidy dark head above the back, cried an aghast "Sophia! Oh gad!" and, jumping up, grabbed for his jacket. There was a mad scramble of activity. Ridgley rushed to assist Damon in the obviously difficult process of putting on his jacket, hissing apparent denials of any knowledge of Sophia's intentions as he perpetrated a ghastly cravat upon him. The two gentlemen, who'd been standing arm in arm, hurried to bow and apologize for their "ha...hum...unpreparedness to greet so lovely a member of the fair sex." They ushered her into the room, all but trampling the man from the sofa, who claimed her hand and bowed over it, then dropped a kiss upon her upturned cheek, a surprised grin lighting his lean features.

"Hello, Harry." She smiled on this distant cousin. "How very nice to find you here."

Damon came over and said a formal "You honour us, my lady." But his eyes blazed at her as he bowed with considerably less grace than his friend.

Looking down at his dark hair, she suspected that he was extremely uncomfortable and guessed rightly from the way he moved that his ribs were badly bruised. She realized, also, that, far from the shame she would have hoped he would feel, he was infuriated by her presence. There was little doubt, however, that the others present reacted differently. She had selected her gown with care. It was of pale-pink silk, tightly fitted about her bosom and descending in a slim sheath over a gossamer petticoat. That the neck was a little lower than she usually affected appeared to offend no one; the gentlemen's eyes, in fact, positively glowed with admiration. Her golden curls were caught into clusters at each ear. The only jewellery she wore was a gold necklace her Papa had brought back from India: a heavy band wherefrom a cunningly wrought translucent red gem dangled, catching the light in such a way as to draw attention to her breasts. She had dressed for men, and with one exception she had them eating from her hand.

The one exception straightened carefully, having touched

169

her fingers to his lips. "You need not have felt obliged to come all this way, ma'am," he said with a chilly smile. "Ted brought me the word that Whitthurst was too ill to come."

"My brother wished me to convey his apologies to the gentlemen." She withdrew her hand with rather obvious haste and stepped back. That dreadful magnetism was as strong as ever, but she was fully forewarned this time. She knew what she risked by coming here, and the pistol in her reticule was her bulwark against his depravity. Nor did she carry it as an empty gesture. Stephen and Papa had taught her well; she was a fine shot. God send she'd not need to prove it.

A chorus of approval had greeted her words and was followed by impatient demands that they be made known to her. The first to be presented was a stout, jolly individual of middle age, Mr. Harold James. The second man, square and powerfully built, with craggy features and a deep, sonorous voice, was Sir Philip Wilton. These two, who had first escorted her into the room, were both so obviously struck by her that they could scarce tear their eyes away. The bald man, a Mr. Ben Blanchard, seemed equally impressed, while the young ex-harpsichord recliner was bashfully silent. Damon introduced him as Lord Jeremy Bolster. Sophia had heard Redmond speak of him and knew he'd been gravely injured at Badajoz, and was still not fully recovered from the shock. She smiled on him kindly. Ridgley, making his bow with a puzzled look in his eyes, muttered that she might have done him the honour of riding with him had she intended to come. She explained, she hoped convincingly, that Stephen had become so upset about missing the meeting that her only means of placating him had been to promise she would come in his stead and convey to him what had transpired.

"In which case," smiled Damon, "let us not keep the lady waiting, gentlemen. There's no cause to delay our meeting longer." He cast a pointed look at his 'niece'—a look she missed since she was busily mesmerizing Sir Philip.

"Right," Redmond agreed. "I've to be in Brighton tonight without fail. If you will excuse us, little coz, we'll get at it and let you know—"

"But I shall enjoy it," said Sophia, fluttering her fan at Mr. James.

The gentlemen eyed one another uneasily.

"That is quite impossible, ma'am," said Damon, his eyes glinting.

Sophia cast him a terrified look, shrank, and put her handkerchief to her lips.

"Come now, Cam," bristled Wilton indignantly. "Can't dismiss the dear soul!"

"Beastly manners lately, Damon," James protested. "Don't know what's come over you!"

Sophia, her eyes huge and frightened, whimpered, "I would not intrude, but Stephen is...so very ill. We thought—you would not be too...angry..."

It was the last straw. Damon's hawk glare lingered with baffled fury on her injured innocence. She was swept into the library, and three of the gentlemen practically acquired a concussion as they each jumped disastrously to pull out the same chair for her.

When the laughter died down, Damon, torn between vexation and amusement, called the meeting to order.

Chapter 16

Thirty minutes later they were all seated around the library table, and Sophia was trying hard not to yawn as Sir Philip read the minutes of the last meeting. She kept her eyes demurely downcast, well aware that the eyes of every man in the room were turned upon her, their obvious admiration rendering it doubtful that they had heard one word of Sir Philip's efforts. But one pair of eyes held a frown, and knowing this, she took care not to meet them. Undoubtedly, he was wondering why she was here. Perhaps he was afraid she intended to unmask him for what he was. It was apparent from a few teasing and faintly admiring remarks that he had explained away his bruises by telling them of an encounter with an irate tradesman who had mistaken him for a gardener. He must have been convincing. Indeed, to have used Mr. Jenks as his alleged antagonist had been a shrewd stroke because the Earl remembered their previous disagreement and lent weight to the tale. Damon would not dare admit he had actually fought Ariel, of course. They probably knew of the big man's devotion and would have realized that only a matter of gravest import could have made him turn against his master.

Her reflections were disrupted as Damon called for approval of the minutes and proceeded to the business at hand. His report on the progress made thus far was impressive. His statement of spiralling costs was very obviously less well received, although Sophia was secretly awed by this small revelation of the details and expense involved in such an undertaking.

Some corner of her mind registered that Horatio was honking somewhere, as her cousin Redmond, with an impatient glance at the clock, said, "Cam—are you asking us to lay out more blunt? If you are, old fellow, I'll have to turn you down. Sorry, but..." He shrugged wryly.

The rest of the investors hastened to offer comments of much the same nature, each having some pressing reason for withholding further funding. Only Bolster said nothing, his hazel eyes, turning shyly from time to time to Sophia, reflecting neither dismay nor approval of the as-yet-unspoken request.

A very thin, melancholy-looking individual entered the room at this point. Clad in a black jacket and black pantaloons, he had a clerical air and gazed at the Marquis with intense anxiety as he requested a private word.

"By all means, Gilly," frowned Damon. "When we have finished."

Mr. Gillam's expression became so agonized at this that Damon leaned forward and asked intently, "What's wrong, man? Does this concern the Spa?" A convulsive bob of the head constituted his answer. "Then speak out, if you please. Lady Drayton and these gentlemen have a right to hear it." He added a curt "Mr. Gillam handles my business affairs, ma'am."

Gillam bowed politely, but his response was barely audible. "There's a...new fence, my lord."

"Scarcely momentous news," Damon observed dryly.

"All around the property!" finished the wretched Gillam.

"Jolly good idea," Redmond approved. "Steal you blind else, Cam!"

Damon, his narrowed eyes fixed on Gillam, said, "Go on."

173

"It's posted, sir," Gillam croaked. "The signs read: 'Keep Out! Property of Merrick Corporation.' Your workmen cannot...get to work, sir!"

All the investors were on their feet, and everyone seemed to be shouting at once. Sophia felt a little stunned. She hadn't counted on the cost of a long fence. And who on earth was the Merrick Corporation?

Of them all, the Marquis appeared least disturbed. At length, he drew a small knife from his pocket and gently struck the goblet beside him, the bell-like sound bringing the heated faces of his friends around to him.

"Gentlemen, may we have quiet, please?"

They resumed their seats with much grumbling, Wilton saying testily that it was all very well for Damon to be so blasted calm. With his fortune, he wouldn't be hard hit should it prove to be anything more serious than a confounded practical joke. James put in a heated observation that it was undoubtedly the work of revolutionaries; and Harry Redmond, afire with indignation, proposed that they all at once sally forth and tear the blasted fences down, this course of action winning much approval and the eager endorsement of most present.

"It would be good sport, I grant you," smiled Damon, "but you surely must realize, gentlemen, that it is a mistake of some kind. I own the property on which the buildings stand, and there are no liens against any of my holdings, I do assure you. Sir John Black owns the parcel north of mine, and—" He saw anguish in Gillam's gaunt face, paused, and lifted one quizzical eyebrow.

"Sir John sold out a month ago, my lord. To the Merrick Corporation!"

A mutter of unease arose. Damon's expression was unchanged. Only his fingers tightened a little about the knife he held, and something deep within his eyes became very still. Sophia, peeping nervously round the table, saw the other gentlemen sit straighter, their anxious glances flashing from the Marquis to his man.

"That's odd," said Damon softly. "John said nothing of it. I would have thought he'd at least have come to say goodbye. What happened, Gilly?"

"I went to see his steward, my lord. He seemed most upset but would only say that Sir John had 'no choice'."

"By God!" cried Mr. James, mopping at his brow. "I don't

174

like the smell of this! Who holds the land to your west, Damon?"

"As of last August," said Damon thoughtfully, "an old—er—acquaintance of yours, James. Prendergast."

Sophia felt a tingle go up her spine and listened intently.

"*Josiah...Prendergast?*" gasped Mr. James, whitening. "God help us!"

Ridgley, his own face strained now, leaned forward and said harshly, "Cam, he'd give his soul to—" He stopped before the flash of Damon's warning glance.

Frightened, Wilton jumped to his feet, his impassioned appeal for the Marquis to tell them exactly where they stood being echoed by several angry voices.

Damon looked thoughtfully at Gillam. "Who controls this Merrick Corporation?"

Gillam wet dry lips. "It is a subsidiary corporation, my lord. Named for a minor stockholder. And...and owned by..."

"Oh, dear," murmured Damon. "Prendergast Associates, *sans doute.*"

"From your manner, sir," said Mr. Blanchard, one eyelid twitching with nervousness, "one gathers this—Mr. Prendergast—will not deal fairly with us."

"You forget, my friends," Damon pointed out, "our access road and our lakefront acreage are both owned by our fellow stockholder, Lord Whitthurst."

Through the chorus of relieved exclamations, Sophia kept her eyes down, her heart pounding madly. She heard poor Mr. James gasp, "Thank God! I've poured twelve thousand into this spa—I cannot afford that kind of loss!"

"Thanks to Whitthurst," said Damon, "we shall none of us have to take a—"

"Seems curst odd to me," interrupted Sir Philip. "We *do* hold a legal deed to the Viscount's holdings, I trust?"

"Of course," answered the Marquis. "D'ye take me for a flat? Gilly delivered the papers to my solicitor months ago. Though I had Whitthurst's hand on it, which is enough for—" Again, he was given pause by Gillam's twisted and pained expression. The lightness in his manner vanished. "Now what?"

"The transfer was not...legal, my lord," gulped the unfortunate Gillam. "Sir Horace says it was not properly signed."

"Not...properly," echoed Sir Philip, and exploded. "Dash it all, the poor lad lost his right arm! Cannot expect him to write—"

"The deed was sent to him in Belgium, *before* Waterloo," said Damon bleakly. "What in the devil was Horace about all this time?"

"He said, my lord," Gillam replied, "that there was a clause to Lord Whitthurst's ownership of which he was previously unaware. He returned the deed to Lord Whitthurst with a letter of instruction and sent a note to you here."

"A note I never received," Damon growled. He stood and, amid a deathly stillness, turned to Sophia. "Can you help us, ma'am? You must certainly be aware that your brother owns that property and deeded it to our venture?"

They were all waiting anxiously, and she had no need to pretend nervousness as she faltered. "I am at a loss to understand any of it, gentlemen."

Damon's mouth tightened, and one hand gripped at the edge of the table. His eyes were fixed upon her, and she met that unblinking stare, trying unsuccessfully to find one particle of pleasure in the shocked disbelief she read there.

"Your brother," he said softly, "*does* own the acreage—does he not?"

"No, my lord." Her voice sounded thin and far away. "He does not."

Never afterwards would she be able to forget his stunned look, the bruises dark against his suddenly white face. Never would she forget the resultant chaos, the furious accusations of carelessness that were hurled at him. Yet when at last he raised one hand for quiet, such was the power of the man that, despite their total dismay, it was granted him. "Are you saying, my lady," he asked quietly, "that your brother—broke his sworn word to me?"

"No! He just did not know...*I* did not know..." Good God! Now what a mess she had stumbled into! She folded her wet hands and stared down at them. How could she have been so foolish as to assume that only Damon would suffer the consequences of her actions? Why had it not occurred to her that others might be hurt? At all costs, Stephen's reputation must not be tarnished! "The property," she half whispered, "was left to us—jointly." She heard gasps and a smothered groan and went on hurriedly. "I suspect Whitthurst simply...forgot. It is necessary that I sign anything to do with

176

the acreage, as well as Singlebirch, which is also jointly owned. When I came home, he was...near death." She gripped her hands tighter. "Our finances are...are not—very good. I had to raise cash somehow, and I dared not worry him with such matters. I found the deed together with a pile of other papers—perhaps there was a letter from Lord Damon's solicitor, I could not say. I only saw the deed. Stephen had already signed it for a transfer of ownership, but the details had not been filled in. I thought he had probably been trying to...to raise funds, too. So..." She flashed a scared look round the circle of intent faces. "I know," she said chokingly, "that it was very wrong...of me. But—"

"Good God!" Wilton groaned, "you sold to Prendergast!"

"We're finished!" gasped Blanchard. "He'll squeeze us to the last sou!"

"No, by gad!" cried Ridgley loyally. "Damon's land ain't encumbered!"

"What the devil is that to say to anything?" Wilton roared, thumping his large fist upon the table, his face thunderous. "What good is an hotel built on the shores of a lake whose guests cannot reach the God—" He noted the Marquis's frigid glare, glanced to Sophia, spluttered, and fumed, "—the dashed lake?"

"Or more to the point," frowned Redmond, "whose guests cannot reach the hotel!"

Sophia felt crushed by guilt, but before she could say anything, Redmond burst out, "How could you be so birdwitted, coz? You must have heard of the spa since you come here! Didn't it occur to you that your lands were in the locality?"

"Oh, Harry," she said with a small and very real sob, "I do not understand all those legal property descriptions."

"'Course she don't," snapped Wilton, who was clearly growing more panicked by the minute. "Place the blame where it really lies. Of all the cork-brained starts as to go ahead with construction when you'd no clear title to the lands surrounding us! A fine great mull you've made of it, Damon!"

Mr. James gasped, "My God!" and, losing all his colour, sat down. "I'm ruined! This spa was my last hope. I sank every penny I could raise!"

"Then," said Damon kindly, "you shall be reimbursed, Harold. At once. See to it, please, Gilly."

"I trust," Wilton snarled, "that offer holds good for all of us?"

177

Gillam turned frantic eyes to his employer, opened his mouth to speak, encountered a steady stare, and closed his mouth hurriedly.

"Hold up a bit," said Redmond. "That ain't fair, Philip. We all agreed to go ahead and try to beat the weather. We all thought—"

"Do not seek to place the blame on my shoulders," Wilton retaliated, his face scarlet." He shook a fist at the Marquis. "The responsibility was—"

"But of course," Damon smiled. "The fault was mine. I should have been more cautious. And none of you shall pay for my—error. You shall have my notes within the week."

Damon came back into the music room and closed the door. Sophia, standing beside the fire, turned to face him, her pulses racing again. Except for Horatio, who had galloped behind the drapes when she entered the room, they were quite alone. Ridgley had accompanied Redmond and Bolster to the stables. Wilton, James, and Blanchard had left very soon after the meeting had broken up, Sir Philip's angry eyes and stiff bow conveying his resentment at having been placed in such an unhappy situation even while his polite words ensured that Damon not forget his pledge to cover their losses. Redmond had said he would not withdraw his backing, pending negotiations with Prendergast, and Bolster's blond head had nodded a vigorous agreement. Ridgley had made it very clear throughout that he placed complete trust in his kinsman.

The Marquis had been affability itself, apparently confident that his attorney would sooner or later bring matters to a satisfactory conclusion. Now, however, watching as he locked the door and slipped the key into his pocket, Sophia felt a surge of fear. She had a fair idea of what she had cost him today, and every instinct had told her to leave with the gentlemen when he would not dare to wreak his fury upon her. But she could not bring herself to strike at even so unprincipled a man and then run away like a coward. She *must* face him. She must play this game out by her own rules even if he was without honour.

"How valiant of you," said the Marquis in a cold dispassionate voice, "to wait." He wandered to the terrace door, turned the key, and pocketed it, also. "And how very fool-
178

hardy."

His smile was silken and terrible, and despite the pistol, Sophia felt her palms grow wet. "I stayed because there is something I have to say to you."

"At the very least ... And I shall be most interested to hear it. But first, if I may ask ..." He sauntered a little closer and paused at the far end of the harpsichord, one slim hand resting nonchalantly on the top. "You were, in fact, fully aware of the location of your property, were you not, ma'am?"

She looked him straight in the eye. "Most assuredly, my lord."

"My compliments, niece. You are a most accomplished liar. So, from the first moment you came here, this fiendish little plot was slithering about in your mind?"

She felt faint and sick and could not answer, striving for a haughty stare to convey her dislike of his choice of words.

"Tell me, my lady," he purred, "do you feel elated? Is revenge truly sweet?"

"Unutterably," she lied. "And yet, alas, it is not nearly enough to repay you."

"Console yourself. You have done better than you may think. And how you must have enjoyed it. Feigning affection for my family while all the time you were gloating over your shabby scheming!"

Sophia's cheeks were burning. How white and enraged he looked. How fierce the glare in his eyes! Surely, he would not dare attack her knowing his father admired and respected her? Gathering strength from that thought, she managed to say without a tremor, "I will tell you this, sir, since I was not able to finish what I started to say at your meeting. I have not sold the property."

He tensed and waited.

"I merely borrowed against it. Possibly, I shall be willing to negotiate a sale at some future date."

"How very gracious of you. And this sale would be at your idea of a fair price. Predicated upon the amount you were able to borrow, perhaps?"

"Perhaps," she said, trying to sound nonchalant.

"And—forgive me—how high is your loan, ma'am?"

"Twelve thousand pounds."

Shocked out of his cynical derision, he gasped, "Twelve ... thousand! Rubbish! Your property isn't worth half that amount even if it were sold outright!" His brows drew

179

down into a fierce scowl. "There's more to this. Let me see your note."

"I shall do no such thing!"

He took a step closer, his eyes like flames. "Then I shall have to take it from you. Unless your brother has it, in which case—"

"My brother knows nothing of this!" she cried hastily.

"Of course, he does not. You little fool! You've made Whitthurst seem a veritable idiot! Many people know he gave me his hand on this! You've properly fouled his honour!" He began to move toward her, that terrifying set look about his mouth. Frightened, she backed away. "By God!" he grated, "were you my sister, I'd spank you 'til you couldn't sit down for a week! That you sought revenge against me was foolish hysteria and a chronic underestimation of Whitthurst. That you carelessly brought near ruin on six other gentlemen is unforgivable!"

She had never in her life been confronted by real rage, and the menacing tone of his voice, the thin hard line of his mouth, the coldness in his eyes were petrifying her. One must never betray fear with such a man, she knew, and, wetting stiff lips, she said an unfortunate "Men who...l-lie down with dogs, get up with fleas!" The resultant blaze of his wrath was so unnerving that she took several quick little steps away from the fire, her courage quite deserting her as she choked a desperate "Do not dare to strike me!"

"You've a wicked tongue, ma'am" he breathed through set teeth. "And I do believe I shall favour Whitthurst by administering the spanking he is unable to mete out! Now—give me that note!"

"No! I shall not!"

He smiled unpleasantly. "If I know you women, you have it in your reticule. You'd not dare leave it where Whitthurst might discover it!" His eyes gleamed as her terror betrayed her into an instinctive tightening of her hold on the reticule. "So I was right!"

For answer, she clutched it to her bosom and gasped, "No! I do not have it with me! Stay back!"

Instead, he moved closer. "I intend to see for myself! I warned you!"

With a whimper of fear, she ran toward the door. Despite a slight limp, he moved very fast to block her path, then stopped abruptly as, seeing herself trapped, she levelled the

180

small pistol at him. "Stay back!" she repeated, her voice shrill with hysteria.

Those heavy brows lifted. The turquoise eyes widened and were lit by a reluctant admiration. "Egad! You did, indeed, come prepared! Had you a duel in mind, ma'am, or were you hoping to find it necessary to defend your virtue?"

She said nothing, though she shrank a little farther from him.

"Silly child," he said, amused. "Put that stupid thing down before you break something else in here."

"Do you really imagine I shall? Or that—knowing what you are, I would c-come here unarmed?" she stammered breathlessly. "Do you think I do not know that little N-Nancy was just one among your many v-victims?"

His amusement faded. "Do *you* really imagine I have the remotest intention of assaulting you in my music room? Don't be ridiculous!"

"I would not place you above the basest treachery in this or any other room! Ah—no! Stay back! I do not want your death on my conscience!"

"Oh, my God! What dramatics! I'll be damned if I'll stand here and let you wave that popgun under my nose!"

His eyes held inflexible purpose, and her finger tightened on the trigger. "I shall shoot," she half sobbed, "if you t-take one more step!"

"Shoot, then! I'm safe enough so long as you're aiming at me! I will have that note. And then, ma'am, you shall pay the price of your naughty scheming!"

He advanced relentlessly. How grim was his mouth—how deadly his eyes. She realized he had not the least intention of halting, and he was of Cobra! In total desperation, she aimed and squeezed the trigger.

The roar of the shot echoed and re-echoed, hurting her ears. Horatio squawked frenziedly and rushed madly up and down behind the drapes. Damon, clutching the scorched sleeve of his jacket, uttered a howl of torture. "You miserable wretch of a woman! Look what you've done!" He raced to the harpsichord and began to inspect it, moaning his anguish as he raised the top and peered inside.

Trembling, Sophia gazed at the large hole in the beautiful wood behind the keys. The pistol fell from her nerveless hand. Sickened by the thought of just such a wound in the Marquis, she mumbled, "You . . . you dared me to shoot . . ."

181

"I thought you were going to shoot *me!*" he groaned, touching the shattered wood caressingly.

He sounded positively indignant that she had not; despite herself, a tearful smile quivered on her lips. "I w-was afraid I...m-might..."

Damon swung around. She looked very small and white and shook visibly, her teeth all but chattering. He should cling to rage but, like a fool, felt instead an all but overpowering impulse to take the brave soul into his arms and comfort her. The best he could do by way of compromise was to speculate, "If I thought you had *deliberately* shot my poor harpsichord..."

"I did." She was weak in the knees from the reaction, but her chin lifted. In a thready voice, she said, "And I'm glad, because it was much more effective. If you're anything like my brother, and I had succeeded in wounding you, you would undoubtedly have been...much too stoical to make a sound. That heartfelt wail was some compensation for our ill usage at your hands."

Mirth crept into his eyes. "I must admit, it is painful in the extreme!" A quirk beside his mouth spread to a grin. "I've never been shot in the keyboard before!" And he broke into a hearty laugh.

Sophia knew she had totally frustrated his hopes and plans today. She'd threatened his life and hurt the one thing she was sure he loved. A man of his type should at the very least have shaken and slapped her or driven her away in a torrent of abuse. Damon, however, looked charming; the menacing anger quite vanished from his battered face, his deep merry laughter as contagious as it was unexpected. She was unable to restrain an answering smile.

He stepped forward at once and took her cold hands into his vital clasp and, being caught so off his stride that he was temporarily defenseless, asked gently, "Why don't you admit you're a very poor shot?"

"*Au contraire*, my lord. The bullet took you squarely above middle 'C'."

Incredulity widened his eyes, and he turned to look. "By Gad! You're right! You really can shoot!"

"I have won two Ladies' Day trophies," she said proudly.

"And I almost dodged aside! Why—you vixen! You *must* be punished!"

"I spared your life!" She pulled back in alarm. "You

182

wouldn't—"

He would, as he proceeded to demonstrate. She was swept into arms that seemed little impaired by this morning's brutal encounter and crushed against ribs that no matter how painful were apparently able to survive this pressure. His lips, damaged but effective, found hers. Her hands clawed toward his face, only to relax, hang motionless in the air, then sweep round his neck, those clawing fingers closing gently in the thick, crisp hair.

Everything else faded, and she was aware only of his mouth, his arms, the tender gentleness of this strangely unlecherous lecher. She marvelled at the strength that was so firmly held in check, the need and hunger in her that reached out in a passionate response she had never dreamed was inside her. He released her lips at last, after an eternity of sweetness, but still held her close against him, his hand cradling the back of her head, his cheek against her hair.

She was weak and trembling. Everything she believed in and held dear was crumbling: every concept of honour and decency; every trust in a code she had always held inviolate; every prayer that someday she would find a man to whom she could look with respect as well as love. Yet her heart was shouting what it had whispered from the start. She looked up into his eyes, and all the yearning, all the adoration she had dreamed of, and so much more, was there.

"Sophia," he breathed. "Am I really...just a little like Stephen?"

"I begin to think," she murmured, "you are far more like him...than..." But a small, cruel voice gibbered, 'Cobra! You weak, spineless fool! Cobra!' And in a sudden return of panic, she tore free.

Damon drew the key from his pocket and held it out. She took it and ran for the door but, opening it, looked back to find him watching her wistfully,

"Amory Hartwell handled the loan for me," she choked, her eyes blurred with tears. "Prendergast is his family solicitor."

And she fled.

Chapter 17

For the entire two days since their arrival at Bodwin Hall,
Whitthurst had been confined to his bed. He had managed
to convince Sophia he was suffering a slight relapse of his
illness; a subterfuge since his real ailment was panic, brought
on by his having discovered the identity of one of the guests.
Today, fortified by a determination to confront her and have
done with it, he had gone downstairs to watch the riders
leave, but his victory over terror had been for nought. She
did not accompany them although the morning was fair and
cool, perfect weather for the ride Lord Phineas had planned
so as to remove his guests from a house humming with prep-
arations for the evening ball. The Viscount's thoughts were
soon diverted from his own concerns, however, and when the
horses were out of sight, he wandered frowningly toward the
house and re-entered the back garden.

Kicking a stone he had guided from the stableyard, he
sauntered across the grass. Sophia seemed totally unaware

that the elegant Bodwin, with his grey hair and grey eyes and grey house, looked at her with an expression that was ageless. He was their host, and his generosity knew no bounds. But Whitthurst's initial dislike of the man was deepening. Perhaps he was merely a well-meaning but egotistical bore, perhaps he was just a foolish gossip; but he had visited the "sick" man several times, and some of his "innocent" remarks—particularly in regard to Damon and the Priory—had bordered on the malicious. Because of his wealth and his impeccable lineage, he was regarded as a great catch for any girl, but the thought of him attempting to fix his interest with Sophia made Whitthurst's jaw set, and his eyes become very grim, indeed.

Head downbent, he kicked the stone savagely and tried to convince himself that he was letting his imagination run riot, as he'd often accused his sister of doing. But, gad, he'd be pleased when they could decently get away from—

"Ouch!"

He looked up and checked, frozen and terrified.

She knelt on the lawn and frowned at him, her hand clutching her injury unaffectedly. "*Ma foi!* But you are sudden, sir!"

She was even prettier than he remembered, laughter lurking behind the indignation in her roguish eyes and a smile hovering about that little mouth he found so delightful, the upper lip very slightly outthrusting. He tried to answer but was tongue-tied, partly from fear of her reaction to his injuries and partly from pain because she quite clearly did not recollect him in the slightest.

"Have you no apology, monsieur?" she demanded, piqued by his silence.

"Very...s-sorry, ma'am," he croaked.

She peered around. "I bring a book. It is...somewhere."

A green leather-bound volume was lying in plain sight just inside the shade of the tree. She began to crawl around gropingly and whisked a small pair of spectacles out of sight a second before she knelt on them. So she did not see very well! He'd not realized it, but perhaps she hadn't yet recognized him. He picked up the book and handed it to her. Mrs. Radcliffe, of course, he might've known. How the ladies loved her romances. "Yours, mademoiselle?"

Genevieve tensed. The voice was different this time. Deep

185

and surer and very familiar. Her heart turned over, and she spun around, holding up a hand against the sunlight. "Is it? Can it be? Ah! It is!" She held out both hands eagerly, then let one fall. Horror plunged a knife through her. "*Mon Dieu!*" she cried as he lifted her, "you have lost your arm! Ah—*mon pauvre!* What a terrible nuisance that must be! But how pleased I am to see you here. And why is this? Have you the acquaintance with our Phinny?"

A tremendous relief swept the Viscount, and he was freed from the despair that had weighed him down for months. She *did* remember! And she did not seem to be repulsed! Her hands were clasped on his arm. Her sweet face smiled up at him, her eyes as radiant as before. "My . . . my sister is here," he stammered. "You know her, I believe. Sophia Drayton."

"Sophia? I *know* I have see her somewhere before this!" The ache in her heart was intensified because the virile young officer she remembered was this thin, ill-looking man, aged by suffering, and so humbly grateful that she had remembered him. As if she could ever forget! If he but knew how many nights she had prayed for him. How many tears she had shed because her wretched aunt had made her run from Brussels only hours after she had met him at the Duchess of Richmond's ball. How she had hoped that he would seek her out. And now . . . Emotion brought blinding tears, and her awareness of his ordeal was choking her. He did not need tears now! Somehow she forced away the lump in her throat and said brightly, "It is *you* I see in Sophia!"

Joy was making him seem to float as they strolled along. He was sufficiently emboldened as to offer his arm and ecstatic when her hand slipped within it unhesitatingly. "You wouldn't recall, I am sure," he said, "but—I'm Stephen Whitthurst. We danced once, just before—"

"*Oui,*" she said sadly. "Just before they come and tell you all to go quickly to Quatre Bras! And all you fine young officers go running out—and I have not the time even to discover your name. It was of the noisiest, you recall? I do not quite understand what poor Uxbridge say when he introduce us . . ." She gazed up at him and said softly, "So you are named . . . Stephen."

His senses swam with happiness at the softness in her eyes. Could this really be happening? Now—when he had given up all hope? "I've never forgotten," he murmured, "how beautiful you looked in that orange gown."

"And how horribly it clash with your scarlet jacket." She giggled. "I take it home and give it to my maid, I am so mortified! I have the dance with the most handsome man in the room, and my gown fight with his splendid jacket! *Tragique!*"

Whitthurst stopped walking and gazed down at her. "You are too kind, ma'am," he breathed.

"Ma'am?" Her lashes drooped coquettishly. "Have you forget my name, perhap? Or did you not hear it also when first we meet?"

"I heard it. And indeed I have *never* forgotten—nor ever could! But I had no idea you were related to Damon, Mademoiselle de la Montaigne."

"Such a mouth full of names, is it not?" She blushed prettily. "My first name you may call me, sir. It is Genevieve."

"You do me too great an honour, Mademoiselle Genevieve," he said worshipfully.

With a shy new diffidence she murmured, "How very nicely you speak it. And—you deserve far more honour than I may give you, Lord Whitthurst."

Infuriated, Damon sprang from the leather chair and pounded a fist on the desk of his estimable attorney. "*Not* next month! I want fast action on this!"

Sir Horace Drake blinked his pale eyes, peered over his spectacles at the young face glaring down at him, and observed, "Damme, but you're confounded hot on this! I tell you I shall unravel it all in time. What's in it I don't know?"

Pacing the luxuriously conservative office, Damon told him, briefly and to the point, ending, "I want to see that note Lady Sophia signed! I want that blasted fence torn down—or by God, I'll have my men tear it down! I want a right of way, which I was assured I had! And dammit, Horry, I'll give you a week!"

Sir Horace, unintimidated but shocked out of his usual calm, answered, "I am most sorry it happened. Cannot think what became of that letter I sent you. I know my man delivered it to your place in Dorset. Water under the bridge, of course. And you'd best resign yourself to a year, my lord."

"A year—hell! One...damned...week!"

"Impossible. Unless perhaps your father, with his powers, could—"

"No!"

"I see." The stocky old gentleman pursed his lips and folded his hands. "Then be reasonable, Camille. These legal matters take time. I realize I bungled it to an extent. Still, you should not have—"

"Have relied upon the word of a gentleman?"

Sir Horace looked into his grim face and smiled. "Yes, damme! I'd have done the same, under the circumstances. But as for Lady Drayton—there's absolutely no legal ground there. If she refuses to show you her note, I am powerless to ask another solicitor to violate his client's confidence."

Fuming, Damon growled, "You know what Prendergast is."

"I know that he is Craig-Bell's lifelong friend and counsel." The pale eyes of the great man of the law became bleak. "And Craig-Bell, my dear boy, could buy and sell you *and* your noble father several times over."

"Which puts him above the law?"

"Which makes him excessive powerful—even when out of England." Sir Horace leaned forward and admonished, "You were a witless fool and will likely pay for your folly the rest of your life! If I'd had my way—"

"Well, you didn't," Damon interrupted rudely. "And you're just as bound, I'll remind you, to respect *my* confidences."

"Such as?"

"My father. He's to know nothing of any of it."

"I'd tell him, anyway, had I the slightest moral integrity," Sir Horace sighed.

"But you have not!" Damon burst into his sudden swift laugh. "You're just a shifty solicitor."

Sir Horace frowned, then gave an answering laugh and came around the desk to place an affectionate hand on his client's shoulder. "You're one of the very few men I know who would dare talk to me like that, Camille. I'll do what I can—and as fast as I can. But do not rush in blind—you'll likely cause more trouble than I can remedy. And...have a care, lad. Guard yourself!"

From Lincoln's Inn, the Marquis drove to Hartwell's London house, but the porter told him Sir Amory was visiting Lord Phineas Bodwin at Bodwin Hall in Dorsetshire. Frustrated at every turn, Damon rejoined his groom and proceeded to thoroughly demoralize that unfortunate individual in the ensuing wild ride to his own large and seldom-used house on Green Street.

Mr. Quinn fared little better the following day and was, in fact, shivering noticeably when the Marquis pulled up the horses behind the Priory, thrust the ribbons at him, and clambered awkwardly from the curricle. Limping across the terrace, his face dark with anger, he halted. The lathered horses were unmoving, and Quinn still watched him, round-eyed. With a twinge of contrition, he realized the man looked scared. "My apologies, Tom," he called. "I drove 'em too hard, I see. You should've checked me."

"N-not at all...mmmilord," stammered the groom, rousing a little. "Most—most enlivening." As he later told an intrigued audience in the servants' hall, one could as lief put a check on the devil as try to slow down his lordship with that black scowl on his face! And, after all, if his lordship preferred that his curricle travel mostly in the air, it was A Experience! Was a body fortunate enough to survive it!

Damon flung open the door to the music room and went inside, pulling off his gloves, his reflections bringing his black brows even lower. Amory was dangling after Sophia again, damn him! Well, there was nothing for it, he'd have to go—

"Well, here you are at last, Cam! Gad! What a magnificent coat! Why do mine never fit like that? And where in the devil have you been?"

Astonished, as the object of his thoughts rose from the chair in which he'd been snoring, Damon scowled. "Looking all over Town for you!"

Hartwell's welcoming grin faded. "From your looks, I collect I'm in for a prime setdown! Cheerio! I'll see you in—"

"Hell—most like!" Damon tossed hat and gloves onto the harpsichord as he advanced into the room.

Hartwell exclaimed, "Good God, man! What's happened to your face?"

"Devil with that!" Attempting to shrug out of his many-caped driving coat, he swore. "Lend me a hand here, will you?" And when his friend had complied, and his temper was worsened by that painful endeavour, he deposited the coat beside his hat and gloves and demanded wrathfully, "What in God's name made you go to Prendergast to arrange that blasted loan for Lady Sophia?"

Hartwell stiffened. "Don't see it's any of your concern, actually."

189

"Do you not? Well, that land you encumbered happens to damn near surround my spa! Is that sufficiently 'my concern'?"

"Surround your...? By Jupiter! I *am* sorry! I'd no idea! I didn't bother to fizzle out the lots and all that nonsense. Didn't Sophia—"

"She didn't know," the Marquis lied. "But—why Prendergast, of all people?"

"He's handled my uncle's affairs for donkey's years, and I knew he arranged loans." Hartwell looked increasingly troubled. "Cam—didn't you check your rights of way before you—"

"Yes, dammit! But never mind that now. Did Prendergast give you any arguments?"

"Naturally. Offered practically nothing at first, but I stood right up to him! He put me off for a couple of days, but..." He gave a sly grin. "I'd things in Devon to occupy my time..."

"So I hear. Like a certain *jolie* cousin of mine."

"Come now, never look so pious! I seem to recall a certain mademoiselle named Gabrielle...To say nought of Celeste and Margarita and—who was that little bit of muslin—that choice tit that no Buck or Corinthian could bed until you winked your eye at her and—"

"Her name," said Damon, a film of ice in his eyes, "was, as you are very well aware, Blanche. And I neither believe I was the first, nor the last. None of which has the least to do with either a lady of quality—or your good friend Prendergast."

Given pause by that chill blast, Hartwell's smile died. He went over to the side table and poured himself a glass of Madeira. "Sometimes—Damon," he said in a brittle voice, "you can be devilish offensive."

"I guarantee you, Hartwell," replied the Marquis grimly, "you have never seen me when I am truly offensive! Now pray tell me what the note took as collateral."

Hartwell took a sip of wine and stared at him. "Well, the lands I suppose. How the devil would I know?"

"You mean," snarled Damon, "you let the lady sign without reading it?"

"I don't understand all that legal flummery! Told the gal to let her brother read it! She said she had, so it's his bread and butter, not mine!" He searched Damon's intent face with narrowed eyes and, his own features flushing angrily, said,

190

"Concerned about her, are you? How gallant! But if I have caused the Lady Sophia Drayton to lose so much as a groat, my fine and noble Marquis, I—personally—will refund it! And if there's one thing that lovely little filly don't need in the meanwhile, it's a rake like you dangling after her! Let her alone! I've offered for the lady twice, and—"

"And," asked the Marquis in a caressingly soft voice, "has she accepted?"

"As good as," Hartwell said defiantly.

Murder flared from Damon's eyes. "You lie!"

The gauntlet was thrown, and the room became hushed. Hartwell, staring into the face of death, was appalled. But it was the turquoise eyes that eventually flickered and fell. It was Damon whose shoulders drooped and who muttered, "I'm most devilish sorry... Hartwell."

For another long moment, Sir Amory regarded him, and there was neither smile nor anger upon his pleasant features now, only an odd emptiness. "Why, I may have exaggerated... just a trifle. Damon."

"And I've no claim on the lady. None in the least, Amory," said the Marquis, looking at him wistfully.

"Damn fool gudgeon." Hartwell grinned. "What're you after, Cam?"

For a space, they smiled upon one another, and after that very brief pause, "I know Prendergast," said the Marquis. "He's slippery as an eel. The property Lady Sophia put up isn't worth twelve thousand even if it were sold."

Hartwell frowned thoughtfully. "In that case, I'd better toddle down to Kent, get hold of that note, and have my man of business look it over."

Damon crossed to tug at the bellrope, thinking that was what he should have done in the first place. "Excellent idea. But Lady Sophia is not at Singlebirch. She and Whitthurst visit with Phinny Bodwin."

For an instant, Hartwell's eyes held an arrested expression; then he smiled. "Well, that's good news. I'll go right over there."

"How long have you been here?"

"Arrived last evening. Hate to criticize, Cam. But your new cook don't hold a candle to Ariel. You really shouldn't have let him go."

191

Whitthurst won their game of croquet, and when Genevieve laughingly accused him of having beaten her by trickery and deception, he pointed out it had been her idea that she use only her right hand. "I have not the suspicion," she admitted, "that your left hand it is so much surer than my right!" She stretched out that same small hand eagerly and, as it was just as eagerly clasped, asked, "What do we do now? Should you wish a small ride? I know of such a pretty view by—" But the happiness had left his eyes, and, aghast, she begged that he not consider her "the fast lady."

"Heaven forbid I should ever think such a thing," he denied. "It's just that I haven't—er—done any riding for a long time."

"Ah," she said with a slow smile, "you have this thing in the common with my Damon, *n'est ce pas?*"

Whitthurst became very red and looked away from those eyes that could not see, yet saw so much.

"My dear friend"—she laid her hand gently on his sleeve— "there is nothing so wrong with being afraid. You were the hussar officer of the most *magnifique*. It will come back to you...when the time she is right."

She had called him her "dear friend"! This darling girl he'd not dared to hope would glance his way again was looking up at him as if he were a whole man once more. And by God! with her he *felt* a whole man! "Mademoiselle de la Montaigne," he grinned eagerly, "may I beg you will accompany me on a small ride?"

They parted briefly, to rendezvous in the stables where, despite his new-found resolution, the gelding looked enormous, the saddle very high, and his own heart fluttered with nervousness. Genevieve, adorable in the riding habit she had changed into with record speed, raised her hands to the horn and glanced expectantly toward Whitthurst.

The Viscount prayed as he bent, well aware that many in the area watched anxiously as he held that little boot. Genevieve's heart was also pounding with the fear that he might not be strong enough to boost her into the saddle with his one hand; and so, as he threw, she jumped. Unfortunately, Whitthurst possessed a good deal more strength than she had supposed. She shot up into the air and, with a shocked squeal, disappeared over the far side of the horse. The Viscount gave a cry of horror. The horse looked around in some surprise. Suddenly, the entire area was devoid of people, although from

192

behind the doors of stalls and the Tack Room came muffled sounds that told of suppressed hilarity. The groom holding the horses looked steadfastly, if tearfully, the other way.

Whitthurst bent to peer under the mare. Genevieve, on hands and knees, her pert little hat gone, peered back at him. "You have," she gasped, "the deuce of a strong hand, my lord!"

He raced round and helped her to her feet, and she leaned against him, thrilling to the feel of his arm about her.

"My poor girl! Are you hurt?"

"Well," she said, her eyes a'sparkle. "I have hear of being the bruising rider, but..."

There was no restraining himself. He burst into a shout of laughter. Genevieve joined in, hugging him. They laughed until they cried.

Chapter 18

The riding party returned to Bodwin Hall to encounter a scene of total frenzy. The stables were being prepared for the tide of vehicles and animals that would descend upon them that evening. In the house they were met by a small army of people decorating the Great Hall with hanging baskets of flowers and large Oriental vases that were a blaze of blossoms. Carpets were being laid on the front terrace and steps, while the gardeners were busily trimming the hedges—his lordship having at the last moment decided that they looked ragged and shabby.

En route to her room, Sophia passed through a welter of industrious cleaning. She was quite relieved to find her maids occupied elsewere and sat down, wearily thinking over the events of the morning. It had been a pleasant ride insofar as fresh air and dewy scenery had been concerned, but Lord Bodwin's tendre for her had been distressingly apparent. Never venturing beyond the bounds of politeness, his solicitousness, his eagerness to win her approval, and, above all, the adoring look in his grey eyes had spoken so eloquently that she had felt uncomfortable on more than one occasion.

So preoccupied had she been by this development that she had paid little heed to their route and had been beyond words shocked when, rounding a tree-clad hillside, they had quite suddenly come upon the spa. It stood upon the north bank of a large lake, surrounded by a lush sweep of meadowland. The buildings loomed huge amidst a cluster of lovely old oak trees that had been preserved among the structures. To the rear, beyond another cluster of trees, stood a large barn, complemented by more stables and outbuildings, sturdy and bright with fresh paint. Sophia was charmed by the potential beauty of the spot despite the fact that the unfinished canals yawned raggedly; the windows, empty of glass, looked inward like blind eyes; and the raw newness of the construction was as yet unsoftened by the gardens that were planned. But despite its size and obvious promise, the spa presented a forlorn appearance, shut off by the wire fences that girded it about, the many large signs warning that "Trespassers Would Be Prosecuted."

Bodwin had reined up at once, voicing an astonished "What on earth?"

"Why, the blasted place is under siege!" Feather had roared indignantly. "Who would dare to do such a thing? Is it not Damon's land?"

Ridgley, his keen gaze fixed on Sophia's flushed and miserable face, had murmured, "Apparently... not."

"I don't understand," Sophia said worriedly, accompanying Genevieve up the stairs. "He's been quite ill again because of that terribly exhausting journey from Kent. He should have had more sense than to ride today."

"Ah—you are angry! And the fault is mine! Ah! *C'est plus qu'un crime, c'est une faute!*"

They reached the first landing, and Sophia slowed her steps, looking at the distraught girl in total bewilderment. "Your fault? Crime? Blunder? What—?"

"*Oui!*" Genevieve clasped her hands and began to speak rapidly while gazing up into Sophia's face with a pathetic entreaty. "I cannot believe when I see him again, my chevalier! He hit me on the *derriere* with a rock, but this I do not mind because love for him have stay in my heart since so long. We meet in Brussels, you see, but I am kidnapped away because my stupid aunt fears your fine Wellington will lose and we of the french aristocracy shall ride in the tumbrils again. I pray for him at the battle. We hear the drums and then the cannon...on and on, *Mon Dieu*...so horrid! And afterwards, we hear is not the *big* battle, which have come three days later! Yet I feel he is alive, and I pray he will seek me out. But he does not, and so I flirt with all the silly boys who do come, but my heart it break into my pillow every night. And then today, *voila*! He is there—before me! With his dear arm gone. And my heart it break again."

"S-Stephen?" Sophia managed. "And...*you*?"

Genevieve nodded so vehemently that her rather rumpled hair became even more disarrayed. "He look so sad and humble—but I make him laugh a little bit. He beat me with his mallet and throw me over the horse and—"

"Good God!"

"And we laugh and laugh about it all, and my chevalier he ride so *bon* and start to look like his own self a tiny bit. Only—" Her big eyes began to swim with tears, and she sniffed and said jerkily, "We ride to a place I know, but I am afraid because...his beautiful face is now so white..."

Sophia gave a gasp and hurried on, Genevieve trotting along beside her. "The groom help me get him in the back way because my chevalier cannot scarcely walk, and I know he will not wish for others to see this. But now—he just lie there!"

Sophia shot her a harried glance and began to run, and running, also, Genevieve gasped, "I do not know that he is your fine, brave brother. Ah—do not hate me, Sophia. I love him so!"

"Of course I do not hate you. Indeed, I should have guessed, for often I have thought him unhappy, his thoughts far away."

The bedchamber was very quiet, the curtains drawn. Mr. Byrnes let them in, a finger held to his lips, his faded eyes kindly. "He's asleep, my lady," he whispered. "Just worn out, I think. No great harm done."

Together, they tip-toed over to the bed, neither concerned with the shocking impropriety of Genevieve's being there.

The Viscount lay very still. He was pale and tired-looking and, even as they watched, heaved a great sigh and snuggled

196

deeper under the coverlet.

Sophia's eyes blurred. Stephen was smiling. Even in sleep he looked quite ridiculously happy.

After twenty frustrating minutes, Sophia got off the bed and walked over to the open windows. Her mind was just too full for her to nap. She had left a blissful Genevieve, but the thought of Stephen having found his lady was so new, so bewilderingly unexpected, and opened so many avenues for conjecture that she found herself, as Hettie Adams would have said, "all atwitter." Genevieve could scarcely have been more perfect for him. And yet—Her brow furrowed. With typical romantic impracticality, she had forgotten the all-important matters of family and finances. Would the Duke approve? She shook herself mentally. Crossing her bridges again!

She gazed toward the southeast. What was happening at the Priory? Was Horatio trundling irascibly about? Was Damon at the harpsichord, running those impatient fingers through his rumpled hair? She closed her eyes, trembling, and at once saw him bending to kiss her, felt the tender pressure of his lips, the strong arms about her. And knowing her cheeks were flaming because of that bittersweet memory, put her hands to cover them, whimpering a little because of her helplessness...and hopelessness.

"Had I waited out in the hall much longer, my dear," said Lady Branden in an unusually gentle voice, "I should likely have took root! Which would be not only unfortunate but startling since one don't find Feathers growing out of Persian carpets—or not very often, I am persuaded!"

Sophia stammered an apology, was hugged gently, regarded by two shrewd eyes, and commanded to sit down again.

"I am vexed to discover that I am become rather disgustingly fond of you, child," Lady Branden admitted. "Irritating. I do dislike becoming maudlin about people. Well, you need cheering up, so I shall tell you some old family secrets." With a frown, she muttered, "Lud! Come to think on it, I may thereby succeed in making you even more miserable!"

Laughing at this mixed speech, Sophia assured her that she loved to hear secrets. "Especially about such an interesting family."

197

"Hmmmmn," said Feather. "I rather thought you found it so. Your brother already knows the story but has probably said nothing. Damon should tell you, of course—but will not." Quick to note the shyness in the lovely face beside her, she nodded and said, "I decided it was necessary to tell you because of three pairs of eyes. Yours—when you saw my craven nephew shrink from that splendid stallion the other day—"

"Oh! But—ma'am—I assure you, I—"

"Damon's," Feather went on inexorably, "when he knew you had seen it..." Here Sophia's lashes dropped, and she stared fixedly at her hands. "And—Phineas Bodwin's," Feather concluded, "when *he* looks at you!"

"Oh, dear," murmured Sophia.

"Quite. Now I have already told you about Ninon and Vaille—and the tragedy that took her from us. Only I did not tell you all of it. And I know all of it... almost. I have known the family all my life, you see. We grew up on neighbouring estates—my sisters and me and the two Branden boys. We had such happy times, and then Ridgley was orphaned and came to live with them. He was their cousin, but very soon he and Philip were more like the two brothers. Roland, the younger Branden boy, was quiet and bookish. The bond between Philip and Ted I never thought to see broken..." She paused, her eyes looking into the past.

"It was Roland whom you married, I think?" Sophia prompted gently.

At once, that booming laugh rang out. "The quiet one, you're thinking! Married to a great, clumsy creature like me! No, no, child—never get into a taking! It's what everyone thought. Still, we loved one another. We had twenty wonderful years. And then—he was killed at Talavera. I grieved for him, but he died as he would have wished, fighting for the country he loved. A noble dying. If only we'd been blessed with children, it wouldn't be... quite so..." She broke off, shook her head, and said impatiently, "D'ye see how maudlin I get? And this isn't my story but Vaille's. I shall never forget the expression on his face when he met Ninon again. It had been almost five years since he'd saved her life in France. His first wife had died eighteen months previously, and we were all down at Hollow Hill for the week. Harland had many guests, and one day Ninon and her Mama walked in. I don't know what made me look at Vaille, but he was staring at Ninon as if he had glimpsed something... holy. The only trouble was, Ridgley had the same look!" A sad smile flickered over her face. "Trouble, trouble! They both courted her. Bets on which would win were laid at all the clubs, but I don't think Ted ever had the slightest chance."

"One would think, with such a love, there would have been few problems," Sophia interjected. "Yet you said the marriage was unhappy?"

"Not at first. Philip's life revolved round her and their child. And when Ninon became withdrawn and afraid of him, I think it broke his heart. To add to his sorrow, she would use any and every excuse to keep him away from Camille until the child himself became—and I think is to this day— afraid of his father. Even so, he worships the man. But will not acknowledge it. Which is what provokes me so that I wish I might strangle my arrogant, cold, top lofty, much too good looking, and altogether beloved nephew! That surprises you, I see. My dear, never doubt it. I am putty in those beautiful hands of his, and well he knows it, however I harp and rail at him! At all events, it was Ninon's fear of Vaille which caused the final rift between the cousins. Poor Ridgley, you see, was still completely in love with her, and to see her so unhappy was unbearable to him. It was wrong, of course. He should have gone away and left them to manage their troubles; and he would, I'm sure, had she been happy. As time passed, however, Philip and Ninon grew ever farther apart. When Camille was nine years old, there was, as I told you, a dreadful quarrel. For better than a year, Vaille had wanted the boy sent away to school, but Camille was frail, and Ninon dreaded to be parted from him."

"But this is our custom. Did she not realize British families send their boys to boarding school?"

"I'm sure she did. But she would not agree. Vaille was patient at first but became increasingly angry, especially since Ridgley stood firmly with Ninon in the matter. They were at the Priory for the summer when it all came to a head. Ted arrived to find Ninon in tears. He lost his temper and Vaille...well, he can be very cutting in a quiet way, but when he is really furious, the ice flies in all directions, I do assure you! From what I heard, they almost came to cuffs— at the very least! The next morning, Ninon—poor child—took Camille and ran away." Her lips quivered, and she stopped abruptly.

The large hands were tightly gripped, and Sophia realized

how soft was the heart that hid beneath the bluff exterior. "How sad," she said gently. "It must have been a most ghastly thing."

"Yes . . . The chaise went off the highway and rolled down a bank. One of the horses broke free, but the other went down with the chaise. Mercifully, Camille was thrown clear. He was not badly hurt, but his arm was broken, and he was pinned beneath the animal's neck. He struggled bravely, dear child, but could not win free. He could see . . . his Mama but could not help her."

Horrified, Sophia whispered, "Dear God! How awful!"

"It was hours before they were found. The groom was unconscious and unable to help. The rain was very heavy, the chaise half concealed by shrubs. . . . And that, my dear, is why Camille cannot abide horses. He can drive 'em and does exceeding well. But to touch one is more than he can bear."

There was a brief silence, each woman engrossed in her own thoughts. Then Sophia asked, "Feather, you said the Comtesse would not allow Damon to return to his Papa. Was she bitter about her daughter's death?"

"Perhaps. But, basically, she and her husband were kind people. She never forgot that Vaille had once saved her life. She wrote to him regularly—long letters with much detail of the boy. And she made Camille write, also. But each time Vaille tried to bring his son home, she outwitted him. The Comte had lost most of his wealth during "The Terror" but still wielded great influence throughout Europe. When Vaille finally became completely out of patience, the courts in Belgium would not support him. Eventually, Vaille took desperate measures and stormed to their chateau. He could not have chosen a worse moment. The Comte was critically ill and the Comtesse sick with fear that she would lose him. There was a bitter confrontation. Camille rejected Vaille and refused to return except by force. He was seventeen then, and I don't doubt was capable of being just as cutting as he often is now—beastly creature! Vaille came home alone. When his Grandmama died, Camille finally returned to England, but that was the hardest blow of all, I think. Because he would not live in the same house with his father. And now, alas, will not even share the same city."

"Does he perhaps lay his Mama's death at Vaille's door?"

Lady Branden frowned thoughtfully. "Perhaps. Or perhaps he knows something of their relationship that none of us suspected. The only one who knows for sure where Ninon was running that day is Camille. Would that he could remember!"

"And this is the reason why the Duke and Ridgley hate each other?"

"Reason and enough, Sophia. When Vaille came home and learned of the tragedy, he almost went out of his mind with grief. He sat for days and nights in the music room...just staring at the harpsichord Ninon had so loved to play. One night, he went to Town in search of Ted. He found him at a Ball at Lucinda Carden's house. Frightful! They went into another room. Nobody 'noticed' of course, but that cat Anne Hersh followed and watched. She told us that Philip accused Ridgley of coming between them and implied that Ninon had been running to him when the accident happened. Ridgley said something stupid—to the effect that he prayed to God that was truth!" Her eyes flashed, and she snorted an impatient "Men!"

"I'm amazed that Vaille didn't call him out—cousin or no!"

"Did. Roland and I, in a very desperate struggle, were able to stop that final disaster. But they've been on the brink of a duel a dozen times since. I...I wouldn't mind it so much, but..." Her twisted smile was woeful. "They are quite equally matched. Probably kill each other. And that I simply...could not...bear."

At first, Sophia thought the gallery empty, but looking around, she at last saw Lord Phineas contemplating a display case containing splendid antique jewellery. She called to him, and he hastened to join her and express his profound gratitude that she had interrupted her rest to come and talk with him. He expressed himself so profoundly, in fact, that she began to be bored by his gratitude and was quite relieved when he, at length, drew her to a sofa beneath a magnificent tapestry and asked her with a rather overdone humility if she would grant him just one small favour. Afraid that this might evolve into the offer she now dreaded to receive from him, she said cautiously that she would hope to be able to oblige any good friend were it in her power to do so. She was considerably surprised, however, when he enquired what she planned to wear to the ball. With the smallest of frowns, she replied that she would probably wear an ivory-lace gown, refusing to admit even to herself that she had no intention of doing so. The look of horror that flashed across his face was so ludicrous that she burst into laughter. "Good gracious, Phinny! Shall I spoil your evening?"

"Yes! Absolutely!" He possessed himself of her hand and, patting it, said, "I have planned a—small surprise. One of your maids was kind enough to tell me you own a truly magnificent blue gown. I was sure you would wear it."

Sophia removed her hand gently and said with quiet emphasis that she preferred not to wear that particular gown. She was taken aback when Bodwin voiced an eloquent plea that she do so. "For the colour is perfect, and I vow I can scarce wait to see you in it."

"You...have *seen* it?"

"I must confess that I have and could not help but admire it."

Considerably annoyed by such flagrant presumption, she said stiffly, "How kind of you to plan a surprise for me."

He gave a sad little answering smile, and she was at once seized by remorse. The poor man was kind and well intentioned. He planned to honour her at his ball and had been a considerate host. All he asked in return was that she wear a gown which, in her heart, she longed to slip into. She smiled and capitulated. "Very well, Phinny. I will wear the blue gown."

His face lit up, and he clapped his white hands ecstatically. "Dear lady! You are so gracious! How may I reward such magnanimity? Ah, I have it!"

He minced over to the display case he had been inspecting when she arrived. Without looking around, he snapped his fingers, and a gorgeous footman at once floated into the room, unlocked the glass door of the cabinet, and drifted soundlessly away.

Bodwin removed a flat jewel case and carried it to Sophia. "This is very old," he said, placing it in her hands. "You would honour me by wearing it this evening, dear lady."

She knew that she should simply hand it back with a polite refusal but was unable to resist a peek at what lay inside. A magnificent necklace of sapphires and diamonds that must have been worth a fortune winked and sparkled at her. Worn with a very plain gown, it would still have been ornate; worn on the gown Damon had sent, it would be downright vulgar. "It is perfectly lovely." She closed the case and held it out to him. "But I cannot wear it."

"Nonsense," he smiled, waving the case aside. "It will not put *you* in the shade, my dear."

She stood despite the fact that he did not step back, and she was obliged to come closer to him than she would have wished. "You are very good, Phinny," she said quietly. "I shall wear the blue gown but not the necklace."

She prepared to walk past, but he tossed the case down, the lid falling open and the jewels spilling onto the gleaming floor. As she paused, shocked by this careless gesture, Bodwin gave a groan and, to her horror, dropped to his knees and pressed her hand to his lips. "I have offended you! Sooner would I die! Ah, my most beautiful Sophia, when you consent to become my bride, I shall be the proudest man in all England!"

"Phinny!" She struggled to free herself. "This is most improper! You should have spoken to Whitthurst before you so addressed me!"

"Why? The boy's ill. You are a mature woman and can reach your own decisions. From the moment we met, we have been more than friends! Though I doubt you'd expected to bring a strong man to his knees."

Such a speech should have enraged her, but she had to fight a wicked impulse to giggle, an impulse strengthened by having caught a glimpse of the footman's impassive features transformed into a gigantic grin before they were whisked from sight. She could scarce blame him—Bodwin looked so utterly ridiculous, kneeling there in all his finery, the necklace sparkling beside him. "*Do* get up, Phinny! I am truly sensible of the great honour you pay me, but—I wouldn't really suit you at all."

She was impressed by the agility with which he regained his feet, springing up in a way that many a younger man would have envied. "You must have more confidence in yourself, my dear," he said with tolerant condescension. "You are lovely now and will grow in grace and beauty under my guidance. Your family is quite presentable, and your lack of an inheritance is of little moment with me. With you here, presiding over all the pretty little feminine functions that have gone unattended for so long, my house will be complete!"

Torn between irritation and amusement, she thought, 'He doesn't want a wife, he wants another object to display!' And she said aloud, "It is much too soon, my lord. I scarcely know

203

you, and—"

"And there is someone else, perhaps?" It was softly said, yet his gaze became fixed and oddly brilliant.

'...there is someone else, perhaps?' The words seemed to echo in her ears. "I have received other offers, sir," she evaded, lowering her lashes, "but never one I have considered accepting."

"Then can it be because there is some slight discrepancy in our ages? I assure you, my dear, you will not find me wanting in virility. You are not just out of the schoolroom, and I am considered quite a prize in the matrimonial stakes, you know. Many a lovely girl has dropped her handkerchief for me; many a trap has been set by a hopeful Mama—but in vain. Always I have waited for the perfect partner."

He was all but preening himself. Sophia, having been made to feel quite matronly, was less vexed than amused. Unable to resist the temptation, she said demurely, "But— alas, I am not perfect."

"I shall make you perfect!" he vowed, striking a pose. "I shall take your natural beauty and refine it! The greatest couturiers in the world shall clothe you! I shall import skilled cosmeticians to enhance your loveliness. There are those, dear Sophia, who know just how to make a mouth..."—he tapped the side of her cheek gently—"just a teensy shade...less wide. Or to bring a nose to perfect scale! Your father's recklessness, your brother's wildness, are not necessarily traits you must pass on to your children. You shall never know worry again. Money, Sophia, is the softest cushion the world offers, and you shall be one of the richest women in England. Your word will be law absolute—second only to my own—in all my vast possessions and estates. You shall have..."

She had gone from incredulity to anger to mirth during this speech. Now, as he went on at great length, she found laughter bubbling up inside her and thought, 'Oh, Camille! If only you could hear this!' She realized that he had finished his oration at last and was watching her, probably expecting her to fall at his feet! He was an insufferable bag of conceit! And not once, in all the puffing off of his consequence, had he said the one thing that might have disposed her more kindly toward him. Not once had he claimed to feel the tender emotion. But just the same, he was her host, and in his own pathetic fashion he had paid her the greatest compliment a

204

man may pay a woman, and she would not hurt him for the world. Therefore, she lowered her eyes and stood in meek silence, striving to think of something she might say without giggling. Fortunately, she was spared the effort.

"Ah"—Bodwin smiled indulgently—"I have overwhelmed you, have I not? I am too sudden, too masterful! It was ever thus with the men of my house. Take your time, my dear. Become accustomed to this palace of mine and allow yourself to think of it as...ours!"

Chapter 19

"Like dark pools..." sighed the Viscount, a hand behind his head on the pillow, his eyes smiling up at the canopy above him. "And that delicious upper lip..." He turned a look of complete idiocy upon his amused sister. "Did you remark that, Chicky? Have you ever in your life seen such a delightful little mouth? Reminds me—"

"Of a little rabbit." She nodded. "You told me."

His bright-eyed happiness caused her to bless Genevieve's absent head. He loved her all right! How wonderful to be so sure. To have pride and joy and love. And no doubts. And how could she spoil this bliss by confessing her own sins? How could she admit that she had brought shame upon him, fouled his given word, had so little faith in his judgment that she had—

"Chicky?" Anxiety clouded Whitthurst's eyes. "Nothing wrong, is there? You do like her? I mean—" He looked very shy suddenly. "I mean—just supposing she should honour me—Not that I think she would. But—you wouldn't—er—Oh, dash it all! You know what I'm trying to say, you ninny-hammer!"

"Of course I do. And I love Genevieve already. I did, in fact, before I knew you two had met. It's just..." But the eagerness with which he waited was her undoing. She could *not* tell him! Not now. He deserved this new found joy, bless his dear soul. She forced her own misery to the back of her mind and stammered, "Well dear, we're not exactly plump in the pockets. If Genevieve—"

"Needs a rich husband?" he grinned. "'Fraid the shoe's on the other foot. She may not be the wealthiest heiress in Europe, but she's never going to have to worry about the price of tea! I shall feel positively guilty about offering for the sweet girl, in fact." A shadow crossed his face. "Everything considered."

"Speaking of offering..." said Sophia with a twinkle.

Whitthurst looked at her sharply. "You'd best give me the office, Chicky. He's liable to come asking permission to address you, and I should—"

"He already has."

He sprang up in bed, his eyes flashing. "He—*what*?"

"He offered to—er—bestow upon me one of the oldest names in England. And"—she tossed both arms wide and said dramatically—"all this!"

"By God!" cried Whitthurst, her humour escaping him. "How dared he approach you without first asking me? Fellow's uncouth, Sophia!"

She stared at him and thought of Phineas and the condescending proposal he had made her. "Uncouth?" she gurgled. "Oh! How that would enrage him, Steve!"

"I'll enrage him!" he muttered wrathfully. "What the devil did he say?"

"Well, he first showed me the most magnificent diamond and sapphire necklace I have ever—"

"I'll break his filthy neck!" cried the Viscount, tossing back the bedclothes and exposing a very hairy leg.

"Please do not," she said with amused affection. "Though I thank you for the impulse. It was not a gift. I suppose even Phinny would not be that gauche. He wanted me to wear it to the ball tonight. But I refused."

"So I should hope!" growled Whitthurst, settling back.

"And I refused *him*, dear. Though he was willing to overlook a great deal." She went to the dressing table and leaned closer to the mirror. "Do you think cosmetics could help my poor mouth?"

"Help it? What humdudgeon are you talking? Ain't hurt—is it?"

"No. But he was right, I do believe. It *is* a shade too wide."

She turned and found him gaping at her. "He never did!" A little light began to dance in his eyes. "You're making it up!"

"But, no. He will even forgive me my—huge nose, I collect."

Whitthurst gave a great whoop of laughter. "Oh, gad! This is rich! Don't he know our dear Regent wants Lawrence to paint you?"

"Apparently not, but he does have a discerning eye." She touched her nose doubtfully. "You don't suppose it really is—?"

"Poor Chicky! Such a bulbous monstrosity!" He succumbed to hilarity once again as she flew back to the mirror.

"You may laugh and tease, sir," she said with mock severity, "but our host was also quite willing to forgive my pitiful dowry!"

Whitthurst, wiping his eyes with a corner of the sheet, sighed, "You are a naughty puss is what you are, Sophia Drayton! And will be punished for making up such shocking whiskers!"

"It *is* fortunate, is it not, that I have several wealthy suitors? Dear Phinny and Lord Owsley and that kind Mr. Buckingham, and—" From beneath her lashes she slanted a glance at her brother. "You seem to think—your uncle . . . ?"

"Poor old Cam ain't in that league," Whitthurst said regretfully. "Properly in the basket, from all I hear. Serves him right, stupid gudgeon. He'll be lucky if he can get his spa finished in time to save his fool neck, and—Sophia! Are you ill?" He sprang up, all genuine concern, and crawled down the bed toward her. "Dear soul, you're white as a sheet!"

"Stephen," she gasped, clinging to him. "Camille's rich! He must be!"

"Was. But he's got too many dipping into his pockets. A bunch of leeches was you to ask me. And you'd not believe the blunt he's spent to improve the home farm and the village. Besides the Priory and the spa! Now he's thoroughly antagonized Vaille—blasted fool!"

'Good God!' she thought numbly, 'the Duke has cut him off! What have I done?'

Stephen's voice echoed as though she stood on one side of a great canyon and he on the other, but the words were indistinguishable. All she could think of was Camille's strained white face at that ghastly investors meeting...His searing rage when he'd locked the doors to the music room...the unutterable tenderness in his eyes just before he had kissed her.

She could all but feel that sweet embrace and, blinking up through her tears, exclaimed, "Oh! Stephen!" as she abruptly returned to reality.

"Yes—I'm here, dear. Whatever is troubling you?"

She clung to him for a moment, fighting for composure. And then, frantic lest she weaken and tell him everything, mumbled, "I'm just a...a silly chit, you know, Steve. I'm—" she pulled away and wiped at her eyes impatiently. "I'm just—jealous, you see. I had you back with me for...for such a short while. And now, I'm going to have to...lose you again."

Whitthurst scanned her face narrowly. She was closer to becoming a watering pot than he'd ever seen her. Whatever had so upset her was, he suspected, of a far more serious nature than a simple dread of his possible marriage. On the other hand, what she said was true. They'd always been very close, and had been reunited for a comparatively short space of time. Perhaps she really *was* grieving. He shook her gently. "Silly little girl. Even should Genevieve accept me, it would likely be months—if not years—before we could wed. You'll have me to fuss over until you are glad to see the back of me, never fear."

Sophia smiled, sniffed, and dried her eyes resolutely, while all the time conscience screamed, 'What have you done? You wicked jade! What have you done?'

Lord Edward Ridgley leaned back against the reference table in the library, folded his arms, and watched the distraught girl in silence. His confirmation of her fears had left her white and shaken, her eyes tearful, her hands tightly clasped. She looked small, alone and frightened. A situation of her own making had completely run away from her. And even so, she was more beautiful than any woman he had seen since Ninon...

"If I may make so bold, m'dear," he said kindly, "you underestimate Whitthurst. Do not now underestimate Damon, also. He's inclined to be top lofty, I grant you. But he's no fool. He'll find a way out of this mess."

Sophia regarded him uncertainly and, dabbing at her eyes with her dainty handkerchief, quavered, "I just do not understand. The Duke seems a kind man. Even though I could tell they were not exactly—close, surely he wouldn't turn his back if the Marquis were in desperate trouble?"

Ridgley scowled but said nothing. Sophia noted in an absent fashion the carefully colour-matched leather covers of the books. Very neat and very clinical. She thought of Damon's library and the many dog-eared, shabby books, the worn and broken backs, the oft-read and beloved favourites.

"Vaille don't know," said Ridgley gruffly. "Nor is Damon like to tell him. All the Brandens are mad." He gave a wry smile. "I thought you'd already realized that. But if you're wondering why I don't tell Vaille about the fix Cam's got himself into—good gad, I'd not dare! The boy has a ferocious temper! He'd never forgive me. And I am—rather deuced fond of him, d'ye see."

"I do see," she sighed. "He has made you promise you'll say nothing. Then I must try and do something." But what could she do? She'd given the money to Marcus, and the poor darling needed it so badly.

Watching her, the Earl said shrewdly, "Already spent, eh, ma'am?"

"I don't think so. But—I cannot give it back, I'm afraid."

He realized that she had given it to somebody else. Not Whitthurst—Clay? Of course! She doted on the man, and he'd been deep under the hatches. Bless the chit! Despite her fiery impetuousness, she'd a good heart!

"I shall have to tell my brother," Sophia said miserably. "I had so hoped he could have a few more days here, for he is much improved. But...there is no one else I can turn to. *Someone* must go to Devon and try to make Mr. Prendergast take down the fence, and I fear he'd not pay much heed to me."

Ridgley frowned. It would be a bitter blow to Whitthurst to discover what his sister had done. And a greater tragedy if the shock and humiliation sent his health tumbling once

210

more. Whitt looked happy again, and God knows, he deserved it. Camille had Thompson and Ariel at the Priory, or there could be no contemplating this. But he certainly needed help, and it just might be possible to throw a scare into that wicked old Prendergast . . . "Ma'am," he said tentatively, "if you have that note with you, I could go to Devon at once and try to effect some compromise—though I don't promise I'll succeed."

"Oh! Would you? Thank heaven! I do not have a copy of the note. Mr. Prendergast said he would send one, but it has not come. If I were to give you a letter, appointing you my agent . . . would that do?"

Sophia was unaccustomedly silent as her two maids fussed with the finishing touches to her toilette. Their awed exclamations woke her from her reverie, and standing to survey the results, she was pleased by her appearance. The gown Damon had sent was *not* too small. It fit so exactly, in fact, that she knew he must have borrowed one of her own and had careful measurements taken. The rich blue-violet enhanced her violet eyes. Connie had brushed her hair into a high cluster of curls atop her head, with one fat ringlet swooping to her right shoulder. Even the Viscount, escorting her downstairs, had nothing more critical to say than that the ladies would hate her with a passion. "Must say I still like the wide skirts and all those fluffy petticoats you was used to wear," he observed cheerfully. "Still, that's a good colour on you—dashed if it ain't." He grinned and added, "Might even win Phinny's approval—though I wouldn't refine on that!"

"Wretched one!" she scolded, squeezing his arm affectionately. "Good heavens, are they dancing already?"

They walked around the landing and started down the last spiral of the stairs. Music drifted pleasantly through the huge room. The air was sweetly scented by the fragrant blossoms of the great bouquets and hanging baskets. Already the hall was filling, and near the foot of the stairs, Lord Phineas and his sister, an angular lady named Mrs. Bridgley-West, who had come down from Bath for the occasion, stood receiving their guests.

Whitthurst, looking pathetically thin in his dark-maroon jacket and knee breeches, searched the throng eagerly. Glancing at him, Sophia's heart warmed, and she enquired

211

teasingly, "Do you see her, dear?"

"No. But—Oh...my...good...God!"

"What is it?" she demanded, her anxiety for him returning.

"Don't go into the boughs, Chicky," he implored. "For pity's sake—do not lose your temper!"

"Lose my temper? Why, Stephen—have you ever known me to—?" And she stared, immobile with shock. The ballroom was colour-matched to *her!* Instead of the black jacket she had expected from so formal an individual, Bodwin wore a peerlessly cut jacket of almost the exact shade as her new gown. The footmen wore blue waistcoats, the lackeys sported blue boutonnieres, even the maids hovering in the halls wore blue flowers in their hair. The bouquets, she now realized, were predominantly blue!

"Dear heaven!" she gasped. "I am part of a display! Oh! That *odious*—that *pompous*! Oh! How *could* he?"

"Rich as Croesus," Stephen grunted, misunderstanding. "Must have cost him a mountain of blunt, though, to have all those damned silly outfits tailored in jig time! Chicky!" He grabbed her arm. "Where are you going?"

"To change, of course!" she said furiously.

"You cannot! There's no time. Besides—you promised him you'd wear the frippery thing!"

"Let me go! I will *not* be put on exhibition like one of his prize possessions! We shall seem a *couple*! Stephen! It might almost be an *announcement*! *Oh*! How *dare* he!"

"Because he's a pompous damned ass! If he weren't so blasted well meaning, I should punch his head. But— They've seen us!"

"Ah," cried Lord Bodwin eagerly, "there you are, my dear Lady Sophia. And how exquisite you look!"

Mrs. Bridgley-West's pale face was upturned, her hard eyes filled with malice. Stephen hissed, "Please, Chicky! It's a devilish trick, but the poor old fool don't know how clumsy he is."

Seething, she knew that if she left, Stephen would also leave. And this was the first ball he'd wanted to attend since his illness. "Very well," she grated, baring her teeth in a tigerish smile, "but never—as long as I live—shall I forgive that insufferable windbag!"

"Dear Lady Sophia," crowed Bodwin. "Come and enjoy your moment of triumph!"

The dancers, gliding through the complications of a quadrille, created a brilliant, shifting pattern against the gleaming floor; the air rang with lilting music and the pleasant chatter of the glittering throng. Taffeta and satin rustled, feathers nodded, jewels sparkled. Beautifully decorated fans fluttered in dainty hands; jewel-encrusted quizzing glasses swung from strong, gloved fingers. And everywhere speculation was rife. Sophia Drayton and Phineas Bodwin? Was it possible? He was fabulously wealthy, true, and what lady would not desire such a magnificent home—such a dozen, in fact, of beautiful homes? But—Sophia Drayton? The toast of Italy, the darling of London, the girl who was known to have reproved the Prince himself and earned only a laugh and a wink from that notorious gentleman? Bodwin was old enough to be her father. He was handsome, admittedly: a fine figure of a man. And many an ardent beau gazed enviously at the elegant Lord Bodwin, while many a lovely lady looked with curiosity upon the incredible beauty of The Drayton.

Feather, beset on every side, was irked by the enquiries until she realized what had triggered them. She made her way to Whitthurst and, drawing him apart from a noisy group of young men, said urgently, "The *ton* is agog! Is Sophia like to murder our host?"

"At the very least," he answered with a rueful grin. "Can't say I blame her. She didn't notice it in time, y'see, ma'am, and couldn't very well create a scene at the last minute."

"She's handling herself very well. See how she smiles upon him."

Whitthurst saw and shuddered. "Poor Bodwin. By tomorrow we'll be on our way back to Kent." A vision in a cloud of pink silk and chiffon came toward him. His eyes took on a glazed look. His lips formed her name, but no sound could be heard. Feather watched mistily as they drifted to one another and, with a sigh for yesterdays, went in search of her good friend, Lucinda.

"What I should do," Sophia gritted as Harry Redmond handed her a glass of punch, "is leave this fiasco! Never have I been so mortified! Look at all those spiteful cats. See how they smile at me, then titter behind their fans!"

"Then laugh," advised Sir Harry wisely, his green eyes dancing with mischief. "Bodwin ensnared you very neatly and has announced his intentions and your apparent acceptance without saying a word. I find it hilarious."

"Then you, cousin," Sophia remarked with a trill of insincere laughter, "are as odious as Bodwin is foolish."

"In which case, my dear," he countered, "I am not in the least odious." She glanced at him, her head tilted questioningly, and he warned, "Bodwin may appear foolish, and self-opinionated he most certainly is. But he's as safe to cross as a Bengal tiger."

"You jest, surely?"

"No, ma'am. I do not. Aha!" His sober gaze brightened. "Now Phinny's ball is an assured success. Look who just arrived."

Sophia looked, and her heart turned over. Damon stood near the stairs, his intent gaze turned to her. Their eyes met across that crowded room and, for an instant, it was as though none was between them. Then he bowed politely over the hand of the Countess of Carden, and friends pressed in, surrounding him.

Sophia tore her eyes away from his dark head and realized with a sudden ache of grief that Redmond was murmuring something. "Your pardon, Harry?"

"It was of no importance—and I'd not thought to bring you to tears!" Dismayed, he stepped closer. "What's wrong, love? Can I—"

"No, no. It is nothing. Please do not—"

"Lady Sophia . . . ?"

How that deep voice plunged an arrow through her heart. Fighting for composure, she turned to meet eyes that glittered in a face pale with rage and powder. His bruises were effectively hidden, but—Camille in powder? She felt an hysterical urge to giggle and only with a great effort managed a cool "Lord Damon, how pleasant to see you again."

"You look very lovely, ma'am," he said with a sardonic smile, straightening from the briefest touch of his lips upon her hand. "And the colour becomes you far more than some of those you have permitted to copy it."

"Evening, Cam," said Sir Harry politely.

"Camille," Sophia begged, low-voiced. "If you will let me explain, I—"

"Egad, my lady, I am not blind." His brows lifted, and he drawled, "And must not allow myself to become confused. I'd come to think Hartwell was to be the lucky man. Now it would seem I must offer my congratulations to Phineas."

214

Looking from the cynical hauteur of the Marquis to the flushed features of his cousin, Sir Harry smiled, "Awfully good to see you, Cam."

"Does it indeed, my lord?" frowned Sophia.

The Marquis lifted his quizzing glass languidly to inspect her, the flowers, and the distant form of Lord Bodwin. "What a charmingly coordinated picture." And he added wickedly, "Almost a uniform—you would look so well, side by side, atop a wedding cake...Or—do I detect a treat in store? Is there to be some kind of group entertainment later in the evening?"

"I am sure you will both excuse me," Sir Harry grinned.

"Group entertainment!" gasped Sophia.

"Cheerio!" Redmond laughed and deserted the field of combat.

"All you need," sneered Damon, eyes glittering, "are the Bodwin sapphires, and your costume would be complete."

"If you must know, I refused them. It would have been most improper!"

Damon appraised a passing footman, glorious in his blue waistcoat, and said with a curl of the lip, "Belated awareness, ma'am?"

"You," she hissed, "are extreme offensive tonight, sir. Did you come purely to be odious?"

"Apparently, since I am sadly at odds with your colour scheme. I do possess a blue jacket. Would you wish, ma'am, that I go home and change?"

Sophia drew a deep breath and, knowing that many eyes were upon them, opened her fan with a snap that almost rendered it in twain and, with a forced smile, grated, "Thank you for this beautiful gown, my lord. Though I will admit I had no least intention to wear it tonight."

"What a great pity," he said in a bored fashion, "that you changed your mind."

"So there you are, Damon."

They had been so wrapped in their quarrel that neither had noted the Duke approaching, and they stared at him, equally astonished.

Sophia dropped a curtsey in response to Vaille's bow. Rising, she shot a glance at the Marquis and found his attention fixed upon a lady virtually surrounded by admirers, whose answering gaze seemed to hold a warning. Charlotte Hilby had surely never looked lovelier, gowned in an exquisite misty chiffon that seemed to an irritated Sophia exactly the

215

shade of Damon's eyes.

His father's presence astounded the Marquis. He knew he had always disliked Bodwin, but before he could speak, Vaille murmured gently, "A private word with you, if you please, my lord."

Sophia experienced a surge of nervousness, wondering what sins the Duke had now discovered in his errant heir; and then Genevieve was hurrying to join them, aglow with happiness, her hand on the arm of a so obviously lovestruck Whitthurst even Vaille's stern countenance softened.

Bodwin appeared at Sophia's elbow, begging that she keep her promise and sing for them. She was ushered to the dais, willy-nilly; the orchestra struck up, and she sang. Conversation was busy in the room when she began. By the time she finished, total stillness prevailed. A storm of applause rang out, with shouts of "Encore! Encore!" She sang again, the old Zingari air her father had particularly loved. And again their response was tumultuous. Bodwin, delighted by this success, prevailed upon her to sing "that lovely piece" she had sung for them at the Priory. She agreed and, glancing to Damon as the orchestra struck up, found his brooding gaze upon her. Somehow she made herself look away as she sang the words that would, to her, always belong to him. At the end, knowing she had never sung better despite her heartbreak, she looked again to Camille. He was bending to listen to something Miss Hilby whispered, apparently paying no least attention to the song. A knife turned in Sophia's breast as she was practically carried from the dais by a swarm of admirers. The ovation was deafening. Deluged with compliments, adored, flirted with, worshipped, she was swept into a refreshment room and plied with ices, cakes, and delicacies. From the corner of her eye, she saw Damon come in, at once creating a center of attention. He was in a light-hearted mood now, and she heard his deep laugh ring out several times. Not once did he seem to glance her way, and eventually he returned to dance attendance upon an obviously worried Miss Hilby.

Sophia's cup should have been full. Many of the *ton*'s most eligible bachelors were vying jealously for her smiles; compliments upon her talent, her beauty, her charm, were showered upon her; less successful ladies cast her envious looks; hopeful mamas put up their lorgnettes and viewed her with disapprobation. But her triumph was hollow. At last, she excused herself, slipped away, and all but ran to the back stairs. Climbing to her room, her heart felt like lead. How cold he had seemed. Well, why not? She had let Bodwin trick her into what must have seemed a mockery of his kindness in buying her such a lovely gown—*and* she had ruined the man! But he'd known that at Cancrizans after the meeting, and his tenderness had been...so...She blinked away tears and hastened her steps. She must not forget what manner of man he was. She must not forget poor little Nancy...

She secured herself in her room and was about to indulge herself in a good cry when the door opened and a maid hurried in. Sophia turned quickly away, dabbing at her eyes with her handkerchief.

"I seed ye come in here, m'lady, and seein's how it do be—"

She spun around with a shocked gasp, "Nancy!"

"Aye, Lady Sophia," the girl beamed. "Though I see ye've no need for me—ye look that beautiful!"

"But...how?" Sophia struggled to gather her wits. "I mean—I thought...Well, it must have been such a...ghastly experience!"

Nancy nodded, her face sobering. "That it were, ma'am! Proper scared I were. Not to say cross as crabs!"

It seemed an odd reaction, but Sophia held out her arms. "Poor child" After a second's hesitation, the girl came to be hugged, and Sophia stroked her soft hair and said comfortingly, "You need never be afraid again. I shall take care of you!"

Nancy looked at her wonderingly. "Ye be very good, m'lady. But—'tis over now, and no cause for'ee to look so dreary-eyed."

She seemed quite in spirits, and Sophia thought wretchedly, 'Oh, Camille! How could you abuse her when she is so innocent?' "You shall come back to Kent with me," she smiled, and added nobly, "You will not have to face shame alone!"

Nancy grinned. "Why, I doan't reckon it do be that bad, ma'am."

"You don't. Oh, my," said Sophia in failing accents. "You are...more worldly than I...had thought."

"Ar—now that I be! Very worldy! Why, I been to *Paris*, m'lady! Last spring—'fore Old Boney went on the rampage again, Miss Hilby taked me with her!" She nodded proudly. "I bean't no country pumpkin, Lady Sophia!"

There was little doubt but that the poor girl's intellect had become disordered. Fighting tears, Sophia murmured, "I am so relieved to find you looking well. And how very kind of Lord Bodwin to take you in."

"He bean't have taked *me* in, m'lady!" Indignation dawned in the blue eyes. "Not as how he hasn't tried. Very quick with his hands be his lordship! If Miss Hilby hadn't of asked me to come and help Lady Branden and the little Mamzelly, I'd— Oh! M'lady! Come'ee now—sit ye down! Oh, my gracious! Maybe'ee should put your pretty head 'twixt your knees. I see the natural do that to Mrs. Grimsby once when she come over queer with her fourth—right in the middle of the curate's sermon on sin!"

Sophia heard the words but dimly. She felt faint. Before her eyes was Camille, lying under that tree, so battered and bleeding...and she'd not even stayed to help him...She clutched at the girl's hand. "Why are you here? Miss Hilby did not send you!"

"But she did, ma'am. 'T'were that day as the Duke come so unexpected like. I own I were disappointed 'cause my Mum and Dad live outside of Cerne Abbas, and usually when we go to the Priory, Miss Hilby lets me slip home for a bit. I knowed once the Duke come as how I wouldn't be able to get away. Well, anyways, I likes to take a little walk afore dinner—always has if the weather be fine—so as soon as Miss Hilby goes down that afternoon, off I hops. I was by them trees along the road when a chaise come flying up, and there's me old carpet bag alongside o' the groom, and he's a'telling me to pop in, smart-like 'cause I'm to go to Bodwin Hall and take care of the Mamzelly and Lady Branden, who was a'coming the next day."

"But..." said Sophia dazedly, "Miss Hilby thought...we all thought...But—surely they had their maids at Bodwin Hall already?"

"Aye. That's what I thinked, too—though they're not the best I ever did see, ma'am...always making sheeps' eyes at the footmen and a sight too uppity—"

"Your father! What about your poor father?"

Nancy looked at her uneasily. "My—father? I never did get to see him, to be sure, nor me Mum, bein's I spent the night under the hedge! That were the worst of it! Mr. Taylor took a 'short cut,' he says! Long way to Brummagem, more like! First the wheel come loose, then the team broke free

218

while Mr. Taylor was a'fixing of it. And I must say as he was slow, was that there Mr. Taylor. My Ariel could've done it in jig time! I was fair froze, and the end of it was we had to walk all the way to a farm miles from nowhere, and Mr. Taylor comes and gets me when the chaise is repaired and the horses found. Only that be the following evening!"

"But—you sent word that your Papa was ill, and—"

"I never did! Why—that would be fair asking for me Dad to get struck down. If you'll excuse me for saying so, ma'am!"

"But—weren't Lady Branden and Mademoiselle Genevieve surprised to see you?"

Nancy considered this carefully. "Come to think on it, m'lady, they was a little put about at first. But when I explained, they didn't go into a taking. And next day, Mr. Taylor come with a message from Miss Hilby that I was to set here and wait 'til she come back. Though how she'll go on without me, I cannot think! No one but me knows how she likes her hair, especial when—"

"This—Mr. Taylor," Sophia intervened, "do you know him well?"

"Never do have seed him afore... he must be new." Wrinkling her brow, Nancy knelt beside Sophia's chair. "I bean't a clever maid, ma'am. But something do be wrong, I think. I'd take it kindly if ye'd tell me of it."

Sophia pressed a hand to her temple distractedly. "I cannot think. My head feels so stupid...The note! The note you sent to Ariel, telling him that Lord Damon had molested you in the wood! Didn't—"

Nancy gave a little shriek and, throwing both hands to her scarlet cheeks, cowered, crying, "Oh! What a dreful bad thing for ye to say! How could'ee think such wickedness of him? Or—of me! Oh...my...*Lor'*!" She grabbed up her apron, buried her face in it, and burst into tears.

Sophia gazed blankly at that bowed head. So he had been blameless, as he'd told Luke. She'd known somehow that he just couldn't be that kind of animal. But something was terribly wrong. *Someone* had written the note. Why? And why hadn't he explained when she'd all but begged him to deny it? Had he been affronted because she'd believed the filthy lie? Was that why he'd let her go on thinking...

"M'lady?" Damp fingers touched her wrist. Nancy, her eyes abrim, stared at her in terror. "You said...I sent a note...to *Luke*? Ma'am—I cannot write, but I never let him

219

know that. I—didn't want him thinking I'd nought in me head but hair. Did—does Ariel think—?"

"Yes. I fear he did think it—"

"Oh, God! Oh, my God!" Nancy sprang to her feet in a frenzy. "Then Lord Damon do be dead! Or dying! I knowed the minute I seed ye so sorrowful as there be something wrong. But I never thought...Oh, how *could* he believe it? Lord Damon, who has always treated me so kind and good. And never put a naughty hand on me. Oh! Oh! Oh!"

"Hush, dear." Sophia went swiftly to the hysterical girl. "They fought be—"

"Fought! Oh, ma'am—Luke loved Lord Damon like he was his own brother! He knowed his lordship couldn't fight him back!"

"But he did, and quite well, really," said Sophia, pride overtaking her. "I—"

"Doan't ma'am," Nancy sobbed. "Doan't'ee tell me of it. I can't bear to hear! No man could never stand up to my Luke. Oh, poor Lord Damon...such a fine handsome man to be cut down so young..." She raised a tear-streaked face. "Be they after him, m'lady? Be the Runners after my Luke already? Oh, may God forgive me for teasing him! I should've married the dear soul long since. And now—it be too late! And I do so love him."

"Stop, stop, my poor child, and listen to me!" Sophia forced her own quavering voice to be heard above the violent sobs. "The Marquis was *not* killed. I haven't seen Ariel since, but he is trying to find you. And I know Lord Damon has men trying to find *him*. And that he does not intend to have him punished."

Nancy fell into her arms, and they wept together.

Chapter 20

Sophia paused on the last flight of stairs, her eyes searching the ballroom. She had summoned the housekeeper and placed Nancy in her reluctant care, requiring that the girl be conveyed to Cerne Abbas at once. Nancy, her swimming eyes bespeaking her gratitude, had mumbled a promise that she would take Ariel to the Priory as soon as she found him. Now, seized by a frightening sense of urgency, she looked in vain for Camille. A boulanger was in progress. Bodwin was Genevieve's partner—fortunately. She continued to the foot of the stairs, and at once several gentlemen started hopefully toward her. Foremost among them was Whitthurst, and she blessed him mentally for coming so swiftly to her side.

"You look like the devil, Chicky," he said quietly, drawing her away.

Accustomed to such brotherly admonishments, she asked if he'd seen Damon.

"Went off with Vaille just a minute or two ago. One of the

221

anterooms, I think. Sophia! Wait—you must not—"

But she was already hurrying into the side hall, eluding the friends and acquaintances who sought to detain her. The occupants of the first room, locked in a passionate embrace, were not even aware of her having opened and closed the door. The lady in the next room let out a shriek that betrayed her uneasy conscience, and there was not need for any enquiry. The third door opened onto a double room in the outer chamber of which stood a pale and frightened Charlotte Hilby. The closed connecting door betrayed the presence of an extremely vexed gentleman beyond it. Recognizing Vaille's voice at its most acid, Sophia hurried to clasp Charlotte's outstretched hands.

"...moved heaven and earth," Vaille was saying, "to get you to Oxford where you might have learned how a British gentleman behaves! Since I did not do so, I can now only rely upon whatever the French have bred into you. Which, I might add, seems precious little! Be silent, sir! Nor dare to interrupt me again! You know how dear to me are your Mother's possessions. Instead of selling these—" A small clatter was heard. "Why in the name of God did you not come to me and explain that you felt beholden to repay your investors? Oh, do not look so shocked. I have ways of discovering such things."

"So...I see." Damon sounded breathless.

"And that," Vaille rasped, "is no answer!"

Charlotte drew Sophia to a love seat and they sat together, holding one another's hands, each heart beating very fast. In a remote fashion Sophia realised how incongruous it was that she should cling to this woman she had often felt impelled to scratch. A woman she now knew she would fight tooth and nail to prevent winning Camille. Yet, at this moment, the only thing that mattered was that he was in great trouble, and that each of them loved him.

"Since I have no intention of accepting your terms, sir," Damon responded coolly, "I felt I could not approach you in the matter."

"Indeed! And would prefer to be cut off entirely, I take it!" Receiving no audible reply, the Duke went on in a voice that made Sophia's heart ache. "Am I then...so repulsive to you?"

There was a pause, after which Damon reiterated in a flat, unemotional tone, "I cannot accept your offer, sir."

Charlotte gave a little whimper. Sophia moaned a faint

222

"Why does Camille persist in antagonizing him?"

"In that case," Vaille said harshly, "I must insist upon a prior claim to the rest of your Mother's jewels. They mean a great deal to me, at least. But you will not be out of pocket. I will purchase them from you."

Sophia winced, and Miss Hilby whispered a reproachful "Oh, Philip!"

Damon's response was markedly uneven. "I sold...them all, sir."

"*You...what*? The rubies, also? Now if I do not discover and *re*cover 'em speedily, by God, you'll rue the day!" That whiplash of a voice was stilled, and then Vaille resumed, in a purring tone Sophia found even more terrifying. "But I forget to whom I speak. Damon—oblige me by removing your jacket."

"Dear heaven!" Miss Hilby was on her feet, her face white as death.

Sophia thought wretchedly, 'She knows...and still she loves him.'

The seconds seemed to stretch into minutes. Damon's reply was calm. "May I ask why, your grace?"

"You may not." And after a few more nerve-wracking seconds, "Thank you. It grieves me to disturb so impressive a shirt, but—roll up your left sleeve, if you please."

Miss Hilby gave a sob. Sophia was shaking, dreading what must follow.

"That will not be necessary," Damon said slowly. "I was a member of Cobra. My code name was Scorpion."

"Dear God!" The Duke's voice was hoarse. "How I prayed it was a lie! For five hundred years, not one major blemish on our family name. No madness, no cowardice, no deformities, and, above all—no disgrace! And now...For Christ's sake—how can you stand there and say nothing? Look at me, sir! Look me in the eyes and tell me the truth. Did you join willingly? Or were you forced into it? Blackmailed? Tricked?" That pained voice broke, and, on a near sob, the proud Vaille gasped, "Only tell me and I'll believe you."

"I joined...willingly."

Vaille groaned. "You cannot have...enjoyed it. Give me that, at least."

Damon said haltingly, "I—thoroughly...enjoyed—"

Tormented, Vaille uttered an inarticulate cry. There was the distinct sound of a loud slap.

223

Sophia was on her feet now, her hands pressed to her mouth. Charlotte rushed to fling open the door. Vaille, his expression a mask of anguish, stood with one hand swung back for the return blow. Damon, very erect, watched him unflinchingly, though his face was almost the colour of his shirt.

"Philip!" Charlotte implored. "For the love of God!"

The Duke's blazing eyes shot to her. Somehow he was able to restrain that upraised hand. The thin fingers clenched, then lowered.

The quivering silence held until the Duke's flushed cheeks paled, his tumultuous breathing quieted, and the rageful grief faded from his eyes. He took up Damon's jacket and tossed it to him. "You—sir," he said with low-voiced contempt, "are no son of mine! If it was in my power to cut you out of the succession, I would do so. You have left me only one thing for which to be grateful...that my beloved wife did not live to see this day! For her sake, I shall see to it that you are provided with an allowance. Sufficient to live without shame. Outwardly, at least. Should we meet in a public place, I shall thank you to refrain from addressing me!" His voice failed him a little as he saw the flinch that his son was unable to repress, but he ended remorselessly, "It will be better for us both, my Lord Damon, do I not set eyes upon you again."

The Marquis stood silent and unmoving. His hands clenched until the nails bit into his palms, but the white, drawn face, the suffering in those blue eyes, were more than he could bear, and his head went down. He felt the movement of the air and closed his eyes as the Duke strode past him.

Charlotte, grasping Vaille's arm with a heroism that awed Sophia, pleaded, "Do not go! Philip, I beg of you. Do not let such terrible words lie between you! Oh, Philip...please..."

Vaille detached her hand and swept on. Tears beading her lashes, she turned from proud and stately Duke to shattered Marquis. "I'll try to talk to him," she promised chokingly. She put a hand on his arm, but he did not move. "Don't worry, Camille. I'll try to make him see reason."

Damon whispered something, and she gave a little sob and ran down the hall.

Sophia's knees were jelly, and she sat down once more, waiting. Damon's shoulders sagged, but for a minute or two he made no other movement. At last, as though he sensed her presence, he turned to her. His eyes were dulled, and he looked exhausted. The mark his father's hand had left was glowing on his face beneath the powder, and she was reminded of the first time she had slapped him, never dreaming what the future held. He ran a hand through his hair in the familiar gesture of exasperation and muttered, "If you heard it all, ma'am, why do you stay?"

"Because I must talk to you." She was surprised that she could speak so steadily.

"Not now," he said wearily.

She walked swiftly forward, blocking the doorway as he shrugged into his jacket. His eyes moved past her, and from the empty room behind her, a man coughed discreetly. Sophia stepped aside, and a footman, gazing at a point some inches above the Marquis's telltale face, intoned a sepulchral "A note for your lordship. By special messenger." He handed Damon a folded paper, bowed in acknowledgment of the crisp thanks, and took himself off, his eyes sliding sideways for just long enough to register the name and rank of the lady involved.

"Well, now we're properly in the soup," Damon muttered, breaking the seal. "Between my face, your presence, and the fact I was putting my jacket on when that dolt—"

Sophia's gasp was echoed by the Marquis as he read the letter, crushed the paper, and stood glaring down at his clenched hand. "Where's Ridgley?" he demanded. "Here—yes?"

"No." Taken aback by the fierce light in his eyes, she said, "He went to Devon to try and reason with Mr. Prendergast. As my agent."

He took a pace toward her, those dark brows downdrawn in a heavy scowl. "Alone? Wasn't Hartwell with him?"

"Amory? Why—no. Lord Ridgley went with Major Henderson."

"Buzzy Henderson?" he asked keenly. "Of the Seventh?"

"Yes. He was staying here, but his wife is increasing, and he became worried and decided not to remain for the ball. He lives in Torquay. They journey together."

He stared at her for another long moment, then started for the door.

"I *must* talk to you!" she cried.

"I haven't the time, ma'am. Stand aside, if you please."

"No! Camille, I want to know—Oh! Put me down, sir!"

He did not put her down. He held her for a moment, close

225

against his heart, his eyes searching her face with a yearning desperation. Her own anger faded. She forgot about Nancy and Ariel; she forgot poor Vaille and his grief; she forgot Cobra. All that mattered was the handsome face before her. All she knew was the need to throw her arms about his neck, to feel the dear pressure of that sensitive mouth...

Damon set her down and said with a bitter smile, "What a damnable fool I am! What a weak-kneed failure! I shouldn't have come. But—I did want to see you in that gown..." His eyes drank her in hungrily as he held her at arm's length. With a short laugh, he said, "It will be something to hold in my memory..." She stretched out her arms appealingly, and he stiffened and turned away. "Gad, how I forget myself still. The complete cad! What would my affianced think?"

Sophia had heard men talk of having been kicked by mules. She knew now how it must feel. "Your...affianced?"

"I'm to be married. Quite soon, I suspect, if the lady has her way." He strolled to a corner table and affected to inspect a paperweight that lay there.

Recovering a little, she followed and tugged at his sleeve. He faced her, a cynical half smile still upon his face. She said firmly, "You are *not* going to marry Charlotte." He looked astonished, and she went on. "I am sorry that she will grieve, but you love *me*— I know you won't admit it, but then you lie so much, it's hard to know where you begin! You lied about Nancy!"

Blinking dazedly, he said a low-voiced "I said nothing of it."

"Which was in itself a lie! You lied to your father about Cobra!"

He sighed and, putting down the paperweight, reached for his sleeve.

Sophia placed her fingers over his hand. "I have seen your scorpion. You may have been a member, but I shall never believe you joined willingly."

Damon pulled quickly away and said with a bored shrug, "Why would I lie about such a thing? Do not be ridiculous." Glancing up, he smiled unpleasantly. "I assure you, ma'am, I was a most—active...member."

"One would never guess it," she flashed, "considering that *I* am pursuing *you*! And it is you who profess to be the filthy, lecherous libertine who...Camille? What are you...doing?"

"Realizing you are right." He moved very close, his smile

226

incalculably evil. "Because I am your uncle, I have held you in high regard. But you inflame me, I'll not deny it. Nor any longer restrain my natural instincts."

"Good!" she cried, and threw her arms around his neck.

Several eons later, he lifted his head from the glory of her mouth, looked yearningly into the glowing tenderness of her eyes, joyed in the firm young beauty of her, leaning so trustingly in his arms. And pulling her even tighter against him, he closed his own eyes and after a long, precious moment murmured, "What a fool I am, not to have realized you have already found a way for us."

She smiled happily and snuggled her cheek closer under his chin.

"Sophia, beloved. How I adore you. But—we'll have to wait—just a little while. For appearance's sake, my heart."

She looked up at him questioningly. "Appearance's—?"

"Well, I can't very well—ah—arrange things just at first. I shall have to take her to Spain, I think. But as soon as we're home..."

A chill touched her. She pulled herself away. "Camille? What is it?"

"Why, our arrangement, dearest. I dared not suggest it, though I've wanted you...you must know that—almost from the first instant we met. I'd not dreamed you would be so sensible, so understan—"

"So," she said, her lips cold and stiff, "you will marry Charlotte for her fortune. And I...will become your...mistress..."

"*Bien-aimée*. I shall cherish you forever. And how shall it matter? You will have everything money can buy—for Charlotte has a great deal of that, at least. Ah, do not look so sad, my heart. I can set you up in style once she is my wife. Were it not for that curst immovable father of mine, *you* would become my Marchioness. But he's cut me off altogether. We have no alternative, you see."

"Perhaps...we do," she said faintly. "I have a very fine emerald, Camille. We might manage...quite well without—her...if we were careful."

He gave a muffled sound and swung away from her and after a second said harshly, "Scarcely. Would your emerald give me back my spa? Enable me to complete the Priory?"

"It would last us—for a year. And then—Marcus will pay me back."

"Clay?" He tensed, and glanced at her. "You gave the money to Clay? What a joke! I cannot wait a year! The roof is not on the stables, nor part of the hotel. The barn is complete, but there is much still to be done on the main buildings. The canals are dug but not paved. Were a whole year of rain and weeds and wind to have their way, half the work would be ruined. If I could complete the spa at once, we might manage...but I cannot—and Vaille is a relatively young man, Sophia. A vigourous man. For as long as he lives, I would exist on a pittance. I could not endure that." He turned to her, his smile eager, his eyes very bright and hard. "No matter. This way is surer, with less effort. Sophia—most beautiful and desired of women—what a life we shall have— you and I."

"It would...break...Charlotte's heart," she whispered.

He gave one of his small, graceful, and very French gestures, and she thought achingly that he had never looked more handsome—or more ruthless. "Come, now, *ma chère*,"— he took her by the shoulders—"we do not live in the Middle Ages! It is, after all, quite the thing. Charlotte must eventually agree to whatever we—"

She spun away and sobbed out, "How could you be so cruel? She worships you! How could you believe I would suggest anything so...so crude...and immoral?"

He looked bewildered. "But—I thought...you said—"

"You thought me a cheat! A wanton who would betray her friend! Can you think I would take my happiness by breaking the heart of someone else?"

He stepped closer, his eyes anxious now. "Such a dramatic child...But it is done all the time, my heart. You have only to look around."

She backed away, one small step at a time, knowing all her hopes lay in ashes and her future would be a dreary emptiness. "Do not..." she said in a gasping little voice, "*ever*...come near me again!" And on the words, she turned and left him alone.

The fire was dying in the beautiful parlour fireplace, only an occasional flicker of flame lighting the gold leaf of the mantle. Sophia made no move to add a log, although the room was growing chill, and she shivered a little as she huddled on the doubtful comfort of the Louis XIV sofa. Her brows

228

were knit above her dulled eyes because her efforts to recall the evening were proving useless. The last thing she remembered with any real clarity was that ghastly little ante-room, the terrible quarrel, and her subsequent idiocy. She had a vague impression of having seen Damon stalk across the ballroom, his face a thundercloud; of having danced a good deal and laughed too much and too shrilly. She had flirted outrageously with Phinny, poor man, and God knows who else. Longing to creep away and hide like the poor wounded creature she was, she had forced herself to see it through, to deny them all the pleasure of another *on dit*. Stephen had not interfered, though he had seldom been far away and watched her with a worried frown; and twice Genevieve had come and slipped an arm about her, enquiring if everything was all right. Dear fortunate little Genevieve...loving and loved.

Self-pity was deplorable, and she knew she was unutterably foolish to feel such a horrible sense of loss. She should be glad to have discovered in time that he was just as she had initially imagined him. Selfish and utterly without honour.

She wiped automatically at her reddened eyes with her sodden handkerchief. She would not have thought she'd any tears left. She had made a total fool of herself—but one learned from one's mistakes...surely? She had imagined herself in love with an unworthy and evil man, an aristocratic, soulless gigolo. And yet how tenderly he had held her. How ineffably dear that kiss. And—God help her! How she loved him! Even now! She put her hands over her face and bowed forward, weeping again and wondering that her mind did not fail her, so torn was she between love and loathing. And she realized at last, with a forlorn helplessness, that there was no real loathing. Only grief—and despair.

A hand touched her shoulder. A beloved voice said, "Chicky...do not."

In a second, she was clasped tight against her brother's shoulder, sobbing her heart out, grateful beyond words for the comfort of his presence.

After a while, she took the dry handkerchief he offered, wiped her eyes, sniffed unashamedly, and finished. "And that's all there is, dearest. Only...I feel so sorry for...poor Vaille." She blew her nose, afraid to tell Whitthurst the whole, having omitted all reference to Charlotte and the shameful proposal Damon had made her after the Duke had gone.

"And you, dear?" he asked kindly. "Do you realize now that Damon is not the man for you? That you will find somebody else?"

His eyes were very intent, and Sophia blinked rapidly, struggling for control, but two great tears spilled over and streaked down her cheeks, and her brother, his arm tightening about her, said, "Oh, Chicky...my poor darling!"

Clinging to him, she whimpered helplessly, "It's no use...you see. I have tried so hard to hate him, Stephen. But—somehow it always...goes wrong. Each time I am determined to quarrel with him, I wind up...loving him a little bit more. I must be witless. I know what he is, and still I cannot help it. No matter how low...and vile...and contemptible! I cannot—"

"Be still! Dammit! That's enough!" He tore away from her and strode to the mantle, glaring down at the smouldering fire. His hand formed a tight fist. He slammed it repeatedly against the mantle and swore softly, as she had never heard him swear. Her mouth dropped open in bewilderment. This raging, snarling, bitter man could not be her gentle Stephen? This blast of profanity could not be issuing from that sweet mouth that had never cursed before her—except for small oaths at times of great provocation.

Whitthurst drew his hand across his eyes, was briefly silent, then turned to face her fully. And she was afraid because he looked grim and older—not at all like her light-hearted, happily-in-love brother.

"I should have told you long ago," he said in a hard, forced voice, "but I lacked the courage. And then Cam said I must not...for your own safety, so—"

"My...what?" she gasped.

"So I took the easy way," he went on wretchedly, "and convinced myself that he was right." He took a deep breath, his chin came up, and his shoulders drew back. "Do you remember what you said when you described Cobra to me?"

Sophia stared blankly, and he gave a bitter smile. "I do. Oh, so well! You said they were the dregs of mankind. The lowest, most wretched beasts that ever walked this land. And it was true. They were—they are—just as you described, and worse. And I suppose that's why...knowing that you knew of them, knowing what Papa had said, I—could not bear to..."

230

Her brother bit his lip and, as if the words were torn from him, groaned, "Sophia—*I* was a member!"

The breath caught in her throat. *Stephen*? "No!" she cried ringingly, jumping to her feet, stretching out her hands to him. "I don't believe it! Not you!"

He watched her in abject misery but made no move to touch her. How horrified she was—and rightly so. God forbid she ever knew the full story of what had gone on in Green Willow Castle! God forbid she ever had to lie awake at night, remembering...as he did!

"It was Damon," she cried frenziedly. "*He* got you into it! It was—"

"Do you not understand yet? Cam joined but only to protect me! Were it not for your contemptible Viper, I would be as dead today as the man they murdered and the dogs they killed to torment him! He saved my life, Sophia! And thereby—God help him—has ruined his own!"

Her knees gave out under her. Her throat was dry, and the room seemed to fade into shadows. Vaguely, she realized Whitthurst was helping her to sit down.

"I do not understand," she whispered, clutching at him. "What—?"

He sat beside her, his face white and strained. "Don't talk, my dear. Listen. And—try not to hate me—too much."

Chapter 21

Thompson carried the silver tray into the music room and paused, scowling toward the chair where his master sprawled, his long legs thrust out before him, one hand over his eyes, the other trailing over the chair arm, loosely holding an empty goblet. It was the chit who'd brought his lordship to this pass. He'd knowed the minute he'd laid eyes on her, with her looks and her shape and Quality wrote all over her. A fine damned mess! He stalked forward, and his scowl deepened as the Marquis lowered his hand, leered up at him, and said thickly, "Took y'time!"

"Thought you was asleep, milord," Thompson growled.

"Almos' was. Poten' stuff this brandy." He waved his glass and mumbled, "Pour me'nother, if y'please."

"You've had too much a'ready," his devoted minion observed.

"That'll be'nuff outta you!" warned Damon, shaking one finger in owlish reproof. "Bring th' damn brandy...an' ...sight less disrespec'!"

Holding his master's hand steady while he half filled the goblet, Thompson announced coldly, "I been thinking on re-tiring."

"Good idea," choked Damon, a little watery-eyed from having taken rather too large a gulp. "Y'may now... retire, an' curl up in y'r li'l beddy." This deliberate misinterpretation amused him, and he chuckled foolishly.

"To a farm," clarified Thompson, aiming a polar stare at the top of his lordship's windblown locks. "And if you pour it down yer gullet like that, you'll be drunk as a wheelbarrow 'fore you can say—"

"Jim Ro-Robinson!" said Damon, and raised a triumphant cheer.

"About my farm," Thompson glowered.

Damon waved a dismissing hand. "Farms—smelly places. No self 'specting butler'd be s-seen dead in one!"

"*You* got three," Thompson pointed out sapiently. "An' if you'd not put more into 'em than what you've took out, bringing 'em up to snuff—"

"Never cared much f'snuff," Damon mused. "Vaille uses it, though. Spanish... Spanish Bran, mixed with a li'l Br-Brass...?"

"Brazil!" snorted Thompson.

Damon peered up at him. "You try that, too? Never would've thought it! An t'think you use th' same 's *Mon Pere*. Whoops! Mus'n call him that!" He chortled merrily at this fine joke.

"I take leave," said Thompson in his best London accent, "to tell your lordship as how your lordship is foxed." He slanted a reproving glance at the hilarity this remark elicited and, feeling safer now, ventured scathingly, "What I'd like to know is—how you going to get up early in the morning? Which is a whole fat four hours from this here minute!"

"*Get... up... early?* Good God! Why should I do... 'gusting thing like that?"

"To meet your foreman on the site is why! Going to pay off all the contractors. Remember?"

"Pay 'em off!" Damon agreed, waving his glass with di-sastrous results. "Jolly good've you, Jack! Know where the blunt is. Don't mind, d'you?"

Perhaps it was as well, thought Thompson. His Nibs

looked a bit better now, even if he was going to pay the perishing piper in the morning. When he'd first come home, he'd looked like he'd been pulled through a knothole! "Come on," he offered. "I'll get your lordship to bed."

"No, no. Comf'able here. Lots o'drinking t'do yet! You go on up."

The valet regarded him narrowly, then, satisfied, withdrew.

Damon waved his glass with great deliberation, singing happily to himself.

He awoke to find it quite cold in the room, the grey light of dawn frosting the edges of the drapes. He was alone and comparatively sober. Recent events came back to him gradually. He had done what he'd set out to do. Vaille would not come here again. And Sophia would probably . . . marry Hartwell. He clenched his fists against that awareness. But she would be safe. He'd not have to live with the nightmare fear of her beauty being marred or her precious self hurt or killed. That was all that mattered.

His eyes lifted to the harpsichord. He stood, holding his head on, and wandered to the instrument, touching the blackened hole wistfully. Now what? If he died, the lack of funds would be immaterial. But supposing his luck held? His father had said "a small allowance"—and if he knew Vaille and the feelings he must hold for his disgraced son, it would be small, indeed. He had so hoped to complete Cancrizans. He glanced fondly around the gracious room. Mama had loved the Priory, and now it held new memories—memories that made it infinitely more dear to his heart.

His attention was caught by the old parchment on the music rack, and he picked it up idly. If he could decipher it, his worries would be over. This weird unmelodious music held the key to the location of the treasure, he was convinced of it. At first, he'd thought there was a secret panel somewhere in the room and that the sequence of notes, played in some rhythm or volume or with some certain repeat might cause it to open. Far-fetched, perhaps, but he'd struggled with it for weeks totally without success.

His fingers wandered over the keys, and he smiled faintly as he recalled what Sophia had said of the "music." The notes seemed to have been arranged without rhyme or reason . . . "much as a child might toss a pile of alphabet blocks onto the floor and hope to find them arranged into words . . ."

234

Arranged into words! Suppose the poor Jacobite gentleman had used notes to spell out his message? His heart beginning to race, he sat at the bench. The first note was middle C. What if he used the A below it as his base and went on up the alphabet from there? The next note, in the bass clef, was A! His excitement mounted. C...A...! Now, by Jupiter, it *might* be! He stood, seized a branch of candles, and hurried into the library, music in hand. He seated himself at the reference table, pulled over the inkstand, a quill pen, and a fresh sheet of paper and went to work.

Whitthurst stood by the mantle with his back to Sophia, unable to endure the stricken look on her face. She had, he knew, always looked up to him with trust and love. What must she think now? Would she ever again be able to think of him without disgust now that he'd told her the whole miserable story? It had begun with the old demon of boredom: too much money acquired too young; a spendthrift, easygoing father; a gentle stepmother who, adoring him, had only remonstrated mildly at his extravagances. The parties, the gambling, the seasons at Bath or Brighton, the entire social whirl couldn't fully satisfy his youthful energy. Longing to go to Spain, yearning to get into the fighting, he had bowed to his stepmother's pleas that he not leave England. After his father's death, the ties binding him to their country seat in Kent had tightened further. When Sophia went to Italy, her absence had left Singlebirch even less exciting. He had plunged ever more wildly into gaming and, a little frightened and much too dangerously in debt, had begun to run with too fast a crowd.

He hadn't realized at first what he was getting into. Frequenting ever-seedier hells, drifting closer to the dock areas, roaming the streets late at night, kicking up all manner of minor disturbances, exhilarated by the excitement of encounters with the Watch. Waking sometimes with an aching head in some filthy, verminous parlour or rooming house, not too sure what had happened, revolted by his surroundings, yet always returning to his friends when boredom took him again. And then, one never-to-be-forgotten night, he had found a distinguished gentleman beside him at one of the more gruesome hells and, succumbing to the ingratiatingly polite attention of this stranger, had by dawn been deep in debt to him. Very drunk very soon, he remembered little of what transpired but had awakened next afternoon in a luxurious bedchamber, waited upon hand and foot by bold-eyed maids and inscrutable gentlemen of the chambers. He had learned he was at Green Willow Castle, and his host, the notorious Lord Sumner Craig-Bell. Horrified and eager to get away, he hadn't known he was already trapped. Not until later had he learned that Craig-Bell was the leader of Cobra and he himself a helpless captive, so incriminated he dared not make his escape; blackmailed and threatened into everdeepening crimes; forced to attend the meetings—masked, of course, as they all were, but with Craig-Bell and the six lieutenants aware of his identity and ready to make it public if he refused their demands.

And what demands! Small pieces of information about members of the *ton*. Access to business or personal papers in homes where he was a trusted visitor. Scraps that made no sense to him but that, added together, became choice sources of revenue to the club. The luring of others into deeper involvements; the wild, sickening parties. The girls—about whom he said very little to Sophia. One night had almost driven him to self-destruction. A little village girl, stealing innocently away to a meeting with her sweetheart, had been tricked into the castle, made drunk, and so degraded that her poor mind had given way. How they had laughed, Craig-Bell and his cronies! And he had gone back to Singlebirch, sick and shivering, and had become so ill that his stepmother had summoned Dr. Upton and had him cupped, not realizing his fever was the result of mental rather than physical ills.

This, because of his self-disgust, because she must understand how low he had sunk, because of his inherent honesty, he did tell Sophia. Her grief so unnerved him that he'd had to stop and now stood there, staring at the dead fire, wondering if she would ever speak to him again.

"Is that," she quavered at last, "why Mama went...to India?"

"No!" He swung around. "I had to talk to someone before I ran mad! But not Mama! She is so frail—I dared not. And if I'd told almost anyone else in the family, they'd have been sure to confide in their wives. You know how they are. So—I sent word to Damon."

Trembling, Sophia looked up at him and waited.

"The summer Papa took me to Europe and then fell out
236

of the carriage in Marseilles and broke his ankle, Camille was in Florence. Papa sent me down there, perhaps you remember me writing of it? Cam had a lovely villa, and we all—" He thought of the lovely Gabrielle and broke off in some confusion. "And, he was very hospitable," he went on lamely. "We hit it off extremely, and after he came back to England—you was in Italy then, of course—we became close friends. It was always a joke between us that he was my uncle. Still I looked up to him, I suppose. So when I got into this frightful mess, I turned to him. He came down to Kent at once, and I told him everything. Lord, what a brutal scold he dealt me! Then he bought me my colours, and—I was in the hussars before I knew what had happened!"

Sophia, her handkerchief pressed to her quivering mouth, could scarcely see. Camille had decided—so wisely—that a noble dying was far preferable to the nightmare Stephen faced. What his continued association with that hellish club might have led to did not bear thinking of. And how she had hated Camille, little dreaming what he had spared them.

"I didn't know," the Viscount said heavily, "what he was going to do."

She stiffened and, dashing the tears away, breathed, "What *could* he do?"

"He joined Cobra," he said tonelessly. "I don't know how. Perhaps Craig-Bell thought he'd be able to get his hooks into Vaille. It don't signify."

"But—why? Surely, after what you told him—?"

"He despised 'em long before that, Chicky. A friend of his had been a victim of one of their...funny little pranks. I'd come to know Cam quite well by then, and I didn't trust him, so before I sailed, I made him give me his solemn word he'd say nothing. I...know what Craig-Bell does to people who cross him."

Sophia's hands were twisting frantically at the soggy handkerchief. Her face very white, she moaned, "He ...Camille...wasn't the one who—started that fire? Who destroyed them? Stephen? My God! It wasn't *Camille*?"

"It was! It was! The blasted fool! The Runners had been after Cobra for years but couldn't find the smallest clue. Nobody dared speak—we were all so hopelessly incriminated, and we all had loved ones who would have been...disgraced. Craig-Bell is incredibly vicious. You do not know, Sophia..."

She did know, to some extent. For, at last, it was all falling

237

into place. Camille had withdrawn to country obscurity after a famous statesman, standing next to him, had been shot down on a London street. They'd been aiming at the Marquis, not Rondell! For their own protection, he rebuffed the visitors he must have longed to welcome to his lonely home. He lied constantly; had they guessed the truth, nothing would have kept them away. Vaille, certainly, would be firmly installed at Cancrizans! And Feather? Nothing would drive that grimly devoted lady from his side if she suspected he was in danger! So many things became clear. That wicked note to Ariel and the resultant battle had been Cobra's doing, of course—the big man had been a tool for murder! Did that mean they had tortured Camille long enough? Was his death now decreed?

Stephen's arm was about her; something cool and refreshing was at her lips. She swallowed and coughed. "My dearest," he groaned, "I am so sorry!" He knelt beside her and, as she reached out to touch his haggard cheek, begged, "Can you ever forgive me?"

"Foolish boy! Did you think me so righteous I wouldn't know it was but a mistake? You were young and foolish merely. And they were merciless enough to use your inexperience. My poor love, how terribly you have suffered."

He pressed her hand to his lips. "God bless you for your sweet compassion," he said huskily, "but do not excuse me. I was a very great fool!" He sat beside her, but as far away as he could, as though any contact must be repellent to her. "I was afraid, you see, Sophia, that they'd do—as they threatened. That they would tell Mama."

"How unspeakable they must be! And how proud I am of Camille! But why did he join? Could he not have sent word to the Runners, anonymously?"

Whitthurst stared fixedly at his clenched hand. "Aye. And should have. But would not. He intended to destroy them, but he was afraid they would suspect me because I was the only one who'd got out—alive. He joined only to protect me. And then he discovered that Craig-Bell kept dossiers on each one of us. I know it must sound impossible, but there were some very decent young chaps. Good fellows, hopelessly trapped, who were living a life of pure hell. If the Runners had found those files, some very fine families and many innocent lives would have been destroyed. So Cam stayed a member until he found Craig-Bell's hiding place for his dossiers." He shook his head soberly. "He prowled that castle...alone. Knowing well what they'd do if they caught him!"

Sophia, hanging on his every word, scarcely dared to breathe.

Scowling, Whitthurst went on. "He found the records at last, but he had to break into a safe to get at them. It took too long, and he was missed. They caught him burning the miserable stuff, and he had to fight his way clear. That's how the fire started."

His eyes began to glow. "Gad, but I'd love to have been there! Cam is spectacular in a close fight. I saw him once in Paris. Anyway, he stood 'em off for a while and managed to get outside in all the smoke and confusion when the fire really took hold. He got halfway across the courtyard, but Craig-Bell spotted him and shot him down. Thompson was waiting nearby with the racing curricle just in case Cam needed to get away fast. Cam had given him strict instructions not to go in after him. Jack says he didn't hear! He drove that damned curricle hell for leather across the courtyard, got between Craig-Bell and Cam, and hauled him in. Jove!" His face alight with excitement, he looked young and boyish again. "Can't you just picture it, Chicky? The castle burning, men in their masks rushing madly about, and that curricle racing to get to Damon before they did?"

Sophia could picture it—too well! She shuddered. "And now they mean to kill him."

Whitthurst's expression sobered at once. "Cam knew they'd go after him, of course—that it would be self-defence until they were all caught. It just never occurred to him that—" He frowned and said, "Well, he's a sportsman, you see. And those six lieutenants of Craig-Bell's are...barely human! They're sworn to destroy Cam. But they don't want to make it too easy. So they've had some 'fun' with him. They may execute him tomorrow...or next year. But, meanwhile, anyone close to him must take the consequences. He felt awful when Rondell was killed, though the man had a beastly reputation. So he put himself where others wouldn't be hurt."

"But—surely, he could employ guards?"

"Yes. And he did, at first. It drove him wild to have them lurking about all over the place. And then one man was found, half dead. They'd put a pistol ball through both his knees. He'll be crippled for life. That was enough! Cam sent 'em packing."

"And his dogs?" she asked in a very small voice.

"He had two and loved them dearly. Géant was a bloodhound. Cam brought him over from Belgium. They shot him. He wouldn't let Satin go out after that. She was an English setter, beautiful creature. He decided to give her to Lucian St. Clair. He found her one day...down in the catacombs. Poison. He had to shoot her himself."

Sophia leaned to hide her face against his shoulder; patting her gently, the Viscount went on, "Thompson was deafened at Badajoz. He'd been a stagecoach driver before he got into the fighting but was so badly wounded that when he came home, he couldn't handle the ribbons, and no one would give him work. Ariel was in the same fix. His back used to be pretty painful, I gather, and he turned to gin. Soon he was good for nothing. They met and took to the High Toby together. One night, they held up Damon's carriage. Thompson was known as "The Hampstead Horror" in those days. Old Cam tossed him clear over the backs of the team and had a pistol on Ariel before either of 'em knew what was happening. When he learned they were both war veterans, instead of turning them over to the hangman, he gave them work."

"Yes." Sophia smiled tenderly. "He would. And so they stood by him. And Mrs. Hatters?"

"She was his nurse. She loves him as if he were her own."

Blinking rather rapidly, she asked, "When did you find out about it all?"

"When Harry came that day. That was why I come tearing down here. I knew it must have been Cam...but he'd given me his sworn word he'd stay out of it. When I taxed him with it"—he grinned ruefully—"he told me that, being a halfbreed, he never feels bound to keep his word unless he repeats the oath in English *and* French! Stupid gudgeon!"

Somehow she managed a smile. "Who else knows of it? The Earl, I collect."

"Yes. And I believe Miss Hilby knows some. Though I'm not sure how much." Sophia's expression changed subtly, and, curious, he asked, "Sophia? I thought you liked the lady."

"I do. Poor soul..."

"Poor? With *her* fortune? Oh—you mean her *amour*, I collect. Well, at least nobody cuts her. He may make an honest woman of her yet."

"Lud!" she gasped. "I didn't know things were—that way."

"I don't either. Shouldn't have said it. But—wherever he

240

goes, sooner or later she turns up. And she's adored the man for so long...can't help but think—"

"Was she in Florence with him? Is that why you hesitated to speak of it?"

"Charlotte? Gad, no! Vaille wasn't there."

"V-Vaille? The *Duke*?"

"Of course. Who did you think? Chicky! You never thought—*Cam*?"

"B-but...but yes! He said..."

The Viscount gave a crack of laughter. "I wonder *she* didn't tell you! Everyone knows she's been in love with Vaille for years. He won't offer because he thinks he's too old for her. That...and other things."

Numbed, Sophia cast her mind back. Surely Miss Hilby had said— But, no. In the conversation she'd overheard Charlotte had said, "Camille says we will be wed..." The 'we' she'd referred to had been Charlotte and *Vaille*! And tonight it had been she herself who'd named Charlotte when Camille had claimed he was soon to marry. His astonishment had not resulted from the fact she'd guessed the truth, as she had supposed, but because she was so unaware of it! He had used her misapprehension for all it was worth. That note the footman had brought had upset him badly. It had been another warning, no doubt. One of their vicious little threats—probably against Ridgley this time, because Camille had at once demanded to know where Ted was, and been so vastly relieved when she'd said he travelled with Major Henderson. She wondered dully if the threat had been put into words this time, or if it was another taunting drawing like the one she'd found that rainy afternoon in the library. They'd all been there—Rondell, the two dogs Camille had so loved, and the woman. Who was the woman? Charlotte? No, of course not, for they'd known the truth of poor Charlotte's devotion to Vaille. Who then...? *Herself*! Of course! *That* was why he had come up with his nefarious plot to marry the "faithful" Charlotte for "her money"! He knew he had revealed his love, and he'd had to push her away somehow. How shamefully he had played his part. How gallantly. And how it must have torn his dear heart to watch her turn from him. She swallowed a lump in her throat and thought mistily, 'My own...Viper...'

Her heart was so full she could not express it, her world bright beyond belief, her love vindicated as she'd never dreamed he could be vindicated. And refusing to acknowledge the dark threat that hung over him and that soon would threaten them both, she smiled at her brother radiantly.

"I cannot let you go to him," Whitthurst said with unfamiliar gravity.

Her heart seemed to turn over, but her smile did not waver. "I shall marry him, Stephen—if he will have me."

Her face was more beautiful than he had ever seen it despite its tears and the rather grubby look. He thought, 'Camille won't let her. He'll find a way.'

Holding the branch of candles high, his heart hammering with excitement, Damon hurried through the dank blackness of the catacombs. Beside him, Horatio muttered a squawky complaint at being thus rudely drawn from the warmth and comfort of the hearth. Damon scarcely heard him. He had broken the code at last! Thanks to Sophia's casual remark, he had been able to convert that awful music into a very succinct message: "Catacombs. North wing. Bottom level. Last room on right. Pivotal stone. East wall." The low heavy door was before him now, and it swung open smooth and silently to his touch. The blackness was absolute, but with his eyes glued to the east wall, he stooped and stepped forward.

Horatio burst into a frenzied honking. Damon, whirling, knew too late that the very soundlessness of those well-oiled hinges should have warned him. He caught a glimpse of a dark hooded figure, hideously faceless in the light of the flickering candles; an upraised arm; and a heavy club flashing down. A staggering shock, a fleeting sense of pain, and the world exploded in a great sheet of flame that caught him and spun him into total darkness.

Chapter 22

"Milord was up very late last night, ma'am." Patience wiped her hands on her apron and closed the front door, her eyes reflecting astonishment at the arrival of a caller before nine o'clock in the morning. "I do reckon as how he will sleep 'til noon at the very soonest."

Sophia, looking around happily, felt at peace again. What a relief to be in this silly old house instead of Phinny's magnificent and cold art gallery. She'd not had to pretend weariness when Stephen had finally left her, but directly she was alone she had rung for Louise and left strict and confidential instructions that she was to be awakened at seven and would need a horse by eight. She had slept deeply and could have slept three times longer, but her need to see Camille would not wait. She had told the awed Louise to inform no one of her departure and had horrified Phinny's grooms by refusing an escort.

Patience informed her that Mr. Thompson had gone to the spa on an errand for my lord and that Mrs. Hatters was in the village. Sophia said she would wait for Lord Damon in the music room and gratefully accepted an offer of tea and some muffins.

The room was chill, but a shy-eyed boy hurried in and started the fire, which was already laid, then slipped away. Sophia glanced round her, the memories associated with this room rushing back, now fraught with such intense meaning. She wandered over to touch the sofa upon which, despite Mrs. Hatters' best efforts, the mud stains were still faintly visible. The harpsichord, with its black hole unrepaired, sent a pang through her. If only he would come. But she must not wake him. He would be exhausted after that dreadful night. She sank down contentedly beside the fire and was beginning to drowse by the time Patience returned with a tray.

"I must get out to the smokehouse, ma'am. The new cook don't know his way about and wants me to help him down there. Be there anything you needs?"

Sophia assured her she was quite comfortable and would need nothing except perhaps a short nap. Patience bobbed a curtsey and left her. She nibbled on a muffin, poured herself a cup of tea, and sighed luxuriously. It was wonderful to be... home. Wherever could Horatio be?

Damon awoke to intense blackness and intolerable pain. He could not think where he lay, nor what had happened, but he was shivering with cold, and the slightest movement sent a new lance of agony through his head. The darkness was so absolute that he began to wonder if he was blinded, but his efforts to look about brought a sick giddiness, and the pain increased until he was nauseated and lay still again.

It seemed that all this misery had something to do with music. It was so hard to remember clearly. If only he could see... the darkness was like a tomb... The catacombs! That was it! And that ghastly hooded figure! He had been struck down. Was he, indeed, blind? Panic spurred him, and with a costly effort, he managed to lift a hand to his head. His hair was wet and sticky, the flesh torn and excruciatingly painful. He wondered how long he'd been lying here. If the wound continued to bleed, he would soon be too weak to get out. No one knew he was down here. They would undoubtedly think he'd gone to bed and, after his drinking bout last night, would hesitate to disturb him. It might be hours before they initiated a search.

Gritting his teeth, he fought his way upward but, after a struggle that left him panting and soaked with sweat, had only managed to get one elbow beneath him. It took all his willpower not to collapse again as the icy floor heaved and pitched and the pain mounted.

Horatio had been with him, he was sure, but there was no slightest sound, no disgruntled squawking. Had they murdered the poor beast? Poor innocent goose. He was shocked to realize that he was sinking down again and with a tremendous effort got to his knees. But his struggles were useless. He was spinning helplessly, and the pain was fiercer than any he'd ever experienced. Consciousness was leaving him; slumping down, he felt only a vague shock as his head struck the floor. His lips were cold and numb but formed one word in a sigh so faint he barely heard it. "Sophia..."

Sophia's eyes flew open. Her pulses were racing, and she was frightened. Yet she was here in the dear, familiar room, and the house was silent. No workmen now; Camille was without funds. Sunlight streamed through the windows. The drapes were wide, for he was not seated at the harpsichord, presenting an easy target. With an involuntary shiver, she stood as the old grandfather clock chimed the half hour. She had thought she would sleep for hours once she dropped off and was surprised to discover it was only half-past nine.

She went over to the harpsichord and with one finger began to play, her thoughts remote. The yellowed sheet of parchment was gone, and she looked for it in a vague searching. If only he would come! She started for the door but stopped. She was being hysterical. He was safe in his bed, and there was no need to rob him of sleep to confirm his love. She knew very surely now that she had his heart. Yet this taut restlessness made it impossible for her to be still. She wandered into the hall.

All was calm and peaceful. The library looked inviting with its dear old books, and she walked inside. The maids had not yet been in here. The fire was not set, and the reference table had been left hurriedly, the chair still swung back. The missing parchment from the music room lay on the table. Beside it, a piece of paper held Camille's scrawl; reading the words, she gave a small cry of excitement. He had deciphered the message! He most assuredly would not have done so and then gone nonchalantly to bed—he was in the catacombs now! Afire with eagerness to see what he had found, she lit a branch of candles, hurried along the corridor, and turned toward the north wing.

Not until she reached the fateful flight of stairs leading to the lowest level did Sophia hesitate. Only then did it dawn on her that she was all alone. What if Camille had already found the treasure? But if that were the case, the household would have been agog with excitement. Besides, the Priory was empty of servants at this moment; there was nothing to be gained by going back in search of someone to accompany her. Resolutely, she hurried on, eager to find Camille.

She had never gone into the real depths and was struck by a growing sense of something amiss as she crept down the worn stairs. The darkness was absolute—a stifling blackness that is encountered only in places never touched by sunlight. However firmly she chastised herself, she could not keep her steps from slowing, her breathing from becoming rapid and uneven.

The cypher had said "last room on right," and there it was finally, just a few yards ahead. She stopped, seized by a strong compulsion to turn and run. Instead, she called, "Camille?" Her voice echoed eerily, but there was no answering shout, no sudden flash of light. She saw, in fact, that the door stood partly open and that it was totally black inside. He was not here! Disheartened, she started swiftly back the way she had come. But wait, suppose that pivotal stone led to a secret room or hidden stair? She turned again and, coming to the door, gave it a timid little push.

A scream was torn from her. Camille sprawled on the floor, his face streaked with blood. Sobbing incoherently, she was on her knees beside him. "Oh, my dear love—do not be dead!" Touching his cheek, she found it warm and gasped a fervent "Thank God!" The wound had bled profusely, and her hand shook as she set down the branch of candles. A sick faintness swept over her, but she fought it away and investigated gently, only to utter a horrified moan as she saw how cruelly the flesh was torn. Only the thickness of his hair had saved him.

Her first thought was to get help. She started up but sank back again. Blood was still creeping slowly down his face; she must fashion a bandage. He was clad only in shirt and breeches and there was no large handkerchief available. She sat down and, in tried-and-true manner, ripped at the flounce on her petticoat. Either her hands were weak or her petticoat a lot stronger than such garments are supposed to be. It resisted her efforts with sturdy indifference. This was no time for modesty. She pulled her skirts up and her petticoat down.

Standing on the hem, she tugged with all her might, and it gave with a loud rip. She folded a small pad and, kneeling close beside Camille, wound the cloth about his head and pulled it as tight as she dared before tying the knot.

Now she *must* get help! She sprang to her feet and then thought of him perhaps regaining consciousness to find himself alone in this terrible darkness. She removed a candle and, tilting it, allowed some hot wax to drip onto the floor. Placing the candle in the small resulting puddle, she took up the branch and started for the door.

Damon moaned and stirred weakly. She flew back to his side. "Camille..." Her voice was thready, and she fought to steady it. "I'm here, my beloved..." She knelt, took up his limp hand, and holding it, felt a faint answering pressure; then the long dark lashes fluttered, and he looked dazedly up at her. "Oh, dearest...my dearest love," she choked.

"Mama is...very worried," he muttered. "About my foot...you know."

She fought tears. "Yes, dear one. But it's all right now."

He moved fretfully. "Did they get her out? They will not tell...me."

She bit her lip and gulped, "They—got her out, my darling. Do not—"

Damon frowned and said in a surer voice, "Sophia? What...on earth?" He tried to sit up, stifled a groan, and sagged down again, his face ghastly white.

Frightened, she cried, "Lie still, darling. I'm going for help."

His hand detained her. He whispered faintly, "How...did you...?"

"I found your music and followed you. Camille, can you understand me? I must leave you, dearest heart. Just for a little while."

"No! Stay...here." His eyes were so filled with pain that her heart constricted. "Must be careful. Monk...he's out there, Sophia. Do not..." The words trailed into a weary sigh, and he lapsed again into unconsciousness.

It had not dawned on her that whoever had done this terrible thing might still be down here! That she was alone, two floors beneath the ground, in this musty, chill blackness, with a man near death—and a murderous intruder! She felt frozen with fear. She must get help, or Camille would surely die. Yet if his attacker had been interrupted by her coming, he might be lurking somewhere, ready to complete his savage work the instant she left. She glanced to the hall fearfully. The faint light from the candles was cut off by a solid wall of blackness beyond that open door. How could she dare venture into it with the monk waiting? She looked down at Camille and knew a searing anguish to see him so desperately hurt and helpless. She raised his hand again and pressed it to her cheek, murmuring her love even though he could not hear her.

She *must* go! She picked up the candelabra, hurried to the door, and peered into the corridor, her heart in her throat. How dense was the darkness, hushed and menacing, as if something ineffably evil waited just beyond the small area lit by the wavering candlelight. She started off, quaking, her hands wet, trembling as she approached each small dark doorway, any one of which might hold a terrible threat...a savage murderer, crouching in wait to spring on her.

She was soon so frightened that she could scarce set one foot before the next, but she went on, her ears straining for the least sound, her eyes striving to pierce the impenetrable darkness. She came at last to the foot of the stairs, and her heart missed a beat. A faint glow was approaching! Had Stephen followed her already, found the music, and—?

Her knees turned to water, her blood to ice. Hooded, tall, and menacing, the monk drifted down toward her...with candles held high, and...*no face*! Her mind reeled, and she felt suffocated. He had seen her! Her lips parted, but even her attempt to scream was thwarted, not a sound escaping her throat, so frozen was she with terror.

Only the thought of Camille saved her and, with the memory of his helplessness, came new strength. She began to run frenziedly back to him. Pounding footsteps were following, gaining on her. The corridor seemed to stretch out endlessly. Breathing in sobbing gasps, she reached the door at last, but he was much too close. His arm stretched out to grab her. With a courage born of desperation, she hurled the candelabra at his head. He threw up one arm and drew back with a startled shout. She sprang inside, wrenching the door shut even as his dark form leapt at her. She shot the bolt. The door shook to a thunderous assault, and she leaned against the damp wall, sobbing wildly, her face pressed to the stone, her brain spinning.

"Sophia...are you...all right?"

Damon, propped on one elbow, was gazing up at her, his white, blood-smeared face desperate with anxiety.

248

The sounds outside had ceased. She tottered to him, sank down, and gathered him gently into her arms, pillowing that battered head against her heart, looking lovingly into his strained eyes. His hand moved weakly, and she took it and pressed it to her lips, managing somehow to smother her panicked weeping.

"You should not...have come back...to the Priory," he whispered.

"I should not...have left!" she gulped. "And I never shall again, sir! No matter what lies and nonsense you tell me!"

He frowned deeply. His eyes closed, and she thought he had fainted again, but he breathed a gasping "Sophia...I loved you...from that first"—he looked up and with a twitching attempt at a smile, finished—"that first...slap."

She bent and kissed him very gently, but when she drew back, he had gone from her again and lay like a dead man in her arms.

Her eyes flew at once to the flame. They must wait here until help came, but the candle was terrifyingly short. An hour—two at the most—and they would be enveloped by the horrible darkness.

The minutes dragged by. Her thoughts wandered chaotically, reliving the events of these past crowded days. Yet always, like a steady thread through her reminiscences, ran fear for this beloved Viper. Had she found him only to lose him so soon? Scanning his face, she saw a relentless creep of crimson down his cheek and strove once again to tighten the bandage.

Her thoughts turned to Vaille. Damon should have told him the truth. He would be utterly devastated if...She cringed away from finishing that terrifying thought and, glancing to the door, was petrified to see the latch lifting silently. Her heart jumped into her throat. She held Camille closer as a soft scratching sound came from the door. And, in that moment, the candle guttered and went out.

A snarling shout. A barrage of blows thundering on the door. Sobbing with fear, she bowed over Camille, knowing that if the monk succeeded, they must both die. She would be helpless against him! But at last the attack ceased, and silence prevailed once more.

Time became an endless nightmare of darkness and despair. Camille had not moved for what seemed hours, and she knew now, fully, what love meant, for if he died, her reason for living would be gone, also...Fighting the dread that threatened to become total hysteria, she began to sing. Her voice was faint and quavering, but it seemed to give her a little courage, and she sang on. English folk songs, French, Italian opera. She was halfway through "The Sands of Dee," her voice becoming hoarse, when she screamed to a renewed pounding on the door.

"My lady! My lady! Be ye in there?" The voice was a deep rumble.

With a sobbing prayer of thanks, she slipped carefully from beneath Damon's dead weight and, staggering on cramped legs, swung the door open.

A blaze of light blinded her. She heard a shriek and a hoarse cry. And there before her, huge and powerful and comforting, with Nancy peering from behind him, stood Ariel.

The Priory was silent in the hush of early morning, but on the bench outside the door to Damon's bedchamber, two people sat in a forlorn waiting, while others were seated on the stairs. Lord Whitthurst sprang up at the sound of flying feet, and Mrs. Hatters, her eyes red and swollen, stood also.

Rushing to join them, Sophia gasped a fearful "Camille?"

"No change, my dear." The Viscount took her outstretched hand and spoke with a calm reassurance he was far from feeling. "And before you eat me for letting you sleep—you were exhausted!" He forced a smile. "Don't even remember Hartwell coming, I'll wager?"

She put a hand to her temple. "Amory? No." Glancing to that closed door, she asked urgently. "Was Mrs. Gaffney able to tell if—"

"She's gone. Hartwell found us a doctor, and he—"

"Doctor?" she echoed stupidly. "But there isn't one for miles!"

Whitthurst drew her to sit beside him on the bench. "A retired London surgeon lives hereabouts. Amory went into Pudding Park to discover his direction."

"And brought him? Thank God! Is Amory here? I must thank him."

For answer, the Viscount handed her a note, and she unfolded it and read:

Sophia, my dear,
    I found Dr. Twine's house, but he is from home and
250

no word on when he will return. I have left a message
with his butler and at "The Wooden Leg" that he is to
come to you at once. Meanwhile, I am riding after Vaille
and his personal physician, Lord Belmont.

Ever yrs. to command,
Hartwell

Sophia folded the page and returned it to her brother. "How very kind of Amory. Is Dr. Twine with Camille?"

The Viscount nodded. "Evidently don't care to be called on nowadays, but I collect he didn't dare turn down a person of Cam's consequence."

Relaxing a little, Sophia leaned in the circle of his arm. With a famous surgeon tending Camille, his chances must surely be improved. Seized by a sudden thought, she asked why Mrs. Gaffney had left, and the Viscount replied that Dr. Twine had brought his own nurse.

"Hatchet-faced old crow," sniffed Mrs. Hatters. "Cruel it were for them to upset Maggie Gaffney that way. Regular heartbroken she is, poor soul."

Sophia turned a puzzled look on Whitthurst.

"They'd a slight disagreement," he explained. "Poor lady really was beside herself, I admit. Twine's a crusty old chap, and she should not have argued with a physician about the cupping, however experienced she—"

"Cupping!" gasped Sophia. "My God! She must have been out of her mind!"

Mrs. Hatters, wringing her hands nervously, said, "Weren't *Maggie's* wish, ma'am. And if you was to ask me—"

A terrible coldness enveloped Sophia. "Stephen! He didn't! You didn't *let* him? Oh—my dear heaven! You surely must have known—"

"Chicky!" He shook her gently. "The man's a great surgeon. You don't tell a physician his business. Cam quieted down soon enough, I assure you."

"Quieted...down?"

Sophia stared at him blankly, then with a stifled sob, rushed to the door. It was locked, and she wrenched frantically at the handle. "Let me in! I am Lord Damon's betrothed! Let me in!"

Shocked, Whitthurst pulled her back. A woman's angry voice cried, "You will be admitted as soon as Dr. Twine has finished!"

251

Sophia struggled to escape, and the Viscount's grip on her arm tightened. "Sophia! The man's fighting for his life in there! Control yourself!"

"He called to me!" she sobbed. "Did you hear him, Steve? Oh, God! The doctor must be in his dotage! He must be stopped! Help me! Please!"

She looked so wild and distraught, and his own fears making his heart ache, he mumbled, "I know how terrible this is for you, love. But—you must face reality. Poor Cam might not—"

He was wasting time while Camille's precious life was being drained away! With a sobbing cry, she left him, running madly back to her room. She tore open her bureau drawer with such desperate haste that it fell, the contents spilling on to the floor. She snatched up that which she sought and flew back down the hall again. She concealed her hand in a fold of her gown as Whitthurst came toward her, his face tired, pale and contrite. "Chicky, dear—forgive me. I'd no thought to—"

She smiled wanly through her tears, but as he reached out to her, she eluded him with a pantherish leap and again pounded on Damon's door. A man roared, "Quiet out there, dammit!" Mrs. Hatters was weeping with fright, and from the corner of her eye, Sophia saw the small crowd of awed faces that watched from the stairs. Whitthurst, groaning with mingled sympathy and irritation, was trying to force her away, but again she had thought to hear Camille's faint voice call her name beseechingly; wild with desperation, she shoved at her brother with all her strength and swung up the pistol, aiming at the lock.

Slender but strong white fingers grasped her wrist, forcing her hand away. Vaille, his voice very gentle, said, "My poor child, have you lost your mind?"

She swung to him with a sob of near hysteria. "Thank God you are come! You *must* stop him! Hurry! Hurry!"

The Duke, his own face haggard, his eyes haunted by dread, glanced at Whitthurst's helpless shrug and said kindly, "Twine is a splendid man, Sophia, and he's here to help Camille. If you care for him, you must—"

"*Care* for him?" She gripped his lapels and tugged at them furiously. "I *worship* him! And that monster in there is cupping him! Don't you understand? I held him in my arms in that horrid...little room...for hours! I couldn't stop the bleeding!" Vaille stared at her twisted, agonized face in mute horror. "Oh, my...dear God!" she sobbed distractedly. "Why will no one listen? My dearest love is being...murdered. And you tell me I'm an hysterical woman! *Help* him! For mercy's sake—*help* him! Or stand aside—and let me!"

Ariel ran up and looked anxiously from one to the other. Whitthurst muttered, "Sir, poor old Cam *had* rather messed up the place. Perhaps?"

The Duke's mouth hardened in the manner he shared with his son. He strode to the door, pounded on it, and announced clearly, "I am Vaille! Open this door!"

A deep voice called, "In just a few moments, your grace."

Vaille, his face bleak, lifted one imperious finger. "Break it down!"

Ariel ran back, then launched himself at the door. With a great tearing of splintered wood, it crashed open to the accompaniment of a screech from within.

A short, heavily built, white-haired man scowled beside the bed, surgical knife in hand. A gaunt, hard-eyed woman, holding Damon's wrist over the bowl, stared in rageful astonishment. Damon, struggling feebly, looked at Sophia with hope dawning in his horrified eyes.

With an inarticulate cry, she ran to push the woman away and, lifting that drooping arm, bent protectively over her love.

"Hell and damnation!" roared Twine, the knife glistening in his hand. "How dare you burst in here with this madwoman? Get out! Or, by God, I'll not be responsible for Lord Damon's life!"

"To the contrary, sir," said Vaille icily. "I shall hold you personally responsible. And heaven help you if he dies!"

Sophia awoke with a guilty start and straightened in the chair, her gaze flying to the bed. The shade on the lamp was tilted so as not to disturb the sufferer, and in the dimness of the room she thought for a moment he was asleep. She leaned closer. He lay very still, with closed eyes, but the pucker between his brows and the hand twisted tightly in the coverlet betrayed him. She longed to hold him in her arms, to be able to ease his pain. The only thing she could do was to bathe his burning face very gently with lavender water, taking care not to wet the bandages.

Damon's eyes opened, and a puzzled frown eased into a tender expression. Her heart lightened. He knew her! This time he knew her! Her vision blurred, but she saw him attempt to speak and placed a finger over his lips, saying huskily, "You are not to talk. Lord Belmont says you may have a...touch of the headache." A wry quirk touched his mouth at this massive understatement, and she went on quickly. "We don't know who it was, love. Nor how he got in. Stephen and Ariel went down there, but there were only some silver bowls and urns remaining. Everything else, and they think there must have been a great deal, had been taken. Whoever your monk was, he escaped with your treasure."

"No," he managed faintly. "It's here...beside me."

He tried to reach out to her, but the effort sent his hands clutching convulsively at the coverlet and, when his breath returned, he gasped out, "I haven't the...strength of a kitten! If I am dying...I want to be told of it."

Sophia dug her nails into her knee. "You would not dare!" She smiled, though tears were blinding her, and added with a brave attempt at levity, "After all the dreadful lies you have told, the devil is probably waiting eagerly to receive you!"

The shadow of his grin flashed at once, but his attempt to speak was cut off in the middle of the first word, and terror sent Sophia's heart to fluttering. She had heard the half-finished name and, loving him the more because of it, said reassuringly, "Stephen found Horatio in that hideous room in the catacombs. The coward had squeezed into one of the silver urns, and we could not get him out. We had to pour melted butter inside. All over him. And he hated it. The little beast gave me a good peck when he finally escaped."

Damon knew he dared not laugh, or his damned head would likely fly into a thousand pieces. Somehow, he controlled the impulse, but meeting the dearest eyes in the world, which watched him with such sweet anxiety, he whispered irrepressibly, "Probably was afraid...you were going to...cook him!"

He had the satisfaction of hearing her silvery little laugh as he sank into an uneasy darkness. A long sleep followed, troubled by strange dreams of a demoniacal man with white hair who threatened him with a knife. He moved restlessly, half waking. Damme, but his head throbbed! Weary and hot and uncomfortable, he gave a sigh of relief as a gentle hand bathed his face. He caught at those ministering fingers and breathed, "Thank you...darling." The fingers were gently but firmly withdrawn. A startled masculine voice exclaimed, "The devil!" It sounded like Vaille, but could not be, of course. His mind was wandering again. His head pounded so brutally

254

that a groan was torn from him. The cool fingers closed again over his own, and the bathing was resumed.

Sunlight was bright round the sides of the curtains when next he awoke, but he could not see clearly. Sophia was still sitting by the bed. She must not stay! The monk, surely, was of Cobra, and they would not hesitate to strike at *her* if they knew how deeply he loved her. He started up feebly, wincing to the immediate and savage thrust of the sword through his head. "You must leave here!" he panted. "My dearest beloved, you must—"

Strong hands restrained him, and an odd odour assailed his nostrils. Not lily of the valley. Definitely not! Spanish Bran...and Brazil! He peered eagerly, trying to pierce the thickening mists as he was eased back against the pillows.

"You know, Camille," drawled Vaille, "I really do think I prefered *'Mon Père'*. 'My dearest beloved' is a trifle ridiculous!"

Sophia gave a gasp and stood as the door opened. Blushing, she said shyly, "This invalid of ours will not believe he may not have a beefsteak for breakfast, your grace."

Vaille trod gracefully into the bedchamber. He noted that his son's sunken eyes were clear this morning, if suddenly anxious, and that the feverish colour was gone from the cheeks. Relieved, he gave no hint of it as he asked calmly, "Are you sure he is rational, Sophia? I've no pressing need to be mooned over by a lovesick lunatic."

Sophia's colour deepened. She withdrew her fingers from Damon's clasp and, having assured the Duke that his son was quite level-headed, excused herself, saying she must see about Camille's breakfast. She slanted a warning look at Vaille and moved to the door.

Damon wrenched his gaze from his beloved to his formidable sire and waited tensely. Vaille walked to the bedside and stood scowling down at him, saying nothing. Tentatively, Damon held out his hand. Vaille ignored it, and it was withdrawn. Frowning, Sophia hesitated.

Vaille drew himself up and then swept into a low and dignified bow. "I salute you, my son. You are a brave gentleman and have made me the proudest man in all England."

Damon flushed and stammered an uncomfortable "Thank...you, sir."

Vaille's amused glance turned toward Sophia. She met his

255

eyes for an instant, then fled.

"Mon Père—" Damon bit his lip in irritation at this *faux pas*, and corrected hastily. "Father—I could not tell you . . . but—I had no thought—I didn't mean—"

Vaille lifted his brows and, with a gentle smile, assured him it was of no least importance.

"And yet—you would not take my hand, sir."

The Duke moved closer. The wistfulness in the thin face warmed his heart. Their hands met in a long, firm grip, and there was a moment of emotional silence through which blue eyes held steadily to eyes of turquoise. "I am," said the Duke, "at a most vexing disadvantage. St. Clair tells me you have a right. Were you in good health, my boy, I would compel you to put on the gloves and demonstrate it. Instead, I am instructed that you are not to be upset. The look your lady just now bestowed upon me has so terrified me, in fact . . .". He paused, and Damon chuckled.

In the hall, Sophia removed her ear from the door, gave a sigh of relief, and went downstairs.

"How thankful I am"—Damon grinned—"to have so invincible a champion!"

"And how fortunate," Vaille nodded, sitting in the chair the champion had vacated. "She is, I am convinced, wholly responsible for the fact that you look much better than when we returned on Sunday." He saw bewilderment in Damon's face and vouchsafed the information that it was Thursday.

"Oh, gad! Five days?"

"Yes. We passed Friday night at 'The Bull' in Winchester. Charlotte was in a fine taking, I can tell you. But it was not until the following evening that my suspicions of your deplorable play acting became certainty."

"Then—you came back even though you had *not* learned what happened? I understood Sophia to say that Hartwell rode after you?"

"Your friend apparently assumed we had gone direct to Town, and so missed us. Meanwhile, having bullied poor Charlotte into telling me as much as she knew, we returned to this house and"—Vaille's frown was grim at that memory—"utter chaos!"

"You . . . do understand, sir? I could think of no other way but to—"

"Set yourself up as a sacrificial offering?" Vaille rasped. "Shut out everyone who loves you, including your magnificent lady, in an effort to carry that whole horrible burden on

256

your own shoulders? The devil I do, sir! And when my conniving, lying cousin shows his miserable nose, I shall—" He saw distress in Damon's eyes and shut his teeth with a considerable effort. "I must not give you the setdown you deserve...while you are ill." For a moment he sat in silence, his lips tightly compressed. Then he burst out, "But—by God! When I consider what a cork-brained, reckless, stupid, damned—" He broke off, seething, then catching a glimpse of Damon's grin, laughed ruefully, stood and, placing a hand on his shoulder, said, "I went roaring out of Bodwin Hall believing I possessed an immoral coward for a son, a black-hearted villain who would have broken his dear mother's heart! I returned to find I had damn near lost an heroic...idiot!" Damon blinked rapidly, and was speechless. Vaille's grip tightened. "I should have you consigned to Bedlam, but—by George, boy—I cannot tell you how...proud—"

Damon put up his own hand to cover those white fingers. Vaille turned abruptly, strode to the window, and blew his nose. Damon, now very tired, closed his eyes for an instant, his self-control slipping dangerously.

"I wish," sighed the Duke, "I had not slapped you."

"Yet it suited my purpose, sir. And did not signify, at all events."

"Compliment to your performance, eh? Well, it was masterful—I own it." He strolled over to close the partly open door of one of the presses and asked, "What possessed you to take them on, single-handed?"

Damon answered slowly, choosing his words with care. "I've not been of much use to...my country. This gave me the chance to do something...worthwhile."

It was the answer Vaille had prayed to hear, but he observed dryly, "Even a General does not confront the enemy alone, Camille."

"I assure you it was not the way I should wish to have dealt with it. But too many innocent lives would have been ruined had I put it in the hands of the Runners. My only chance to destroy those records was from the inside."

Vaille's jaw had set during this small speech, and his eyes held an angry glint. "Did it not occur to you that instead of rushing in like a rash and quixotic young fool, you could have come to me and—" He choked back the words once more. The boy looked very ill; this was no time for a trimming. After a minute, he said in a kinder tone, "I really am sorry, Camille—about your dogs. And the guard."

257

His well-meant attempt was disastrous. Those memories were too raw to be endured with equanimity, and Damon, his nerves beginning to shred, flinched perceptibly. "You will be glad to know," the Duke went on, sublimely unaware of the havoc he was creating, "that Mr. Rust gets about a little now, with the aid of a cane. I drove over to see him and discovered that his son is one of your gamekeepers, a steady young chap. I have promoted him—temporarily, at least. He is now one of the guards." He turned from his wanderings to meet a flashing look of anger and admitted, "Yes, I have caused the estate to be surrounded by armed men—which should have been done long since. I trust you do not object."

Damon thought it doubtful that his objections would be heeded. Watching the Duke's rambling progress about the room, he had thus far seen his medicines arranged tidily, the window curtains straightened, a smudge removed from the mirror and a hairbrush turned bristles down.

Vaille, meanwhile, was thinking that the carpet in this room was all wrong. He would instruct Orpington to have one installed that was more in keeping with the prestige of the head of the house. He checked his thoughts guiltily, all but hearing Charlotte's indignation, and, smiling to himself, knew he must leave before his son became tired. But one matter must be rectified first. He returned to the bedside and stood for a moment, fiddling with his emerald ring.

"Camille," he said with unaccustomed diffidence, "I rather suspect I owe the French an apology. Oxford, I doubt, could have done any better."

Damon was lying, passively watching the trees toss against a cloud-dotted sky when the door opened stealthily and Whitthurst's apprehensive countenance appeared. Damon shot a look to Mrs. Gaffney. The good woman was snoring softly in her chair. He gestured impatiently, and the Viscount crept in, sat on the bed, and peered at him. "Ain't going to have another spasm, are you?" he enquired. "Your sire is still smarting from the dressing down he received at the hands of old Belmont because he tired you yesterday! Lord! What a tyrant!"

"If I don't damned well find out what went on in this house," Damon grumbled, "I shall have two spasms and a convulsion, at the very least! Why was Belmont called from Town? I'd have sworn there was another old duck muddling

258

around." His brows knit thoughtfully. "Seem to remember swearing at him—though I'm dashed if I can recall why..."

Whitthurst, emboldened by the fact that his sister and Genevieve had gone for a ride with Vaille, undertook his uncle's edification. Damon listened in silence, but he paled, and the horror did not leave his eyes until at last he breathed, "Then, that valiant, darling girl saved my life!"

"Well, I ain't all wood upstairs, y'know," Whitthurst pointed out. "I began to think she might have the right of it." He scowled and muttered, "Just like Craig-Bell to have come up with such a loathesome idea."

There was a small, grim silence. Then Damon asked slowly, "Was Twine one of 'em, do you suppose?"

Whitthurst's finger traced the pattern of the coverlet. "Twine was never here, Cam."

"But you said— And I remember—"

"We hauled Mrs. Gaffney back, and first thing next morning, Hartwell come galloping in with Belmont, who confirmed that Twine is—as he says—the hell of a fine surgeon. Cannot understand what possessed the man, he kept saying. Your father demanded to know if that meant Sophia had been right." He looked up and, meeting Damon's steady gaze, shrugged, "Belmont admitted that if that last cupping had been done...there'd have been no saving you."

"So that's why I've been so pulled," muttered Damon.

"That's why, old fellow. When Vaille heard it, he informed Belmont that he intended to seek Twine out and strangle him with his bare hands—white hairs or no!"

"Did he, by God!" said Damon, brightening.

"Would have done it, too," Whitthurst grinned. "Only..." He looked down again. "Only Belmont said there must be some mistake. Twine don't have white hair, he said. He don't have *any* hair! For a good twenty years, that *walking skeleton* has been bald as an egg!"

Damon felt chilled. They regarded one another for a long moment, and then he whistled. "That was a close one! Jove! They were fast this time!"

Whitthurst nodded and pointed out quietly, "If your monk was of Cobra, also, they have been *inside* this house, Cam. Twice!"

Damon was silent, but his thoughts turned to the portrait of his Mama. Whitthurst was wrong: Cobra had invaded the Priory more than twice.

Chapter 23

Leaning heavily on Ariel's arm, Damon came to the balcony and hesitated, glancing at the stairs uneasily. He'd never before realized how steep they were.

"Upsy daisy!" quoth Ariel cheerily. He swept Damon into his arms, took the first step, and paused. Damon put a hand over his eyes and groaned. Beside them, Whitthurst asked an interested "Don't think your back's going out, do you, Ariel? I can't catch the old fellow if you drop him, y'know."

"You are," observed the Marquis with a nod of his bandaged head, "a great comfort to me, Whitt."

At the foot of the stairs, Sophia watched anxiously and, heaving a sigh of relief when her love's feet touched the floor, hurried to open the door to the music room. "We have a surprise for you, Camille. Close your eyes, please, dear."

Obeying, he kept them closed until he was comfortably disposed on the sofa and the attentive Mrs. Gaffney had placed a blanket over his knees, her shake of the head expressing her disapproval of the entire affair.

A chorus of welcoming shouts opened his eyes. He was swooped upon by a radiant Genevieve and warmly embraced. Feather kissed him and muttered that he was a "wicked liar." Charlotte Hilby, pressing her lips to his brow, said archly, "My betrothal kiss, dear fiancé!" which drew an unrepentant laugh from the invalid. Whitthurst enquired how it felt to be "among the living again." Answering him with a brief and fervent "Splendid!" Damon's eyes sought out his father. Vaille stood beside the fire, Horatio snoozing at his feet. He smiled on his son, turned slightly, and glanced up. Damon stiffened. The portrait of his Mother, in all her glowing beauty, hung once again over the mantle. Through a hushed silence, he faltered. "I cannot conceive how...even you...found an artist able to repair it."

The tremble in his voice brought Sophia hastening to sit beside him and slip a hand through his arm.

"It is from my drawing room in Vaille House," the Duke smiled. "I am having another painted, and—"

Thompson threw open the door, and Ridgley rushed in, closely followed by Amory Hartwell. The Earl strode to Damon's side, took his hand as though it were fashioned from sheerest glass and, peering into the ravaged face, groaned, "You stupid damned gudgeon! I should never have left you! Why in God's name did you not tell me Ariel had deserted? I'd never have let you be alone here—you know that, Cam!"

"How charming," murmured Vaille acidly. "And what a very great pity that you had not the common decency to inform a father of his son's peril."

Ridgley whirled on him, his brow thunderous. Sophia felt her beloved tense and placed her other hand gently on his arm. Miss Hilby said a cautionary "Philip..."

"Come and give me a kiss, you blasted clumsy clod," Feather demanded.

Obviously containing his resentment with an effort, the Earl obliged.

Hartwell came to take Damon's hand and say unhappily, "I collect you know I was almost responsible for your—"

"How very kind in you to have gone for Doctor Belmont," Sophia interrupted, her eyes flashing him a warning. "And then to go on for Ted. You are too good!"

He straightened and, taking the hint, said smoothly, "I do

261

at least have good news for you, ma'am. Ridgley and I were successful to some extent. Your beloved Singlebirch is safe. Full title has been restored to Whitt, and—"

"S-Singlebirch?" she gasped.

"Prendergast was busy, I take it," said Damon cynically.

Hartwell nodded. "The old rogue had slapped a lien not only upon your spa but on all the Drayton properties and estates. I'm sorrier than I can say, ma'am."

Sophia turned a distressed face to Whitthurst, and Sir Amory asked a perplexed "Didn't you tell her of it, Whitt?"

"No," said the Viscount sternly. "I've not yet taxed her with her misdeeds."

Sophia went at once to stand before him, hanging her head like a chastened little girl. "I was very stupid—and wicked, Stephen. I *meant* to tell you..."

He lifted her chin. "Yes, of course, but you'd...other things on your mind." She smiled at him gratefully, and he added in a very low voice, "Your 'wickedness' was minute, dearest, compared to my own!" He gave her a quick buss on the cheek and said gruffly, "Silly chit! Get on back to your beau."

She obeyed, and Damon drew her close to him, saying in tender accents, "You see what happens when you go Viper hunting...?"

The adoration in his eyes drove all other considerations from her mind. For an instant, it was very still in the room, everyone watching the young lovers; each heart touched. Then Vaille gave a small amused cough, and Sophia, glancing vaguely at him, became aware of his laughing eyes. She blushed and stammered, "Sir Amory, you have been more than kind. And now have come to my rescue once more. I—"

Hartwell threw up a deprecating hand. "My efforts were small, Sophia. The Duke threw his entire legal staff into the effort to untangle your property."

Her startled gaze flashed to Vaille, and before she could speak, he said fervently, "Dear lady, do I live to be a hundred I shall never be able to repay you. Not only for your intrepid bravery in the catacombs but for your unbelievable willingness to shoot the lock off that damnable door, while the rest of us held you to be hysterically unstable!"

Ridgley's jaw dropped. "A gun...in the house? What the devil?"

"I am amazed," murmured Vaille, "that *you'd* not foreseen

262

such an eventuality..."

Hartwell, noting the swift angry flush on Ridgley's face and the imploring gaze Sophia shot to him, said, "I must beg you will all excuse me. I've business I can no longer neglect." He turned wistfully to Sophia, having bade farewell to the others, and sighed, "He don't deserve you, you know. If you ever change your mind—"

"She will not!" Damon intervened with mock indignation. "And *you* do not deserve her either, so *adieu, mon faux bonhomme!*"

They all laughed, but Hartwell eyed Damon searchingly for a moment. With a faint smile, he turned to leave, only to stop again. "I forgot to pass along something that might be of small interest—if any of you knew of him. One of England's most colourful individuals has left the current scene. Sumner Craig-Bell died yesterday."

There was a total hush. Whitthurst, his face almost as white as Damon's, drew in his breath audibly. The Marquis, his unblinking stare riveted to Hartwell's comely face, breathed, "The devil, you say!"

"Craig-Bell?" Vaille said mildly. "Of Green Willow?"

"Yes." Hartwell cast a curious glance round those taut faces. "It was believed he was out of the country. Strange. They found him in his carriage. Not too far from here, as a matter of fact. Terrible tragedy. Did you know him, Duke?"

"I did. And I agree. It was a terrible tragedy. That he lived so long." He glanced at Whitthurst's stricken face and murmured, "Do you not agree, Stephen?"

"Totally, sir. How did it happen, Amory? Heart?"

"Might say so. Don't know who or why...but—a bullet stopped it."

Sophia walked slowly down the hall. She had accompanied Hartwell to the front door for the express purpose of thanking him for all his efforts in her behalf. He had been gallant, but the sadness in his eyes had been intense and had cast a shadow over her own happiness.

She had little time to dwell on the matter, however, because she returned to the music room to find Vaille and his cousin practically at daggers drawn. A small reference to Ridgley's loyalty had brought the Duke's simmering anger to the boil, and it was all that a suddenly militant Charlotte

Hilby could do to restrain them from throwing the gauntlet there and then. Feather and Sophia rushed into the breach, and the danger was averted, but the strain wrought havoc with Damon. An infuriated Belmont later told Vaille in no uncertain terms that the best thing he could do for his ailing son would be to take himself and his entourage back to London. "Wounds, germs, and disease I can fight," the surgeon snarled. "I do my possible for all my patients and will concede to no man my score of victories! But relations I cannot combat! They are, sir, the worst plague ever to drive a nurse to hysterics and a doctor to drink!"

There was little doubt but that the Marquis had suffered a setback, and for the next few days, he enjoyed Mrs. Gaffney's competence, the serene companionship of his devoted Sophia, and the total absence of his fond but disruptive family.

Vaille refused to leave the Priory, however, and found much to occupy him. He set about learning from the local constable the details of Lord Craig-Bell's death and electrified the household by bursting in one afternoon with the news that the dead man's coach had contained several items believed to have been part of the Jacobite treasure, plus a hooded robe and head mask that Sophia, with a shiver, later identified as the garments worn by the "monk" who had all but written finis to the life of her love. Vaille's powers and agents were many and by some means next unearthed a list of Craig-Bell's infamous lieutenants. It was then discovered that each of these could be accounted for. Two had already been sentenced and imprisoned; one was dead of natural causes; one had been shot by a grieving farmer who'd held the man responsible for his daughter's suicide; and the remaining two had fled the country and were not likely to return in the face of the widespread public anger over the entire ugly affair.

There was great rejoicing at the Priory. The threat that had hung for so long over the Marquis was banished. Sophia was the blushing recipient of much teasing about her future plans and went in hourly expectation of an offer from her beloved.

The Duke, ever cautious, augmented the screen of guards he had caused to be thrown round Cancrizans. Sophia was rather surprised that Damon raised no objection to this when the danger was past. Secretly, however, the Marquis was relieved. Perhaps Cobra *was* defunct, but while Sophia and his family and friends dwelt at the Priory, the presence of the guards allowed him to sleep easier. Ridgley, on the other hand, took a very dim view of the matter, complaining indignantly that he had been all but refused admission to the grounds by one of these intrepid gentlemen. Vaille murmured a smug "Deuced fine idea!" when he heard this, which again all but precipitated the threatened duel.

Inactivity was anathema to Vaille. He had developed a deep affection for Sophia, and it was his practise to select a rose for her each morning and, having supervised its placement in a proper receptacle, to present it to her personally. This charming and apparently innocuous pursuit involved both gardeners, who not only accompanied his grace in a painstaking search for the most perfect bloom available but were also kindly instructed as to how to improve their efforts in the garden. Never one to stint himself in behalf of others, Vaille also suggested his man should educate Mrs. Hatters in the more modern and efficient methods that might be utilized in the operation of a large house. The Duke was quite willing to point to those areas needing improvement, and Mr. Orpington even more willing to pass along his grace's remarks—suitably embellished. Nor was Vaille the man to leave a task half done. Aware that his son rarely stepped within sniffing distance of the stables, he directed his coachman to "look into matters" out there.

By the end of the week, Sophia was struggling to soothe chaos in the kitchen, mutiny in the stables, a totally incensed Mrs. Hatters, a Thompson whose hearing appeared to have failed him totally, and gardeners who had begun to resort to hiding rather than endure the torture of being compelled to find a perfect rose that must be cut to an exact twelve inches.

"He is the very dearest man," she moaned to Miss Hilby, "but is there nothing you could do to persuade him not to be so generous with his—er..."

"Interference?" smiled Charlotte. "Of course, I could, my dear. But is it not better that he keep busy irritating the servants than that he and Edward face one another over the glitter of small swords or sighting along those hideous duelling pistols?"

Sophia shuddered and, in total agreement, made no further mention of the matter.

Gradually, the Marquis crept back to health. The blinding

headaches that had lingered on for days after the wound itself was outwardly healed became less frequent and diminished in severity. He was patient through his convalescence, for he was a happier man than he had dreamed possible and seldom looked at Sophia without marvelling that he had been so fortunate as to find her and win her love. Three matters still plagued him, however. The first and most important of these was the haunting sense that he had not heard the last of Cobra. Second was the sustained and potentially deadly animosity between his father and Ridgley. And, third, the matter that had so tormented his lovely mother. However he wrestled with these problems, he could find no solutions and was obliged to resign himself to their existence rather than attempt to cope with them.

Whitthurst, also, was a happy man. The drawn, weary look had vanished from his face, replaced by a radiance that was echoed in Genevieve's worshipful eyes. He had not formally offered for his lady, but he told Sophia that he intended to seek the Duke's approval just as soon as Camille was up and about again.

On a brisk morning a week after Damon's first venture downstairs, Sophia went to the library to find a book he had asked for. Returning to the hall, she saw Vaille, her daily rose clasped in his hand, strolling gracefully before her. She was about to call to him when he stopped before a painting, and she watched in amusement as he clicked his tongue and straightened the frame with careful precision. She smiled fondly. How impossible he would be to live with—yet how very dear. She tensed then as Ridgley appeared at the far end of the corridor and started down, surveying his cousin with a swift frown of resentment.

Sophia took a step back into the library, watching them anxiously. Vaille, becoming aware of the Earl, stiffened and bowed slightly. Ridgley gave a terse nod. Vaille sauntered majestically toward the Great Hall. Ridgley walked to the picture and stared up at it. His gaze flashed mischievously toward the Duke's disappearing figure. With careful deliberation, he tilted the painting to a rakish angle, dusted off his fingers, and with a triumphant grin, proceeded down the hall. Sophia stepped out to face him, and he stopped, askance. She stood in front of him and shook her head chidingly. Ridgley, well aware of her dimples as well as her frown, grinned but, as he went on past, looked very much like a naughty little boy, discovered at his pranks.

Damon's voice answered Sophia's knock, and she entered the bedchamber to find him sitting in the armchair before the window, the habitual blanket across his knees. She was surprised to find him alone, but he explained that Mrs. Gaffney had gone on an errand and finished with a twinkle. "You are surely not afraid to be alone with me *en pantoufles*...in my bedchamber, are you, ma'am?"

"It would be only proper if I were, my lord," she answered primly, crossing to sit in the windowseat and hand him the book. "After all—we are not...affianced." Lowering her lashes, she waited hopefully. Surely—if he loved her—he would offer? But he said nothing, and venturing a shy upward glance, she surprised such a troubled expression in his eyes that she abandoned coquetry and, reaching out, cried, "Oh, my dear! What is it? Does your head—?"

"No, no!" He clasped her hand in both his own, gazed deep into her eyes, then placed a kiss in her palm and said haltingly, "Oh, Sophia, I'm such...a coward!"

"Coward! What nonsense! If there was ever a man less cowardly, I—" But there could be no doubt but that he shivered, although she had thought it unseasonably warm; too warm, in fact, for him to be fully dressed and still have the blanket over his legs. Alarmed, she reached for the pull on the open window.

"No. I'm n-not...cold," he stammered. He set the book aside, took a breath, and drew up his head in that slightly regal fashion she so loved. "Would you please...p-pass me my boots?" he asked faintly. "A brown pair will do."

Too worried to wonder why he would need boots inside the house, she crossed to the press. The brown boots seemed awfully heavy. Perhaps another pair...And then it dawned on her. Only the right boot was heavy! She stared downward and knew at last why the Marquis of Damon never walked faster than a stroll; why he did not ride or fence or..."do almost anything a gentleman should do." In a dazed, automatic movement, she replaced the boots and remained for a moment, staring at the one that was so cunningly built up.

Watching her, taut with anxiety, his heart hammering,

Damon said hoarsely, "It's hereditary, I'm afraid. On my mother's side. Sometimes, several generations escape unscathed, but every so often, one of the males..." He shrugged, then, seeing the tears glittering on her lashes, shrank a little and muttered, "Don't pity me, Sophia! For God's sake—don't pity me!"

She stiffened, and the tenderness had gone from her voice when she spoke. "It must be very expensive to have such boots made, Camille."

"It is of no consequence."

Fear laid its cold hands about his heart as she walked to the windows and stood with her back to him. "And must, I would think, be exceeding uncomfortable."

"I've grown accustomed to it. Mama had a shoe built for me when I was quite small, and the same man made them until he died two years ago. Since then...I've not found anyone quite so skilled."

"And so it pains you. I see." She seated herself in the windowseat and, eyeing him dispassionately, asked, "Does Vaille know all this?"

"Good...God...no!"

"Your Mama must have had to struggle very hard to keep it from him."

Damon searched her face anxiously. She looked different somehow, her lovely eyes regarding him with an intent, almost judicial expression. "It was not apparent when I was an infant," he explained slowly. "I began to...to drag the foot a little when I was about four years old. Mama took me to a surgeon, but—" He gave a small Gallic gesture of resignation. "There was nothing he could do. It simply did not...grow properly, and as the years went on...became..."

"Stunted," she said calmly.

He winced. "Yes."

"And so she had those shoes made. And forced you to walk...normally."

She seemed so very remote that his fear deepened. "You find that hard to understand?"

"Yes," she admitted quietly. "I confess that I do. All I can understand, Camille, is how difficult it must have been for you to have disguised it all these years. Indeed, I think your Mama must have been just as prideful as the Duke!"

Anger touched him at those words, and a small furrow appeared between his brows. "Try to understand, beloved.

268

She was little more than a child when he rescued her from a shameful death. In that moment, he became to her a combination of Sir Galahad and saint. But you see how he is. Everything must be—perfect. And I believe their marriage was just that until—I was born. When Mama realized I had the Montaigne foot, she lived a nightmare. She was sure if Vaille discovered it, he would turn from her. That he would obtain a divorce, have us sent back to France, and find himself another wife, and a more...acceptable heir. When she found she could do nothing to correct my infirmity, she did everything possible to keep it from him. She managed somehow to see to it that he never entered the nursery until I was dressed. She moved heaven and earth to keep me from being sent away to boarding school, and—"

"Ah," breathed Sophia. "I wondered!"

"Her very secretiveness made him suspicious. In her fear and grief, she turned increasingly to Ted, who had always worshipped her. She drew comfort from him, and he wanted only to protect her—to ease her burdens."

"Ridgley knows?" she asked, much shocked.

He nodded.

"And...said nothing?"

"She swore him to secrecy. He was furious because she had been driven to such measures, and they began to see more and more of one another. It was," he sighed, "*inevitable*, I suppose."

"And so," she frowned, "at the end, she ran to him. *He* would not have expected...perfection. Is that it, Camille?"

He stared at his hands. "Probably. I cannot remember."

"I see." There was a definite chill to her voice. Shooting an oblique glance at her, Damon noted that her firm little chin was very high, her lips tight. He longed to pull her close to him, but his pride forbade it, and he asked softly, "Would you prefer I not...say—what I was going to say?"

"Camille," she evaded, "is this what has kept you and your father apart?" He looked away and was silent. "She has been dead these twenty years," she said. "Do you still feel obliged to deceive him?"

His hands clenched, and for a moment he said nothing. Then, with every instinct screaming a protest, he tossed the blanket aside and stood. Only stockings covered his feet, and Sophia's eyes, irresistibly drawn to them, reflected both shock and sympathy despite her effort. Very pale, he walked across

269

to his great bed, his limp painfully pronounced. He held to the carven post and, standing with his head high but his back towards her, asked levelly, "Can you imagine how he would regard such a performance?"

"I cannot imagine," she replied, "that there can be any family in England cursed by such a surfeit of pride! Do you so fear him?"

"Yes. I suppose I do." He spun to face her. "But also I love him. Do you remember the way he looked at that pink rose? Do you remember how it disgusted him? I could not bear to see that same look in his eyes...because of—me."

"Oh!" She sprang to her feet. "How detestably top lofty! You are his only son! He was denied the joy of watching you grow up. Now you deny him the joy of your presence because you are afraid he will discover your secret—as if it was something vulgar! He *loves* you! He should have been told of this from the start and allowed to help cope with it. Not shut out like—like some savage interloper! What do you think he would do? Announce in the middle of St. James's—" She flung her arms wide. "Hear ye! This afflicted person is *not my son*! I deny him!'?"

"Of course not!" He limped to take her by the shoulders and shake her, smiling slightly. "Stop ripping me up, you fiery little savage! I know exactly what he would do. He would accept it—outwardly. He might even pretend it did not upset him. Inside, he would be sickened. Now be quiet, ma'am! You've had your say—allow me mine! You do not know him very well as yet—you could not begin to know what the name 'Branden' means to him! To see me hobbling about all over Town, to let his friends, and his enemies, become aware that he had a—a crippled son...would tear his heart out."

"That," she said fiercely, "is what your Mama told you, isn't it, Camille?"

"And my Grandmama and Grandpere—and what I have seen for myself. Do you not remember Phinny's ball...and what he said? That in five hundred years there have been no major blots on our family tree. No madness—no cowardice...no deformities."

Sophia gave an impatient exclamation and pulled free.

"I cannot," Damon went on firmly, "I *will* not cause him humiliation. Nor give him cause to remember her—with anything but—Now, why do you look at me like that?"

270

"I am beginning to understand what Lord Ridgley meant when he said all the Brandens are mad! Good God! What kind of family do I become involved with?"

He smiled. "A very fine one, I dare to think." It was not the time to speak, but he was afraid and, in a bid for happiness, reached to take both her hands and say humbly, "Sophia—most adored of women. Will you share this madness? May I ask Stephen for the honour of your hand in marriage?"

It was the moment she had so longed for—and now wished had not come. She could not find the words to answer him and looked away from his worshipful gaze. Damon's heart plummeted, and the dreams he had dared to build shivered into fragments. But because he was the man he was, he at once drew back and said lightly, "I rush you, do I not? And, after all, what young lady wishes to marry her uncle?"

"Or," she smiled, matching his effort, "accept a proposal in a bedchamber?"

He swung the door open for her and, bowing, said, "I must find a more suitable location the next time." He watched her in a wistful silence as she started down the corridor.

Sophia, the lump in her throat choking her, wondered if there would be a "next time"—or if that terrifying Branden pride would forbid he ever offer again.

Chapter 24

Sophia retreated to her room, and it was perhaps as well that her sorrowful reflections were interrupted by a request for her mediation in a kitchen disturbance. Following Patience downstairs, she discovered an infuriated Ariel, a mockingly scornful Nancy, and a troubled Mrs. Hatters, who conveyed to her in a hoarse whisper that it was "that there horrid Orpington what done it, no matter what Luke do say!"

Luke was of a different frame of mind. Horatio, he announced, had attacked him for the last time! Horatio was due to become an early Christmas dinner!

Nancy uttered a snort and tossed her pretty nose into the air. Sophia's enquiries were answered by Ariel, who swung the flat of the meat cleaver against his muscular thigh and, with a darkling glance at his love, announced the feathered varmint had "tore me poor leg to shreds!"

"I be a'going for to buy Luke a whip," volunteered Nancy acidly. "A big whip. So he can protect his poor feeble self."

Suppressing a smile, Sophia murmured, "He has a powerful beak, Nancy."

"Ye might say so, ma'am," the girl retaliated, regarding her betrothed with disdain. "Perhaps that there beard hides it!"

The fireboy's shriek of mirth was interrupted as Genevieve burst into the kitchen, her face taut with anxiety. "Sophia! Come! *Vite! Vite!*"

The angry voices were audible even as Sophia ran up the stairs with Genevieve beside her, gasping out a garbled story of a messenger and a box and of Vaille having flown into a towering rage. Upstairs, Genevieve went to join a frightened Mrs. Gaffney, who waited farther along the hall. Her heart pounding, Sophia knocked and, receiving no answer, went inside and closed the door swiftly behind her.

Camille was sitting as she had found him earlier, the book open on his knees. His eyes were fixed upon Vaille, who was thrusting a diamond and ruby bracelet at an infuriated Ridgley.

"...to explain," rasped the Duke, "why it should be inscribed with *your* name—and dated six years after Ninon became my wife!"

The Earl said harshly, "It was her birthday, and there was no reason why I should not give her a small gift. What did *you* ever give her but grief and tears?"

"She was *my wife*!" Vaille countered, as icy in his wrath as the Earl was blazing. "And the man who steals another man's wife—who creeps and skulks and connives to win her away from her loving husband—is *despicable*, sir!"

Ridgley's jaw tightened. With narrowed eyes, he stepped closer to Vaille. Damon leaned forward and flung out an arm in desperate appeal. "For God's sake! Don't say such bitter things! Why must you—"

"You lured her to her death!" Vaille overrode his son as if he had not spoken. "Deny if you dare that she was running to you when she was killed."

"She likely was," the Earl flashed. "For the poor dear soul was heartbroken because of your insane obsession with perfection! Terrified you'd—"

Vaille's face lost its hauteur and became dark with passion. *"Terrified?"* he thundered. "Of *me*? Now, by God, sir—you shall answer for that! It's past time for you and I to—"

"Stop it!" Damon sprang to his feet and, forgetting everything but his need to keep them from the final confrontation, started forward. "I won't let you—" He stopped. Vaille's horrified eyes were fixed upon his foot. The moment of truth was upon him, and he stood paralyzed by that awareness.

"*There's* your explanation!" roared the Earl with a wild gesture. "*That's* what drove her to her death! That—and your mania!"

For an instant, the quiet was so intense that Sophia felt her heartbeat must deafen them all, and she clasped her hands to her breast, watching Damon's face, so deathly white as he confronted his father's stark horror.

"How...long?" breathed Vaille at last, "how...long was I—deceived?"

Damon wet dry lips and, meeting those glaring eyes somehow, answered, "Since I was four—sir."

The Duke's handsome features twisted in such anguish that the trembling Sophia could not bear to watch, and she looked down. "Now, by God!" he gasped.

"Is *that* all you can say?" Ridgley snarled. "Hasn't he—"

Sophia, glancing swiftly at Damon, saw his proud head go down, and a searing rage drove fear away. "How dare you!" Her ringing voice cut through Ridgley's fierce words. Pale with anger, her narrowed eyes shooting from one to the other, she moved forward. "How *dare* you bring your stupid jealousies, your carefully nurtured hatreds into this room? Shall you never rest until you have murdered each other? Or destroyed him?"

"Ma'am," said Vaille in a tone he had never used toward her, "I appreciate—"

"Oh, no, your grace," she interrupted boldly, "you do not! Or you would certainly have more consideration for your son!"

Vaille flushed slightly and, slanting a frigid glare at Damon, said, "My—son, ma'am, is—"

"Your *son*, sir," she interrupted again, driven by fury because of his brief hesitation, "is an invalid still! And far from ready for such behaviour as has been exhibited here!"

Guilt-ridden, the Earl began to edge toward the door. Damon, not looking up, muttered, "Sophia, do not—"

"I shall leave at once," Vaille announced coldly.

"Thank you, sir," snapped Sophia. "And I beg you will return—both of you—when you can come with

274

consideration and love in your hearts."

Ridgley avoided her flaring gaze and crept miserably away.

Damon, daring to look up at last, searched his father's face and discovered only a cold disdain.

The Duke of Vaille stalked from the room without a word.

The ensuing days were peaceful, a calm settling over the old house and its occupants that Sophia prayed was the calm after the storm, not the calm before a hurricane. She wrote to Mrs. Adams at Singlebirch, informing her that she would stay the month out, by which time she believed Lord Damon's health would be completely restored. She pointed out that she was well chaperoned since Lady Branden and the Viscount stayed on also, even though Vaille had taken both Charlotte Hilby and a rebellious Genevieve with him to visit the Earl of Harland at Hollow Hill.

The Marquis made no further mention of marriage to the lady he loved more deeply with each passing day. The humiliation of the encounter with Vaille was a bruise on his spirit, deepened by the fact of Sophia's having been present to witness it. He drew much consolation from the fact that her tendre for him appeared undimmed despite her refusal to respond to his declaration. She had been shocked, he told himself. It had been too sudden for her. But she had not left him. If he was patient, and if she loved him still, there was hope. Meanwhile, each day became a gem to be treasured, and he hoarded his happiness, driven by a subconscious fear that this pleasant interlude might cease all too soon.

The Viscount had no intention of leaving without Sophia. The absence of his chosen bride created a new and deep emptiness in his life, but the vows of eternal devotion they had exchanged kept him from sinking into a slough of despond. Secure in his love, his former buoyancy returned. Having wrapped the gruff Feather about his little finger, he became her constant companion, their mutual fondness for the Marquis, horses, and dogs binding them in a deepening affection. The long, quiet days, the relaxed camaraderie, were doing much to give back to Sophia the cheerful young Corinthian her brother had once been.

On one count, Sophia was reprieved: Both Vaille and Ridgley had forgiven her furious indictment of them. During the week following the quarrel, two small boxes were delivered to her at the Priory. The first contained a magnificent gold and emerald bracelet and a note from Vaille apologizing in flowing terms for having been so crude as to lose his temper before her and assuring her that he valued her friendship and would look forward to the day when she and her fine brother would visit him at Vaille House. The second box held a brooch, fashioned in the shape of a harpsichord, with diamonds forming the keys and one deep ruby centred above the keyboard. Ridgley's note was, like the man, clumsy but endearing: "Forgive me. I lack the proper words to express my remorse. I wish I could—" (this crossed out). "I am a fool. But ever yrs to command. Ridgley."

At the end of the week, Whitthurst received an invitation to spend a few days with the Earl at his estate near St. Albans, to be climaxed by a trip to Tattersall's to see what they might have to offer in the way of "bang-up bits of blood." He took himself off in high fettle, a very different young man from the crushed semi-invalid who had so dramatically arrived. Four days later, he returned, bubbling over with news. Genevieve had been in Town with Miss Hilby, and he and Ridgley had "happened to drop by" and been accorded a royal welcome. So royal, in fact, that just to think of it sent him into a daze of rapture, prompting an amused Damon to suggest they get him outside quickly where he "might cool down a trifle."

This was accomplished by means of a picnic. It proved an unsuitable day for "cooling" purposes, however, being very warm for the lateness of the season. They settled down, all four, on the gentle slope of the bank above the stream, shaded by a venerable old oak tree. The picnic basket, having served nobly, was eventually set aside, taking with it an interested wasp. Feather, finding it difficult to stay awake, repaired to the house and the cooler comfort of her room. Damon sprawled contentedly beside his love, a serviette across his eyes; and Sophia and Whitthurst, their shoulders sharing the obliging trunk of the oak, chattered drowsily.

"Never saw such a place, Chicky," he averred for the third time. "I'd no idea Miss Hilby was so well set. That house! Gad! I do believe it's even grander than Phinny's Hall, but more comfortable, thank the Lord!"

"I wish them well of it." Sophia smiled. "Does Genevieve admire it?"

276

"No! And I could never keep her in *that* style! But I *do* think she will like Singlebirch. She's—" He checked and, reaching for her hand, gave it a brief squeeze. Craning his neck around to grin at her, he said, "All I do is talk of *my* journey and *my* plans and *my* lady...Not a word about you! Shall you mind living here when you and Cam are—"

"Who knows what the future holds?" she intervened, with a sidelong glance at Damon. "What about Marcus? Did you discover how little Douglas goes on?"

"Yes—by Gad, I forgot! Douglas is quite recovered and Esther happy as a lark. Clay was appalled when I told him what had happened and says he shall visit us when they come to Yolande Drummond's country ball."

"What splendid news! I shall so look forward to seeing them."

Whitthurst, watching the play of light and shadow across the meadows, said quietly, "I had hoped to call upon the Duke, also, but he was at Brighton with the Regent." A frown touched his face as he spoke.

Sophia said encouragingly, "He will not object, I'm sure, dear. He spoke of you most kindly."

"Perhaps it won't come to that, Chick. If...things go as people think." He paused, looking even more troubled, and leaned closer to all but whisper, "Deuced lot of nonsense, I hope. But there are some heavy bets entered on the books. Ridgley said not a word, but men talk of little else in the clubs. They are so evenly matched, it's said!"

She paled. "Dear heaven! Is a meeting arranged, then?"

"Word is it's only a matter of time."

Sophia turned to remove a fallen leaf gently from Damon's rumpled hair. "My Viper does not need that news. But if it becomes imminent, we must warn him."

"That's what Phinny said. Cam would be the only man might stop 'em. Though I'd not give much for his chances do those two fire-eaters clash!"

The thought made her shiver, and eager to change the subject, she asked, "Was Lord Bodwin in Town? He called three times to visit Camille and was the soul of consideration, yet looked at me—"

"Like a moon calf," Whitthurst grinned. "Sorry, Chicky, but shall I ever forget the sight of him in that ridiculous blue costume. And Cam's face!" He gave a hoot of laughter, forgetful of the sleeper, and Damon, without opening his eyes,

277

tossed the serviette with swift and unexpected accuracy and voiced the opinion Whitthurst was a "pestiferous young cub."

"You are awake!" Sophia said accusingly.

He rolled lazily onto his side, propped his head on one hand, and smiled. "How may a poor man sleep with your braying brother close at hand? What is my intrepid rival about in Town, Whitt?"

The Viscount sobered. "Arranging for some kind of small memorial to be built in honour of Irvin Ford. He still mourns him."

"And if I know Phinny, his 'small memorial' will evolve into something only slightly less pretentious than the Taj Mahal!"

"To hear Genevieve talk, one would think Ford rated it." Curious, Whitthurst asked, "What *was* he like, Cam?"

Damon sat up, looked unseeingly at the wasp that still hovered hopefully round the picnic basket, and said slowly, "He was the salt of the earth. England lost a great deal when that blasted gun misfired."

"Do you suppose his death—er—affected Bodwin?"

Damon threw him a quizzical look. "Phinny has always been... Phinny."

Whitthurst nodded, suddenly snatched out his pocket watch, and groaned that his head would be forfeit if he did not leave at once. "I promised to ride into Farnham and meet Hartwell. There's a team of chestnuts he has his eye on."

"Sidmoor's?" asked Damon with interest. "I heard he was letting them go. Amory will be hot after 'em all right. Does he come on here afterwards?"

The Viscount, assuring him this was the case and that they would return in good time for dinner, took his leave.

Sophia watched him stride cheerily away and refused to turn even when a long tufty strand of grass tickled persistently at her ear.

"You are angry," sighed Damon, dropping the strand of grass.

"You were listening." Her eyes searched his with keen anxiety. "Camille—did you hear—?" and she paused, frowning a little.

Realizing she was not going to divulge whatever it was that he might have heard, Damon asked, "Why does Whitthurst call you Chicky? You never told me." She fixed her troubled gaze upon the stream and made no answer. "You

278

have no need to hesitate," he smiled. "*I* am not plagued by fears of heredity, you see..."

She turned an indignant glance on him, but the quirk beside his mouth was irresistible. She laughed and in a second was clasped in his arms. And when he had kissed her satisfactorily, whispered of his love, and apologized for "whatever it was" he had done to offend her, he repeated his question.

"It was because of our Uncle James," she said. "He came home from the Americas full of tales of the New World and the Indians. He told us how one tribe shaved their heads and left only a long strip of hair running down the middle of the scalp. Stephen and I were fascinated. We just had to try it. I started on Steve, but, alas, I was no great hand with a razor. He accused me of trying to scalp him, and the end of it was that he shaved *my* head, instead! All except the middle." She ran one slim finger from front to back of her lovely head. "It looked perfectly delicious, though my dear Mama and Papa did not find it so." She chuckled at that memory and went on, "When my hair began to grow back, it was like fuzzy down all over my head, and the center, having grown longer naturally, stuck up like a cockscomb!"

"Aha!" Damon's eyes danced with laughter. "How I should love to have seen my little...Chicky!"

"Do not dare start to call me that!"

"Why not? You have a far less kindly nickname for me!"

"And well deserved," she nodded with a flash of dimples. "My...Viper."

Her voice softened. Damon's eyes became ineffably tender, and he leaned once again to her lips.

The afternoon was still, and the countryside, beginning to be touched with russet, was peaceful, with no sign of menace or danger. Yet, fifty yards to the east, an apparent gamekeeper strolled, with hunting gun on one arm and eyes keen; and to the west were two more such vigilant guards. Damon, having schooled himself to find such intruders invisible, was managing to ignore them, particularly when so happily occupied. But in the pocket of his jacket, now discarded and lying on the grass beside him, resided a small but efficient pistol. Just in case.

Sophia opened her eyes, gazed into the finely chiselled face above her, and murmured, "Camille..."

"Yes, beloved?"

"It is... very warm."

He looked around and, getting to his feet, went to a nearby tree and broke off a branch of leaves. Returning to fan her gallantly, he was rather taken aback to meet a ferocious scowl. When he enquired as to the reason for this, he was told an explicit "Nothing!" He knew his ladies quite well, wherefore he smiled faintly and continued to fan her—thus providing the spark that was to launch a campaign.

"You," she nodded thoughtfully, "are just as bad as they are."

There was no doubting to whom she referred. "They are not 'bad,' Sophia."

She sat up and, taking the branch from him, began to fan herself rapidly. "They are proud and arrogant and... childish! And so are you!" Her sudden violence shaking the leaves from her impromptu fan, she glared at the bare stalks and cast them aside.

The Marquis sighed, leaned back against the tree and, pulling up a strand of grass, stuck it between his teeth, closed his eyes, and said nothing. Such provoking conduct must naturally lead to reprisals, wherefore, opening one curious eye in a few moments, he opened the other in a hurry and gasped, "Good God! What are you doing?"

"Taking off my stockings, silly," she giggled. "Turn your naughty head, sir!"

Horrified, his eyes reconnoitred. The guards were not facing this way. "Sophia! You must not—"

"Oh, don't be so high in the instep! They're not looking. And, at all events, you told me to pretend they are not there."

"I know, but I didn't mean... that is—I—Gad! *Now* what are you doing?"

"I am about to paddle in the stream. Come!"

"Sophia!" he protested, "a lady of quality don't—"

"Deirdre Breckenridge does. And she's a lady of quality!"

"Yes—and delightfully so. But always was as wild as—"

"She is the reigning toast! And I heard you fluttered about her campfire before you disappeared from the social scene. Which was natural enough, I suppose, since she—like yourself, sir—is a halfbreed."

He flung a sharp look at her, then grinned. "Vixen!"

Sophia ran down the slope, stepped gingerly into the clear water, gasped, then splashed happily, holding her skirts so that he could see those shapely ankles. "Come, dearest—it's lovely!"

He stood and followed her to the water's edge but said a firm "No."

"You are afraid," she taunted.

He frowned a little, then smiled and shrugged. *"Assuré-ment!"*

"Proud...and arrogant...and childish!" she verified.

Refusing to be baited into a quarrel, he bowed and started away.

Desperate, Sophia called, "Why do you still wear that special shoe and punish yourself by walking...normally? Because—you *are* a coward. As you said!"

Stunned, Damon halted but did not turn to her.

Her heart contracting, she said, "Feather told me that your foot doesn't hurt if you limp. But you never limp if other people are about. Is pride that important to you? Had people known you had a...a..."

He whirled around. "Crippled?" he supplied between set teeth.

"Crippled foot"—she gulped—"nobody would have thought you should have been in the fighting. But you would not let them know preferring instead to live a lie so as not to fail his impossible standards!"

White-faced, he drawled, "Are you quite finished, ma'am?"

"Why do you love me?" she demanded, dreading lest he walk away from her.

He bit his lip, scowling.

"Is it because I am beautiful?"

She was very beautiful, standing there with the sunshine waking golden lights in her hair, her lithe and lovely body swaying, her bare feet white through the clear water. But..."No," he said honestly. "Not entirely."

"Why, then?"

And remembering so many precious moments, he could not hold his hurt and anger and said, "Because...you have a bright and happy nature. Because you have a clear, intelligent mind. Because I honour you for your virtue and respect you for your courage. And because—when you are my wife—I shall be able to talk with you...as well as...make love to you."

Sophia blinked, and the lump in her throat so choked her

281

that for a moment she could not speak, and then she asked, "And why do you think...I love you? Because you are said to be the handsomest man in London—and will become one of the richest? Because of your high title?"

He watched her, his heart in his eyes, and asked humbly, "Why *do* you love me, my most precious woman?"

"Because," she replied, her voice a caress, "even when you sought to frighten me and drive me away, an innate decency shone from your dear eyes. Because you are as gentle as you are strong; and as good as you pretended to be evil. Because you are kind to those who have nothing and as courteous to a serving maid as to a Duchess. And—because I would not settle for any less than a man I could...honour...for his gallantry."

Recalling her words that morning such a little—yet such a long time ago—his eyes misted, and he begged huskily, "Sophia, my heart...come to me."

"And," she went on, her pulse racing, "my love for you has little to do with whether you have one arm or one leg...or are...crippled."

Damon froze.

"Oh, my dear," she cried yearningly. "I cannot bear to see you struggle for so foolish a cause. Will you not come into the stream with me?"

He knew now that this was why she had refused him. That if he did as she wished, it must mean that he never wear that cunningly contrived yet so cruel boot again. And that his father would be obliged to own that he had a crippled son. He stood for a long moment, torn by conflicting emotions. Then he frowned and said a harsh "No!"

"Go, then!" she cried fiercely. "Take your pride and clutch it to your heart, as they do! Make it the most important thing in your life—as they have! Wear that horrid boot for the rest of your life—no matter how it punishes you! But you will walk through life without me, Lord Damon! No son of *mine* shall be sacrificed on the altar of pride, as your Mama sacrificed you!"

She knew at once that she had gone too far. He stood utterly still for a few seconds, his face a livid mask. Then his head tossed back in that familiar haughty gesture—so like Vaille. He turned from her without a word and started up the slope, walking very straight and steady. Sophia threw

282

both hands to her mouth and, shrinking, stifled a whimper of despair.

Damon, rage struggling with a bitter desolation, reached blindly for his jacket—and paused.

She was singing, her voice gaspingly uncertain but that rich, glorious soprano piercing his heart:

> It is not while beauty and youth are thine own
> And thy cheeks unprofaned by a . . . tear,
> That the fervour and faith of a soul can be known
> To which time . . . will but make thee . . . more dear.
> No . . . the heart that has truly . . . loved . . . never forgets
> But as . . . truly . . . loves on . . . to . . . to—

And her voice broke and choked into silence.

"Oh—hell . . . and blast . . . and damnation!" he groaned.

The Most Honourable the Marquis of Damon sat down and tore off his shoes and stockings; then, standing, rolled up his breeches. Shamelessly, he limped down the bank and into her arms.

Chapter 25

Damon's eyes opened as the first thread of light split the darkness around his door. Silently, the light widened. He saw a man's shape black against the shielded glow from a candle and, his blood tingling, slid his hand under the pillow, fingers closing around the reassuring chill of the pistol.

The door was closed. The figure crept closer. The hand was removed from the candle flame, and looking into the yawning mouth of a steel barrel, Amory Hartwell yelped, "Good God! D'you want me to have a seizure?"

Lowering the weapon, Damon reached for his watch on the table beside his bed, peered at it, and said quietly, "Whatever gets you up at this hour is not like to be good news."

His friend proceeded to kindle the flames on a branch of candles. "Had I known I was about to get my head shot off, I'd not have come at all!" Then, abandoning his aggrieved manner, he said regretfully, "Truth is, I wish I'd *not* to be the one to bring you word, Cam."

Damon was already up and limping toward his press. "My father?"

"Yes. I left my man to keep an eye on things, and he just arrived with word that they meet at sun-up. It's almost four now. You'd best hasten."

"Blast!" Pulling on his breeches, Damon asked a terse "Where?"

"Tottenbury Castle. Of all the miserable places! I collect they were both guests at Parapine—you know the Drummonds, do you not? Yolande's come-out is to be next month, and—"

"Gad! They never quarrelled at Yolande's party?"

"'Fraid so. Never should have sold your Mama's locket, Cam. Vaille traced it down day before yesterday. Bad *ton*, dear old boy. Not the thing at—"

"Locket?" Buttoning his shirt with icy fingers, Damon said impatiently, "What the devil's that got to do with it?"

"Lockets, y'know. Personal things. Why in thunder did you not take the miniatures out?"

Damon's fingers ceased their fumbling, and he stared at his friend in mystification. "There were no miniatures, or you may be sure I would have done so!"

"Oh, gad! What a gudgeon! I collect you only opened the front compartment! Yes, you clunch! There was another—on the back! Inside were—" Hartwell stared uncomfortably at the candles. "There were two paintings. One of your Mama and one of—Ridgley. And, inscribed around both, the words 'Ninon and Ted—one love... one heart... Forever!'"

"My God!" Blanching, Damon gasped, "Vaille read *that*? How do you know all this?"

"Everyone knows. One of his agents delivered it to him at the ball. Vaille opened it and seemed turned to stone, my man said. Then he tossed it aside and plunged off after Ridgley. He came back for the locket eventually, but, meanwhile, several of the ladies had seen it. Word spread like—"

"Say no more!" Damon reached for his jacket. "Did my father simply demand satisfaction—or just knock Ted down?"

"I collect Ridgley was seen wiping his mouth," Hartwell sighed, "but that for the rest of the evening they smiled upon one another..."

The night wind was chill and carried a smell of rain, the promise heightened by the halo round the moon hanging just above the black clouds building on the horizon. Buttoning his many-caped driving coat, Damon strode onto the terrace. The carriage stood ready, seeing which, he grated furiously, "Dammit! I said my racing curricle!"

"Trouble with a wheel, my lord," said Thompson staring at the horses.

"Blast! Well, it's too late now. Who's up? Rust?"

"Trask." Thompson's voice was miserable. Damon slipped a hand onto the worried man's shoulder, and stuck out the other. It was caught in a hard grip. "Guard her for me, Jack. Whitthurst is a fine fighting man, but—he's rather slowed nowadays. She must not be left alone—not for an instant! I charge you with that!"

Thompson swore under his breath, but nodded and, watching that tall figure move towards the luxurious vehicle, muttered a forlorn "Good luck, sir!"

Damon waved and swung inside. At once, the steps were put up, the door slammed, and the carriage plunged forward. He was thrown down before he had a chance to take a seat. Starting up, furiously angry at such tactics, he checked. Amory Hartwell sat opposite, watching him gravely.

"Didn't think you were going all alone, did you, Cam?"

Damon settled himself and, touched, said a gruff "Idiot! You must have had very little sleep. When I went upstairs you and Whitt were still throwing dice and more than a little foxed."

"He was. I wasn't."

"At all events, I doubt I properly thanked you for warning—" Damon's eyes were becoming accustomed to the dimness, and he detected a large trunk balanced on the seat beside his friend. "What's this? Are you leaving us so soon?"

"Care to see what's in it?"

"Why in the devil should I want to look at your small clothes?"

"Not mine, old fellow. Yours."

Damon watched curiously as Hartwell loosened the straps and raised the lid.

The moon was half obscured by clouds, yet even that feeble illumination awoke sparkles from the contents of the trunk. Leaning forward incredulously, Damon saw gem-encrusted bowls and vases; exquisitely wrought sterling and fine old jade pieces; and fat leathern bags, bulging with the shapes of coins.

"Found your treasure for you," Hartwell beamed.

"Did you, by God! How splendid! But—where? How the deuce—?"

"In the catacombs—second level down. Ain't you going to say 'thank you'?"

"I most assuredly am!" Damon leaned at once to clap him on the shoulder. "And I can do better than that! You shall have half the profits! Now what the hell are you scowling about? And—why did you bring it along?"

"I thought it would be safer if we salted it away in your bank—as soon as you take care of your—er—obstreperous relatives."

"Quite right." And less danger for Sophia, he thought, and said awkwardly, "Amory, I wish—there could have been two of her."

"I'll drink to that!" Hartwell pulled a flask from his pocket. "Jove, but it's getting cold! This'll warm us up! Here."

Damon took a good swallow and coughed. "Cognac. And not my best, I fear!"

"Ingratitude," Hartwell said dryly, retrieving the flask, wiping the top and upending it uncomplainingly, "thy name is Damon!"

The Marquis laughed and apologized. "That trunk must weigh a ton. Did Ariel put it in for you?"

"Gone to his bachelor party, old lad. Trask helped me with it. I always thought"—he again wiped the flask fastidiously and returned it to his friend—"that your loot was still down there somewhere. I kept prowling around until I discovered it. Ah—that brandy ain't so bad now, eh?"

"You're right. But what a damned risk to take. We never did find the secret entrance Craig-Bell must've used. Suppose one of his friends had been crawling about down there? I hope you took a pistol with you?"

"Never without one. Matter of fact, I have a Manton with me now."

The carriage rounded a curve much too fast. Damon frowned out the window. "What's that lunatic about? He's going the wrong way!" He picked up his cane and rapped sharply on the roof. "Trask! What the devil d'ye think you're doing?" There was no response. They were heading toward the spa instead of having branched off to the west. He reached for the window. "By God!" he cried wrathfully, "I'll give the fellow a—"

"Cam," said Hartwell, "why get into such a pucker?"

"You know damned well why! I must reach Tottenbury ...before..." He was seized by an odd dizziness and sat down.

"Ain't it a pity," smiled Hartwell, "life is so full of disappointments?"

Damon looked up slowly. The Manton was aimed unwaveringly at his heart, but Amory's familiar smile was unchanged. Treachery from such an old friend struck so keenly that he could only stare in speechless disbelief.

"Beastly, ain't it?" Hartwell commiserated.

Finding his voice, Damon said unsteadily, "Yes. Why? The treasure only?"

"Only!" Hartwell gave a sardonic laugh. "There speaks the man who has never gone hungry!"

"You are not like to starve."

"Only thanks to you, dear old philanthropist. Oh, yes, *you* were my wealthy relation from the Americas. And what a good life you provided me! I found your treasure when we first came back from Europe. This is only a tenth of what there was at the start. I took the lightweight stuff first. You've such a dashed devoted little staff, Cam. It was the very devil to sneak it out under their noses. I filched a little each time I came down. There was no real hurry. But when you began to mess about with that music, it occurred to me that there *might* be some code in it, after all. I'd have burned the blasted parchment, but I knew you'd probably memorized the notes, and if it disappeared, you would have known you were on the right track. So I decided I'd best move what was left. You came barging in right in the midst of my efforts."

"So *you* were the monk!" That knowledge hurt more than he would have cared to admit, and he said frigidly, "You hated me that much?"

"Not at all. I really am very sorry—didn't intend to hit you so hard. But you were always so damned fast with your fists in spite of that foot of yours."

Damon stared at him. The shock was affecting him strangely, and his head felt muddled, but he said cuttingly, "That Twine business was pretty raw—my friend."

Even through the dimness, he detected Hartwell's flush. "It was Sumner's idea," he said defensively. "He liked it. And when Sophia spoiled it, he realized she was in love with you. He was delighted. He'd found a way to really repay you, he thought. Unfortunately, his 'way' was to kill her. I knew he

288

was right when he said it would break you, but—Now don't get violent, old boy! I don't want to shoot, but—if I have to... That's better." He leaned back, eyes watchful and, when the deadly glare in Damon's eyes faded, remarked, "It so happens I really do care for Sophia. I couldn't let him hurt her. I got him down to Pudding Park by a ruse—shot him, and left 'evidence' to indicate he'd been the monk. No loss, so don't look at me like that, Cam. He was utter slime."

Impatient with himself, Damon realized his recent illness must be responsible for the fact that he felt utterly drained of strength. He must have been blind not to have seen this coming. Hartwell had always appeared so loyal, yet there had been incidents—several—that had caused him to question the man's character. He'd taken him for a weakling, but years of friendship had compelled him to ignore such traits. "My dogs?" he asked wearily. "That note to Ariel? You?"

"Certainly not! I loved Géant—and Satin! And I do not send anonymous notes! Nor did Craig-Bell. But more of that later."

"Is... is Trask to die as well?"

"No need. He's been our man for some time." Hartwell regarded his companion with real sorrow. "I bear you no malice, Cam. I wish you will believe that. But—it's your life or disgrace and prison for me. No choice, you see."

"Had you no... choice... in the matter of the beam? Sophia might have—"

"'Fraid I must plead guilty there. It was a little delaying mechanism I'd rigged in case anyone should come creeping after me while I was down there. I honestly didn't know she'd followed me. When I heard her voice, I ran back and damn near got caught in my own trap. Damon? You're not going to fall asleep, are you?" He chuckled softly. "At a moment like this?"

Damon, comprehending his sick weakness, groaned. "Damn... you!"

"Clever, wasn't I?" Hartwell's voice seemed very far away. "Wouldn't have done it—except I know how difficult you can be. Didn't you notice how carefully I wiped the flask? Was simply inserting a stopper. Beastly stuff!"

"Was it..." Damon asked thickly, his head sinking, "poison?"

"Gad, no! I couldn't kill a friend. Cam? Have you gone... out?"

Damon could no longer see.

"Out?...Out?...Out?"

The word echoed into silence.

To walk was a tremendous effort. Damon's head ached, and his mouth felt like dusty wool, yet he was stumbling along willy nilly, shoved from behind when he slowed. His mind was too dulled to sort it out. All he could see was the ground, which seemed very uneven and stony; and boots. His own and a pair of gleaming, tasseled Hessians that kept pace with him. Men laughed raucously as the owner of those boots murmured something. The voice sounded vaguely familiar, if only he could think...The ground was becoming clearer, as though—It was almost dawn! That realization brought his head up, and with it came memory. He halted, staring at the dapper gentleman, elegant in a many-caped coat, who surveyed him through a jewelled quizzing glass.

"Good morning, my dear friend," said Phineas Bodwin in a soft, silky voice. "By Jove, but you cannot know how excessive pleased I am to have you here!"

Damon returned no answer and was again pushed forward. With every stride now, his head felt clearer, and with every stride, his amazement grew. Bodwin! Of all men—the last he'd have suspected of being associated with Cobra! He shivered and realized with faint surprise that he wore neither coat nor jacket.

Bodwin's neighing laugh rang out. "Cold, Damon? Your garments have been spoken for, I fear." He gestured toward Trask, who followed, swaggering in the Marquis's driving coat. "Murray has your jacket, old chap, but you won't be needing it...Confess now—you'd no idea I was Craig-Bell's second-in-command, had you?"

Damon reflected grimly that he also had no idea what they were doing at the spa; why they were now approaching the barn; nor how in the devil he was to get out of this mess. He was by now aware of the powerfully built round-eyed man who trod just a step behind him, a lethal-looking club in his hands; of the musket Trask held pointed at his back; and the pistol Hartwell dangled with apparent nonchalance. Another man, stoop-shouldered and narrow-faced, had remained with the carriages. He must be the "Murray" Bodwin had referred to. Five in all.

"I would not have imagined," he answered, "that any man related to someone as fine as Irvin Ford could—"

Bodwin stopped, his gaze turned upon the Marquis with savage malevolence. "You swine! It is because you murdered my loved nephew that I have gone to such pains with the manner of your dying!"

"*I* . . . murdered Ford?" Damon gasped. "You're mad! I wasn't even in Dorset!"

"He found out," snarled Bodwin. "When you stuck your long and noble nose into our affairs, he found out. About me! He overheard poor Stover when he came to the Hall half out of his wits with fright, poor lad. The Runners were hot on his tail. A fine young man like that—from a fine old family! Thrown to the wolves! And for what? Because we rousted a few peasants about—of whom there are untotalled numbers starving every day? Because we had a little fun with some village trollops? Because we kicked up a little hell that gave the Watch something to occupy their time? What the devil was that to you?"

"He was avenging his friend," Hartwell put in mildly. "You remember Hilary Flanders, don't you, Phinny? Foreign Office. Shot himself."

"Ah . . . yes. That little ploy. A very foolish young man who refused to help us."

"So you ruined him," said Damon. "Which broke his father's heart, and—"

"And for that reason alone, you dared to—"

"Reason enough! But it was only one of a hundred reasons! And if you're going to tell me Irv committed suicide because you were involved, I do not—"

"But, my dear boy, I tell you no such thing. Irvin did not commit suicide. *You* murdered him! He might have betrayed me, so I had to stop him. It would not have been necessary but for you. It was *your* fault, Damon."

The Marquis stared at him in horror. "*You* killed him? Your own nephew? Why, he was worth ten of you! You dainty, murdering bas—"

He lunged for Bodwin, but the musket rammed into his back, staggering him. Hartwell cautioned softly, "Careful, Damon—no time to be high in the instep."

Damon had been extremely fond of Irvin Ford. His fingers fairly itched to wrap themselves about the throat of the dandy who had so mercilessly wiped away that promising young life. But, again, he was shoved with bruising force toward the barn. Bodwin, picking his fastidious way over the rubble left by the workmen, said, "That was merely my first score against you. But there are other matters between you and I."

"You mistake it," said Damon. "I make it a point to avoid dealing with persons of...questionable taste."

The words were uttered with cool disdain and could scarcely have been better chosen to inflame his captor. A smothered chuckle escaped Hartwell. Bodwin, obliged to look up at the Marquis, discovered in the contemptuous lift of the brows, the droop of the eyelids, no trace of fear, but, instead, the very hauteur that so infuriated him when evidenced by Vaille. "Oh, but you Brandens have a top-lofty air," he jeered. "It has always amused me, considering that my House predates your own."

"Do not trace it back too far," Damon murmured, "else you will doubtless discover creatures dwelling in caves and glutting themselves on raw meat." He cast a scornful look at his companion. "Who might be offended by the relationship, at that!"

Trask broke into a rather doubtful coughing. Bodwin checked, colour flooding into his face, his hand tightening about the gold handle of the fine Malacca cane he carried. Hartwell watched him narrowly, but, after an instant, Bodwin resumed his stately pacing. "So you like a jest, do you, Damon? Then here's one for you. Twenty years back, your father entertained lavishly at Cancrizans, yet not once, in all the time he dwelt there with his little French tit, was I—"

Damon tensed. Knowing him, Hartwell jumped forward and grabbed his arms. Bodwin, who had retreated a step, moved closer again. "Did I speak disrespectfully of your dear Mama?" The tip of his cane tapped very gently under Damon's chin as he smiled into those narrowed eyes. "But that is *my jest*, you see, my friend. The foolish lady also made the mistake of cutting me."

"Naturellement," said the Marquis, his nostrils flaring slightly. "My Mother was a lady of excellent discernment."

Bodwin leaned nearer. "Wherefore," he hissed, "she is—dead!"

Something very cold gripped Damon's heart. "Filth!" he grated. "What are you saying?"

292

"Why Camille, dear boy," Bodwin giggled. "Do you not recall why the chaise spun off the road that day? A wheel came right off!" He giggled once more. "Such a tragedy! And so nicely...timed."

"Bastard!" raged Damon. With all his strength, Hartwell could barely hold him. Trask grabbed an arm, and they hung on as the Marquis fought them savagely.

Bodwin shook his head. "You've a naughty mouth, and *I* am the injured party here, my lord. History does repeat itself, you see. Recently, I chose a lady for my bride, and you had the unmitigated gall to attempt to lure her away!"

Still trembling with passion, Damon said breathlessly, "Gad, but you've a rare sense of humour! Sophia don't much care for your brother club member here, but she'd sooner wed him than you, any day of the week!"

"And you, sir, are an insolent puppy who wants for manners!" Bodwin's eyes glared his hatred. "As for club members—Hartwell was not one of us."

Hartwell had moved aside but still held his pistol aimed steadily at Damon. "I was an unwilling accomplice," he shrugged. "Phinny discovered I'd been bartering your treasure. He's been blackmailing me ever since. But I am to keep all the loot, Cam, so do not seek to promote a quarrel between us over Sophia. T'would be a foolish waste of breath."

"Perhaps, but I'm not so foolish as Bodwin if he harbours such pathetic delusions. Sophia would run a country mile before she'd wed a degenerate old man."

"You arrogant clod!" Bodwin snarled. "I paid the lady the supreme compliment of offering for her, but when Hartwell had the good sense to smash your wretched skull, she ran to you! And you wonder I intend to destroy you? By God, but when I'm finished, you will wish you'd never raised your hand against your own kind!"

"I have not done so," said Damon with indignation. "Whatever 'kind' you are, Bodwin, I refuse to be numbered among it!"

Lord Phineas gave a strangled cry, and the cane whipped upward. Stepping quickly between them, Hartwell laughed. "Cam—*will* you behave? I'm trying to keep this on at least a fairly polite level!"

"Because you're gutless!" raged Bodwin. "Well, there's no reason I cannot—"

"It's almost dawn, Phinny," Hartwell pointed out mildly.

Damon's heart missed a beat. He'd thought the duel part of the plot to lure him here. Was it indeed to take place?

"True..." Bodwin gave a soft laugh and turned to the man with the club. "Doak—fetch Whitthurst. Hurry, or I'll be late for the second act."

Whitthurst? Damon stiffened, and noting the reaction, Bodwin's eyes lit up. "After you retired last evening, dear boy, the Viscount became quite foxed and, thanks to Hartwell's clever baiting, insisted on galloping to Parapine to see his love, regardless of the hour. Unhappily, he never reached his destination...and will die with you. So sad, but with both of you gone, Lady Sophia will be only too glad to accept my devotion and—eventually—my hand."

The Marquis gave him a pitying look but was thinking that if he brought it off, this would kill Sophia. Enough she should have to mourn him, but her adored brother as well? He *must* get them out of this!

They had reached the barn. Trask swung the huge door open, and Hartwell bowed Damon inside. There were only three of them now...probably the best chance he'd have.

Bodwin turned up the wick on an oil lamp that hung on a peg beside the door. "After we are wed," he mused, "I may have to be quite harsh with Sophia. For a while, at least. She's a fiery chit and must be brought to heel."

Hartwell frowned. Damon, appalled by the thought of Sophia as the helpless wife of this satyr, laughed. "You poor fool! You make her skin creep. The only emotion she feels for you is amusement!"

Hartwell laughed outright. Bodwin's lips pulled back into a grimace of hatred. His hand darted into the pocket of his coat.

Trask, levelling the musket, cried in a stentorian tone, "Lord Phineas Bodwin—Sir Amory Hartwell, I arrest you in the King's name, for complicity in—"

Damon gasped in astonishment. Hartwell stared with utter disbelief. Bodwin swore, whipped the pistol from his pocket, and with a shove sent Hartwell plunging against Trask. Damon leapt forward, but even as he did so, there were two distinct shots: the roar of the musket; the sharper bark of the pistol. Clutching at his arm, Hartwell reeled backward. Trask gave a grunt and fell. Bodwin, his pistol smoking, ran from Damon's charge, wide-eyed with fright. Damon sprang in pursuit. Bodwin flailed at him with the pistol as he fetched up against the gate to a stall. Damon swayed lightly aside, sent his right smashing into that slender middle, and, as the man doubled up, connected with a solid left to the jaw. Bodwin straightened out, crashed against the gate, and, as it burst open, shot through it and went down, vanishing noisily into a welter of painters' equipment.

A harsh voice shouted, "Hey! Your lordship!"

Damon spun around. Whitthurst stood just inside the open door. His hair and clothes were wet; he looked half frozen and shuddered violently, his white face reflecting helpless misery. Doak gripped his arm, and the narrow-faced man held a pistol low against his side. "One more move,"—he leered—"and—he'll die slow."

Doak swung the door shut, and the Marquis stood motionless.

Hartwell, leaning weakly against a post, clutching his arm with crimson-stained fingers, groaned, "Can't help you now, Cam. You and your fancy...fists."

Damon knew with grim certainty that he was in a most devilish situation. Bodwin was getting to his feet, groaning curses. Doak came up swiftly behind Damon and wrenched his arms back. Bodwin, his jaw red and swelling, his eyes slits of hatred, stepped forward. "Hold him, Doak." He drew back one fist. "I'm going to enjoy this."

"Da...mon" The voice called from a very great distance. He was extremely uncomfortable and had no least intention of responding, but the call was repeated and, at last, sighing plaintively, he opened his eyes. The round glow above him resolved itself into a face, the features becoming clearer as full consciousness returned. He tried, fruitlessly, to sit up.

Bodwin, bending over him, murmured, "At last!"

Damon could remember little after the first few blows, but the salt taste of blood was in his mouth; his jaw felt as if it might be broken; and his head was splitting again. Wherefore, naturally, he summoned a grin and said in a far away voice, "Want to go another round, Phinny? I should be...about down to your speed."

He heard a faint cheer and, looking around, eventually made out Whitthurst dancing around a nearby tree. This puzzled him until he realized that his vision was at fault. The Viscount was, in fact, leaning against a heavy supporting beam in the center of the barn, waving to him. There was much noise in the barn—a deal of banging and clattering about that echoed in his ears. He sighed again.

"You miserable swine! *Will* you wake up?"

"What?" he said thickly. "Oh...you still here, Phinny?"

"Yes, damn you! And you're making me late! It all took so much longer than I thought, and I really *must* be at Tottenbury by sunrise!"

"Poor fella," said the Marquis. "Do not let us detain you." And he frowned, wishing it was a little less noisy.

"Look, Damon," urged Bodwin. "Can you see what I have arranged for you?"

Damon looked and, as objects became clearer, felt hope drain away. There was a line of stalls along the left side of the barn and, on the right a central area intended for feed and supplies now held stacked cans of paint and varnish. This section was set off by a five foot fence consisting of horizontal rails threaded through sturdy supporting posts about seven feet apart. The lowest rail was some six inches above the ground, and to this his wrists were separately tied, while his feet, tightly bound together, were secured by a rope stretching to one of the stalls opposite and knotted round a gatepost. Whitthurst was as helpless, the bonds that pinioned him against the massive centre beam leaving only his arm free. And that arm was stretched high above him; not waving, as Damon had supposed, but holding Doak's club. A small hinged shelf had been attached to the upper part of the beam, and the club was just long enough to restrain that clumsy shelf from folding downward.

"Do you see, my dear Camille," purred Bodwin, "what is on the shelf?"

Damon saw and realized with a weakening of the knees why the oil lamp had been placed there.

Bodwin gave a happy little crow of laughter. "There should be brackets to hold that shelf upright. But so long as Whitthurst can support it, the lamp will not fall. On the other hand"—he glanced upward, his eyes glistening with pleasure—"should he weaken..." His cane indicated the bales of hay below that unsteady shelf. "Doak is so clumsy. He accidentally dropped quite a lot of oil on those bales. It ran, in fact, all the way to that other stack...by the horses."

Damon wrenched his head around and felt the blood drain from his face. The far end of the barn had been roped off;

296

beyond the rope, many horses milled about uneasily. He realized that they were the source of the clattering sounds, and he stared, sickened by the awareness of what would happen when the lamp dropped, as inevitably it must. His gaze shot to Whitthurst, and, very briefly, the Viscount glanced at him, his eyes strained, his young face haggard and beaded with sweat. The shelf tilted, and Damon gave a gasp as the lamp slid to the side.

"Careful!" called Bodwin, and the Viscount's attention returning to his desperate task, he clicked his tongue regretfully. "He's tired, poor lad, and I'm afraid became thoroughly chilled while we had him in the canal, awaiting your arrival. But," he smiled kindly, "he'll warm up very soon...I've no doubt."

Keeping himself well in hand, the Marquis observed, "Phinny, you've a perfectly frightful black eye...poor chap."

Bodwin gritted his teeth and struggled to contain a boil of rage. "Have you ever," he asked silkily, "seen a stable fire? Have you ever seen horses maddened with fear? They'll be through that rope in a flash...And just think...here you will be, Damon, lying between them—and the doors. When they cannot get out, they'll rush madly back...and forth..." He waved his cane over the Marquis and smiled. "A plan tailor-made for you, dear Camille."

Damon could only pray he didn't look as petrified as he felt. "I imagine you shall stay to see the...fireworks?" His voice was cool and mercifully without a quaver. "Your sick little soul will doubtless gloat over us." But as bravely as he spoke, his glance slid to the side in a last faint hope. Trask was sprawled motionless, just to one side of the doors. He looked dead. There was no sign of Hartwell, but perhaps because of his own deeply ingrained adherence to the Code, it was almost inconceivable to Damon that Amory could be a party to this final savagery. He had done all he could to protect his ex-comrade from Bodwin's fury enroute to the barn. Was it possible that, objecting to Damon being struck with a cane, he could yet turn his back on this brutal murder? Hartwell was a weak, greedy man, but surely he would not—

Bodwin had not missed that searching gaze and offered smugly, "If you are looking for Hartwell, he's gone. He wouldn't have helped you, anyway. He is quite totally spineless. He needed you dead but couldn't bear to watch it. I rather fancy he is at this moment driving your coach hell for leather toward Weymouth and the first ship he can find."

Receiving only a bored stare by way of comment, he sighed. "I really must go. Such a lovely morning for a duel, don't you agree? Cheerio, Whitthurst. Keep your chin up!"

The Viscount's breathless response was pithily explicit, and Damon laughed. Bodwin shook his head reprovingly, then started for the door. Outwardly calm, he was inwardly in a raging fury. They were being so very stoical! He bethought himself of a detail and, smiling, turned back to tap his cane gently against Damon's lacerated cheek. "I forgot to tell you, old fellow. You were so very cooperative to sell your Mama's locket. It was made to order for me! What a pity you will not see the miniatures I commissioned—you'd have liked them. And they did the trick so well. My timing, you know, never fails. Now I shall go to the funerals and weep. I weep so convincingly..."

Damon's poise vanished. Struggling against the ropes, he gasped with rageful futility, "By God! If I ever get out of this!"

"But you cannot, poor lad. We shall replace the fences as we leave, and no one knows you are here. I should so love to stay and watch. But I shall see the fire from my coach...I mustn't be greedy, must I?"

"Cam..." Whitthurst's voice was a sob of despair. "I can't hold this damned thing...much longer!"

"You must!" gasped Damon. "I've...I've nigh...got it clear! Hang on, Whitt!"

He wrenched frantically. He'd had no intention of ever again donning the built-up boot, but the prospect of attempting to stop the duel while he limped about had been repugnant. Now he could only thank God he'd worn it, for by an ironic quirk of fate his infirmity was their one hope. Whoever had tied him had made his bonds cruelly tight. His left foot was already numbed, the rope having bitten deep into the soft leather. The reinforced boot, however, had not been crushed at all, and if he could but drag his foot out and push the boot clear, the resultant slackening of the ropes must allow his left foot to escape, also. His efforts were agonizing, but to be trampled beneath countless iron-shod hooves would be incalculably worse, wherefore he clenched his teeth and pulled savagely.

"The horses!" choked Whitthurst, slanting a look at the nervous animals. "They must...smell the...oil!" His face was streaked with sweat, and his arm shook visibly, the lamp essaying a crazy dance on its small shelf.

It was a miracle, thought Damon, that the poor fellow had been able to last this long, for it seemed an eternity since Bodwin had minced out of the barn. "You've done splendidly. Whatever...happens, it's not—" His struggles ceased, his heart thundering as a white stallion, plunging away from another animal, broke through the rope. The horse trotted toward him, pranced to the side, stamped about uncertainly, then came closer. The great head swooped down; the nostrils sniffed at him. Damon, sick and nauseated, managed to shout, "Get back! Damn you!" The stallion reared, the powerful hooves smashing down scant inches from the prostrate man. It was all the impetus Damon needed; one racking effort and his foot was free. He kicked desperately at the still-trapped boot, shouting again so that the stallion's eyes rolled, his ears laid back, and he moved uneasily toward the two mares who had started after him.

"Cam...old sportsman..." Whitthurst's voice was a sob of despair. "I...I can't hold my...dashed arm up...any longer! Cam, I...can't...I—Oh, God!"

The club fell from his hand. His arm dropped helplessly. Damon's throat constricted with horror as the lamp seemed almost to float down. For an instant it did not catch, but then one flicker exploded into a column of fire. Whitthurst shrank away as the blaze licked up beside him. Fighting madly to free himself, Damon succeeded in pushing the boot through the ropes and tore his left foot clear. The stallion jumped away from the fire and he and the mares ran back towards the other animals. A line of fire was streaking to the bales, and the terrified horses screamed as another great pillar of flame shot up amongst them. They raced for the doors, collided with the stallion and his mares, and milled in a plunging, rearing panic. Damon, twisting his body frantically, had one brief second before that frenzied confusion became a ravening stampede for freedom...over him! His wrists were still hopelessly tied, but his fingers gripped the rail, and with a strength born of desperation, he half scrambled, half flung himself to the side.

The thundering mass of horseflesh was upon him as his knees struck the fence. He hooked one foot over the bottom rail, but there was not sufficient space to squeeze through,

299

and he could only flatten himself against the rough wood and pray. Sound was deafening; the floor shook; smoke and dust choked him. His heart all but jumped through his chest as something smashed against his back, beating the breath from his lungs. Splinters drove into his cheek as he was rammed against the rails. A hoof whipped through his hair, missing his scalp by a whisper; another stunning impact seemed to crush in his ribs, and his senses swam, his grip weakening. Sagging helplessly, he knew this was death and begged it might be quick. A terrified screaming...a tremendous crash...

"Cam!" The agonized scream sliced through the mists in his brain. Whitt! He peered about disbelievingly. He had slumped down from his desperate hold on the rails and was sprawled on the floor, yet his body was not being sliced to pieces under those plunging hooves. The horses had gone! Contrary to Bodwin's plans, they'd beaten the doors down with their first thundering charge. He was still alive! Through clouds of acrid smoke the Viscount was barely visible, cringing away from the flames, coughing, his streaming eyes fearfully riveted to what he had obviously thought the lifeless body of his "uncle."

"I'm...all right!" Damon howled, and began to fight the ropes about his wrists. The heat was incredible. When the flames reached the stores of paint and varnish, they were done! His hands were very strong. With all his might he wrenched and tore at his bonds. Had his wrists been bound together, he may have succeeded; as it was, however he struggled, he could neither reach the knots nor loosen the rope; even the slippage that blood provided failed to allow him to pull free. His heart sank; it was taking too long. The fire was closing in on Whitt. Another minute or two and he'd be enveloped. Abandoning the useless effort, Damon twisted until his knees were under him, and, gripping the bottom rail, fought to drag it from the end post. With his wrists bound he could not get a proper hold. The smoke was blinding him, and he coughed and spluttered, his eyes streaming. The end post was heavier than the regular supports, and the rails rested there in deep sockets. Reversing his tactics, Damon used the rail as a battering ram, and pounded savagely at the post. He thought his wrists must break, but—had the post shifted a little, or was that the shimmering heat distortion? He rammed the rail home again and this time the post definitely tilted. Another slam. He swore in anguish, but the end of the rail slipped from the socket.

Hope flaring, he heaved desperately. If he could pull the entire length of the rail through the other posts, he would be able to get to Whitt. He succeeded briefly, but then the rail refused to budge. He could not see through the smoke, but whatever impeded it was quite immovable. Cursing with frustration, he threw himself back, striving with all his might to break the rail off short, but for all he achieved, it might have been cast of iron. His last alternative was to drag his hands along to the end, but in this he was foiled by the ropes catching on the rough wood. It was his only hope, however. Ignoring the pain of torn flesh, he strove with all his strength. Slowly, jerkily, the ropes began to move. He'd been secured not too far from the end post and the rail narrowed where it had been shaped to fit into the socket. The last foot was easy. He slid the ropes over the end, clambered to his feet, and tottered toward Whitthurst.

Coughing incessantly, blinded by the dense smoke, he flung an arm across his eyes, fear that the flames had won making him lurch into a run, only to trip over a sprawled shape and fall heavily. Whitthurst, lying beside him, gasped, "Ropes...burnt...through!"

Damon sat up, peering at him. His jacket was charred and his eyebrows and hair singed, but a quivering grin and a wink attested to his indomitable courage. A can of paint exploded with a boom like a cannon, and Damon bent protectively over Whitthurst as blazing sprays shot through the smoke. "Come...on!" he wheezed, and on hands and knees they started to where he prayed the doors were. They had gone only a few yards, however, when the Viscount crumpled in a paroxysm of coughing. Half smothered, Damon turned back, slipped an arm about him, and pulled insistently.

"No...use," croaked the Viscount. "I'm...finished. Get out, Cam! Must think...of Sophia!"

"I *am* thinking of her! *Move*! You damned...lazy sluggard!"

Whitthurst gave a faint, weary smile, struggled up, and collapsed.

"Blast your...miserable...hide!" groaned Damon. He dragged the Viscount's arm across his shoulders and crawled on, choking, through the inferno. Sparks rained down. Another boom outroared the flames, and the glare and heat intensified. His lungs were on fire...he was near blinded...his

301

knees were giving out, his strength too far gone for him to be able to carry Whitthurst's dead weight. He sprawled helplessly but, refusing to give up, tugged at him, cursing him in faint, sobbing gasps.

A large boot rammed into his side, and he uttered a cry of mingled pain and shock. Startled hazel eyes peered down at him. A mighty arm came to aid him. Ariel! The tears that filled his eyes had little to do with smoke. He shoved the big hands away and gestured to the inanimate figure of the Viscount. Ariel bent. Whitthurst was swung up and over his shoulder. His other hand slipped under Damon's arm. The Marquis leaned on him gratefully and somehow found the strength to stumble along. The billowing smoke was suffocating...he was vaguely aware of scorching heat and the deafening voice of the sheeting flames; and ever, that blessed, supporting arm.

He was outside, under lowering, cloud-heavy skies. It was cold, and with a dull sense of incredulity, he saw that the sun was not yet risen, although the skies were lightening to the touch of dawn. Had it then been only a very short interval? Was that possible? It had seemed a lifetime! Rain was falling, and he could have kissed each drop. Ariel left him, and he sat thankfully in the rain, coughing and spluttering, drawing in great gulps of the beautiful, cool air. Whitthurst lay close by, coughing hoarsely, and Damon was astounded to see Marcus Clay kneeling beside him but with his gaze riveted to the holocaust of the barn.

Following that gaze, he saw Ariel silhouetted against the pulsing glare, Trask's limp body in his arms. Even as he watched, a section of the loft collapsed. Ariel ducked but failed to straighten up. He was only a few yards from safety, but his shaggy head lifted, the glare illuminating an expression of agonized helplessness on his broad features.

"Christ!" Damon struggled to his feet. "His back!" He tottered forward while Clay sprinted madly for the barn. But they could never be in time. Another section of the loft came down; clouds of fire roared round the big man. Damon groaned aloud as a blazing board plummeted down. It slammed across those broad shoulders.

"That's the dandy!" roared Ariel and with one mighty leap was clear.

Chapter 26

"Esther and I were at Parapine for Yolande's Ball," said Clay, gingerly cutting away the ropes that still encircled Damon's wrists. "When I heard about the duel, I rode like fury to get here in time to warn you. Thompson told me you were already on your way, and I decided to follow and see what happened. Fond of 'em both, y'know. Gad! What a mess you've made here! We'd best—"

"Never mind that," said Damon urgently. "How did you find us?"

"Met Hartwell driving your carriage and looking deuced rum. I give him a hail, and he come down on me like a load of bricks. Poor fellow had a beast of a hole in his arm. I bound it for him, and when he woke up, he started yowling that Bodwin had gone off his upper works and intended to put a period to you two. He kept screaming that I must hurry or I'd be too late. Tell you the truth, if it hadn't been for that arm, I'd have thought his intellect had become disordered!"

303

"Amory..." breathed Damon, a twisted smile lighting his smoke-blackened face.

"What? Oh—quite. Well, at all events, I rode here at the gallop and met Ariel coming home from his bachelor party, very well foxed. When I told him what Hartwell had said, he sobered up in a hurry and ran along behind. We got to the spa in time to see smoke begin pouring out of the barn. We were about to tear the fence down when what looked like all the remounts for the Household Brigade come roaring out of that barn! They took down the fence for us, but my Rajah spooked, and by the time I'd managed to bring him back to earth, Ariel was already inside and hauling you and Whitt— Cam! Good Lord! I *must* get you home. These wrists are—"

"No time!" Damon stood and peered through the rain. "Where the devil is Whitt?"

"Rest easy. If there are any hacks about, he'll spot 'em. I'll tell you frankly, when I saw Luke haul him out of the barn, I thought he was done for! Remarkable that he could have come that close to being fried and escape with just a few burns."

"Yes. We were both lucky. Luckier that Ariel found us." Damon felt his ribs tentatively, and Clay laughed.

Ariel was working over the prone Trask. The Runner looked up as Damon walked over and managed a quivering grin. "Really knocked up a lark...didn't we, sir?" he muttered. "Had me fambles almost on the perishers and...let 'em diddle me! Never hear the end on it, I won't!"

"Don't worry," said Damon. "We'll get 'em!"

The man's face brightened. He sighed, closed his eyes, and lay still. Damon shot a look at Ariel. "Never worrit, milord," said the big man. "He'll be right as rain." The cook's hair was all but singed away, his beard a remnant, his shirt hanging in scorched tatters, his face blackened by smoke. "You"— he grinned—"look like you been run through a mangle, sir."

Damon slipped a gentle hand onto one blistered shoulder. "Were it not for you, my friend, I'd look a hell of a sight worse."

A heart-stopping roar and a great gout of flames and sparks announced the collapse of the barn's roof. They all stared at that pulsing nightmare, knowing how close tragedy had come.

Damon swung around, looking anxiously for Whitthurst.

304

"I must get my racing curricle, and fast, if I'm to reach Tottenbury in time!"

"Never!" Clay said gravely. "Even if I rode to the Priory and brought your curricle back, we could not be in time! It's better than fifteen miles, Cam! And it's almost sunrise!"

Damon groaned, glancing frantically at the lightening sky.

Whitthurst rode up and, slipping wearily from the saddle, gasped, "Not a blasted...nag for miles! I'll have to take Rajah, Clay. If I ride cross-country, I can lop seven miles off the journey. I just might—"

"Devil you will, you shatter-brained cinder!" Clay expostulated. "I'll go!"

"Neither of you shall go," said Damon quietly. "I'm the only one who has the least chance of stopping them."

Ariel turned and gaped up at him. Whitthurst and Clay stared at one another, then faced him in stunned astonishment.

"Go...? *You?*" The Viscount looked from the ragged scarecrow that was Damon to the splendid and spirited bay gelding and back again. "You never mean...*ride?*"

"I refuse to carry him," said Damon dryly. "Why does he dance about like that?"

"Scared," said Clay. "Told you."

Damon looked at Rajah, shuddered, and started forward on rubbery legs.

"You cannot go, you gudgeon!" said Clay. "You've lost your boot, and—" He checked with a strangled gasp.

Whitthurst caught his breath. Damon smiled. "I'm lame," he said calmly. "Always have been. Sophia won't allow me to conceal it any longer."

"Is *that* it?" Clay beamed. "By Jove! I thought you'd have been over there with us if you'd had the choice!"

"Wouldn't I just." It hadn't been so hard. And Clay didn't look repulsed—not with that great grin spreading across his face! Damon proceeded to commandeer Whitthurst's right boot and, having found it to be a size smaller than his own and the fit not totally hopeless, again forced himself to approach the bay. He took two brave strides. The gelding laid back its ears and eyed him with loathing. He felt sick. Try as he would, he couldn't go any closer.

Whitthurst, having experienced pure unreasoning terror, said sympathetically, "Get out of the way, Cam. You cannot!"

"I...must!" gritted Damon. But his feet would not obey

305

him. His hands were wet. And Rajah, sensing fear, pranced and snorted. "Clay," said Damon hoarsely, "hold him steady."

Clay shoved his pistol into Damon's belt, grunted, "You may need it!" and moved to take the reins and speak softly to the beautiful bay.

"Luke," quavered the Marquis, "you shall have to lift me into the saddle. My...my damned feet have...taken root!"

Ariel begged, "Milord...let *me* go! Even if I *was* to lift ye up there, wouldn't do ye no good!"

"You *have* helped me, my friend. This...is something...I must do myself."

"But—sir...first time he kicks up his heels, ye'll be head over tail! Ye ain't rid since ye was a little shaver!"

"All...the Brandens," said Damon faintly, "have a good seat. It'll come to me, Luke."

"But—"

"*Lift* me, dammit!" he roared. "Lift me!"

At once, those mighty arms closed around him. He shut his eyes tight, but the smell wafted to him. Hands were thrusting his feet into the stirrups. Fighting a sick weakness, he bowed forward.

"For God's sake!" Whitthurst pleaded. "You cannot ride to Tottenbury with your eyes shut!"

"Oh, hell!" groaned Clay. "Catch him, Luke!"

But Damon got a grip on the pommel and somehow dragged his failing body upright. He could feel sweat pouring down his face; horror was rushing over him in debilitating waves, but he slapped the reins feebly against the glossy neck and croaked, "Come...on!"

The bay trembled and ignored him.

Clay, his face grim, reached over and gave Rajah a swat on the rump. The bay lunged forward. Whitthurst shuddered and awaited the inevitable.

Damon was flung back. He gave a gasp and wrenched himself forward. The animal's mane slammed against his bruised face, awakening a sense of *déjà vu* as brief as it was terrifying. He twisted his shaking hands in that coarse hair and hung on somehow, the smell gagging him. His brain reeling with the nightmarish need to escape, he dug in his heels.

Whitthurst, watching that indomitable effort, gave a slow smile.

Clay said softly, "By God! Old Hookey never fought a battle more valiantly!"

Ariel's face was twisted with anxiety. "Look at him, milord! He'll break his neck surely. Already, his boot fell off!"

Whitthurst said gravely, "All the Brandens have a good seat."

Ariel groaned.

By half past five the rain was being swept into flurries by the gusting wind. A sullen daylight touched the hill with grey fingers, and the crumbling ruins of Tottenbury Castle crept stealthily into view and crouched there, grim and forbidding.

A luxurious carriage already waited beneath the dripping trees, lamps burning brightly. Inside, the Duke of Vaille trimmed his fingernails with a steady hand. Seated opposite him in the chill interior, Geoffrey, the Earl of Harland, watched his friend, his smoky blue-grey eyes, unusually beautiful for a man, now shadowed with worry. "Philip," he murmured, "is there nothing I can say to dissuade you?"

Without looking up, the Duke replied, "Nothing."

Harland leaned forward persistently. "But he is your cousin!"

Vaille lifted his head, ice in his blue stare. "And Ninon was my loved wife."

"But—surely...after twenty years...?"

"Admittedly, a regrettable delay." The Duke unbuttoned his magnificent coat and pulled his watch from his waistcoat pocket.

"And what," frowned Harland, "of poor, patient Charlotte?"

Vaille's fingers clamped convulsively over the timepiece. "Damn you, Geoff," he said unevenly. "To remind me of...of her...at this moment! Damn you!"

A low rumble of thunder delayed Harland's response, but he had no intention of neglecting the chink in Vaille's armour. "You love her, you blasted idiot!" he accused angrily. "Oh, save your breath! You may fool everyone else but not me! I've seen it in your eyes this year and more whenever you think she is not looking at you! You push her away because your nonsensical moral values say you are too old for her! Much *she* cares! If you die today—*she* will die an old maid! And not very long after you, I'll warrant!"

"Be done!" Vaille snarled, his face twisted. "Good gad, but you've a merciless tongue, Harland! Lucian has my sympathy!"

"We do not speak of my tongue—nor of my son! *Must* you add this folly to—"

"To my incredibly long list of follies?" Vaille's smile was bitter. "Yes! This has hung over all of us for too long. Now I've proof of Ridgley's treachery! He must be dealt with—and...if I do not...emerge victorious..." He shrugged. "As well, perhaps. Charlotte will—eventually—find someone of her own age."

"Fool! She adores you! Must you break her heart, as well as—"

Vaille's eyes narrowed a trifle, the sudden glare stilling his friend's impassioned utterance. Harland sighed, gave a helpless shake of his handsome head, and leaned back against the squabs. Vaille held his watch to the lamplight and peered at it. "Half an hour. Typical!" He replaced the watch and frowned into the gloomy morning.

A chaise splashed up. Harland said, "It's the surgeon, I believe. With Moulton." He put on his high-crowned hat and buttoned his coat. "I'd best get over there." Stepping into the rain, he muttered, "Beastly morning."

Ridgley's carriage tore into the clearing. He alighted and came toward them with his seconds. At once, Vaille joined them, also. "My apologies," said Ridgley with a nod to his cousin. "Overslept." Vaille's brows rose, but knowing the man, he didn't doubt it and assured him gently that it was of no least importance.

The surgeon, accustomed to these early-morning encounters and far from entranced despite the fat fees they paid him, begged them to reconsider and, this plea having fallen on deaf ears, assured them he would do his best in behalf of whichever of them might require his services. He then acquainted them with the fact that they were a couple of damned fools and he'd say the same if it was the King of England and the Pope he addressed. Vaille murmured that he believed this an unlikely confrontation. Ridgley, a twinkle appearing in his brown eyes, allowed that "By Jove! That would be something to see!" The other gentlemen, exchanging resigned glances, indicated their readiness, and the small, grim group stepped into the rain.

The protagonists having disdained to have the distance

308

paced off and the preliminaries having been dispensed with, Ridgley, his back to his cousin, waited out a grumbling peal of thunder, then said softly, "Philip—whatever you may believe—I did nothing of which I am ashamed."

"It grieves me to learn that," said Vaille acidly. "But—I suppose we all have our standards."

Harland's clear voice began to count off the paces. The two straight figures moved steadily apart, in each hand a gleaming duelling pistol; blue eyes and brown drinking in the glories of this morning that most men would have found dismal. Again, thunder pealed ominously, as on the count of ten they spun around.

A muddied, lathered bay gelding, his rider more out of the saddle than in it, galloped over the far side of the hill and halted between the duellists. A croaking voice was raised indistinctly; one hand flung upward in a restraining gesture. But in vain. The thunder was echoed by the sharp and deadly reverberations of two shots. The bay horse reared with a scream of fright, and the rider toppled to the ground, started up, then slumped back and lay motionless.

An agonized cry was torn from the Duke. He threw the smoking pistol from him and rushed forward. Ridgley was already running. Together, they fell to their knees beside the sprawled figure.

"Now—may God forgive me!" cried Vaille on a near sob.

Damon, watching that tortured face between his thick lashes, lay as one dead.

"Oh, hell! Oh, hell!" Ridgley groaned. "Where is he hit? Don't say... *Please* don't say... we've killed the boy!"

The surgeon and the seconds ran up as Vaille raised that limp and battered head into cherishing arms.

Harland, appalled, gasped, "Camille! Dear Christ! What the devil's happened to him?"

Damon, peering up at the ring of horrified faces, sighed, "*Mon père*...thank God!"

The doctor knelt beside him, heedless of the mud, and said an astonished "Sir—you look more like a man who's walked through the fiery furnace than the victim of a duel! Where are you hit?"

"Nowhere," Damon murmured. "Awful shots... both of 'em. Didn't even come close to—" Through the wet shrubbery nearby, he glimpsed a hate-contorted, scowling face—a hand that aimed a long-barrelled pistol at Vaille's back. With an

309

inarticulate cry, he wrenched upward, shoved his father roughly aside, and pulling Clay's pistol from his belt, fired with lightning speed.

For an instant, Phineas Bodwin stood rigid. His fingers tightened about the weapon he held. A shot rang out, but he was already falling. By the time the surgeon reached him, it was too late. Lord Sumner Craig-Bell's second-in-command had slid into whatever dark future awaited him beyond the fringes of this life.

Standing with one hand on the mantle, the Earl scowled into the fire in this best parlour of "The Oaken Bucket" in Tottenbury and breathed, "Bodwin!" He glanced to where a grim-faced Vaille was engaged in converse with the village constable and, shaking his head for the fourth time, said, "I still cannot credit it!"

Damon, sprawling in the deep armchair, was feeling considerably better. His head still ached; his face felt raw and painful; his bandaged wrists throbbed; and he was aware of the discomfort sustained by those who, not having ridden for a number of years, suddenly undertake a lengthy journey on horseback. But he had bathed and, thanks to his father's crisp and unquestioned commands, now enjoyed the comfort of clean clothes. A hearty breakfast, washed down by scalding coffee, had also gone a long way to restoring him. He started up as Vaille approached, only to lean back to the authoritative wave of one white hand. The Duke scanned his son's unfortunate features and swore. "When I think of what that animal did to you...and young Whitthurst!"

"Do not forget...Ninon!" grated Ridgley.

Vaille drove a fist into his palm. "Damme! I'm not likely to!"

"Speaking of Mama," said Damon. "While I was...more or less...riding here—"

"More or less?" Ridgley interrupted curiously.

Damon shifted uncomfortably in the chair. "There were some hedges, you see, Ted. Clay's horse and I parted company—several times."

Vaille smiled thinly. "I noted that your arrival was—somewhat precipitate. As well as being damn ridiculous. Your death scene, especially."

Damon flushed. Ridgley sprang to his defence. "Ask me,

310

it was dashed spunky! If you had any feelings at all, Vaille—which you ain't—you'd have some idea what it must've cost the boy to climb into that saddle! And as for—"

"Any man," Vaille sneered, "who rides a horse between two individuals aiming loaded pistols at one another is a blasted fool."

"Yet you are both alive," Damon murmured.

"And you, sir," the Duke snapped, "interfered in a matter of honour which—"

"Which had no business taking place at all!" And having interrupted his sire in this daring fashion, Damon stood. He moved slowly and painfully, yet—somehow he seemed taller. "If you will permit me, sir—I shall explain."

Ridgley watched him in considerable astonishment. Vaille, his face thunderous, closed his mouth, but those blue eyes surveyed his heir with blazing anger.

"I have," Damon said quietly, "remembered that whole lost week, nineteen years ago."

All traces of colour faded from Vaille's face, and he sank into the nearest chair.

"Good.... God!" Ridgley gasped. "Cam—you've taken the devil of a beating. Are you sure?"

Damon sat down again. "I'm quite sure." He gazed at the fire. "Once I was on that bay, I was too petrified to do any more than point him in the right direction and hang on. But then...gradually, it began to come back to me. And so clearly that I can picture it as if it was yesterday...I'd gone to Mama's bedchamber that morning to wait for her." He slanted a quick look at Vaille. "You were both in the music room, and I could hear you arguing." The Duke winced, put a hand across his brow, and waited in silence. "You were quarrelling," Damon went on, "about me going away to school. I remember that I didn't want to go. I knew the other boys would mock me because...I am a cripple. When Mama came upstairs, she was weeping." His eyes returned to their preoccupation with the flames, and he murmured, low-voiced, "I can even recall that she wore a pale-blue gown and how very beautiful she looked when she called me over to her. She held my hands, and she said that if I went to school, you would find out...about me. And we would both be sent back to France..."

Ridgley swore under his breath, stalked to the window, and stood staring out at the rain. Vaille's eyes closed very briefly, his head bowed, his hands fastening like claws on to each arm of his chair.

Damon was aware of none of this, seeing only that elegant bedchamber and the lovely woman, now so clear in his mind's eye. He had tried to comfort her, and she'd gathered him into her arms and had said in French in her soft, pretty fashion, "I am going to do what Cousin Edward wishes, Camille. He has a good friend who is also very clever. He is going to make your foot well again so that your Papa will be proud of you, and you can go to school like other boys and play the cricket, and he will not be angry with us anymore. You must be very brave because it will hurt quite badly. But you will never again have to wear that horrid shoe. You will walk easily—straight and proud. Do you think you can do that, my dear, brave son?"

He had assured her that he could do it as easily as the cat could flick her tail. Mama had dried her tears, kissed him, and summoned her abigails, and they had begun to pack for their sudden journey.

Through the breathless quiet, Damon looked up and said, "And that, Papa—is why she was leaving you... Only to take me... to have surgery done."

"B-but..." gasped Vaille, "I thought... Did she say... anything to you—?"

"She said that you were the most valiant gentleman she had ever known and that—no matter what it cost, we must never... either of us... fail you—or—or make you ashamed of us." A groan was torn from his father, and he went on hurriedly. "She said that Ted was ever dear to her heart because he loved us both and was trying to help—even though she would not do as he wished and tell you—about my foot."

"Oh... my... God!" cried Vaille. "Ted—*why* did you not tell me? You damned *idiot*! All these years!"

"Couldn't," Ridgley said in a husky, shaken voice. "Death-bed promise, y'see, Vaille. The dear soul was in a coma for two days, but—just before the end, she roused a little. She made me promise never to tell you—so that you would not remember her... with disgust."

A strangled sound escaped Vaille. Damon was aghast to see tears on his father's cheeks, and then the Duke swung away from them and, stumbling to the fireplace, leaned there, head bowed upon one hand. After a minute or two, he said hoarsely, "It would appear... that I owe you a—most pro-

312

found apology, Ted. She was not...running away from me, after all."

"Not with me, at all events," said Ridgley. "Though I'll admit I would have been the happiest man in the world if she had."

"No," Vaille argued. "I do not believe you would have run off with her—even had she gone to you. Not—loving her, as much as you did." His tearful eyes fell. He drew something from his pocket and, staring down at it, said brokenly, "I am ashamed to say that I had intended...to throw this in your face—after you'd fallen. Now—" He lifted his head and, his face working, held out the locket. "You may have it. It probably means as much to you...as it would to me."

Ridgley stared down at it in puzzlement.

"It means nothing to Ted, *Mon*—er—sir." Damon stood and added softly, "He's never seen it before." Vaille's shocked glance flashed to him, and he explained, "Bodwin bought it when I was so stupid as to sell it with—all the rest. He had the miniatures painted purely to provoke you two into killing one another!"

Ridgley, having opened the back, gave a gasping cry and, looking at Vaille, said, "By thunder! So this is why...?"

"Damn his twisted soul!" Vaille's face was a study in hatred. "And I almost fulfilled his hopes!" He brightened suddenly. "Then—Ninon had *not* forsaken me!"

Damon said, "You were her world, sir. She loved you to the moment she died."

Wordlessly, Vaille again turned away. Ridgley, still staring down at the locket, wandered toward the door.

Vaille glanced round. "Edward!"

Ridgley stopped but did not turn.

Vaille came up behind him. "We came damned close to killing one another today. I know—it was all my fault. That my curst...pride. My—as you've said so often—my *mania* for perfection...caused the entire tragedy. I...don't know if I can change, Ted. But...I could try." His voice petered out.

Damon, watching breathlessly, wondered if this grieving, humble man could possibly be his proud father. Ridgley neither moved nor spoke. Vaille sighed, started to move away, then stopped again.

"Edward," he pleaded, "I'd have you know...that I always—" He checked and stepped closer, his gaze sharpening. A small loose thread hung from the back of Ridgley's jacket.

313

Vaille frowned a little and pulled at it. Unhappily, it gathered before it broke, opening a gap in the arm hole. Vaille gave a guilty gasp and drew back. Damon shook his head in a mixture of mirth, affection, and incredulity.

Ridgley swung about, clapping a hand to his shoulder, his face flushing with irritation. "Damme, Philip! If that ain't just like you! Tidying me up when you're supposed to be down on your infernal knees, grovelling an apology!"

Recovering himself, Vaille drew an impatient sleeve across his face. "I *am* apologizing, blast your eyes! Are you going to accept it or not?"

They glared at one another.

"What amazes me," murmured Damon, "is that you stood twenty paces apart—crack shots—and could not so much as graze my horse!"

Two angry faces suddenly became very red. Vaille looked away. Ridgley said, "Well...It was...Ah...humph!"

"The one who should really be cursing and stamping about"—Damon nodded—"is me! What I went through: wallowing in mud, being tossed around on that blasted nag's back, thinking of you killing one another...Did you both intend to delope?"

"Certainly not," said Vaille haughtily. "I chanced to see you at the last instant and was able to swing my pistol aside."

"I see. And you, Ted? Did you also swing your pistol aside because of me?"

"Well..." stumbled the Earl unhappily. "I—er—that is to say..."

"You...swine!" raged Vaille. "You'd have stood there like a blasted martyr and let me kill you! How the devil d'you suppose that would have made me feel?"

Amused by this rather quaint reasoning, Damon grinned.

Ridgley, however, hung his head. "When the time came...I just couldn't bring m'self to aim..."

For a moment there was a deep silence. Then Vaille leapt forward, seized Ridgley's right hand, clasped it within both his own, and pumping it up and down, cried, "Damn you, Ted! You *shall* shake my hand!"

Ridgley broke into a deep, glad laugh. "I shall, by gad!" He clapped his free hand on Vaille's shoulder. "Like old times, eh, Phil?"

"Yes," said Vaille gruffly, "like old times!"

The Earl beamed on him. Vaille blinked mistily. "I'll go

314

and call up our vehicles," said Ridgley.

"We'll return together," said Vaille. "If you please, Ted."

"Aye, aye, sir," grinned Ridgley, and took himself off.

For a moment, the Duke stared after his cousin. When he turned, his pleasant smile was gone. "Well," he said bleakly, "what do you expect of me, Damon?"

Damon's nerves tightened. "Nothing, sir. You do not have to—"

"To acknowledge publicly my...crippled son?"

A knife turned in Damon's heart, but his chin lifted. "I know it must cause you humiliation. And I am, indeed, sorry. But—I will not hide it any—"

"*Sorry*—are you!" The blue eyes fairly sparked. "By God, how noble! I was angered with Ridgley for near twenty years and find my anger was unwarranted! In your case, I am fully justified! And fiend take you, Damon! I may *never* forgive you!" He took a step towards his son, and the Marquis blinked and retreated. "How *dared* you?" Vaille went on in a quiet voice more deadly than the loudest shouting. "How *dared* you imagine that I would be offended by such a trite affliction? Or by *any* affliction in my own son! How *dared* you think I would view you with any less fondness—or give a hoot in hell what others thought!"

Damon's heart began to quicken. His eyes searched that handsome face eagerly.

"When I think," Vaille snarled, "of all the years I have longed to have you beside me! Of all the misery to which I have been subjected purely because of what others laid to *my* pride—never admitting their own! Well, sir? Never stand there like a deaf mute! What have you to say for yourself?"

"But...but..." stammered Damon, "I always thought...I believed...But, father, I—"

"*What* did you call me?" thundered Vaille.

"Father—sir."

"You was used to coin another name."

"Yes." said Damon apologetically. "And I know you—"

"Say it!" Vaille scowled.

Wonderingly, Damon said, *"Mon...Père?"*

Vaille, his smile suddenly tender, said, "By Jove, Camille, I do rather like the sound of that—after all!"

He held out his arms and, in a most undignified manner, clasped his son to his heart.

315

Chapter 27

"Took us half an hour to catch some of those blasted hacks!" grumbled Clay.

Whitthurst, drinking hot coffee with much pleasure, his scorched self deposited in a fireside chair in the pleasant parlour of "The Oaken Bucket," nodded. "Whole damn barn full of horses one minute. Not a nag for miles the next..." His words trailed off, and he paused, his thoughts turning back to the thundering charge of those maddened animals and Damon lying helpless in their path.

The three young men exchanged grim glances, noting which the Duke frowned, and the hand he leaned on the mantle tightened into a fist.

"Well, I'm glad you came up with us," Damon smiled.

"And I'm relieved your—er—problems are so happily resolved," said Clay, with a sidelong glance at Vaille.

"So I'm become a problem, am I?" the Duke retorted. "Well, problem or no, I am forever in your—"

316

The door burst open, and Charlotte Hilby rushed into the room, her face pale and hunted looking, her cloak swirling out behind her. Oblivious of all but the Duke, she cried tragically, "Philip! Oh, my darling—I bring the most ghastly news! Poor Camille has been—" She broke off, her eyes widening as the Marquis stood and faced her. Vaille jumped forward, caught her as she swayed, and half carried her to the sofa.

Clay raced to the door and shouted, "Brandy! Quick!"

Seating himself beside the beauty, Vaille gathered her into his arms and said, "My dearest girl, whatever has happened now?"

And when Miss Hilby had sipped a little of the potent brandy, coughed, and a trace of colour had crept back into her cheeks, she gasped, "I had gone...to Cancrizans to beg Camille's aid in the matter of this senseless...duel." Again, she stopped, her frantic eyes searching Vaille's calm face.

"There will be no duel, my love," he reassured her. Surprised by such a public term of endearment, she glanced swiftly at the others present. "I have been a very great fool," the Duke went on. "Indeed, why you have borne with me is more than I can understand. But—unless the prospect of becoming a Duchess displeases you—you and I have much to plan..."

Her eyes widened joyously. A flush brightened her lovely face. Disregarding the others, Vaille raised her hand and kissed it with betraying tenderness. Charlotte swayed closer, touching his cheek, her eyes adoring. Ridgley's embarrassed cough recalled her to the present, and she cried, "Oh! What a henwit I am! Camille—you must go at once! Phineas Bodwin sent one of his grooms to warn us you had stopped at the spa and been caught in a flash fire in the barn! We mourned you as dead!"

"My God!" gasped Damon. "Sophia never believed that?"

"But—my dear, the groom told us Phinny had been on the way to find you and tell you of the duel when he saw your carriage race by, empty, but the horses mad with fear. He followed the tracks and then saw the fire but could not get inside to help you. What else were we to think?"

"But...didn't Ariel tell you—?"

"Ariel came with us," Clay interposed. "The good fellow's so devoted to you, Cam. He was half crazed to know if you'd broken your neck falling off my Rajah or got yourself shot. He's in the kitchen now, for his back was quite burned, and his grace's coachman insisted the doctor must look at him."

Stunned, Damon asked, "Does Sophia know Whitthurst was with me?"

"No! Thank heaven! We went at once to the barn..." Charlotte clasped her hands. "I shall never forget her face when she saw that...that ghastly...glowing mass. We were both weeping...praying there was some mistake. But then—one of the men began to...rake the embers. And he found—" She shuddered, and Vaille patted her hand comfortingly. "Found the charred remnants of...your special...boot," she went on. "It was almost gone, Camille, but there was no...mistaking it. Thompson had gone with us, of course, and he broke down completely and said you'd insisted on...wearing it. Even now, they are attempting to search the wreckage. But—the heat was so fierce, they told Sophia it might be hours before...they could—Oh! How could Phinny have made such a dreadful mistake? Is he here? He was coming to try and stop the duel and tell Philip of your...your—Camille! You must go at once! Dear Sophia is breaking her heart!"

Damon was already limping to the door. "Ariel! Ah—there you are, my good friend! Lord Ridgley's chaise and my father's greys! All four of 'em! And fast!"

Damon refused the services of a groom, knowing that no man would drive as he intended to drive. He took no shortcuts this time, yet reached the Priory in an incredible forty minutes to find two carriages drawn up behind the house, one of which was his own, the other bearing the insignia of the Bow Street Runners. Guiding the team expertly round them, he swung around to the front of the house and was out of the chaise almost before the lathered horses had stopped. The front door was flung open as he limped up the steps, and Thompson and Mrs. Hatters rushed out. For an instant, he thought the man was going to embrace him, but he stood aside, blinking through swimming eyes as the little woman rushed into Damon's arms, sobbing, "Oh, thank the good Lord! We thought...we thought—"

"I know." He kissed her gently. "But as you can see, I am unhurt." Thompson, who was clinging wordlessly to his shoulder, as if needing the reassurance he was indeed flesh and blood, viewed his damaged countenance with a shocked

318

expression, and Damon grinned. "Well—almost!"

The valet drew an arm across his eyes and gulped, "Her ladyship..."

"Where is she?"

"The music room," said Mrs. Hatters. "Hurry, sir!"

Damon cuffed Thompson lightly on the chin and hurried away. In the Great Hall, a crash and a muffled scream greeted him, and he leapt to catch Feather, who swayed beside the stairs, a tray and a broken glass of milk at her feet. She hugged his bruised ribs so hard he was forced to beg for mercy, and when he had kissed and reassured her and told her there had not been, nor was like to be, any duel, she sobbed gratefully, "I was just taking some warm milk to poor Sophia. Oh, Camille—never stand here comforting a silly old woman! Go to her!"

A dark-visaged man, wearing black clothing, said, "Your lordship, there is some questions wot I must put to—"

"Bow Street?"

For answer, the man held out his small baton of office. "Hif I may 'ave—"

"You may, indeed. In half an hour, exactly."

"Yus, sir. But first—"

"And not before," said Damon curtly, and strode past him.

The music room door was open. It was very quiet inside, with no sign of that beloved, golden head. He pushed the door wider and entered cautiously. Sophia lay huddled on the sofa, one tear-stained cheek pillowed on her hand. Her eyes were closed, and a glittering drop coursed slowly down her face. Horatio, fascinated by this strange behaviour, was creeping toward the girl, and as Damon watched, the goose nibbled, but very gently, at the fingers of one drooping hand, for all the world as though he sought to comfort that terrible grief.

Sophia, opening swimming eyes, said brokenly, "Oh, Horatio...he is gone from us. My precious love...And soon—poor bird—you will be alone, for my heart is dying, also..." Her voice broke on a sob. "Oh, Camille...Camille!"

Overwhelmed by the depth of this sorrow, Damon moved closer but found her lying as if in agony, both hands clasped over her face. And he hesitated, fearing to frighten her into a collapse by suddenly appearing.

Horatio looked up at him, trundled back to the rug, and settled himself. Damon's glance fell upon the wounded harpsichord.

To Sophia, the music sounded faint and far away, so sunk

319

was she in grief. Perhaps it was the echo of her happiness that rang in her ears. The memory of her beloved, playing with such tenderness the song he had written for her and claimed was for his fictional Great Aunt. She opened tear-dimmed, aching eyes and thought to see him once again, sitting there, his hair as tumbled as ever, his back so ramrod straight, his handsome face so terribly battered, and...She sat up and wiped at her eyes with a desperate eagerness. The music stopped. Peering, afraid to believe, not daring to accept what she saw, she crept toward him.

Damon swung around on the bench, his own eyes blurring at the full sight of her woebegone little face.

"Do...do not disappear...my own, my love," she pleaded, chokingly.

"Never!" He stood, and held out his arms.

Sophia gave a strangled cry and flew to him like a bird to its nest.

And in a little while the sun, being past the zenith, sent a pale but glowing finger down the diminishing clouds and through the side window, a finger that touched upon two heads very close together, one black and one golden. The man seated upon the bench before the old harpsichord, the girl clasped tightly in his arms.

Horatio, aware somehow that all was right with his world once more, went trundling down the hall in search of food: And never knew that behind him, he left—paradise.